30/98

LOYALTIES

LOYALTIES

Gavin Esler

HEADLINE

First published in 1990
by HEADLINE BOOK PUBLISHING PLC

10 9 8 7 6 5 4 3 2 1

British Library Cataloguing in Publication Data

Esler, Gavin
Loyalties.
I. Title
823'.914 [F]

ISBN 0-7472-0228-1

Typeset in 11/12¼ pt English Times
by Colset Private Limited, Singapore

Printed and bound in Great Britain by
Richard Clay Ltd, Bungay, Suffolk

HEADLINE BOOK PUBLISHING PLC
Headline House
79 Great Titchfield Street
London W1P 7FN

For Tricia

The best lack all conviction, while the worst
Are full of passionate intensity
The Second Coming W.B. Yeats

Chapter One

April, Norfolk

The man in the driver's seat tapped the gun in his waistband for the fifth time. He stared into the rear view mirror trying to pick out some movement in the darkness, but the village was still. He had parked the Ford transit van carefully in the shadows midway between two street lights. In the passenger seat the younger man stroked his moustache, looked at his wing mirror and stuffed a stick of chewing gum into his mouth.

'He'd better walk down this side of the street, McKeever, or we're in trouble,' he said, chewing hard.

Billy McKeever was almost forty, and looked even older. His hair receded in two large scoops at the temples, and at moments of stress his forehead was full of deep lines. It was full of deep lines now. He turned from the mirror and watched the younger man chew the gum energetically.

'This fella's so regular they set the Speaking Clock by him. Don't you worry.'

McKeever had been watching the target for a week and the pattern had never varied. Every evening the light in Gordon Durrant's study burned until ten o'clock. You could occasionally see him going back and forth searching for files from his bookcase. The curtains were never shut. When the theme tune for the start of the ITN news could be heard, Durrant switched off the study light, walked downstairs and sat in front of the television. As soon as the news bulletin finished, he walked his dog, taking the footpath along past the church, between where the transit van was now parked and the church wall.

Half a mile down the road, roughly opposite the lights of the Cross Keys pub, Durrant turned and walked back on the other side of the street. He was always home before the pub closed its doors at eleven and the first of the drinkers staggered out into the cold.

1

'I've seen it so many times, Kelly. The only big mystery is which lampposts the dog is actually going to piss on.'

Both men looked again into their mirrors.

Brendan Kelly was short and broad, with a face that looked as if it had taken too many punches in the amateur boxing ring, or somewhere in the backstreets of Belfast. He sat square in his seat, his hands jammed deep in the pockets of his anorak, tensed so that his shoulder muscles looked even wider than they really were.

'Ten twenty-eight,' he said, looking at the green digits on the dashboard clock. 'Two minutes.' He clacked the gum between his teeth, then grinned. 'Unless of course the dog died since you were here last.'

McKeever tapped the gun in his waistband again but did not respond. A car was approaching from the pub end of the village. It swung noisily through the main street, blowing from a hole in its exhaust. Its headlamps picked out what little there was – the pub, the post office, a little grocer shop and a few houses set back from the road. McKeever followed it in his mirror, watching the headlights touch their second van about four hundred yards behind them on the other side of Durrant's house. He strained to see the two figures he knew were inside but could not make them out.

'I like these English villages,' Kelly said, his hands still deep in his pockets. 'They all look so well planned and neat round the church, and the old pub. How come we can't make 'em like that back home?'

McKeever wrinkled his forehead again. He spoke softly.

'I like them because the street lighting is so bloody awful. Makes the job a lot easier – that's it as far as I'm concerned. Who'd want to live in Norfolk, for Chrissake? Countryside's flat and boring, just like the Brits themselves.'

Kelly popped his chewing gum. In front of him on the dashboard was an unlit cigarette. He had never smoked, and he wondered whether, when the time came, Durrant would notice how odd the shape of the butt would feel between his fingers. It had been one of McKeever's ideas. He hoped it would work.

There was nothing about the job Kelly disliked, except the waiting. Nothing. Not even McKeever's occasional bullshit about how things used to be in the early days of the struggle. He could take all that, no problem, and the rest was a gas. But the trouble with the waiting was that you could never relax. Not properly, anyhow. You could hardly crack a few jokes or let the mind wander in case the

2

moment came and you weren't ready. You could not have a drink, and you could not even hold a proper conversation. Not that conversation with McKeever was any big deal, but it might help pass the time. He clacked the gum again with his tongue. It was passing anyway.

Kelly looked over and watched McKeever stretch his arms and yawn. McKeever splayed his fingers, or what was left of them, across the steering wheel. He had lost the little finger of his left hand a few years before when a detonator he was handling blew up. He had lost a brother even before that when a bomb they had both made managed the same trick while the brother was trying to throw it into a bar in north Belfast. McKeever had been sitting at the wheel of the getaway car, much as he was sitting now, when he saw it happen. Bang! Just like that, he would say. Right in his brother's hand. Blew him to pieces, just a stain on the pavement, nothing much more. McKeever had done the right thing. He had driven away. There was nothing else for it.

'He's coming,' McKeever hissed, his eyes fixed on the mirror.

There was a new pool of orange light in the darkness behind them. Gordon Durrant stood at his open door trying to fix a lead on an excited springer spaniel which alternately bounced on the pavement and fawned at his feet. Ten thirty. Right on time. He looked small and wiry even in the lamplight, with long grey hair that fell in his eyes as he tried to catch the dog. McKeever had said Durrant was about fifty, but he looked younger and tougher than Kelly had expected a professor of chemistry might be. He was something of an early morning jogger, and they had considered hitting him then, but decided that the darkness of the village made the evening safer. Morning or night, Kelly didn't much mind.

Gordon Durrant was staring vacantly up and down the road, first in the direction of McKeever and Kelly and then towards the other van. The dog urinated at the first lamppost and sniffed the air. It was mild for April.

Kelly picked up the unlit cigarette from the dashboard and quietly unfastened the catch on the van door. The dog finished its business with the post, sniffed at a pot of daffodils on a doorstep, and began pulling Durrant along the church wall. If Kelly timed it correctly, when he opened the door it would swing out until it almost touched the wall, blocking Durrant's path. As the dog and master reached the rear of the van and disappeared from view, McKeever slid open the driver's door and walked round behind the vehicle. He could hear Kelly swing his door wide and step on to the pavement.

'Would you have a light?' Kelly said, jabbing the unlit cigarette like a weapon at Durrant, who stood fully upright and took a step back in surprise at Kelly's strong Belfast accent.

As he retreated, McKeever tapped him gently on the shoulder from behind. Durrant turned towards the touch and so missed seeing Kelly's fist pull back and smack him hard in the stomach. He fell gagging for breath on the pavement. The spaniel jumped on top of him, wagging its tail. Kelly pushed the dog aside while McKeever slipped a thick piece of cloth around Durrant's mouth, knotting it tightly at the back. Kelly took one of the sacks from the car and pulled it over Durrant's head, lifting his winded body from the ground while McKeever tied his hands at the back and bound a rope round the sack.

They could see a car approaching from somewhere beyond the pub and kicked Durrant against the van's wheels to keep him from view. Kelly, sweating now, grabbed the dog's lead and held the spaniel while it sniffed at the body through the sacking. When the car passed, they bundled Durrant into the back of the van and threw him with the dog into one of the packing cases inside, and shut the doors. Kelly picked up the unlit cigarette which had been squashed under Durrant's body, and threw it over the wall into the churchyard. The two men climbed back into their seats, McKeever panting heavily at the effort, and mopping his forehead with the back of his hand. He switched on the van's hazard warning lights and let them flicker three times. He sat back in the seat, stretching his neck over the headrest, panting hard. As he caught his breath he tapped the gun butt with his fingertips for the seventh time.

When they saw McKeever's signal, the man and woman in the second van stepped out. The girl was young and smartly dressed in a black trouser suit. Her hair had been blow-dried and fell in waves on her shoulders. She wore too much make up. The man was a few years older, about thirty-five, with a pale, ratty face. He looked smart too, in a dark blue jacket with matching shirt and tie, except that he had a shaving rash which left flaky patches on his neck. The woman hitched her bag onto her shoulder and opened its clasp, resting her right hand on something inside.

'Ready?'

She nodded, and shook back the curls that fell across her face. The thin man knocked at Durrant's door. They could hear the woman inside moving and muttering something about 'forgetting your key again'. She opened the door with reading glasses perched on her nose and a fat book in her left hand.

'Hello,' the girl said, smiling. 'Mrs Durrant?'

For a moment Margaret Durrant thought they were going to try to sell her a copy of *The Watchtower*. Before she could answer, the thin-faced man kicked the door fully open, lunged for her throat and bounced her head against the wall. The book and glasses fell to the floor, and Margaret Durrant slid down the wall to the carpet, a puppet whose wires were cut. The girl slammed the door shut, pulled the pistol from her handbag and rammed it hard into Mrs Durrant's face.

'One scream and you're dead meat, missus. Got it?'

Mrs Durrant nodded.

'We've got your husband outside and we'll stiff the both of you if there's any trouble. Now where's the stuff?'

Margaret Durrant's eyes filled with tears but she made no sound. The thin man left her with the girl and began searching the house from room to room. The tears started to drop down her cheeks.

'Listen,' the girl spat at her, her face white with rage. 'This is the Irish Republican Army. Tell us where your husband keeps his gear and we'll let you go. Fuck us around and it's the last thing you'll do on this earth, I swear to God. Now where is it?'

Mrs Durrant's chest heaved and she began to sob gently. There were three short knocks at the door, a pause and then three more. The girl let McKeever and Kelly in. The thin-faced man came down the stairs.

'A lot of books and papers in the study that we should take with us, but no gear.'

McKeever looked at Mrs Durrant on the floor and knelt beside her. He wrinkled his forehead a little and looked at the mascara smudges on her cheeks.

'Listen, love,' he said tenderly, his face just a few inches from hers. 'We could bring that husband of yours in here and make you watch us beat it out of him. He's in our van outside, wrapped up like a Christmas turkey. But we won't have to make you sit through all that if you point us in the right direction. Now where does he keep the equipment?'

Margaret Durrant looked at the balding Irishman in front of her.

She wiped her face nervously with her fingers, smudging mascara down her cheeks.

'In – the – garden – shed,' she sobbed. 'Keys in – kitchen. Some stuff in garage. Yes.'

They left her with the girl. The garage smelled of oil and sweetly of some kind of chemical. It took them a moment to find the light switch, but when they did they saw the wooden racks and shelving holding a stack of batteries, detonators in a box, and some lying loose on the workbench. There was a bunch of wiring too, and an assortment of chemicals whose use they could only guess at. Kelly found a large paperback book.

'Hey – sleekit old bastard. Look at this Larry.'

The thin faced man told him to shut it.

'No names, for Christ's sake.'

'She can't hear us,' Kelly said. 'Anyway you gotta see this. *The Anarchist's Cookbook*. I haven't seen that since I did basic training in Donegal.'

'Never mind that now,' Larry Kennedy said. 'Get the keys for the hut.'

McKeever unhooked the bunch of keys from behind the kitchen door, found the correct one, then led the way through the garden, down behind clumps of untidy fruit bushes. At the very end of the path where the garden backed on to a thick hedge and open farmland, they found a windowless metal hut. The new season's honeysuckle was just beginning to grow over it. McKeever undid the padlock and slid the door open. Inside they found a switch which lit up a bare light bulb. They could make out in the shadows half a dozen sacks of chemicals, a few unlabelled aerosol cans and a number of bags and boxes. Kelly picked up one of the boxes and tore open the top. It was full of fresh sticks of gelignite. Larry Kennedy held some of the chemical bags up to the light to read the labels.

'Paydirt,' he said, picking them up one by one. 'This one's RDX. This one's PETN. And this one – this is Semtex H.' Kelly watched Kennedy point at the white paste which could have been crushed coconut or possibly soap powder. 'The real McCoy – Czechoslovakian military plastic explosive, their variant of RDX. Who'd have thought he'd have access to that as well?' For the first time it looked as if Kennedy's ratty face might break out into a smile. 'We could have real fun with this. Now where's the magnetic gear?'

McKeever pointed to a heap of coiled brown plastic of all sizes. The coils were flat and shaped like varying widths of curtain rail, neatly folded in two large brown boxes in the corner and covered in cellophane wrapping. Kennedy burst open the wrapper and held one of the coils up to the light. He smiled again as he handed it to McKeever.

'Magnex,' he said. 'We'd better get it shifted. The whole lot.'

Kennedy looked round the store while the other two fetched the tea chests from the transit vans. He found lengths of detonating cord and more boxes of detonators. There were aerosol cans without labels, and bags of what looked like the two kinds of home-made explosives the IRA had taught Kennedy to use when he had first joined the movement back in 1971, one using weedkiller and the other fertilisers.

'Well,' Kennedy said out loud. 'He's got it all. The whole fucking conjuror's outfit. Eastern bloc, NATO, home-made, you name it, we got it.'

They filled the crates with everything from the shed, the gear from the garage and as many of Durrant's books as they could fit on top. While they loaded the vans, the girl forced Margaret Durrant to pack clothes for herself and her husband into two suitcases.

'Where are we going?' Margaret Durrant asked timidly. 'You told me you'd let us go.'

'You're here to pack, missus, not to talk,' the girl replied. 'Get on with it.'

Mrs Durrant pushed back a strand of brown hair behind her ear and glowered at the girl. Nobody treated her like this. Nobody. She hurried with the packing. When she finished, the girl and two of the men forced her to swallow some sleeping pills, threatening to shoot her if she did not co-operate. Before she could feel any effect, they tied and crated her like her husband, boxing the two side by side in one of the vans. When they were ready to leave McKeever took the spaniel from his van into the kitchen, filled its bowl of water, and opened a tin of dog food. He checked round the house one last time to make sure they had left no lights on. The dog whined as he saw McKeever move out the door. He put his head in again, wrinkled his forehead, and smiled.

'Never you mind, old fella,' he said as he put out the last light. '*Tiocfaidh ar la* – Our Day Will Come.'

7

Chapter Two

London

Tony Morgan thought he was going to be sick on the walk from the car park to the office door, but the moment passed. He could never understand why the hangovers which battered other men's heads into dust never hurt him that way. They destroyed his bowels instead, leaving him feeling like a frantic case of dysentery with the taste of old whisky stuck in his saliva. In the morning as he tried to shave, the black stubble sat out from his face, the skin blotchy and with a definite greenish tinge.

'Gooseberry,' he said to himself in the mirror, but his bowels didn't find it funny. He gasped and held himself until the spasm passed. 'Jesus.'

He had two, and only two priorities. The first was to try to survive the morning without actually being sick, which as he pushed open the outer door to the Capital Satellite Television building seemed challenge enough. The second was to finish his expenses and leave them for signature without either Harris or Mortensen – or some other doughhead on the newsdesk – coming up with yet another moronic idea for a two minute film for that night's seven o'clock news. It was a constant battle to steer a course between working too little, which made him feel unwanted and wretched, and working too much on the usual newsdesk crap, which made him feel put-upon and bad-tempered.

As he showed his identity pass to the uniformed commissionaire, Morgan wondered whether there had been any Royal baby, wedding, scandal or illness which had surfaced overnight and would ruin his day. If Donald Harris was driving tonight's show and there was even a whiff of Royal flatulence, some poor sucker would be assigned to provide a full report, plus background commentary from the well-known cast of Royal watchers. Why they thought Europe's satellite television viewers wanted that kind of rubbish,

9

Morgan never understood, but judging from the expanding list of new subscribers, they appeared to lap it up.

Worse still, it might be Sheila Mortensen, whom they used to call 'Thunderthighs' in the days before they realised it was sexist, and whom they now called 'The Neurotic Bitch'. If she were to be in the editorial chair, with her extraordinary love for furry animals and medical miracles, then interesting cats, talented rodents, faithful dogs and parrots with stammers would be in competition with crippled children going to Disneyland, in the fight to get on the air.

Christ, Morgan felt ill. When he caught a look at himself in the rosy-tinted mirror in the lift, he felt even worse. Sometimes he thought it was only the enormous pressure to pay his mortgage every month which kept him working for such a group of deadbeats and dickheads. That, and equal pressure from his wife, Emily, about saving enough to pay for private schooling for both their children, and not just David as he had originally planned.

'Either Louise gets the chance to go to a fee-paying school as well,' Emily had said, 'or neither of them do. And you know I would prefer it if they both went to state schools.'

But not in Clapham, for God's sake. You had to draw the line somewhere.

He stood in the lift, pressed the sixth-floor button and leaned against the side wall. He felt a gentle belch coming and released it. It tasted of whisky. Some days everything in his life seemed to taste of whisky. Or red wine. Sometimes it was red wine. Emily had lectured him about that, too. He was not sure whether he was drinking because his marriage was going wrong or whether, as she seemed to think, the marriage was going wrong because of his drinking. Maybe there would be a divorce. He did not think he could handle that.

Morgan was sure it had not always been so bad. When he first joined Capital Television they had let him work on 'Capital Reports', supposed to be the flagship (which meant the only) current affairs programme sold by the company to the British commercial television network. The half-hour weekly series had taken him all over the world: the Middle East, America, Eastern Europe, South Africa. But since deregulation, the selling of the franchise and the decision to create a new British and European Satellite service called Europe Channel Five, the most recent of the boardroom coups had led directly to Morgan's gloom. It meant the arrival of Gregory Crawshaw, who bought his way in as controller of programmes and managing director. Crawshaw had been a merchant banker, and his opening gambit with any of the people who worked for him now was to reveal that the closest he had come to what he called the 'bright and glamorous world of television' before he took over at Capital was to have watched programmes in the evening at home over a gin and tonic. Crawshaw said it as if it was a unique qualification for the post he now held.

'Business values not show business values,' he would intone gravely. 'That's what we must have. The discipline of the market.'

Most people nodded, and those who didn't were either fired or managed to find a new job before Crawshaw got round to forcing them to it. 'Capital Reports' was transformed into 'Capital Satellite Reports', and most of the old hands left because they said they wanted to work on a proper news programme, not an extended rock video.

'Without the music,' Morgan added.

He had stayed largely because nothing else came his way, and Crawshaw had not pushed him. On one of the few occasions they had spoken together, Crawshaw had simply expressed surprise that 'every one of your reports seems to begin with an intercontinental departure from Heathrow's Terminal Three.' Not any more. Business values now meant that every one of Morgan's reports began and ended with a ride on the London Underground or, if he was lucky, an away-day return with British Rail to exotic locations in Hertfordshire and Kent. The nearest he got to foreign travel was when his one-minute long reports were bounced off the 'Com-Tel 12' satellite into the sitting-rooms of fourteen European countries.

The impact of Crawshaw's arrival led Morgan to conclude that Oscar Wilde had got it wrong. It was not the cynic who knew the price of everything and the value of nothing. It was the merchant banker and the accountant. Beyond knowing the price of everything – including that of his staff – Crawshaw knew exactly how much he could lay off against future profits. He had lumped 'Capital Satellite Reports' together with 'Capital Satellite News Tonight' in a new and extended newsroom, 'to rationalise costs and promote more rigorous journalism'. Rigor mortis, Morgan thought. Dead from the neck up, stiff from the tongue down. The journalists all believed Crawshaw kept repeating the word 'rigour' so the new Satellite Broadcasting Authority might just be impressed enough to renew the CTV franchise next time round. He wouldn't know rigorous journalism if it bit him on the bum, but like motherhood

11

and apple pie he knew he was expected to be in favour of it.

'I don't want any of your crummy sixties idealism,' Crawshaw had said at one of the main editorial meetings. 'If people want to bleed for causes, then they can go and become social workers. We are on the brink of the twenty-first century and times are exciting but competition is hard. If any of you don't like the changes, I will be happy to provide a reference for your next employer.'

The Crawshaw masterstroke, Morgan believed, was not in getting the corporate structure right or even in bluffing the Satellite Broadcasting Authority. It was to create two equal, and equally incompetent, news editors as his deputies – Harris and Mortensen.

Crawshaw must have known they loathed each other and therefore could never cause him any trouble with either the Capital board or the Satellite Broadcasting Authority. They would compete with one another, churn out the stuff, keep it safe and trivial and the audiences would stay tuned. If either screwed up, they would be fired, and they knew it. Their paranoia and mutual loathing was now as indispensable a piece of office furniture as the telex machine.

The other major initiative stemming from 'business values' had been to make the staff pay five pence each time they took a coffee from the newsroom coffee maker, and a cut back on the free booze for guests who came in to appear on programmes. Morgan, suffering now from too much of the latter from the previous evening, couldn't find loose change to pay for a coffee. When he reached the sixth floor he took the drink anyway and tried not to spill it as he lurched into the newsroom. The reek of caffeine and the sudden rattle of a dozen teleprinters and forty computer keyboards made his stomach churn again.

It was a Harris day. You could tell that by looking at the assignments board. It wasn't that Harris put any particular journalistic stamp on the evening news, beyond the swathe of Royal features, which were virtually compulsory for either of the editors, though Harris was alone in being genuinely enthusiastic about them. It was simply that he wrote the stories, the reporters' names and camera crews assigned to them across the board in the neatest and most beautiful handwriting Morgan had ever seen. You would look for your assignment for the day and discover it had been etched in italic copperplate of the type normally reserved for certificates of merit and trust deeds. It was the sort of handwriting, Morgan thought, placing his undrunk coffee in the depths of the wastepaper bin, that

would make you fall in love with Harris if he happened to be your pen
pal and if you didn't know what a dickhead he really was. Full-
frontal, real life, Harris was a less attractive idea. Morgan stared at
him as he sat in the middle of the horseshoe-shaped newsdesk surrounded by stacks of copy from the news agencies. He was already
red in the face, even though there were almost eight hours to go
before transmission. He was trying to smoke, dial a telephone
number, watch a monitor for an incoming satellite transmission and
read a Press Association story all at the same time. It was a good trick
if you could manage it.

'Morning, Tony,' he said, waving one arm high and showing the
armpit of his shirt wet with sweat. 'How are we today?'

All the better for seeing you, you ballocks, Morgan thought,
secretly wishing Harris an early death from heart disease, a nervous
breakdown and piles. He smiled.

'Fine, Donald. And you?'

'Oh, busy-busy. Listen – oh, wait.'

Harris waved the hand with the cigarette in it towards Morgan as if
telling him to sit down. The telephone in his other hand had started to
speak, and he began jabbering to someone about the evening satellite
feed from Johannesburg, and whether the Botha presser would
make the bird, and was it anyway such a big, you know, such a big
deal? Could they cut him a fat minute anyway, and he'd have a look?
The Reuters machine began to spew out something behind Harris's
chair and he waved to one of the subeditors to sort out the folds of
paper. Seizing his chance, Morgan wandered off, hoping to disappear behind his desk and a copy of the *Guardian* until the unruli-
ness in the lower part of his body put itself to rights. He sat at the
mound of old newspapers on his desk, and failing to find a large
enough paper, tried to hide behind a copy of one of the day's tabloids.

' "Why Sexy Sam Quits Page Three," ' it said. Morgan began to
read, but Harris had finished with the problems of Southern Africa,
and yelled over to him.

'Listen, Tony. Crawshaw wants to see you.'

Morgan tried not to show any emotion. He put down his newspaper and thought again of the Building Society, his unpaid mortgage, Emily, David and Louise, his appalling hangover. In that
order.

'Good news or bad news?'

'He didn't say,' Harris replied flatly. 'Just wanted to talk as soon
as . . . Oh, excuse me.'

13

And he was off again, this time fixing coverage for Princess Someone at a horse show. Morgan pulled the newspaper in front of his face again, thinking hard. He could not decide whether to stall for time and hope he felt better, or get in and get it over with. It could be that business values were about to reassert themselves, and he would be looking for another job, with three months notice and not much more to show for it. If that was indeed to be the case, he could not bear the suspense for long. He might manage to prepare himself better for whatever it was Crawshaw had to tell him, by spending ten minutes in the Gents. It was the only place in the whole office quiet enough to allow any half civilised man the chance to think; no telephones, no computer terminals, no paranoid editors panicking because they couldn't get forty-five seconds of pictures of a World War Two Spitfire taking off from somewhere or other. All that, hot and cold running water and utter equality among the users. Not even Crawshaw could be more than moderately pompous in the pisser. Morgan locked the door and sat down on the toilet seat. He rested his head on the wall and experimentally closed his eyes. It was a mistake and made him feel worse.

'If I survive this,' he promised Emily in her absence. 'If my job is somehow saved by a miracle, I swear I will start behaving more like the middle-aged father of two you keep telling me I am. No more the drunken façade of the ageing hack. Promise.'

For a moment Morgan thought that all this solemnity was going to make him sick, but it passed. If it was going to happen, now would be a good time. Doing it on Crawshaw's carpet would be a mistake.

'And if I am sacked,' he said, talking to the vision of his wife again. 'Then I suppose I'd better give up the booze anyway. Otherwise I'll never get another job.'

'You'll never manage to get one anyway,' Emily-vision replied. 'Not at your age.'

Morgan felt the sweat rise on his body and prickle through his shirt. He loosened his tie, took a few deep breaths and started to feel a little better. He was sure he would not now be sick, though if Crawshaw did fire him it was possible both of them and the office carpet would be in for a surprise. When he thought he could survive whatever ordeal lay ahead, Morgan stood up, flushed the empty toilet, and began to wash his hands. He scrutinised his appearance closely in the washroom mirror. The gooseberry face had gone, but he thought he looked every one of his forty years. There was almost as much grey streaked through his hair as brown. The lines round his eyes were obvious, though he supposed they might add to his character rather than the opposite. 'Gravitas,' he intoned at his reflection. 'Rigour.'

Maybe Crawshaw was about to promote him, make him a news reader or some such, beamed into the homes of Europe five nights a week. It seemed unlikely. Besides, he was a journalist not an actor, and there had to be more to life than reading a few headlines on the seven o'clock news. There was no way Crawshaw was going to offer him an anchorman's job, and he did not want that kind of a job anyway, though he would be more than content to spend the money that would go with it. Well, what then? Maybe, he thought, he should follow Emily's advice and get himself a 'real job'. 'If you are miserable,' she had said, 'then leave. Find another job. If you are not prepared to motivate yourself, then things can't be all that bad, so stop making life for the rest of us so wretched.'

Morgan did want another job, but it was not so easy. Where would he find some organisation stupid enough to pay him as well as CTV did for so little work? There were the occasionally interesting bits, but mostly it was a well paid chore. If Crawshaw was right that the sloppy idealism of the sixties had to be replaced with the new, harder business edge of the nineties and beyond, then Morgan was perfect for the job. He would take their money and spend it, while doing as little as possible to deserve it. It was the correct response to their 'business values'. He could not resist, but he could obstruct.

As he sat on the leather sofa on the Programme Controller's outer office, Morgan noticed for the first time that Gregory Crawshaw had made one further major change since he had completed the transformation to a satellite service. Despite the five pence charge for every cup of coffee in the newsroom and the new air of Spartan frugality, Crawshaw had completely redecorated his own office and the corridor surrounding it, repainting the old eau-de-Nil walls, re-carpeting expensively throughout and changing everything from the light fittings to the two matching secretaries. They were both splendid lookers, Morgan thought, studying them from the sofa for the first time. He had seen them before, wandering as if lost through the CTV production offices and all those dangerous bits of the building where television programmes were made. They were two of a type: large breasted, pretty faced, and as good a bit of male jewellery as Morgan had seen in ages. At least Crawshaw had got something right.

Morgan wondered about their legs. The identical secretaries sat behind matching burr walnut desks which, Morgan guessed, were worth at least one week's filming in New York – each. He began trying to work out if any of the newsroom desks, like the one at which he sat, with the chipped veneer and the sawdust centre, was worth any more than a morning's filming in Battersea, when one of the secretaries began to speak.

'He'll see you now.'

'What?'

'He'll see you now,' she said again, without emotion. It was like being summoned by the doctor. Morgan stood up and felt green again. He took a deep breath, opened the door and walked into Crawshaw's office.

The Controller of Programmes was sitting at the far end of the inner office across what seemed like a football pitch of thick beige carpet. In one corner there were six television screens, their pictures flickering silently. There was a full suite of leather chairs and a sofa, a small glass coffee table, and Crawshaw himself behind a burr walnut desk even bigger than the two outside. One week's filming in San Francisco.

'Ah, Tony,' he said. 'Do have a seat. Shan't be a moment.'

Morgan sat down in the leather armchair nearest the desk. He wondered why Crawshaw had said he was ready, only to keep him waiting for a few more moments while he wrote something with his gold-nibbed pen. Was he trying to prove he could write? Morgan suspected it was something Crawshaw had read in an American self-improvement guide on 'How to be a Better Boss'. Or 'How to be a Bigger Bastard', or something.

'Make your staff wait and show 'em who is on top,' he thought. 'Let's keep Management Macho.'

On the desk beside Crawshaw, facing towards Morgan, there was a family photograph, a young smiling wife and a couple of goofy kids cuddling a labrador. Morgan knew this was taken at their country home, where Crawshaw would drive about in a Range Rover and drink real ale at weekends. He did not want to be fired by someone like him. He looked from the photograph back to Crawshaw himself. He had a tall, straight-backed military bearing – in the Guards or something, Morgan had heard, before taking up accountancy and going into the family merchant bank. It was then he had discovered he had no real talent except for piling up lots of money, which Morgan thought was a good enough trick if you could manage it. Now that he had taken up television in his fifties, he was as enthusiastic about it as a thirteen-year-old with a new bike.

'Coffee?' Crawshaw said with a smile that made the flesh creep. He stretched across to his desk intercom, and Morgan noticed he favoured old-fashioned double cuffs on his shirts, held by some kind of regimental or family crest.

'Jean – coffee for me and . . . black no sugar for Mr Morgan.'

Crawshaw sat back in his chair, pulled off his reading glasses and held his fingertips together in an attitude of prayer. Morgan wondered whether he still smelled of booze. He hoped that half an hour in the shower had helped kill it, and that nothing could cross the distance over Crawshaw's desk. He tried not to breathe too hard.

'Tony,' Crawshaw said, fixing him with a sincere stare. 'Let me get to the point. I have a very special project I would like to discuss with you. I would like you to make a programme on terrorism in Ireland. I know you are interested in the subject and have plenty of contacts there. We have had our differences about Irish coverage in the past, and I may have placed some of your ideas further down the scale of operational priorities than you thought justified. I am determined to change that, and I think now the time is right. What do you say?'

For the first time that morning Morgan believed his hangover was starting to come under control. Less than thirty seconds of Crawshaw's machine-gun fire and the Clapham Common branch of his Building Society could breathe again. No rows to come with Emily. Maybe even good news. He cleared his throat and spoke slowly.

'Well, as you say, I have been interested in Northern Ireland for a very long time. The idea of a special programme – certainly anything longer than the usual news coverage – would be just the sort of thing I think we should be doing. Higher profile. Serious. What else can I say, but yes, I'd love to do it.'

The effort of speech made Morgan's stomach churn, but the spasms were weakening. It was not such a bad day after all. The last time they had exchanged a few words on the subject, Crawshaw had made it clear that while Northern Ireland might be important, the viewers found it extremely boring. He could not expect advertisers to pay for slots in some dreary and incomprehensible programme that skated over the great battles in three hundred years of what he called the history and bigotry of the bog men. Northern Ireland was not just low down Crawshaw's scale of 'operational priorities' as he

17

put it. It was not on the same operational planet. Crawshaw was never going to risk the CTV satellite franchise by annoying the Satellite Broadcasting Authority and putting any kind of terrorists on the box. From the moment the British government banned the appearance of anyone connected with terrorist organisations from the land based broadcasters – the BBC and the British independent companies – the satellite channels had played safe and acted as if the ban applied to them in the same way. Under European law it could not, but no one – least of all Crawshaw – was going to risk becoming the broadcasting pioneer who might use the legal loophole, and lose the franchise. Crawshaw would not even discuss it. Now this. Morgan did not understand the flip-flop.

'What sort of programme did you have in mind?' Morgan asked in a spirit of false bonhomie. The churning had completely subsided. He was going to be all right.

Before Crawshaw could answer, the coffee arrived, carried by Jean the secretary who smiled at Crawshaw and ignored Morgan. Morgan was pleased to notice that now she was away from the desk, she had very big hips. Good looking from the waist up, but not exactly, well, not exactly sexy unless you had a preference for the maternal type. Ah, so that was Crawshaw's weakness. He wanted to be mothered. Well.

The coffee smelled like the real stuff, not the usual chicory adulterated mess from the newsroom. Morgan took a sip.

'I know you have been disappointed in the past,' Crawshaw said, placing his hands once more in a prayer-like pose, 'at what you consider to be our lack of adventure on Northern Ireland. I think at least you understand my point of view, even if you do not agree with it. But now I hope there is an opportunity for us to tackle such a difficult and demanding story at the length and in the rigorous manner it deserves.' He tapped his fingertips with an air of purposiveness. 'I am keen to do it.'

Morgan remembered that Crawshaw sometimes spoke to CBI dinners and Institute of Directors lunches about the future of broadcasting in the new satellite age. He wondered if this sort of thing went down well, the air of avuncular reasonableness, the generous gestures. But what did it mean? Crawshaw's 'lack of adventure' meant he did not want any ideas about Northern Ireland at all. Somewhere, somehow, he had experienced a road to Damascus conversion, and Morgan could smell there was something more behind it. Crawshaw took a sip of his coffee and said he

18

wanted to return to the point. Jean the Hippo had given Crawshaw two ginger snap biscuits. Morgan, who was beginning to feel hungry after missing breakfast, had been given none. Crawshaw nibbled a biscuit and continued.

'The particulars are these. As I am sure you know, Patrick James O'Neill escaped with a dozen or so others who broke out of the Maze prison in Northern Ireland last year. I was lunching with someone recently who was telling me that O'Neill is a very big fish within the Provisional IRA.'

'He's on the Army Council,' Morgan confirmed. 'It's rumoured that he is the new Director of External Operations.'

Crawshaw delicately wiped a few crumbs of biscuit from the corner of his mouth.

'And what exactly would that mean?'

'It means he's in charge of bombing England.'

Crawshaw arched one eyebrow.

'I see. Well, that is rather the sort of thing I thought it would mean, and it proves he is indeed a big fish, if that is his role within the IRA.'

Crawshaw paused for a moment, looking at his hands.

'It seems to me that we might consider trying to interview O'Neill, a lengthy, broad-ranging taped interview, of the type that would really make news in this country, in Europe and all over the world. It would establish our editorial credibility, bending the British laws on terrorist broadcasts, but not breaking them, as far as our European satellite service is concerned. Do you think you would be able to find O'Neill, and if so, do you think he would agree to be interviewed?'

The coffee had settled now in Morgan's stomach. He was feeling much better, but he wished his brain was a little more awake. He looked at Crawshaw's face. Then he looked at Crawshaw's fingertips, and at his thick shirt-cuffs. Cautious merchant banker becomes terrorist's pal? This did not square with Crawshaw's image as no-news-is-good-news, on *my* television channel, thank you very much. Morgan was not keen on such surprises from people whose characters he thought that he had already pigeon-holed. There had to be more to this.

'I can find him,' Morgan said. 'But really why do you want him?'

'There are a number of reasons,' Crawshaw replied immediately, sitting forward as if to confide in an old friend. 'Apart from the general one I have mentioned. There are a number of reasons why it is important that we as an organisation manage something a little more ambitious than we have attempted in the past, or the recent past at any rate.' Crawshaw turned for a moment to the six silently flickering television screens as if seeking inspiration. Then he looked back at Morgan, putting his hands together again in front of him like a Buddhist greeting.

'We have now licked the newsroom into shape. I've made the economies and changes the board expected of me, and things are going well. We are, however, a little weak on the hard news front. Our overall corporate strategy is to consolidate in Europe and expand into North America and the Pacific basin. Our soundings suggest the United States Federal Communications Commission wants a better news gathering track record from potential franchisees. There are also those at the Satellite Broadcasting Authority who believe we have done very little original or even serious journalism to date. If they continue with that view, we will have trouble even with our European franchise renewal. The dogs are snapping at our heels. We must build up our journalistic reputation, and I am willing to spend money and take risks to do it. I have decided to initiate a series of projects. This one is the first and most likely to set us off to a controversial start. It will put us in the public eye as a television station which can make the news as well as tell it – able to do what even the BBC cannot do, for all its supposed resources and experience. Just imagine our sales pitch to the Americans – "The Satellite Channel that believes in freedom of speech." Wonderful! Even if it is just a once and forever interview, O'Neill will make our reputation in the world-wide communications business. I am sure of it.'

For his part, Morgan was certain at least half of this was some speech Crawshaw had already given to the CTV board. It had been rehearsed. The quotes were good and pat, the motivation typically Crawshaw. He did not really want the interview at all, but he could see it as a cheap and sensational advertisement for the company. That way it made sense, though Morgan was not entirely clear Crawshaw knew what he was getting in to.

'We'll make the news all right,' Morgan said. 'There will be one hell of a row. The government might be forced to try to change the law and defy the European court over what is or is not permissible on satellite operations.'

'I know. But the row will pass, and what will be left will be the impression that we are the kind of organisation capable of beating the world on a news scoop. This man PJ O'Neill has been on the run for nine months. He is the most wanted man on both sides of the Irish border, yet no one can find him. If *we* can, if we succeed where the Royal Ulster Constabulary, the Irish police and two armies cannot, that will raise more than a few ripples. It will raise our profile to become the best known satellite channel in the world. It will be millions of dollars' worth of free and positive publicity in every market we might think of entering.'

'It won't be positive in Britain,' Morgan said. 'The government will go bonkers. I will have to ask O'Neill if he intends to bomb England again and he will make all kinds of threats. Then the Prime Minister and virtually every Tory backbencher you can name will condemn us as irresponsible for giving – what is it she always says? – the oxygen of publicity to the terrorists. Something like that.'

'Leave that to me, Tony. As you know, my contacts in Whitehall are more than adequate. Of course the Tory party has been sensitive after the Brighton bomb. But their ban on broadcasting interviews with these people was just a cosmetic exercise against the BBC and the British based independents. They admit as much privately and they know they can't win this one in the European courts. Believe me, ideas that looked insane yesterday are good today, and may seem old hat tomorrow. I will take any political flak – gladly. We will be in a good position to do so. We will not be committing any offence in this country, so long as the interview takes place in the Irish Republic. I am sure that is where O'Neill will want to do it. We will have to decide at what point under the Prevention of Terrorism Act we have to notify the police, but that's a matter for the lawyers. I have already run the idea across them – naming no names – and they think it is legally watertight.'

'That still doesn't make it editorially or politically watertight.'

Crawshaw drained the last of his coffee and looked at Morgan, quizzically. 'You do not sound, if I may say so, totally enthusiastic.'

Morgan blanched. 'On the contrary, I am completely behind the idea of doing stories like this. If we do not understand the IRA we do not understand the Irish problem. If we do not understand the Irish problem, how do we expect to solve it? That has always been my view, and that is why the government ban on talking to these characters or their apologists is so stupid. It is the denial of the freedom of speech and the right of people to hear all kinds of political points of view – even those they detest. All of that. I can bring out all the liberal arguments. But what I am worried about is that the people who are going to stamp on us are not to be persuaded by those arguments, and I just want to make sure . . .'

Morgan stopped for a second, then decided he had to continue. 'I just have to be sure that when the going gets very rough – as it will – that you are going to back the project and not throw us to the wolves.'

Crawshaw smiled. 'It's a fair point. I will defend this editorial judgement utterly. It's mine anyway, so I have no choice. I want this story to put us on the map of world-wide television journalism. I want you to do it, and I will back you to the hilt. You have my word on it.'

'Good. Let's do it then.'

Crawshaw dropped his voice. 'If you think you can find O'Neill, how long will it take?'

'Depends,' Morgan said. 'Depends whether the Provos want him to be found, and how badly he wants to appear on television. The IRA may be evil bastards, but they are not fools. They won't believe we will put O'Neill on television anyway, and they will want to check the whole thing out thoroughly. They won't risk putting me into contact with O'Neill unless I can virtually guarantee that the interview will be used and that they'll obtain some propaganda benefit from it. The last thing they want is for him to be arrested again after all the efforts they put into getting him out of jail.'

Crawshaw spread his fingers on the desk. He was going to say something, but Morgan kept going.

'Then there is O'Neill himself. He knows if he is picked up and sent back to the Maze prison he'll never get out except in a box. He will think, understandably, that the warders will want him to try to escape again so they can shoot him in the attempt. On the outside he knows he faces prison or death, with probably three, maybe four years at most on the run. Then someone will get lucky or someone will betray him. The only way to sell this programme idea to him is to play on his vanity and tell him it's a chance for him to make his political will and testament on European satellite television, to go down in history one way or the other. I think, presented like that, he may well agree to do it because, provided his personal security remains tight, there are no drawbacks for him. Only for us.'

Crawshaw leaned back in his chair. He said that he intended to be completely honest. He really had considered the difficulties, and wanted Morgan to know this was not some hare-brained scheme he had dreamed up without much thought.

'Tony, I'm prepared to take your advice on the matter, but you know we cannot absolutely guarantee transmission of anything to anyone. You must tell O'Neill that. We cannot give him a party political broadcast. We reserve the right to edit his words, as always. But I am convinced O'Neill has something important and relevant to say to those of us who live in England, which may be a target for the bombing campaign he is currently organising. Find him, speak to him and make the offer.'

Morgan rose to leave the room. Crawshaw held up his hand.

'Deal directly with me, and for obvious security reasons tell no one in the newsroom or on "Capital Satellite Reports" what you are up to. No one. Just me. Okay?'

'Will you be sending me a memo about this?'

'No.' Crawshaw shook his head emphatically.

Morgan had woken up. 'Who will the producer be?'

'Ah – you'll have to leave that with me for the moment. I'll tell you that when you tell me we have a programme set up. Good hunting.'

Morgan closed the door gently and walked past the two secretaries, wondering whether the other one had the same size of hips as Jean the Hippo. She seemed slimmer. Perhaps they were not a matching pair after all. He had cheered up considerably. He stopped off at the forward planning office and asked for a British Airways shuttle ticket to Belfast, an open return from Dublin, and a hire car. The assignments clerk made shorthand notes.

'Oh, yes. And five hundred pounds in cash to be collected at Heathrow immediately before the flight. No. Make that six hundred. Thanks.'

Morgan felt his belly had settled completely. He would go home soon to pack and tell Emily the good news. He was back on course again. There was no more gurgling. The hangover had definitely gone.

Chapter Three

Belfast

The man in the beige overcoat turned his collar against the rain. He was late, he was wet and he did not want to be in Northern Ireland. The British Airways shuttle from London had been delayed as usual – this time they said it was air traffic control, though he had never known it to be on time. He was travelling under the name of Harry Dunlop, and had decided it would be a good idea to get used to it. Harry was the easy part, since that was his real first name anyway. Dunlop, well, he had to think of something suitably Protestant and that was as good as he could do at short notice. He smiled to himself. It was better than Harry Michelin, or Billy Pirelli.

'It'll be just like going home, sir,' the orderly had said at six that morning when he woke Dunlop. 'Warm welcome from the natives as the exiled favourite son returns to the fatherland, no doubt.'

'No doubt, corporal.'

He had driven from Hereford to Heathrow, and booked a hire car at Aldergrove airport for the drive into Belfast. He stepped briskly across the car park and slid his attaché case into the boot. The rain was driving across from the west, over Lough Neagh and across the airport tarmac. When he started the car, the radio turned on automatically.

'. . . and in Londonderry the security forces have recovered a quantity of arms and explosives from a house in the Shantallow area of the city. Three Kalashnikov rifles, fifteen thousand rounds of ammunition and . . .'

It was good to be home. The Radio Ulster news bulletin could have been delivered any time in the previous twenty years. Maybe they had started repeating the news, too. No one would have noticed.

It was always the same although, despite himself, Dunlop was

25

reassured. Whatever the wars that came and went, the world presidents who were elected or overthrown or disgraced, the floods and the famines and the droughts that other countries suffered and survived, they would still be uncovering terrorist arms and ammunition caches in the city of Londonderry. He chuckled and switched off the radio.

As he reached the security checkpoint at the airport perimeter Dunlop noticed there had been one change. It was now manned entirely by police, no longer by the army. It was a distinction without any real difference. 'The Primacy of the Police,' he remembered, had been one of the great initiatives of the past. It seemed to mean the police were now shot at first, before the army, rather than the other way round. What a God-awful place! He looked beyond the sandbags and grey breeze-blocks of the police post. There was sunshine in the distance on the County Antrim hills.

'A great argument for the neutron bomb,' he once said at an anti-terrorism lecture in Hereford. 'Beautiful country, God-awful people. One neutron bomb causing minimum damage and we could start all over again, using human beings this time.'

There was laughter, and then some of those present told him they thought his argument was at least as credible a solution as any other anti-terrorist policy they had ever heard. So much for Chairman Mao believing the guerrillas were the fish and the masses of people were the water in which they swam. They would just drain the whole bloody pond.

Dunlop took the M2 motorway into Belfast. As he swept over the hill at Glengormly he could see across the city and the lough to the huge yellow cranes of Harland and Wolff's shipyard. He always loved that view – that one more than any – of the lough and the back-to-back red brick terraced houses of east Belfast and the shipyard which dominated them all. It was almost worth coming home to drink in that view again, even in the rain.

He showed his military identification to the guards at the entrance to Stormont Castle, and to his great embarrassment one of them saluted.

'Thanks, pal,' he thought. 'You'd be great at undercover work.'

The Stormont grounds were at their best. The trees were beginning to come into leaf, the new spring grass a deep and rich green. He thought of his unit in Hereford out training in the Brecon Beacons, with sweat on their backs and rain in their faces, half way up Pen-y-Fan or crossing the ridge towards Corn Dhu and enjoying every minute of it. It would hardly be the same, but he wondered if there might be time before he caught the return flight, to walk round the Stormont grounds and taste the air. Anything but the ordeal of the meeting which he was supposed to attend.

A parking place had been reserved, and he was told to step inside the Castle buildings. For all his time in Northern Ireland he had never before been inside the Castle itself. He was surprised to see how well kept the place was – none of the usual civil service drab, this was a proper colonial mansion, with fine oil paintings on the walls and well-worn oak and leather furniture. He sat down on an old brown chesterfield, but almost immediately an efficient-looking secretary with a plummy English accent came down the stairs and led him away. He had been surprised how strange the Ulster accents sounded when he arrived at the airport – the Hertz car hire girls, the baggage loaders, everyone he had overheard. He wondered if his own Ulster accent had simply faded away, or whether he still sounded local. Probably not to the likes of the Hertz girls – but almost certainly to the plummy-voiced secretary. He followed her as she swayed through the corridors of Stormont Castle.

They came to a steel and shatterproof glass door with a security lock on one side. The girl keyed in a sequence of numbers and the door popped open. They climbed one flight of stairs and she opened the dark oak door of the office at the top.

'Captain Dunlop to see you sir,' she said, and showed him inside.

The room was gloomy and wood panelled. Four men sat at one end of a mahogany conference table which could seat twenty. The table was littered with papers and drained coffee cups. The four stood up to greet him.

'Sorry I'm late,' Dunlop said. 'British Airways.'

'No matter,' the middle-aged man nearest him said. He had a round face made owlish by heavy oval spectacles. 'We are all used to it, and make allowances accordingly. What was it this time? Security?'

'No. Air traffic control.'

'I'm Paul Marlowe,' the man added. Dunlop noticed the eyes were bright behind the glasses. 'Your host for today, you might say. I'm Home Office, on attachment to the Northern Ireland Office. This is Brian Henderson from the Ministry of Defence, Christopher Heveley-Martin who is representing Foreign Office interests – since what we are about to discuss refers to the Irish

27

Republic – and James Gibbs who is security co-ordinator here at the Northern Ireland Office. Gentlemen, may I present Captain Harry Dunlop.'

Dunlop looked at the four non-descript, middle-aged gentlemen in grey suits. No, that was not strictly true. Heveley-Martin was wearing a blue suit, but that was clearly an error of judgement. They should all have been wearing grey.

'Coffee, Captain?' Marlowe was saying to him.

He refused it. He always refused it. He had discovered what he believed to be an eternal truth, that wherever the British Civil Service or Army provided coffee, it made him run to the toilet. It was clearly designed to destroy the kidneys, a kind of peacetime chemical warfare which probably meant all those bound to office jobs were incontinent. He wondered about the four grey suits.

'No, really. I'm afraid I never touch the stuff.'

'Well,' Marlowe said. 'Let's get down to business shall we? We have already discussed the preliminary details in your absence, but let me summarise.'

In front of Dunlop on the desk was a blank notepad and pen. He picked up the pen and rolled it round his fingertips. Marlowe cleared his throat and began.

'Professor Gordon Durrant and his wife were kidnapped from their home in Norfolk ten days ago. You will find details in a file we have prepared for you, and photographs. The police believe four or possibly five men were involved, travelling in two vans. We have traced the vans to two separate hire companies, one in Liverpool, the other in North London. Documents used to hire them were, of course, false. There are no worthwhile descriptions of the men. Both vans were found abandoned a few days after the kidnap in Fishguard. Sources in the Irish Republic suggest the couple were taken aboard an Irish registered trawler which had put in to Fishguard the night before the kidnapping, reporting engine trouble. The trawler – the *Roisin Dubh* – is registered in Cork and owned by a man known to be a sympathiser of the Provisional IRA. That is our starting point, and the rest is conjecture.'

Marlowe paused and poured himself some more coffee from the pot in front of him. Dunlop was right. It smelled like burned caffeine.

'As far as we can establish,' Marlowe continued, 'no repairs were carried out on the trawler in Fishguard. Our enquiries about that are continuing, but my role here is as co-ordinator, and this small action group has been convened because this is one of the – what shall I say? – one of the most delicate situations in which we have found ourselves for some years. Let me explain.'

Heveley-Martin produced a pipe from somewhere in his blue suit.

'Mind if I puff away?' he said. No one responded. He began to fill the pipe from an old leather pouch. Dunlop knew by the smell of the unlit mixture that when it burned he was going to hate it, and Heveley-Martin for inflicting it upon them.

'Gordon Durrant,' Marlowe continued, 'was not a civil servant, or rather had not been one formally for a number of years. But he was closely associated with a number of important projects. He was paid a retainer by the Ministry of Defence to continue his research into the development and practical applications of new explosives technology. Durrant was not quite Alfred Nobel, but from what I hear from the MoD he was not far from it, and was particularly useful on some of the special projects being organised out of Hereford.'

Brian Henderson nodded vigorously. Heveley-Martin was almost ready to light his pipe.

'Durrant was not the most organised of fellows,' Marlowe said. 'And so working out exactly what he had in his explosives store has not been easy. His files were not up to date, and he divided his time between lecturing at Cambridge, some freelance work, and the government contracts. He was particularly expert in demolition and blast direction – that is, the use of a shaped charge to produce a blast which could, say, cut through the metal of an oil rig, or destroy the concrete supports of an old building, that sort of thing. He also tried his hand at inventing – there is no other word – inventing new types of explosive. We have produced an inventory of what we think was taken from his laboratory, workshop and store. Let me give you a copy, Captain.'

Dunlop stretched out his hand and received four pages of typed A4 paper. The list began with a large amount of commercial gelignite, two types of NATO standard military plastic explosives, both PETN and RDX, some Czech plastic explosives, wires, detonators, batteries and other paraphernalia, plus two things Dunlop had never heard of, Foamex and Magnex.

'Enough to blow up half of Ireland, if we're lucky,' Heveley-Martin said, smiling.

'I think the problem,' Marlowe said firmly, 'is that it is more likely to be used to blow up half of England.' He helped himself to yet another coffee and Dunlop wondered how long his kidneys could last.

'What are Foamex and Magnex?' Dunlop asked. Marlowe looked at him and smiled.

'They are little inventions of Durrant's, or at least developments by Durrant from existing plastic explosives technology. Foamex is a foamed plastic explosive prepared inside an aerosol can. It looks rather like shaving foam in consistency though normally it is silver in colour. Aluminium filings or something like that within it.'

Brian Henderson, the man from the Ministry of Defence, interrupted. 'The beauty of it is that it is so easy to disguise. It can be scented to make it smell like shaving foam. It is totally stable in the can, but once the foam mixes with the propellant in the atmosphere it becomes a rather effective explosive. Some of our people are rather keen on it.'

'And Magnex,' Marlowe added, 'is even more interesting. It is Durrant's pride and joy – a magnetic, shaped plastic charge which he patented and which is about to be manufactured commercially. He offered it to us a while ago, but our people decided its military applications were limited. He decided it was a more useful tool for those interested in cutting through metal on old ships, destroying unwanted oil rig platforms, cutting through the metal struts supporting skyscrapers that people want demolished. That sort of thing.'

'Sounds potentially nasty,' Dunlop said.

'Yes, very nasty.' Marlowe agreed. 'Not of great interest to us in a conventional military sense, but no doubt the Provisionals might find an appropriate use for it.'

There was a short pause. It was a more interesting briefing than Dunlop had suspected, since in the normal way of things they would drone on with all kinds of theories and make all kinds of rules which had to be followed in the unlikely event of Dunlop having to be used in any capacity whatsoever. This was different. Marlowe seemed capable of rattling through the facts without the usual civil service prolixity. Heveley-Martin had even taken his pipe from his mouth and rested it in his saucer, where bits of ash fell into the stained ring of spilled coffee. Marlowe began talking again.

'The reason we invited you here, Captain Dunlop, is because we are, frankly, in a bit of a mess. Our kidnapping strategy is fairly well known: negotiate, delay, and then if the negotiations come to nothing, attempt a rescue as a last resort. That strategy depends upon one thing – that the kidnappers make some kind of demands, and in consequence have to get into contact with either the family or company of the victim to extort money, or with some branch of the government to extort favours. It simply has not happened. There have been no demands, and there has been no contact. With the Niedermayer case, if you remember it, the IRA wanted to extort political favours from us. In the Don Tidey case they simply wanted a ransom. This time the only inference we can draw is that Professor Durrant is not only the victim but the prize the kidnappers are seeking. They do not simply want his explosives, they want his expertise to enable them to make the most effective use of what they have captured. It is not a very pleasant conclusion, but I think the logic of it is inescapable.'

'You mean the IRA wants him to do for them what he has been doing on an ad-hoc basis for our own soldiers down in Hereford or Wiltshire, or wherever it is?' Dunlop said. 'Train them how to get the best bang from the available kit.'

'Precisely,' Marlowe said, nodding enthusiastically. 'And since Margaret Durrant has been taken as well, we must assume it is not because the Provisionals have developed a sudden enthusiasm for her academic speciality, Norse and Icelandic sagas. We are working on the assumption that she is the inducement for Durrant to co-operate. They will almost certainly threaten to shoot or torture her unless he does as they say.'

The room was suddenly silent. The others had stopped taking notes. The smell of pipe tobacco still held in the air. Dunlop noticed the rain outside was splashing heavily on the window panes, beating in over Belfast and the Castlereagh hills, the sky dark grey. Marlowe shuffled his papers.

'There are various options we have been discussing before holding today's meeting, and since the one which is, shall we say, the most interventionist, involves Captain Dunlop, I thought it best to brief you all in detail now, to save time later. We have still to obtain full political clearance, but I am assured at the very highest level, that in this case we can take such clearance for granted.'

Marlowe looked directly at Dunlop and told him he had been chosen to help not only because of the extraordinary qualities he had shown with his regiment but also because he was an Ulsterman.

'As you can hear,' Marlowe said, smiling to the others. 'He is an Ulsterman who sounds like an Ulsterman. He can blend in, which is more than can be said for most of us over here. And he knows the background with all its complex nuances in a way which defeats most of us however long we remain here.'

Dunlop shrugged his shoulders.

'I may sound like an Ulsterman to you, Mr Marlowe,' he said. 'But to most people in Ireland I sound like a Ballymena man, because that's where I was brought up. And the problem with that, for those of you unfamiliar with the sectarian geography of Ireland, is that Ballymena is in County Antrim, the most Protestant and anti-republican county of them all. I can blend in if you believe Durrant is held by some of the loyalist paramilitaries, but if he really is held by an active service unit of the IRA, then I will be able to blend in about as well as a black man in the Ku Klux Klan.'

Marlowe smiled again. He said he quite understood, and that he knew there were other men in Dunlop's unit in Hereford who were also from Ireland and who might blend in better than he did in particular circumstances, but the general thrust of his point still stood. Some of those on secondment to the SAS and the Intelligence and Security Group were from the Ulster Defence Regiment. There were even two from the Republic of Ireland on secondment from the Irish Guards. From among those Dunlop would select his team.

Dunlop nodded.

'Yes, that's fine,' he said. 'I'm sure we have the men for the job anyway.'

'Well, whatever the details we have decided that it may well become a job for your unit. Our first priority is to *find* the Durrants and I have already begun that process. We are assuming that they are in a PIRA safe house somewhere in rural Ireland, and possibly near the Irish border, but we have no firm information.'

Heveley-Martin lit his pipe again.

Marlowe looked at him with something approaching disgust as the clouds of smoke puffed upwards. The obvious problem, Marlowe continued, was that they were unable to circulate the information of the Durrants' kidnap, since that might preclude any further action.

'Don't follow you there,' Henderson said. 'What do you mean?'

'Let me spell out in full the logic of our position and the risks we are now about to run,' Marlowe said, like a teacher organising a spot of revision for his pupils. 'I do not want anyone to leave this room with any misapprehensions about the importance being attached to this problem. PIRA has been able to add to its stocks of plastic explosives in, we believe, a considerable way. The enhancement to its capabilities which could be provided by a compliant Durrant is virtually immeasurable. There must never be another Brighton bomb, or anything like it. As a result, the decision has been taken that we must ensure that we lay our hands on the Durrants and as much of the equipment that we can recover as soon as possible.'

'But my point,' Henderson tried again, 'is why can't we simply pass on the word right down the line to the Irish police and the Royal Ulster Constabulary. How do we expect them to be found if the security forces do not even know they are missing?'

Marlowe seemed slightly exasperated. Maybe he was not quite so used to dealing with the dogged souls at the MoD as Dunlop had become. He spoke quietly and carefully, as if to a recalcitrant sixth former.

'Because all a hue and cry will achieve is to generate unhelpful media interest and alert the IRA. It will bring in the Dublin government and PC O'Plod, but will also severely restrict our freedom to act. It means that, if the Durrants are held in the Irish Republic, we cannot call on the services of Captain Dunlop since the Dublin government will never allow British troops to be used against Irish citizens on their own territory. It is therefore imperative that we maintain absolute security. If, for any reason, the Irish police do stumble upon the Durrants then all well and good. It seems to me a remote prospect, and rather than wait for such an event, we should pursue other methods in an attempt to find them.'

Marlowe was beginning to sound harrassed, since his decision to proceed without publicity and without a full scale cross-border manhunt, was probably the most important and the most difficult to defend if it went wrong. He had cleared it at higher levels, but the decision was essentially his own.

At the risk of compounding Marlowe's misery, Dunlop said he was curious to know how it was that an active service unit of the IRA happened to pick on a semi-retired academic living in a remote area of Norfolk.

Marlowe smiled again. He said it was an interesting question and one to which they had given a great deal of thought.

'Truth is, we don't actually know. But some of our people have made an informed guess. We think it has something to do with the wonders of television. Professor Gordon Durrant appeared on the "Science Today" programme, extolling the virtues of his Magnex invention. We have a video cassette copy – we'll let you have it before you go. What it shows is a rather verbose but quite engaging man telling the presenter that Magnex is selling like hot cakes in the United States. He says it is wonderful for cutting for down old skyscrapers, greatly saving on labour costs – that sort of thing. We think the IRA were much impressed by this unwitting advertisement. It was filmed at Durrant's home near Norwich. He's in the telephone book under ''D''. I'm afraid you wouldn't need to be to Special Branch track him down. Our inferences may not be correct, but it is a theory which for the moment we find plausible.'

Gibbs, the man from the Northern Ireland Office, spoke for the first time. Dunlop had met a few of these people before and thought he recognised Gibbs from somewhere – maybe at one of the officers' parties at Thiepval Barracks in Lisburn. Of all the civil servants, the English blow-ins at the Northern Ireland Office were the ones Dunlop disliked the most. They were rarely allowed out of Stormont castle except to parties where they met other Brits. Dunlop hated their smart English accents and their superior airs of pretending to know it all after two weeks in Belfast. Gibbs was explaining to Heveley-Martin as a kind of joke why the Irish police could not be trusted.

'You may remember Mrs Lawford's kidnapping last year,' Gibbs said. 'It was a straightforward ransom attempt by the Irish National Liberation Army to raise some money for party funds. Well, the Royal Ulster Constabulary told the Irish police the names and forwarded the photographs and descriptions of the men we believed were involved. There had been yet another takeover inside the INLA with the various lunatic fringes shooting each other for control again, and we believed it was part of the Belfast INLA who had broken off and were desperately short of money. Anyway, the Dublin headquarters of the Garda Siochana imposed a news blackout. We went along with it, of course. The Gardai put into effect their supposedly superb ''National Cordon'' – police officers at every strategic road junction out of Dublin and round the border with the North, that sort of thing.'

Gibbs paused and Marlowe seemed anxious to return to the briefing.

'What happened?' Gibbs went on. 'They kept such a strict news blackout that no one at Garda headquarters told the police on the ground who they were looking for, who the kidnap victim was. They did not even know if it was a woman, man or bloody horse!

Most of them probably thought it was Shergar on the loose again!'

Gibbs laughed loudly at his own story, joined by Henderson and Heveley-Martin. Dunlop smiled politely, and so did Marlowe.

'It's your best hope,' Gibbs said gleefully to Marlowe. 'The Paddy Factor. The ability of the Irish, whether terrorist or police, to screw it up. It is the only way we are likely to find the Durrants in all this.'

Marlowe smiled again and thanked him for his optimism. Then he brought them back to business. He ran through more details of the kidnapping, principally for Dunlop's benefit, and asked Heveley-Martin to go outside and tell the secretary to bring in the cassette copy of Durrant's television programme for Dunlop. He then briskly recounted names and known methods of a list of IRA men who might be involved. Gibbs contributed a few anecdotes on each, and promised Dunlop access to RUC Special Branch biographies of the top dozen or so suspects.

'Maybe he's just remembered I'm a Paddy too,' Dunlop thought. 'Trying to charm me now because he thinks I'm insulted. Damn right I'm insulted. Paddy Factor my arse.'

The briefing began to cover ground they had already discussed. They agreed that such an ambitious plan, the kidnapping and holding of the Durrants for a considerable time, could not just be the work of renegades such as the INLA gang responsible in the Lawford case. This had to be sanctioned at Army Council level within the IRA. All kidnappings were a serious drain on the resources of terrorist organisations. The Royal Ulster Constabulary specialist tracking team, E4A, had tried to provide dossiers on all the IRA active units at around the time of the kidnapping, but most of the top men were outside Northern Ireland and their intelligence was patchy.

Gibbs confirmed that there had been a few changes at Army Council level within PIRA as the Maze escapers re-established themselves within the Movement. Francis Coffey had been moved out as Director of External Operations, and while Sean Hughes remained as Quartermaster, it was thought his days were numbered. The Belfast and Northern Command boys were probably trying to push him aside.

'The changes are all in the files,' Marlowe said. 'As far as we know them. But you'll see the main thrust has been to put some of those who escaped from the Maze prison into positions of power.

They will want to prove themselves, which makes the possibilities in respect of Durrant almost endless. Whether you believe in the Paddy Factor or not, you should know that we do not under-estimate the extent to which personal rivalries and jealousies within PIRA mean that the new hard men will want to demonstrate their toughness. Durrant may be the means to that end.'

'They'll want a big bang,' Gibbs asserted. 'Another Brighton bomb. Or one in the Commons, or at Ascot. Something like that.'

'Well, let's not scare ourselves too much,' Marlowe snapped. 'Anyway, that just about brings us to a close. We'd better let you get back to Hereford, Captain. But I'll be in touch, one way or the other. Even if it is to say that we are not proceeding. It would be useful if you could be prepared to move out when, or rather if, the time comes, with the minimum of delay. You had better choose your team and brief them, whatever happens.'

Dunlop stood up and shook hands all round. He picked up the green file and the video tape, and was shown out by the secretary.

It had been a long journey for a meeting which lasted less than two hours. The rain had stopped but the sky was still heavy and grey. Dunlop looked at his watch and decided there was plenty of time to make the four-thirty shuttle – time enough for a short walk in the Stormont grounds.

In the Brecons they would now be well over Pen-y-Fan and prob-ably descending Corn Dhu, past the Neuadd reservoir and back to the road. They would be soaked with sweat and rain, happy to be on the homeward leg. Dunlop took the alleyway down past the kennels where the RUC kept their Alsatians for the dog patrols and peri-meter security, and then walked out into the main civil service car park at the side of the Stormont Parliament buildings. The rain was easing slightly and there was a blue gap in the sky, a patch of sunshine over Belfast. He walked forward to the statue of Lord Carson at the front of the buildings and looked up at the energetic figure caught in a pose of utter defiance – defying the British of course, insisting that Protestant Ulster should not fall under the rule of the Catholic republic to the south. Dunlop turned and strode up the hill to the Stormont Parliament itself, impressed – despite his usual cynicism about his home province – with the grandness of the building, the wideness of the steps. This was Ulster unionist power, built with love to provide a Protestant parliament for a

Protestant people. It was now empty, the debating chamber shut since the last local elections when the effort to produce devolution had succeeded only in rounding up the usual suspects. The men who had failed before were put into the same room to shout at each other until they failed again. Wasn't democracy marvellous?

Dunlop turned at the top of Stormont steps and looked out over the city of Belfast. His heart leaped, and for the first time in years he felt glad to be an Ulsterman. The rain was sticking to his hair, but it was lighter now, no more than a fine drizzle. The blue patch had widened and he could see the hills of Antrim. Why was it, he wondered, that the English always thought you could solve the Northern Ireland problem by 'compromise' or 'goodwill'? How could a man compromise on the nation he belonged to? He was British. The IRA were Irish, and were trying to expel him and his kin from their own country. It was as simple as that. There was no middle ground – it was not an industrial dispute, where you can settle for one per cent less than you wanted, and everyone goes home happy. No amount of bargaining would make him feel any less British. No amount of talking would make the others feel any less Irish.

He started to walk down the steps and wondered if Marlowe understood. Gibbs wouldn't, or Henderson or Heveley-Martin. Marlowe might. He was bright enough, not flabby in the dull English way of the others. Dunlop smiled. Then, as he once more passed Carson's statue on the way back to the car, a stray thought crossed his mind about why, despite his Ballymena accent, he might be ideal for any kind of illegal rescue of the Durrants from the Irish Republic. If it all went wrong, and if he was leading a bunch of Ulstermen, the British government could write it off as the mad exploits of some loyalist gangsters, acting independently. There would be nothing to link him with the British Army or the government. Once over the border they would be on their own. Dunlop paused for a last look at Carson's eager defiance. He was not sure he believed his own theory, but it did at least make sense.

'Plausible deniability,' he said out loud to Carson's backside, as the statue gestured out over Belfast. 'That's what the Americans call it. Being able to get away with any bullshit because no one can prove you wrong.'

He turned and walked back to the car park. He could feel a sudden quickening of his pulse, partly in anticipation but now a little tinged with fear. He reached the hire car and the rain was starting to gather strength again. There were puddles at the edges of the car park and ripples forming round the heavy drops as they hit the water surface. The engine started first time and he jammed it into gear.

'Plausible deniability,' he said again out loud, rolling the phrase over on his tongue. 'The Paddy Factor.'

Chapter Four

County Louth, Republic of Ireland

The man had a strange, rolling gait as he walked up the gravel path towards the bungalow. He was small and dark, with a brown moustache and a boxer's nose. He had parked his car on the grass verge at the front of the house and pulled three full plastic carrier bags and a brown parcel from the boot. He flexed his arm muscles and swaggered cheerfully up towards the bungalow. When he reached the front door he kicked it gently with the toe of his boot.

Billy McKeever pulled the revolver from the waistband of his trousers and looked out from behind the curtains. No one had followed Kelly up the path, and no cars had gone past. The bungalow was well chosen – near enough town to get what they needed, set far enough back from the road to ensure it stayed private. Brendan Kelly, weighed down with the bags, kicked the door again.

'I'm coming,' McKeever yelled. 'Jesus man, give us a chance.'

He stuffed the revolver into his belt, pulled open the curtain which covered the inside of the door, and slid back the bolts. Then he took the key-ring from his belt and turned the main lock.

'Fort bloody Knox,' he heard Kelly say. 'Is this to keep you in or to keep me out?'

Kelly stood grinning on the doorstep. The hot tang of vinegar on chips caught McKeever's nostrils.

'I got dinner while I was at it,' Kelly said, handing him the brown paper parcel. McKeever could feel the warmth. 'I couldn't face another one of your special fried eggs and bacon.'

McKeever said nothing. He locked and bolted the door behind them and took the parcel into the kitchen.

'She made them up fresh,' Brendan Kelly said. 'Or maybe she reheated them up fresh. I had to wait for them, anyway. You think the prof wants cod or haddock?'

Dipping into the plastic carrier bags, he handed McKeever two

39

jars of white powder and a bottle. All three had chemists' labels on them. McKeever took the chemicals through the hallway connecting the kitchen to the garage. The garage windows were covered by thick curtains, nailed round the frame. When the sun shone directly through the curtains there was at best a poor orange light. McKeever placed the two jars and bottle on the bench. There was a bare bulb in the centre of the ceiling and two anglepoise lamps jointed like black metallic elbows over the workbench. McKeever switched on an anglepoise and checked the names of the chemicals against the list Durrant had written for them. Then he scraped off the part of the label which had the chemist's name and address on it, turning the jars in the light to make sure nothing remained.

In the kitchen Kelly had uncovered the fish and chips and put them on plates under the grill to make sure they were still hot. The smell of fish and vinegar drifted into the garage.

'The hydrogen peroxide is the wrong strength,' McKeever said. 'Durrant asked for ten per cent.'

'It was all Fagan's had,' Kelly replied, turning the chips to warm them properly, and sticking one in his mouth. 'Nothing stronger unless I wanted to wait, or come back. He said he didn't think any of the other chemists would have it either, and I thought we could just see if the prof can make do. Otherwise I'll ask him to make it up special.'

Kelly opened the door from the kitchen into the back of the bungalow, and yelled out. 'Hey, prof you want a haddock or a cod?'

His Belfast accent split the silence at the back of the bungalow. Gordon Durrant lay on his bed reading an old newspaper in the light from a forty-watt bulb. The bedroom window was shut and curtained like the garage, nailed fast. Durrant could smell the dust from the old curtain and longed to stand in the open air. It was a strange fantasy, to stand naked in the cold and fresh air, and breathe and breathe again, or to go for a run until his lungs ached. They had told him insistently not even to try to open the window. It was barred on the outside, shuttered and sealed fast, they said. He had no choice but to believe them. The only way to find out for sure would be to rip the curtain away from the nails. They would notice that immediately and punish him for it. Punish him severely. Of that there was no doubt. In fact Durrant almost found it amusing, an exquisite conundrum for the scientist. Should he begin the most simple of experiments and find out whether the window was barred or not, and try to open it anyway? Or would this attempt at empiricism result in a very unscientific beating? The safest thing was always to do nothing. But was it the most sensible?

He smiled to himself. The imaginary conversations in which he played both parts were becoming part of a daily routine. What would Galileo have done? Galileo now, confronted by the Pope and his Cardinals or stuck maybe with the terrorists. '*E pur si muove*,' and yet it moves. He wondered if he should try it on the Boxer or the Thin Man next time they threatened him. The fate of the scientist in the Dark Ages, to be punished by the fanatics for seeking the truth. '*E pur si muove*.' That was it, you Irish bastards.

'Haddock would be fine,' he yelled back. 'Yes, haddock.'

For the first few days they had spoken to him only when they needed to. There had been no pleasantries, although the one with the boxer's face had once or twice tried to crack a joke. That had been silenced by the others, and the Boxer had not been quick to repeat it. He did not seem very high up whatever pecking order they had, but Durrant thought that the Boxer was warming a little towards him, and he appreciated what he thought were hints of humanity. The bald one, with such a wide and wrinkled forehead that Durrant thought of him as the Skull, had been much more taciturn. Was he quiet, or more likely, just dim? It was difficult to judge.

As for the other two, they lived elsewhere – the thin-faced ratty man and the girl. They were the pair who scared Durrant most. It wasn't just that he saw less of them, and therefore found their moods more difficult to predict. It was also that Durrant believed that the Thin Man was a killer. The Boxer with his bashed face might look like a fighter, yet somehow Durrant could not imagine him pulling a trigger. It took no imagination whatsoever to see the Thin Man pull it. He would be sneering when he did, having a good time. As for the Girl, she was the strangest of all. She looked as if she could be pretty, really attractive, until she scowled or swore at him. Durrant had never heard such viciousness, or suffered such abuse from a woman. He was sure she could pull the trigger. But that was a stupid thing to say – presumably they all could, and still sleep easily.

Durrant could hear the Boxer and the Skull banging around the kitchen preparing lunch. He pushed the newspaper aside and pulled a cigarette from the pack. He lit it and stared round the room. It was like a dim cell, smelling of dust and damp. There was a creaky bed with a sagging mattress, an old wooden wardrobe and a chest of drawers where some previous occupant had rested his lit cigarettes, scorching the varnish. Durrant's old suitcase lay in a corner with a few clothes. The wallpaper must have been garishly bright once, but the purple and maroon and gold had faded now into vague, dull shapes. He often studied it closely, trying to create order from the pattern, fitting the shapes together until they locked to make sensible faces or animals. Sometimes, just to keep his mind working, he would shut his eyes and try to remember every object in the room, reciting them as a list the way he had once recited the books of the Bible at school. At other times he would try to recall the position of all the equipment in the garage, what lay beside it and precisely how it was arranged.

He continued to be surprised at the way they treated him. He had been prepared for threats, but these mainly came from the Thin Man, with a few thrown in by the Girl. The other two were more content, provided he obeyed simple instructions. Durrant assumed from their attitude to one another that the Boxer and the Skull were more like the drones of the operation, with the Thin Man and the Girl in charge.

What he had not expected was that he would be given anything to make his life almost tolerable – an old black and white television set, and newspapers more or less every day. From the start they made it clear this was not some humanitarian gesture. They wanted him to watch and read as much as he liked, to prove to him that he was not big news. He was not news at all. Not once was his disappearance mentioned in any of the papers or on any of the news programmes on television or radio, not a sentence that he could find.

'You're nothing, prof,' the Thin Man had said on the first day. They had taken him into the front room so they could all watch the news bulletin together. The Thin Man was standing drinking tea, talking loudly. 'Not a word, not a single paragraph in any of the papers. Nobody gives a shit whether you turn up again or not. They probably haven't yet worked out that you are missing. So you'd better just remember that, and do as you're told, or we'll make you disappear without trace. Permanently.'

The Thin Man seemed almost drunk, his face flushed with the success of what they had done. Durrant noticed his skin was dry and flaky, his mouth twisted by the intensity with which he spat out his words.

'You're not even Shergar,' he said, and the others laughed. 'There was more of a search for the bloody missing racehorse than there ever will be over you. And if they're not looking for you, then they can't find you. And if they can't find you then there's no chance of a rescue. So don't think you can hold anything back. You are here till we decide otherwise. We want you to tell us everything, got that? Every fucking thing. We want it accurate, and we want it quick.'

They laughed again. The Thin Man finished his little speech by taking a swig of tea. Durrant nodded and agreed where he thought appropriate. He looked around at happy eyes and slack grins.

They had not allowed him to see his wife, Margaret, since the night of the kidnap, though he had talked to her once on that first day. The telephone conversation had seemed the most depressing two minutes of his life, and in the days since he had turned the words over and over in his mind in the hope of finding some meaning he had so far missed. He longed to repeat the conversation, to hear even a few words from her, to remind her he was alive, and to tell her all the things he should have said before. Long before. He took a last pull on the cigarette and stubbed the butt in a Guinness ashtray by the bedside. He put his hands behind his head and lay at full stretch on the bed.

Sometimes when he was alone in the evenings, lying on the bed and smoking, Durrant recalled odd things from his childhood, like random presents pulled from a lucky dip. He could remember without any effort the faces of his classmates at his primary school, the music master playing the morning hymn at assembly, the face of his housemaster as he sang loudly and out of tune. Words and phrases from lectures he had given at Cambridge rolled into his head at odd angles. One moment he thought of his time as a school prefect, the next he would hear himself discussing gas chromatography or the relative values of conventional linear cutting charges. One moment he would be thinking of Margaret, and the next some recollection would butt its way into his thoughts, hold centre stage for a moment or two and then walk away.

He looked at the shapes on the wallpaper and tried to piece together that last night at home in Norfolk. Some things were easy. He could recall exactly what Margaret had been wearing as she sat at the fireside reading some fat and incomprehensible Norse or Icelandic book. It surprised him that he could remember her blue pleated skirt, her thick sweater and dark blue woollen stockings.

She had always complained that he paid no attention to how she looked, and yet she was wrong. He wanted to tell her she was wrong.

She could become so absorbed in a book that anything he did – switching on the television or the radio, or getting ready to take the dog for a walk – simply passed her by. That night he had clipped on Bob's lead, said something like 'I won't be long,' and without looking up from the book, she had made a soft noise in recognition that he had said something. That was all. Blue pleated skirt and blue woollen stockings and soft noise. Fat book and fluffy jumper. He had gone out into an unremarkable night and whatever had happened next, happened. He thought he had come upon the Boxer in the darkness, saying something to him, but he could not remember having seen the Skull until he woke up in his room in the bungalow. He had been hit, he knew that much, and bundled into a bag. He could still smell the sacking and taste the fear, but even the fear was odd. It had never occurred to him that whoever was hitting him was going to kill him, or if it had, he did not really mind.

What did terrify him was the prospect of choking to death on his own vomit, gasping for breath while they stuffed the gag in his mouth and dying for no reason at the bottom of some wooden box. It was not the dying, but the idea of doing so by *accident* which frightened him most. It was the lack of meaning, the sheer unreasonableness of it all, that frightened him. Why me? Why this? Why?

He remembered being worried as he fell to the pavement, that the dog might run out into the road and be hit by a car. He could still feel the lead slipping from his grasp and his mind switching from surprise to fear for the spaniel. He wondered where the dog had gone, and tried to make a mental note to ask them when they brought lunch. The bits and pieces of his first day in the bungalow were coming together, but he found it difficult to remember their proper sequence. They had taken him into the main room. The blinds and curtains were shut, though he was sure it was daylight outside. They sat him in a chair and they had all watched the British television news. All five of them: him, the Boxer, the Skull, the Girl and the Thin Man. The Thin Man had threatened him, and then one of them went into the kitchen and produced a mug of sweet milky tea. He always drank it black at home, but took it anyway. The details of his life no longer mattered.

He looked round the room at their faces. The Thin Man was talking in a loud voice to the Boxer and the Girl. The Skull sat at the table drinking his tea and reading a newspaper. He could not recall what they were talking about. At one point they started to whisper among themselves, and he could see the Skull and the Boxer had pistols stuck inside their trouser waistbands. After a while, long after he had drunk the tea, there was a knock at the door. The Thin Man and the Girl went into the hallway. Someone they called The Boss had arrived. That was how they introduced him.

'Meet the Boss,' the Boxer had said when the man walked into the room. He was tall and wiry and, unlike the others, he hid his face behind a black woollen balaclava. Through the slits Durrant could see nothing of the man's features, nothing at all. All he could remember was that the Boss liked to dress well. He wore a smart tweed jacket and neatly pressed light brown trousers. Durrant remembered distinctly thinking how clean the man's clothes were, compared to the others in their faded jeans and old pullovers. He was no dandy, but he took care to look smart. The Boss sat in a chair next to Durrant and studied him for a minute or two. The others stood leaning against the walls in silence.

'I'm not going to be here for long,' the Boss had said. 'So I want you to listen carefully to what I am about to say. It is very important – for you – that you pay attention.'

He had a curiously soft voice – a Northern Ireland accent, but one which seemed a complete opposite to the unpleasant whine of the Thin Man. He spoke slowly and deliberately, his mouth hidden behind the black balaclava. He said he was a senior member of the Irish Republican Army, and that Durrant was in no danger provided he co-operated fully with them. The kidnapping had been sanctioned by something called the Army Council. Durrant could not believe that this gangster who would not even dare to show his face was lecturing him about 'co-operating'. Durrant countered that he would not be blackmailed into anything by a gang of terrorists, and that they could shoot him for all he cared. He almost threw his empty mug at the balaclava, but thought better of it. The futility of his anger made him smile now as he remembered it.

'We won't shoot you,' the voice from behind the balaclava said calmly, as if foreseeing his reaction. 'We'll shoot your wife instead. And we'll do it in front of you. We will bring her here and execute her and make you watch it all, and before we do we will let you tell her why we're being forced to do it. Then we'll turn you loose so you can spend the rest of your life remembering you were so brave that you got your wife killed.'

The Boss had spoken in such a quiet, measured way that it was difficult for Durrant to take in the threat. He had not really known what to expect, but assumed that people who assaulted him in his own village and then kidnapped him would probably beat him and torture him too. All he had really understood, and this for the first time, was that Margaret had also been kidnapped. He was ashamed to realise that he had not thought of her before, and he stood up in fury.

'Where is she, you faceless bastard?' he yelled at the black balaclava.

'Safe,' the Boss said, calmly. He did not flinch, as if he knew Durrant would not be stupid enough to try to strike him or to attempt to escape. 'For precisely how long, depends on you. Now sit there and calm down.'

There was a moment's silence while Durrant stood looking at the black balaclava, catching a glint from the Boss's eyes. The others said nothing. Durrant felt his courage ebb and sat down. He sighed, bowed his head and closed his eyes. The Boss instructed the Boxer to arrange for Durrant to speak to his wife on the telephone. The Boxer immediately dialled a few digits – God! Durrant had tried to work out how many – but he could not remember whether it sounded like a local call or not. There had been a short conversation with someone at the other end of the line, and then the Boxer jabbed the receiver at Durrant.

From the little she was allowed to say it seemed Margaret had been bundled up and put in a crate too. She was now being held with a gun to her head. She said she was all right and asked how he was. Durrant mumbled a few words which he could not now remember. He thought he was going to cry, but something brave in her voice made him hold back the tears. She said they had made no demands of her, beyond saying that if she were to try to escape they would kill him and it would be her fault. One of them had mentioned that she was what he called 'the penalty clause' in the agreement they were about to negotiate with her husband. She asked Durrant what they meant by that, but the Boss snatched the telephone from him, and banged it down in its cradle.

'Now sit down,' he ordered. 'You understand that we are not bluffing?'

Durrant could not remember if he had started to weep or not. It did not much matter. It was obvious there was no point in being brave or trying to resist. They had it all. He always thought he possessed one real talent as a scientist – an ability to think even the most ridiculous propositions through logically to their conclusion. The conclusion now was obvious. He looked up and asked them to repeat what it was that they wanted him to do. The Boss began again in the same measured tone he had used before. He said they wanted Durrant for his expertise. He was to teach them precisely what they wanted to know about the characteristics of the explosives they had taken from his house laboratory and store. He would ask no questions and he would not fail to answer any of theirs. If he did as they told him he would be treated well, and eventually released. His wife would be unharmed.

'Any other course of action on your part, and both you and your wife will be executed. Co-operate and live, or resist and die. the choice is yours.'

Half an hour later the Boss had left, and that was the last he had seen of him or heard from Margaret. The Thin Man and the Girl left too, and the Boxer and the Skull tried to cheer him up with the promise of a meeting with his wife sometime after he had proved his willingness to co-operate. Then they led him back to his bedroom and locked the door.

'We start lessons first thing tomorrow,' the Boxer yelled through the door. 'Get a good night's sleep.'

A kind of routine had begun from the next day. He woke early and the Skull brought him a mug of tea and some toast. He said nothing. After ten minutes the Boxer would arrive and tell him it was time to wash and go to the bathroom. He could see that the bathroom window was barred and shuttered on the outside. He washed as best he could and then returned to his room to have the first cigarette of the day. At about nine-thirty the Thin Man and the Girl arrived. Durrant, on no evidence, believed they might be lovers and that, possibly, they were also helping to guard Margaret. It was a reasonable guess, and if it was correct then she must be close to where he was. There was a certain logic to it. He hoped it might be so.

Usually, as soon as the Thin Man and the Girl arrived in the morning, the Boxer would let Durrant out of the room and take him to the workbench in the garage. The five of them would sit under the bare ceiling light and the two bright anglepoise lamps. At first the Thin Man would produce articles they had taken from his magazine back in Norfolk – gelignite, detonators, military plastic explosives, and so on. They asked him questions – or rather, the Thin Man asked with the others occasionally making a contribution. Some of the questions seemed to Durrant to be so unbelievably simple that he was sure they were trying to check what he said against things they already knew. Yet he was amazed at how ignorant they were of plastic explosives; genuinely ignorant. The Thin Man, who was becoming more and more tiresome, asked about the relative properties of RDX and PETN.

'I would have thought you might already know that,' Durrant said, with a grin. 'They have been around for fifty years. Or haven't you caught up with Second World War technology yet?'

It had been a mistake. It was the Girl who yelled at him first.

'Skip the sarcasm you bastard and answer the fucking question.'

The words were like needles jabbed deep into Durrant's skin. He did not try to be smart again. Durrant could not understand from their questions whether they were working towards one specific operation, or just trying to learn as much as possible about everything. They were covering a wide range of subjects in no particular depth and in a haphazard sort of way. That first day in the garage was less of a seminar led by Durrant and more an interrogation by the Thin Man. At the end of that day the Thin Man said he wanted Durrant to prepare a series of lessons on different subjects: detonators, home-made explosives, booster charges, Magnex and so on. In effect, the Thin Man was asking for a basic degree course in bomb-making technology, though without any time limit being set on the teaching. Durrant almost wondered whether he should offer to set an end-of-course exam, or arrange for a class project. He had a feeling the class project was already underway. The thought made him smile.

Durrant was about to reach for another cigarette. He sat up at the side of the bed, and then he heard the Boxer turn the key in the door. The most conversation he had got out of any of them at meal times in the first few days was the command to eat. Now the Boxer, in particular, might exchange a few words, and even the Skull had been known to grunt a little. Offering him the choice between haddock and cod today was almost a breakthrough, the nearest he had come to being allowed to make a decision for himself since he had been kidnapped. The Boxer carried in the plate of food on a tray.

'Careful, prof, it's hot,' he said. 'Don't burn those hands. We need them nimble.' Kelly handed the tray to Durrant and turned to leave. 'Sorry about the no-tomato sauce. We've none and I forgot to get some. I got you a copy of the *Irish Times*, and I'll bring it in after you've had your dinner. You can read it all afternoon if you like since the other two have some business to attend to and we decided to give you the rest of the day off.'

'Okay,' Durrant said, pulling the tray towards him. Then, matter-of-factly: 'How's my wife?'

The Boxer smiled. 'She's fine, prof. Just fine. Don't you worry about her. She's being well looked after. Besides we've been keeping the Boss briefed on how things have been going with you, telling him you're sound enough and all that, and he says he's pleased. If you play it right you'll get to see your wife maybe in a weekend or two.'

Kelly turned to go again. Durrant noticed he did not have his gun in his belt. Maybe they were beginning to relax a little.

'Oh,' Kelly said. 'I nearly forgot. I got all the extra chemicals you asked me to pick up, except the peroxide is only five per cent.'

'That's not a problem,' Durrant said. 'It will do at that.'

'Good. Enjoy your fish.'

Durrant thought he would push his luck. Before Kelly could get out through the door he asked how long they were intending to keep him locked up. How could he be sure they would keep the bargain and eventually let him go?

The Boxer stopped smiling. 'I thought you understood that we're the ones that ask the questions, and you're the fella that comes up with the answers. There are no guarantees in this life. Eat your dinner.'

Kelly slammed the door and locked it behind him. Durrant looked at the fish glistening in its batter and the reheated chips. It was better than the fried eggs and bacon they'd been feeding him with, but if they didn't shoot him first, he'd die of heart disease. He smiled at his own foolishness. He had no rights and barely any privileges, and yet he could make stupid jokes. He did not understand it. He pushed a wisp of grey hair away from his face and began to eat. He was hungry. For the first time since the kidnapping, truly hungry. In a matter of minutes he finished the chips and picked the haddock from the greasy batter. He pushed the tray to one side and lay full length on the bed. He lit a cigarette and tried for the dozenth time to live up to his opinion of himself as someone capable of reasoning through problems towards a solution.

There were problems that could be solved and there were those which could be solved in theory, but not in practice. And then there were problems for which no solution was possible, theoretical or practical. Which was this? He tried to take it step by step. He remembered the instruction he used to give to first year scientists when he began lecturing at Cambridge in the fifties – follow Sherlock Holmes, eliminate the impossible and work towards the truth. The trouble was that the only truth that mattered for now was what the Boss said. And even Sherlock Holmes had Doctor Watson to explain his theories to. He wanted to argue out his position with someone or something, or write it down logically, but there was no point. It was actually better when they forced him to work for them, than to give him an afternoon off like this to sit and think and become depressed. That was the misery. To think. To create the illusion that you have free will in anything you do, when you are nothing but a prisoner. He took a deep breath and tried again, from the beginning.

Durrant assumed he was in the Irish Republic, since the news-papers were Irish.

'Well done, Holmes.'
'Not so remarkable, Watson. There is even more evidence. I can receive both RTE and the British channels on my televi-sion set. What do you conclude from that?'
'No ideas Holmes, I'm sure.'
'That I am being held, in all probability, on the east coast of Ireland, or perhaps in the border country with Northern Ire-land. The television reception of the British channels is good. One must assume the British channels are not available in remote country areas in the west.'
'Must one?'

Durrant did not know. He had never been to Ireland before, knew little about the country and cared even less. He told himself he had to stick to what he could be sure about, rather than what he could infer. What did he know? They were most careful not to allow him to find out where he was. They had pulled the number off the telephone dial and always removed the labels with the chemist's address from the chemicals he ordered. He was not allowed to look out of any window, but he was sure he was in the country rather than in a town, although a town had to be close. He heard a tractor or some heavy piece of farm machinery driving around most days, and whatever the town might be, it must be fairly large because the Boxer had twice returned with Chinese food from a takeaway. It had been nearly as lousy as the fish and chips, but at least it was a change, and proved they were not completely isolated. Durrant's thoughts suddenly came to a halt. He remembered what had been nagging away at him, the thing he had not yet been able to understand because it did not seem to make sense. It was that first day with the Boss again. The Boss had been careful to keep his identity hidden. The other four took no precautions and allowed him to look at their faces without any disguise whatsoever.

How could this be? If they had all kept their faces hidden, Durrant would have been sure it was a sign they intended to let him go eventually, and were taking the obvious precaution to prevent him identifying them. On the other hand, if they had all kept their faces uncovered, it would have been more likely that they were unconcerned about being identified because they were going to shoot him anyway, no matter what they had promised or how well he co-operated. Either way, he could make some kind of decision, but for one of them to cover up while the others remained unmasked did not make sense. It meant he could not work out with certainty whether their assurances about freeing him were true or false. He simply could not reason through the contradictions. He would have more chance trying to read the tea leaves in the morning or make sense of the shapes on the wallpaper. It was all, well, it was all very Irish, and very unsatisfactory too. Durrant stubbed his cigarette out on the side of his plate and moved to light another, but there were only two left. They rationed him to a pack a day, which was tolerable when he was working in the garage, but not for a whole afternoon's thinking. He looked at the packet again, put another into his mouth and lit up.

In the past Durrant had felt guilty about smoking, particularly after Margaret had quit. He had taken up jogging in the morning as a kind of compensation or penance. He had tried to give up before, but right now there seemed little point in trying to prolong his health in that way. Preserving his mental health was difficult enough. He lay back and stared at the smoke rising to the ceiling. This line of enquiry was becoming unprofitable. He decided to rest, and to let Sherlock Holmes and Doctor Watson do likewise. He put out the half-smoked cigarette and replaced it in the pack, keeping the butt in a way he had not done since he was a teenager buying penny Woodbines and smoking behind the school lavatories. If the cigarettes ran out he would yell through the door and demand they get him some more. They could hardly refuse him that.

Durrant looked again at the shapes on the wallpaper to try to make sense from the jumble, to fit the purple blotches in with the red and maroon and gold, the balaclava with the rest. It was worse than before, this squaring the Irish circle, hopeless beyond belief. He could not even see the blotches clearly, and he could not understand why. He shook his head and focused again, then rubbed his eyes to clear them. The backs of his hands were glistening and he knew his cheeks were also wet. It was then he realised he was weeping.

Chapter Five

London

Tony Morgan caught the tube train home, staring at the faces of the commuters as they sat bunched in front of him in the carriage. He had moved his family to Clapham at just the right time, he thought, before the sudden rush had more than doubled house prices in two years. He was right to feel reasonably content. If he sold his house now, left London and moved to the country, he could probably make enough profit to invest somewhere and never have to work again. Probably. Except that he would have to find money enough to pay for David's school fees, and also Louise's if that's what it came to. And he would have to find something to do with his life. He could hardly just retire and grow vegetables, without becoming one himself. Still, it did not much matter now. The new project would take up all his time and energy and be properly worthwhile. It would deserve the effort and there were few enough stories like that. He might reluctantly be forced to be grateful towards Crawshaw, even if it was only for recognising talents in Morgan that he should have spotted earlier.

Morgan looked again at the faces round him. He used to tell his dinner parties that he was in touch with popular sentiment because he knew what the man on the Clapham tube train thought, and that was as useful as the man on the Clapham omnibus, but the joke usually fell flat. He wondered if it was true – that he really had any idea what any of these people thought or cared about, or were interested in, and whether it mattered? The old man in his duffle coat, chewing at his own gums. What about him? What did he need to know about to get through his day? The West Indian woman with two children – girls, with their hair in those fancy braids that must have taken the mother an hour each to do. Would she be interested in a film on the Irish Republican Army and the future of the British presence in Northern Ireland? The shifty-looking and

53

spotty twenty-year-old by the door, the one with the personal stereo belting out some daft rhythm that made Morgan's brain feel soft. What did he expect? Could he be brought into the ethical debate on whether it was correct to interview a terrorist on the run, and use Capital's satellite channel to evade British law?

'You have become such a snob,' Morgan said to his reflection in the train window. 'You don't think some of these people are capable of being interested, do you? And yet there must be someone out there who watches the stuff we produce, and they must be in amongst these people somewhere.'

He smiled. Crawshaw, Morgan thought. He watches it. At least he must do sometimes, if only to satisfy himself that the advertisements are appearing in the right places. Anyway, it was better not to be too concerned. Since de-regulation the advertisers kept saying that they wanted to target a more intelligent and prosperous audience, so men in duffle coats or Walkman-wearing zits on legs were probably not what they had in mind. Forget baked beans advertisements and the programmes to wrap round them. The money was to be made from something with a bit more class. That was what they were going to get in any interview with P J O'Neill, something which might appeal to the Euro-Yuppy after a hard day at the office.

At Clapham, Morgan got off and walked home with an almost happy air. He knew that he only worried about the philosophy of his job when he was not engaged in the business of actually doing it. He had long since discovered that the journalism was by far the easiest part. The worrying bit was all the rest. It was less exhausting to be a hack than to think about the supposed 'Ethics of Hackery', and fight them through a terminally haemorrhoidal organisation like CTV. In the end, the punters take what you give 'em, and with few exceptions there are no complaints. Good.

David ran to meet him as he opened the door into the house. He was seven and pushy for his age, with Morgan's wide forehead and Emily's delicate hair. Being at prep school had given David, Morgan thought, a natural composure or ease that he, Morgan, would never possess. It was difficult to decide whether this was fitting their son to survive in a hostile world, or trembling on the brink of creating some kind of English public school monster of the type he and Emily both despised, or thought they despised. Louise, who was just four, waddled in behind her brother. Morgan bent down for a kiss. It was the best part of the day.

54

'Is that you?' He could hear Emily's voice from the kitchen. 'Is that you, Tony?'

She stood at the sink, her hands deep in washing. Her hair was tied back from her face, which was slightly red with exertion. Morgan kissed her.

'You are home early.'

'I'm going to Ireland,' he said.

'For how long?'

'Probably just a week initially. Then I'll have to return if I can set up the filming we are supposed to be doing. Crawshaw called me in to do a special on the Provos.'

Emily dried her hands and yelled at David to stop tormenting his sister. He had produced a plastic spider which someone from school had given him and he knew she was terrified of it.

'Tea?' she said, and put on the kettle. 'When do you go?'

'Tomorrow, for the basic research. Then if we have to film, it should not take too long. No more than another week, later this month or early next I would hope.'

Emily nodded, but seemed distracted. 'I am glad,' she said, without enthusiasm. 'Glad.'

'What's the matter?'

She said nothing, but her body stiffened. He knew there was something wrong, and knew too, with a kind of weariness that came from all their years together, that he would have to coax it out of her. He was in no mood to do so and wondered why, since she was going to tell him anyway, she did not just get on with it. The children were ill? She had crashed the car? She had found herself a job at last and wanted him to pay for a nanny? How was he to guess the unguessable?

'What is it?' he said, putting his arms round her as she filled the tea-pot. 'You can tell me. I'm a friend, remember.'

She turned to face him, leaned back on the kitchen work surface and folded her arms tight under her breasts.

'I'm pregnant,' she said, bowing her head slightly.

There was a scream from the garden as David had found some other way of annoying his sister. Neither Morgan nor Emily moved.

'I'm pleased,' Morgan said with a smile.

'Well, I'm bloody not,' she said. 'I've had enough of it. Day in day out looking after these two while you're out enjoying yourself or tramping round the world. I want to go back to work, and I certainly don't want another two or three years delay while I put our next child on the road to school.'

55

The venom of it surprised him, though he knew she could often be like this, storing up some small thing until it grew and blew up in their faces. They had not planned to have another child, but Morgan could not help smiling. It was not at what she had just said, but the thought of being a father again. The smile was the wrong gesture, or at least she interpreted it incorrectly. Emily was really angry, and began to raise her voice.

'I'm sick of it,' she yelled. 'Sick of being tied to this place. Sick of meeting only other mothers whose sole interest in life is their babies. I want out. *Out*, to escape back into the real world where people think of me as Emily, a real person in my own right and not just some kind of baby machine.'

'We could get a nanny,' Morgan said, defensively. 'I think we can probably afford it. If she lived in.'

Emily scowled. She breathed out hard, as if unable to decide whether to leave the room or not. She let the last words die in the air, turned, and matter-of-factly poured the tea.

'I don't want a nanny,' she said firmly, her back towards him. 'And I do not want another child either.'

'What do you mean?'

'I think you understand what I mean.'

Morgan thought he understood too, but could not bring himself to say the words. The children were still outside, beyond hearing. She turned and handed him a mug of black tea.

'An abortion,' she said calmly. 'The word I think you are groping for.'

He took her by the arm and led her into the front sitting-room. She pushed her long brown hair back from her face again and sat on the settee. He noticed from her eyes that she had been crying, but there was a firmness about her which he had not seen, or did not remember seeing, for years. There was something very odd about all this, which made him feel she was just testing him to see how he would react, but he could not be sure. Sometimes she was so malleable, he could behave outrageously and she would forgive him. But there were a few times when she had such a fixity of purpose there was nothing he could say or do to make her even consider other solutions. He tried to hold her hand, but her arm remained stiff, both hands clasped firmly round her tea mug. Morgan made do with stroking her forearm.

'How long?'

'I'm eight weeks. Got the result this morning.'

'Why didn't you say before that you had suspicions?'

'What good would it have done? Either I was or I wasn't. It turns out I am, and now is the time to worry about it, not before.'

He drank some tea, and asked her why she did not want the child. She repeated what she had already said, and that she wanted to be treated as a human being, not just as a mother. There was nothing he could think of to say.

'I've been offered a couple of freelance jobs on women's magazines. It's hardly what I really want, but I haven't written anything for publication since Louise was born, so it would be a start. I'm not going to give it up now, if people are prepared to make offers.'

'But why does it have to be an abortion?' he asked. He had wanted to say it from the start, but delayed as long as he could until she cooled down and could discuss it properly.

'Because,' she said, staring at her hands. 'Because I do not want this baby, and there is no other way not to have it.'

He put his arm round her shoulder, and this time she softened. She put the mug to one side, and he pulled her to him, kissing her gently. She started to cry, softly and without fuss. He pushed her hair back from her face.

'Just as well I've stopped wearing mascara,' she said. 'Otherwise I'd be in a right mess.'

'Would you even get an abortion?' he wondered. 'I can't think of any reason they might allow it in your case.'

'Oh, they will,' Emily replied, picking up the tea, and becoming matter-of-fact again. 'I made such a fuss at the doctor's today he is convinced another pregnancy might seriously damage my health – mental health, certainly, and maybe physical health too. But I'll have to act quickly.'

'Do I have no say in this at all?' Morgan asked. 'Since I'm the father.'

'Not much,' she replied. 'But I'll listen to whatever you have to tell me. It is just that you don't realise that however much I might love you, and however much you told me that having children would be something we would share, I do it all. I give birth to them, I feed them, I take responsibility for them. You like to do your share, but your share is so pitifully tiny beside the total of their needs.'

Morgan looked at her, shocked not so much by the words but by the precision with which they were spoken, as if she had been thinking along these lines for months without ever having dared say it. It was not an explosion. It was a machine-gun. He stuttered something about loving his children, being a good father to David and Louise, or at least as good as he could be.

'I'm not criticising you,' Emily retorted, making it sound like the most damnable criticism of all. 'You are a good father, or at least good enough. But you are only a father, and you have another life which you enjoy outside this house. I want to enjoy that kind of life as well, and I want to start enjoying it now, not get sidetracked into another couple of years of bringing along an infant that we did not plan and I certainly do not want.'

'But you do not have to have an abortion. You could have the child and then we get a nanny. We can afford one, you know.'

'I know we can afford one, but there seems so little point in having a nanny if I still have to make so many sacrifices to look after David and Louise, because you are to go on the road again making films.'

'I haven't really been on the road for eighteen months, since Crawshaw screwed it all up.'

'Maybe, but you always told me you were going to go back, and now you are off to Ireland I can see the whole cycle beginning again. Research trips of a week which take two. Filming trips of two weeks which take four. Then editing the films under pressure for two weeks in London, though you may as well be in outer space for all we see of you. Then a few days at home in which, during this period of novelty, you rediscover the joys of parenthood. Terrific. Then you're off again. Don't try to tell me different, Tony. It has been too long.'

There was an absence of malice or anger in what she said, more a series of facts that Emily believed were incontrovertible. Morgan did not know what to say, and decided to wait and to think. He ate his meal with the children and they put them to bed together, Morgan reading Louise a story while Emily prepared David's school uniform. Then he packed a suitcase and checked everything for the flight to Ireland. Emily had always been interested in Irish stories in the past. She had written a series of articles on the treatment of prisoners by the Royal Ulster Constabulary in Castlereagh interrogation centre, and on the H-Block protests. She nearly managed a book out of a series of articles she had written for the *New Statesman* on the 'Women Behind the Men Behind the Wire' – portraits of the wives and families of those interned at Long Kesh. Now she was showing no interest in what he was doing. It half crossed his mind that she wasn't telling him everything. Maybe she was tired of him as well as fed up with being a housewife. Maybe the problems were bigger than an abortion.

'Emily,' he said, quietly. She was reading a newspaper he had brought home.

'Mmmm?'

'Could we not do something else?'

'Mmmm?'

'Both of us. How about selling up and moving out of London, maybe down to the West Country. We could buy somewhere really big in, say, Bristol. The past eighteen months have taught me I'm not really cut out for this tabloid satellite crap. I could try for a job with some of the local stations. At least it's proper journalism. You could either go on with your freelance ideas – it wouldn't matter where you were based – or you could try to get a job on one of the local papers.'

She folded the newspaper she had been reading and put it to one side.

'Are you serious?'

'Yes.'

'I don't know whether I'd like to do that or not. All our friends are here. And you have always said all the opportunities are here.'

'That is true,' Morgan said. 'If you think only in terms of a career. But if you start thinking in terms of your life as a whole, then maybe there are places a lot better than this.'

'Maybe.'

'We don't have to decide tonight.'

She laughed, and thanked him for giving her more than a few minutes to decide the course of the rest of their lives.

'No, I don't mean just about that,' he said. 'I mean about anything. We don't have to decide.'

'What do you mean?' she said suspiciously.

'I mean about the abortion too. I will be gone only a week. Let's both think about it. Talk about it on the telephone, too. You needn't do anything for another week. You'll only be nine weeks gone, and that is hardly anything.'

'It is enough. I don't want this thing to drag out. Besides,' she said sarcastically, 'I thought you were in favour of the woman's right to choose.'

'Don't get silly with me, Emily. You know there's a difference between being in favour of liberal laws so people can do something if they want to, and actually deciding to do it yourself.'

'Ah,' she said. 'You mean you just wanted it available. You didn't want it compulsory. Now I understand why we went on all those marches together at university in favour of the David Steel Abortion Bill.'

He shook his head. There was no point going on about it.

'A week,' he said. 'That's all. I have to get the seven-thirty flight tomorrow morning. I will be back in six, possibly seven days – I will phone you every night. We can talk about it every night. It is too important to rush into like this just because you are depressed.'

She was looking at him full in the face. He tried to work out whether his words were having an effect, or whether she was immovable. The fine brown hair fell a little over her left eye.

'There truly is no need to rush. We will decide together a week from now. Agreed?'

She moved her head slightly forward and back in what could have been a nod.

Chapter Six

May, County Louth

There was a game show on the television and Gordon Durrant stared at it grimly. He had tried to avoid watching and to think or read instead, but it was easier to lie back on the bed and smoke and look at whatever happened to be on the screen, letting it flow over him. Two teams representing Gateshead and Harlesden were being asked questions about pop music.

'Who had a big hit with "Da Doo Ron Ron?" ' the presenter was asking. He had a kind of vacuous charm, Durrant thought, and a sharp suit. A car salesman. Or an estate agent.

Durrant did not know the answer. He reached for a cigarette and heard a movement in the hall. It was almost nine o'clock at night, too early for them to tell him to wash and get ready for bed, yet too late for them to want him to teach them anything. It was the worst time of the day, if all they did was let him sit in his room and think. He could hear the key turn in the lock. The Boxer opened the door. He was carrying a glass of whiskey in his hand.

'Listen, prof,' Kelly said. 'We thought you'd maybe like to come in for a drink, into the front room.'

Durrant rubbed his eyes with the back of his hands. He blinked at the Boxer.

'I'd better switch the set off,' he said, matter-of-factly. The car salesman was offering Gateshead a bonus mark if they could also say who recorded 'De Doo Doo Doo, De Da Da Da'. Durrant was never going to find out. He switched off and unplugged the television, then picked up his cigarette packet from the bedside table and followed the Boxer into the front room. It was almost certainly already dark outside. They had drawn the curtains tight.

The Skull sat in front of a blazing peat fire resting his stockinged feet on the coffee table. The room smelled pleasantly of peat and whiskey. On the coffee table there was a bottle of Power's whiskey

61

and a large jug of water. The Skull pointed to the chair next to the fire.

'Sit down, prof,' he said, wrinkling his forehead. 'You can have your choice of anything so long as it's Irish and water. Or you can have it without the water if you want. No expense spared.'

Durrant smiled. You could not tell with these people. A joke, a laugh. Then a threat or something worse. All the same. The Skull's forehead rippled again as he concentrated on filling Durrant's glass.

'Anything'll be fine,' Durrant heard himself saying, as the whiskey was being poured. 'Anything at all.'

Durrant felt grateful, and it surprised him. They had taken him away, locked him up, separated him from his wife, threatened to shoot either or both of them, and he felt grateful. He took the whiskey glass in both hands and pulled at it, sighing as its warmth spread through his belly. Grateful.

'Ach, we'll make an Irishman of you yet,' the Skull said, raising his glass. '*Slainn*.'

'It's Irish for "cheers", ' the Boxer explained, and without any trace of irony added: 'Your good health.'

Durrant wondered if they were already one or two shots ahead of him. They seemed cheerful, and some of the bottle had already been drunk. He looked round the room, taking in its unfamiliar shape and colours. There were a few porcelain ornaments – small horses mostly – on the mantel shelf above the fire. There was a Sacred Heart portrait on the wall and a few books and magazines scattered untidily.

The Skull was showing a hole in one of his socks, waggling his toes in the warmth of the fire. He looked fit for his age, but had begun to develop a slight beer belly. The Boxer sat opposite Durrant and put his boots on the table, his eyes twitching as if the peat fumes nipped them. Durrant wondered if they were trying to cheer him up, and if so, why. The whiskey had already done some of that work, and now he wanted to talk, or rather he wanted them to talk. He needed some kind of proper conversation instead of the interrogation about his work, the silence of his room, or the asininity of the television. Most of all he wanted to hear what sort of life it was they had committed themselves to, because their choices related directly to him and to Margaret. Every time he had tried to raise the subject in the past, the barriers came down. Someone, invariably the Thin Man, would tell him to shut it. But now, in the heat of the fire, Durrant realised the Skull was actually talking to him, initiating a proper conversation. He was asking Durrant about his life at Cambridge, almost like some stranger met in a bar or on holiday, curious to know a few personal details. The Boxer cut in and asked if he had ever used his chemistry skills to manufacture home-made whiskey. Durrant admitted he had distilled alcohol in all kinds of experiments, but had never drunk anything he had produced.

'Ach, prof,' the Boxer said. 'You disappoint me. We'll have to get you some Mountain Dew before you leave us.'

'What's that?'

'What's that? What kind of education have you had? I thought you were smart, or had to be to go to Cambridge. Mountain Dew. Poitin. Moonshine. Illegal whiskey. Get it?'

Durrant got it. The fire was hissing gently and he felt warm and relaxed. Every morning he awoke on command, ate on command, washed on command, and taught them about explosives exactly as they wanted it. Now they were expecting him to play out a new role in an almost domestic scene with them. Very well. He would accept. He would play.

So far the teaching had been the easiest part, because he could forget who they were and why they wanted to know, just give the facts as if it were a Cambridge tutorial group with rather specialised aims. He could not be too technical, because it had emerged over the first few days that they were not at all interested in the chemistry of the reactions. They were simply concerned about the practical effect, and repeatedly questioned him about hypothetical problems: how could you shape a charge to get maximum blast effect? Did detonating cord have any advantages over using a larger detonator in the main charge? How could they boost the effect from fertilisers and weedkiller, or reduce the bulk needed to produce a given blast size? How could they ensure a full detonation of a very large charge – say 1,000 lbs – of home-made explosives? And so on.

They were actually rather able students, more interesting in some ways than many of those he remembered from Cambridge, and more like those he had taught in his time at Hereford. He had been careful not to speak of his association with the British Army. Though they obviously knew a lot about him, they had not mentioned anything of that to him, and he assumed it had remained secret. He could not be sure. However relaxed he became with the whiskey he realised he had better not let his guard slip. If he played it right, he might learn something from them and reveal as little as possible about himself, but he was suspicious of whatever reasons were motivating this sudden outpouring of sociability.

'Top up?' the Skull asked, handing him the bottle.

He could see the gun sticking out from the Skull's waistband. The Boxer was also wearing his, stuffed into his belt. Like him, they were taking relaxation only so far. As the Skull filled Durrant's glass the Boxer began apologising to him. Durrant thought he was not hearing properly, but he was actually being told not to pay too much attention to what 'our comrade' had said earlier in the day.

'He can get a wee bit excited about things,' the Skull said.

Durrant at first could not work out what they were talking about. Which comrade? He decided not to ask. Questions led to trouble. The Boxer picked up the bottle and began re-filling his glass.

'It's just you must never hold anything back, prof. It's better for you that way because we'll always find out, and the other fella has a hell of a temper. He's also our boss, you might say, in the Movement. Not *The* Boss, but our boss – and so it's a good idea not to offend him.'

Now Durrant remembered. That morning the Thin Man had said something in that raspy voice of his which had led to another row. Durrant had been explaining how to ensure that the main charge will always detonate by using the correct size of detonating cord.

'How can we make them?' the Thin Man asked.

'What?'

'Detonators.'

'You can't,' Durrant had replied. 'You have to buy – or perhaps steal – the usual commercial types.'

'Ballocks,' the Thin Man rasped, banging his fist on the workbench. 'You said on that television programme you did three months ago that it was easy to make detonators from chemicals bought at any chemist's shop. Isn't that so?'

Durrant felt the blood rush to his face. He tried to say something but it would not come out. He felt a chill in his bowels. He nodded at the Thin Man.

'Well that's the next lesson, prof. Tell us what you need, and no more lying to us like that or your wife's in real fucking trouble. The next lesson: how to make detonators. And don't ever try to keep anything back from us again, you bastard.'

Durrant was a mass of confusions. He had not tried to lie about the detonators, but to give the most sensible answer. He tried to explain that for most practical purposes there was no point in actually making them. It was difficult to do safely, and could lead to the loss of a finger or an eye. Even the Skull, who had clearly lost a couple of fingers on one hand, seemed unimpressed with this explanation, and like the others assumed there were nuggets of information which Durrant wished to hide but which could be prised from him using sufficient force. Durrant decided it would be better to keep quiet. The Boxer had begun to calm the Thin Man down, and then there had been a break and much whispering. They had taken him back to his room and told him that he was to be given the rest of the day off, as the Thin Man and the Girl had to go somewhere else for the afternoon. To show willing, Durrant had quickly written out a list of chemicals for the Boxer to buy in preparation for the lesson on detonators. It was a calculated piece of grovelling and he despised himself for it. But the past few days had been tough, especially the long afternoons and early evenings on his own. He had been thinking of many things, a scattergun attempt at solving his problems. He had resolved nothing. There was one exception. After the detonator incident he decided that never again was he going to try to deceive them on any matters of substance. They would always catch him out. His answers from now on would be long, pedantic, but correct in every detail. He would act like a prisoner of their war, and he told himself that the first duty of such a prisoner had to be to escape.

Durrant decided that his strategy would have to be never to volunteer information, but always to answer what they asked fully. He realised his enthusiasm for his subject meant that sometimes he told them details he might have been able to avoid mentioning, but there was no real choice. The best he could hope for was that they would not ask him about certain subjects, and he would then not have to take the risk of lying. He still had not worked out what they really did know, and it was therefore impossible to know how much he could cover up. On top of that, they squeezed and squeezed him with their questions until by late afternoon he felt like an old empty skin, sucked dry by the constant interrogation. He did not have the stamina to lie comprehensively. He would have to obey.

Anyway, what did it matter? They would kill people with or without his help. All he could hope for was that he and Margaret would not be among them. He pulled again at his whiskey. The Boxer was asking him, in a good-humoured sort of way, what

Cambridge was really like. Did he ever teach royalty? Was it true the women students were always at it, bed hopping, and half the time they were all stoned out of their minds? Durrant was not sure what he was saying in reply. He almost felt like apologising that he had lost the art of polite conversation, and just wanted to talk about something that did not involve explosives. The Skull threw some peat – they called it 'turf' – on to the fire and sat back in his chair, looking at Durrant and wrinkling his forehead as he listened.

Durrant finished his answer and then asked, looking at neither of them, but straight into the embers of the fire, why they did what they did. He quickly added that he was not trying to push them into forbidden territory, but he was curious to know why people like them gave up their lives to spend time in some little bungalow miles away from anywhere with a chemistry professor from Cambridge. He expected the Boxer to reply, to answer with some flippant remark and then change the subject.That was as much his style as the Thin Man's style was threats, but the Boxer said nothing. Instead, the Skull wrinkled his forehead again, put his whiskey down on the table, and touched Durrant's knee.

'Listen here, prof,' he said, confidingly. 'In 1969 they beat me off the streets during the Civil Rights Marches. The RUC, that is. Beat me for walking down our own streets in our own areas. In 1970 our Protestant so-called neighbours from the lower end of the Shankill Road came across and tried to burn us out. Then where were the RUC when we might have needed them? Nowhere to be found. Skulking in their barracks, or more like lending a hand behind the scenes. Do you know what happened? One man stopped the mob that day. One man. He was in the IRA and he had a gun, and he shot at them and they fucked off. The police, the so-called loyalists and all the bully boys. A few shots and all their strutting and posing, all disappeared. And I learned something that day I'll take to the grave. It's the only way to get any kind of rights for anybody in Northern Ireland. What he done, worked. Shoot at them till they fuck off. I've been trying to follow his example ever since. To do the thing that works.'

There was a long pause, and Durrant did not know what to say. Northern Ireland was just a boring series of pictures on the television screen as far as he was concerned, the bits in the newspaper he always skipped, dead bodies and incomprehensible politics. The Skull was talking again, suddenly animated. It was like a history of all that had happened over sixteen or seventeen years in which the Skull had been part of the 'Republican Movement' as he called it. He talked of the creation of a 'thirty-two-county-socialist-republic in Ireland' as if that long phrase were just one word. At the repeated mention of the thirty-two-county-socialist-republic, Durrant nodded and looked responsive during what he hoped were suitable moments. The Skull seemed to remember every hurt or every slight suffered by Catholics in Northern Ireland during the entire course of his own life and before it. 1922, the 1950s, 1916 and at one point – though Durrant could not remember why – even Cromwell, came into the monologue. The flood gates were really open, and Durrant's concentration was dissipating in the heat and the whiskey glow.

He became more attentive when the Skull said he had been interned in Long Kesh in what he called Cage Five, the same Cage as the Boss. Durrant hoped there might be clues to what was truly going on, clues as to who the Boss might be and the reason for the one man wearing the balaclava. But almost as if the name of the Boss brought him back to sobriety, the Skull moved on to generalities.

'Best thing that ever happened to us,' he said. 'Long Kesh, or the Maze prison as they now call it. That was *our* university, prof, not Cambridge or Oxford. In the cages at Long Kesh, with all the time in the world to think and plan the new Ireland. No prison, just a stage on the road to national liberation.'

While the Skull spoke, Durrant noticed the Boxer occasionally grinning. He was not taking any of this too seriously. Maybe he had heard it all before, and was wondering why the Skull was trying to convert a fifty-two-year-old English chemistry professor to republicanism. At his age it was hardly worth the trouble. The Boxer reached for the Power's bottle again and poured them all a generous refill.

'What about you,' Durrant asked him. 'Why did you join the IRA?' They were opening up to him now, for whatever reason. He wanted to hear as much as they were prepared to say.

'To hit the Brits,' the Boxer said, taking a drink.

'Is that all? You joined just for that?'

'Isn't it enough?'

Durrant said he supposed it was enough, though he must have looked fairly blank because the Boxer was determined to explain. He said that because of all the British propaganda people like

Durrant – decent, ordinary, British folk, as he put it – had no idea what was really going on. He tried to get Durrant to imagine how it would be if the Nazis had invaded England – wouldn't he want to do his bit? Whatever his politics, he was an Englishman and they were foreigners. You had to throw them out, simple as that.

'What I'm trying to say, is that your troops are the foreigners over here. You can hardly object if we treat them like you would treat the Nazis.'

Durrant was beginning to feel the whiskey loosening his tongue, perhaps more than was good for him. He could not believe it was anywhere near that simple, yet he did not want to say the wrong thing. He sighed and looked at the fire. The trouble was, however bad the British might be from time to time, they were *not* Nazis. The comparison seemed ludicrous, and he was surprised anyone could make it, even in anger. If that was the total justification for all the killing, then this Republican Movement was morally bankrupt. It was something about the appropriate response to a certain level of injustice or unfairness. If the British did behave like Nazis, then maybe you could shoot at them. But if they were ordinary British troops under the control of democratically elected politicians, trying to keep the peace between two warring tribes . . . surely these people could see the difference?

It was not worth pursuing. Instead, Durrant thought he might get away with another question. He asked how they thought a handful of them could destroy the British Army, the police and all the rest of it. It had to be a hopeless fight, even if they believed it to be a just one. The Skull said something about politicising people at the same time as carrying out the armed struggle in the Six Counties. The Boxer laughed.

'Our strategy is very simple,' he said to Durrant. 'It is to keep blatterin' away at them. We have nothing to lose, and the Brits have nothing to win. That's it in one. Just keep blatterin' away until they give up. We are not fighting El Alamein or Stalingrad. You don't seem to understand the basic principles of the guerrilla war. We are not out to defeat the enemy in battle. We're just there to sap their will to win. It will happen, sooner or later.'

After nearly twenty years of trouble in Northern Ireland, Durrant thought it most likely that 'later' must be right, unless two decades fell within a republican definition of 'sooner'. It might. They were a peculiar people. Durrant also knew that it was not as simple as their logic tried to make out, but he could not think why. Then he remembered there were more than two sides to this equation.

'What about the Protestants?' Durrant said.

'You mean the loyalists or the unionist community,' the Boxer said. 'Do not confuse them with Protestants. That makes it seem like a religious war.'

'It's not,' the Skull added. 'Really it's not, prof. It's just the British media that likes to pretend it's an old-fashioned religious war. Some of our comrades in the Republican Movement are Protestants, and some are of no religion. We've no quarrel with a man's faith, only with his sense of superiority over us.'

'Well, what about unionists, or the loyalists, or whatever you want to call them,' Durrant said. 'What do they think about all this?'

The Boxer took another pull at his whiskey and then began to answer. The two of them were more intelligent than Durrant had given them credit for in the beginning, but sometimes when they spoke like this it was as if they had rehearsed a little speech, or as if either of them interchangeably would have said the same thing in the same words and with the same emphasis.

'Loyalism,' the Boxer was saying, solemnly, 'is a creation of the British, a Frankenstein's monster which now causes as much trouble to its creator as it does to Nationalists in Northern Ireland. When the British partitioned Ireland they created a mutant state – Northern Ireland. Within it developed a mutant ideology – loyalism. When the British go, both mutations will disappear.'

Durrant could see the Skull was nodding, his forehead a mass of wrinkles. The Boxer continued.

'When the British leave Ireland – and they will leave Ireland eventually – when the British leave Ireland, the unionist community will realise that loyalism has failed them. All that flag waving and pretending they were more in love with the Queen of England than the English themselves. All of that failed to keep them in power and it will fail to keep them within the United Kingdom. When the day comes, unionists will be hard-headed enough to reassess their position and come to the conclusion that they should help to create a new,' – Durrant could feel the phrase again about to be spoken like the chorus of a well-known tune – 'thirty-two-county-socialist-republic.'

Durrant wanted to say it was probably not going to be so easy, but then, what did he know? Or rather, what did he care? He just nodded in agreement, and listened while the Skull said much the same thing in his ponderous way. They talked on and on about all kinds of topics – mainly about his time in Cambridge, and his views, such as they were, about the Irish political scene. They seemed genuinely interested, and Durrant politely played the honest but slightly confused Briton who deferred to their greater understanding. At one time during the conversation he stumbled upon the answer to the question which had been on his lips throughout: why had they invited him to drink with them in the first place?

It was not because they wanted to pump him for information. It was simply that, like him, they were bored. They wanted a change from whatever routine they had been forced into over the past two weeks, and he was it. He was the entertainment. He looked at their faces, flushed and serious, nodding in his direction. He knew they were more than a little drunk, and the whiskey had now completely swirled around in his own head. He suddenly felt old and tired, bereft of hope, depressed that his fate was in the hands of such men.

'You have to seize your chances,' the Boxer was saying, in respect of nothing at all. 'You have got to say to yourself that this must not be the first generation to let the struggle for freedom die. Rather we must be the first generation to bring it to an end.'

Durrant looked at the Boxer spitting out the word 'freedom' in his Belfast accent as if he had just invented it, and at the Skull's belly pressing his pistol hard against his leather belt. Maybe you are right, Durrant thought. Maybe you have to seize your chance, or at least be prepared to do so. Maybe he should prepare himself now, ready to seize his own chance when it came. He waited until the conversation – or rather the Boxer's monologue – reached a natural lull, then said he thought he should go to bed, if they did not mind. It had been a hard day, the lesson on preparing detonators would also be tough and he did not want the Thin Man to shout at him again.

'Ach, don't worry about that ballocks,' the Boxer said. 'You are in our custody, which means you are in safe hands. We think you're dead on. Okay?'

Durrant nodded.

'Thanks,' he said.

The Skull said they understood he would be tired. He sounded almost apologetic for keeping Durrant up so late. They would continue the conversation – and the whiskey – with him another night,

70

if he did as he was supposed to do. The Boxer, glass in hand, escorted Durrant first to the toilet and then back to his room, locking him in and bolting the door with one of the bolts they had fixed to the outside.

'Hope you don't need to piss during the night,' he laughed. Durrant replied he was fine.

'Goodnight, prof.'

Kelly returned to the sitting-room, a little uneasy on his feet. McKeever suggested they might as well kill the bottle now it was almost gone. He poured two large glasses, and topped his up with a little water. Kelly asked whether Larry Kennedy had been right to force Durrant into showing them how to make home-made detonators, before getting on to the magnetic explosives. He thought the magnetic had been the reason behind the whole operation. Billy McKeever looked at his whiskey, then spoke quietly in case Durrant might hear.

'Kennedy is right, Brendan, whatever way you look at it. I spoke to the Boss about it and there's plenty of time. The information about the detonators will be of the most use to the Movement in the future, and there's no hurry on the magnetic stuff. That operation is still being planned and the Boss said he was looking at precisely how we should use it, though I would not mind betting he has something firmer in mind that we don't know about yet. Close man, is PJ.'

'Do you think he's told Larry?'

'Doubt it,' Billy McKeever said. 'Larry may be Officer Commanding here, but I don't think PJ trusts him. He sees Larry as a Coffey man, in league with Sean Hughes and the boys who still believe in abstentionism and all that old shite. I doubt if he tells Larry any more than he tells me.'

'Whatever he's got in mind,' Brendan Kelly said, 'I bet it's a big one. He'll need to prove he can go one better than Coffey and the others. It'll need to be a big one to justify all the expense of holding the Durrants and not just taking their gear like Hughes wanted.'

'Sean Hughes thinks like a quartermaster and acts like a quartermaster. He understands the hardware, and that's about the height of it. Whatever he might think, he'll never make Chief of Staff the way PJ will. He's no vision at all.'

'That's why he *is* the quartermaster,' Kelly laughed. 'What's wrong with that – thinking and acting like he should?'

71

'Nothing,' McKeever replied, annoyed that he had not made himself clear. 'I just mean that Hughes and Coffey and Kennedy all think the same kind of way. That we have to do things the way we always done them, instead of like PJ who is forcing us to think of the future.'

Kelly saw his opening. The whiskey had woken him up.

'I know what it is,' he said. 'Just because they never did time in the Kesh like you and the Boss, you don't rate them.'

'That's not it at all,' McKeever said, angrily.

'Yes it is. You don't think they have been to the "University" like you and the Boss. I suppose you believe I can't think straight either just because all I ever did was six months remand in the Crum? Seems to me the trick is to keep out of the jails, not get in them so you can talk about it later.'

McKeever looked at him in such fury that Kelly thought maybe he had gone too far. He started to laugh, trying to head off a row. McKeever's hands were knuckle-white on the side of the chair. Kelly looked at the stump where the finger had gone on the left hand.

'Sorry, Billy,' he said. 'Only a wee gag. Here, finish the last of it.' He drained the rest of the Power's bottle into McKeever's glass.

'I was only joking. Honest. It's just that you hero-worship the Boss and forget there are others in the Movement who also make it work.'

'Like Larry Kennedy?' McKeever suggested.

'Okay. We agree on that. Larry is a ballocks. But then why did you take his part in agreeing we should push Durrant on to detonators first, before the magnetic explosives?'

'Because if Durrant can teach us how to make them over the next few days then we can get the information down to brigade level in the north within a week or ten days. It makes sense, doesn't it, to do something to benefit the whole movement first? I told you, our mission can wait a few days.' McKeever had cooled down and picked up his glass. Kelly nodded.

'Okay,' he said to McKeever. 'Maybe there isn't any hurry, but you can see why I want to get on with it. When the Boss picked me to join you all on the England team, it was the proudest moment of my life, the best job with the best team in the movement. Then when I heard about this magnetic stuff and Durrant, well, I could hardly wait. If he shows us how to use that stuff properly we'll make the Brighton bombing and blowing away Mountbatten look like side-shows. The quicker we learn that, the quicker we can use it. If Durrant has other stuff to teach us, the Boss should send in another team to learn it. But we're the England team, and we should be hearing what we need to hear from him first.'

McKeever smiled, then drained his glass. He saw in Kelly how he himself had been before, ten years before. All that enthusiasm, and heart in the right place, all accelerator and no brakes. He looked down at the stub ends of his fingers, and thought for a second of his dead brother. Only for a second. He was not going to get sentimental.

'We gotta keep Durrant secure, not go involving other service units in coming here. The more people know where he is, the more chance the Brits find out. He's our catch, and he's our responsibility.' McKeever stood up and stretched himself.

'I'm going to bed,' he yawned, still smiling at Kelly's ambition. 'But I never realised before you were so keen to show your stuff.'

Kelly looked sheepish and said nothing.

'Make sure everything is locked up,' McKeever told him. 'And that Durrant is okay. And don't worry. You'll get your place in republican history. If you don't get your place in the republican plot at Glasnevin cemetery first.'

Chapter Seven

Dublin

The barman took the pint glass and filled it with a gush of black and cream. Morgan waited, feeling his thirst, as the bubbles began to settle and the head formed on the pint. Neary's bar was crowded and noisy with lunchtime drinkers. There were three parts – a tiny snug used mainly by old women, the upstairs lounge where they served hot food, and the serious drinking main bar where Morgan stood among the crowd who could afford the extortionate £1-40p a pint and talked politics. The price of the Guinness was a shock. He had forgotten how big a mess the Irish economy could get itself into because the government had to pay off so many people for all the promises it made in order to get itself elected in the first place. He had forgotten, too, how every Dublin bar seemed to revolve around the most sophisticated discussions of local, British or world politics. In England they talked sex and sport; in Ireland, politics and religion. He wondered if that somehow explained why the English were such poor lovers and bad footballers, while the entire island of Ireland was in a permanent state of political or religious disaster.

Morgan could not understand the causes, but he knew well enough the effects. English drunks always tried to pick up women or fight with rival football supporters. Irish drunks fought over some long forgotten political row and then whined tearfully about the Famine or their mothers. That was very Irish. If Englishmen had mothers, they never discussed them. Irishmen discussed nothing else, except maybe Old Mother Ireland herself.

He stood in anticipation for a full four minutes while the barman poured and then swept off a little of the creamy head, poured and swept and allowed it to stand. Morgan felt pleased to be back in Dublin after all that time, and glad too that no one had devised an automated method of pouring Guinness. It was one reason why the Irish were such creative and patient people. Their minds had so much time to wander while the barman pulled the pint.

Neary's was Morgan's second favourite bar in Dublin, and also in the world. His real favourite was Conway's up near Parnell Square, but that was too near Provisional Sinn Fein headquarters for comfort. Most days of the week one or two Provos would drop in, particularly on Thursdays when they had finished printing that week's edition of *Republican News*. They were not the problem. The problem was that their presence always attracted a few Irish Special Branch men sitting around nursing their pints, trying to look casual, and pretending they were really not six foot three inches tall with a pistol tucked under the left armpit.

Having made his initial approach to the Provos, Morgan thought he should keep away until they contacted him. He did not want to be seen talking to known faces, though the Branch men had probably seen him go into the Sinn Fein offices anyway. Besides, drinking in Conway's might make it look as if he was trying to hurry the Provos along, which was always a big mistake. They were going to make up their own minds, and any hassling would simply annoy them. It could blow the whole job entirely. Morgan therefore took a major editorial decision: he was going to enjoy himself for a few days until they told him whether the interview was on or off. Television producers were paid to have coronary heart attacks. Reporters were paid to look relaxed. He was going to be content and enjoy his vision of Irish heaven – a cool pint of stout, a fresh salmon sandwich, and an hour at lunchtime to read the *Irish Times* properly and in peace.

The first shock had been to discover that the price of the paper had increased even faster than the price of the pint. The *Irish Times* now cost fifty-five pence – twice the price of any English quality newspaper. He worked out that if he gave up the *Irish Times* he could buy a paperback novel every week instead. What a country. 'Dear, Dirty Dublin' – dirty certainly, and dear enough too. Even the Shelbourne was now seventy pounds a night for his room without breakfast.

Screw it. Crawshaw was paying, whatever it cost. The thought was immensely cheering. Morgan might start feeling guilty when the cost of the trip approached that of one of Crawshaw's secretaries' desks. In the meantime he would try to drink his way through the cost of, say, a hundredth of a desk a day, at an exchange rate of one centi-desk to six pints. He would do his best.

The completed pint and salmon sandwich arrived simultaneously, and Morgan drew his stool towards the bar. He took a long, slow pull of the pint and remembered how good it always felt to drink Guinness in a real Dublin bar, paid for by someone else's money. He deserved it. It had not been an easy week.

Belfast had been almost unchanged. If anything it was slightly better than he remembered it. The IRA bombers who used to hit Great Victoria Street almost daily in the old days, must have been playing somewhere else now, or perhaps they were being bought off by some of the traders. It would not surprise Morgan if the Provos had learned they could make more money by not blowing the place up than by planting bombs. Business was business, even for the IRA. Anyway, the whole area round Great Victoria Street had been rebuilt and was full of nice little foreign restaurants and pizza parlours, men's boutiques and health food shops. Belfast had gone twee at last, ten years after everywhere else.

Belfast shipyard was on its knees, as usual. Closure was always 'imminent'. The engineering factories were in terminal decline. The textile industry had collapsed altogether, and agriculture was in a mess. The man from the Northern Ireland Office Morgan had seen for a briefing about the overall situation was 'generally optimistic'. No doubt that meant the Belfast shipyard stagers, the welders and the farm labourers could all be retrained and turned into cocktail waitresses, hairdressers and genuine Ulster-Sicilian pizza chefs. Morgan wondered who the Northern Ireland Office people thought that kind of crap now impressed.

He had been going there on and off for twenty years, and there was no time when the Northern Ireland Office would admit to being other than 'generally optimistic'. Specifically, they could be pissed off, upset, suicidally depressed. But generally they were optimistic. It did not matter. The truth was that Belfast looked better than Morgan could ever have hoped, a slow general improvement as if people decided they should go ahead and enjoy themselves. People had decided the Troubles were not going to end, not now, not soon, perhaps not ever. The conclusion was that you might as well spend your money now, and chase the good times.

It had been in the people themselves that Morgan noticed the biggest changes. He had thumbed through his old Belfast contacts' book trying to work out who to call on, but it soon became obvious that all his best sources were now either dead, in jail or on the run. One of the main loyalist hit men who had personally killed at least seven Catholics and was reputed to have set up half a dozen more for assassination, had been 'saved' and found Jesus before the police had found him. He had left the paramilitaries and was now running a youth club on the Shankill Road, still staying one step ahead of the police but preaching peace and personal salvation through Jesus Christ. He had grown a beard, taken to wearing sandals and told Morgan he should give up the drink. Morgan was gob-smacked. Another former loyalist gunman who was always a good source of background information was now writing poetry and trying to run a magazine reflecting what he called 'genuine working-class culture' in the Shankill Road. He told Morgan he was hoping for a government grant. He would probably get one.

On the Catholic side, less had changed. Morgan had called in to see Martin Anderson, the IRA's West Belfast commander, at Provisional Sinn Fein headquarters on the Falls Road. It was the first logical step in getting to P J O'Neill. Things at Sinn Fein were exactly as Morgan recalled them. No one had found God, and if they were writing poetry it was not obvious. The offices were as shabby, pockmarked, and damp smelling as he remembered them. There was even the constant but indefinable odour of too many people passing through to catch the free buses up to the Maze prison, cramped inside while they waited, warming themselves by a defective paraffin stove. The wire cage doors on the outside of the building, with their double security locks and entrance video cameras, were just as before. Morgan buzzed, paused, the door snapped open, and he was shown upstairs.

Martin Anderson looked older than Morgan would have guessed, his beard flecked with grey. His voice was even rougher than Morgan remembered, but he still wore the same old Aran sweater and faded denim jeans, still smoked the awful tobacco in his stiff little pipe, still looked through you with eyes which must be focused on Ireland's future or on its past but failed to meet yours in the present. On the walls of his office the pictures in the propaganda posters were the same as before. The slogans had moved a little with the times.

The poster with the two gunmen in masks holding Kalashnikov rifles used to say 'They may Kill the Revolutionary, but Never the Revolution'. Now it said: 'The Spirit of the Hunger Strikers will Live Forever. Onward to Victory.' What Hunger Strikers? When he had last been in that same office, in 1982, Morgan could have recited their names, ages and the precise order of their deaths as they followed Bobby Sands into the book of republican martyrs. Now Bobby Sands was the only name he could remember, and that was only because of a joke. A few weeks after the hunger strikes ended, and while the Provisionals were still talking of the 'immortality' of the hunger strikers' sacrifice, some joker had painted a slogan on a wall in one of the Protestant areas. It had read: 'We will never forget you – JIMMY Sands.' That single scrawl on the wall had said to Morgan everything he had ever wanted to know about Belfast. If you could have bottled it, the joke would have been the essence of the city.

In the past Morgan had found most of the senior Provisionals surprisingly good company. Once you forced yourself to overlook the fact that they were all murderers, accomplices of, or apologists for murderers, then the going was easy. True, you also had to forget the intricacies of their political arguments which seemed based on the idea that Ireland was the centre of the universe rather than just one of its many anuses. But if you could do all that, then you might just manage to recognise that they tended to be intelligent rather than stupid, part of the society in which they operated rather than some kind of monster from the outside, and were capable of being witty or showing a self-deprecating sense of humour. All except Martin Anderson. On the day Anderson joined, the humour must have been rationed. He remained cold, brutal and functional in his speech, and Morgan had once told him that his gruff manner was more like that of an Ulster Protestant than a Catholic.

'My grandfather was a Protestant,' Anderson said without smiling. 'The Republican Movement is based on political identity, not on religious affiliation.'

My favourite terrorist, Morgan thought, taking a suck at his pint and looking round Neary's bar. What had that ill-mannered cold bastard in common with these decent Dublin lunchtime drinking folk? Christ knows. How could Martin Anderson hope to liberate anyone from anything when he could not even free himself from his psychotic screwed-up personality? The bar was now beginning to fill up as the offices round St Stephen's Green emptied for lunchtime.

Anderson had been non-committal on the question of an interview with P J O'Neill. He was suspicious, and said he would pass the word along the line, talk to a few people, take soundings. He wanted to know who had dreamed up the idea in the first place and why Morgan thought any Brit broadcasting organisation would transmit an interview with a senior IRA man on the run.

'After Carrickmore, no one wants to try that sort of thing on,' he said, staring unblinkingly at Morgan. 'The BBC got burned there. Now every British company is banned from broadcasting even interviews with Sinn Fein, so why are you wasting my time? Not one of you has the courage to test the law?'

'We don't need to,' Morgan replied. 'It does not apply to satellite broadcasts. We're regulated under the European Convention and the Satellite Broadcasting Authority. The Home Secretary's diktat doesn't apply.'

Anderson looked unconvinced. 'You are not going to tell me you're going to risk a major row with the British government just to get an interview with P J?'

Morgan began to answer, he hoped persuasively. He used all the arguments Crawshaw had used to him, that it was an idea whose time had come, a way of making the news, an important story since two police forces were searching for Ireland's most wanted man, and so on. Halfway through one of the sentences he realised he was talking drivel, and worse, that Anderson realised it too. He had a way of looking at you as if to say: 'I know, I know when you are bluffing. You are doing it now.'

Anderson's was a funny kind of manner that Morgan had only ever come across once before, when he had tried to make a film about British Intelligence. Halfway through a discussion with a former agent who was supposed to be briefing Morgan, Morgan realised that the agent was telling him nothing and instead pumping him for information, that the flow was in the reverse direction. Anderson had the same ability, to create silences and sit through them without embarrassment so that Morgan felt he had to say something if only to fill a space. What filled the space, when he heard himself reciting Crawshaw's arguments, seemed dreadfully thin. At that moment Morgan, in the middle of the Provisionals' offices in West Belfast, began to feel exposed and very alone. He knew he should have forced Crawshaw to set the whole thing out on paper. Under the current agreement with the unions at Capital Television, Morgan could not be sacked for any offence short of setting the studios on fire or an act of gross indecency with another employee in the newsroom toilets. But Crawshaw *could* sack him for meddling with terrorists unless specifically instructed, and oral authorisation from a man as honourable as Crawshaw was about as useful as promises from a prostitute. How could he prove what

Crawshaw had told him to do? Morgan had been through it all before with far better men, and when it came unstuck, the one thing which saved a few editorial careers was that they all kept copies of every memo which referred to the project in even the vaguest terms. These were 'CYA' memos – 'Cover Your Arse' – and he needed one from Crawshaw now. He would demand at least that before he returned to Ireland with a producer and film crew.

'Look, Martin,' he said to Anderson, dropping into his best old-mate sort of voice. 'No matter which way you look at it, there's something in this from the Republican Movement's point of view. If we interview P J and transmit even some of it across Europe, it is a major propaganda coup for the IRA to have Ireland's most wanted man appearing on satellite television while the security forces are unable to track him down. On the other hand, if Capital Television gets cold feet somewhere along the line and refuses to transmit the interview, or cuts it out from the British service and beams it only to the rest of Europe, there is still a yard of propaganda in it for you. "Censored by the biased British media." "Tory government interferes with terror broadcast." "Cabinet Row over Terror Tapes." You know the sort of thing. Heads you win, tails you can't lose.'

Anderson was now poking around in the bowl of his pipe with a matchstick. Morgan was sure this was the only kind of argument persuasive to a hard nose like him. Crawshaw's waffle might cut the mustard at a Rotary Club dinner, but not up the Falls Road. 'Except if we lose P J,' Anderson said, beginning to fill his pipe from a plastic pouch. 'If in setting this up something were to go wrong and compromise P J's security, that would be a loss to the Movement. A grave loss.'

He pointed the butt of his pipe directly between Morgan's eyes, and continued at dictation speed.

'Of course, if we were to lose in that way, you would lose too. I guarantee it.'

The office was bare except for a filing cabinet and a few thousand copies of that week's *Republican News* stacked against a wall ready for delivery. Directly above Anderson's head there was a poster which bore a poor photograph of Bobby Sands. He smiled down like some out-of-focus icon.

'I may die,' the poster quoted Bobby Sands as saying. 'But the Republic of 1916 will never die. Onward to that Republic and the Liberation of our People.'

Follow the Yellow Brick Road, Morgan thought. He wondered whether Bobby Sands had ever said anything of the sort, or if it was some concoction from the Provo progaganda machine. When did he say such a thing? On his deathbed as he refused hot milk and vitamins for the last time during the Hunger Strike? In his brown shit-coated cell during the Dirty Protest? To his Mammy when he had been a six-year-old living happily alongside his Protestant neighbours in one of the new estates just north of Belfast? It was the kind of crap Anderson was likely to speak, not Bobby Sands, but since Anderson was still alive and Bobby Sands was dead, they decided to put the words into the mouth of the one who was safe in the past. Morgan had forgotten how much more important the dead were to the IRA than the living.

'P J O'Neill's security is your look-out,' Morgan said, starting to feel aggrieved by Anderson's attitude. 'You're the experts. You name the time and the place for the interview. We decide the questions and what will actually be transmitted. That's the deal.' He could be a hard ass too, he thought. The only way to make bastards like Anderson sit up and listen was to kick them a bit. 'Personally,' Morgan continued, 'I don't care whether you agree or not. I have done all the political in-fighting back in London to prepare them for the idea of doing an interview with someone the entire country regards as a terrorist. They are prepared to risk the row over it to prove that satellite television can be serious about news and current affairs too. I thought this bit over here with you would be the easy part. But if you don't want to take me up on the offer just say so. It won't be made again.'

Anderson's voice was never going to be soft, but he managed to moderate its rasp a little.

'So it was your idea to do the interview.'

'Yes. Mine.'

'You were a bit vague on that before.' Morgan shrugged his shoulders, but Anderson was not looking for any reply. They had both said their piece.

'Look,' he rasped, 'I don't trust the establishment media. I never have, and they don't give me any reason to change my mind. When you have been in here before the broadcasting ban, you at least tried to be fair, and I've noticed that. But all that means is I trust you personally only a little bit more than I trust your masters in London, since I know that in a few years time, if you play your cards right, you will be one of the bosses in your organisation making all the same decisions as the people at the top now, grovelling to the government just to keep your nice little money factory in operation. I am not trying to get at you, just explain something to you because you do not seem to realise what is at stake here.'

The Anderson pipe was now full and ready to light. He produced a match and began sucking at the flames. His eyes narrowed, studying Morgan's face. When the pipe was well lit, he continued where he had left off.

'P J is on the run. If he is picked up in Northern Ireland he'll go straight back to the Maze Prison and never see the light of day. The screws will let him try to escape again and then stiff him. "Shot while trying to escape." I know that, he knows that. Now you know it too. And if the Gardai pick him up in the south, there will be an extradition case which he may well lose, and he'll end up in the Maze like I just said. Stiffed. We are not going to risk P J for you or for any other television programme. Got it?'

It was like having a conversation with an Armalite rifle. Every time they met, Morgan felt like hitting Anderson, punching the bastard on the nose, stuffing the pipe so far down his condescending throat he would fart smoke for a fortnight. It would at least ensure that Morgan could never return to Belfast. Ever.

'You mean the answer is no,' Morgan said drily from the corner of his mouth.

'I did not say that. But don't take it for granted that the answer is yes. You'll just have to be patient.' Anderson began looking at some papers on his desk, as if mentally he had already moved on to next business. 'Where are you going to be staying for the next few days, the Europa Hotel?'

Morgan told him he was going to Dublin. 'I'll be in the Shelbourne Hotel. And when I'm not there I'll be in Conway's or Neary's or maybe Mulligan's in Poolbeg Street.'

Anderson started to pull out some files from his desk. The meeting was over.

'We'll be in touch,' he said, nodding to a large eighteen-year-old in a leather jacket who stood in the hallway. 'Bingo will see you out.'

On the way down the back stairs Morgan noticed a new poster on the wall. It showed the Provisional Sinn Fein symbol wrapped round a map of Ireland. An Armalite rifle was clutched in a black-gloved fist. '*Tiocfaidh ar la*,' the caption read in Gaelic, and then the translation. 'Our day will come.'

New Provo crap, Morgan thought as he slammed the wire mesh of the security gates behind him. New slogans for the old sacrifice. Always dreaming about yesterday or tomorrow, never thinking sensibly about today. Jam yesterday, jam tomorrow. Today just the revolutionary's three Bs: bullets, bombs and bullshit. He climbed into his hire car, banged it in gear, and accelerated fast towards the motorway and Dublin, back to the real world.

In the four days since then, Morgan had heard nothing. He finished the salmon sandwich and drained the pint, ordering another. He had called in to Provisional Sinn Fein headquarters in Parnell Square, just to remind them he was around, but there was no one available in the Dublin offices as senior as Anderson, and they repeated the advice to go off and be patient. Patience was not one of Morgan's strengths. He had a few journalist friends still in Dublin, but didn't think he should contact them. He could neither tell them what he was doing, nor did he feel he could lie to friends. Avoiding them was the best idea, lying to them only if he happened to bump into them. They freaked out more about 'subversives' than even most British journalists. They gossiped among themselves, and he feared a leak. There were a couple of women he used to spend a night or two with a few years back, but one had moved away from the telephone number Morgan had, and the other was staying with her parents in Galway all week. That meant days of seeing the sights for the umpteenth time and browsing through the bookshops, knowing that he could buy almost anything cheaper in London. In the evenings he telephoned Emily for half an hour at a time, but the conversation was always strained. He could not speak to her freely about what he was doing. She said she did not want to discuss the abortion – 'the other matter' as she put it – until he was back in London. No, she would not do anything before then. No, definitely.

Well into his second pint, it occurred to Morgan to telephone Crawshaw to find out who the producer and the film crew might be. If he managed to push him that far, then Crawshaw could hardly object to giving them all a memo authorising the filming. The trouble was, he could not talk openly to Crawshaw on the hotel phone, and he had nothing much to report in the way of progress. Best not to bother, until he really did have something to say.

Morgan looked up from his pint in time to see a young redheaded girl stride into the bar and order herself a gin and tonic. Her hair was thick and wound in heavy coils round her back, her face pale and freckled the way Irish womanhood was supposed to be. She was not sexy in any obvious way, but she was attractive.

'Oh, serendipitous city,' he remembered some old line, preparing to slide from the bar stool and make an attempt at conversation. Before he could do so, he felt a hand on his arm.

'We have a mutual friend,' a man's voice said quietly. Morgan moved his head back to have a look.

The man was about thirty, slightly pudgy with a bushy brown beard and glasses. A Dubliner, by his accent.

'Finish your pint,' the Dubliner said. 'And let's go and arrange a meeting with him.'

The red-haired girl moved from the bar and sat down in a corner with her gin and a newspaper, an opportunity lost before it began. Morgan looked from her back to the pudgy Dubliner. He picked up his glass and drained it.

'Let's go.'

They turned right out of the pub and right again up Grafton Street. They crossed St Stephen's Green, and it was a full five minutes before either of them spoke again.

'How did you know where I was or what I looked like?' Morgan asked.

The pudgy Dubliner grinned.

'Ah, just put it down to local knowledge.'

They cut through a Georgian square of redbrick houses that had seen better days, and into a large modern housing estate. At the corner of the estate some kids were playing on a car which had no tyres, no bonnet and no engine.

'You wouldn't come round here at night,' the Dubliner said. 'Not if you were serious about wanting to survive. There's that many addicts and thieves here, and if they don't get you, one of the fourteen-year-old joyriders probably will.'

'What do you mean?' Morgan said.

The pudgy face broke out into a grin. 'Some of the joyriders here are so young they can hardly reach the pedals. Couple of months ago they hit a mother pushing a pram, broke both her legs with a Ford Granada estate. Killed the child. That's the way it is here – easy come, easy go.'

Morgan looked inside one of the brown brick alleyways where a scabby dog was eating stale bread crusts through a hole in a black plastic bin bag. There were no adults anywhere to be seen, just dozens and dozens of children.

'Have you tried doing anything about it? Politically, I mean.'

The pudgy man led him up a set of stairs and on to a walkway. 'I know what you mean,' he said. 'When the war in the north is won, then we'll have time for it. But not now. Until then it's as much as we can do to keep the drug pushers under pressure.'

The last time Morgan had been in Dublin one drug pusher who was being kept under pressure by the Provisionals had his kneecaps blown off. Another was held by his ankles over the balcony edge of the sixteenth floor of a block of flats until he decided it was time to quit the estate.

The walkway smelled of urine and faeces. Five or six ragged children were rolling a worn tyre across the yard to each other. Morgan noticed a few teenagers sitting on the stairs, smoking, and at the end of the walkway a man who ran up a flight of stairs when he saw them coming. The Dubliner took him down a further flight, then up two, doubling back on the way they had come. It was beginning to rain gently on the rubbish in front of the flats. The children playing at the car looked for shelter. Morgan was about to ask the Dubliner another question when a door to their right opened, and an old lady led them inside. It was a tiny maisonette, kept clean despite the dirt and smells outside. The main room was small and dark and full of religious ornaments. On the wall there was a Sacred Heart of Jesus, which plugged in and glowed with a weak scarlet light. In front of it sat a man whose face Morgan could not quite make out in the dimness of the room.

'Come in and sit down, Mr Morgan,' the man said, waving an arm loosely towards the sofa. 'I hear you've been wanting to see me.'

Chapter Eight

Dublin

Morgan stretched his hand out from the bed and found the Perrier bottle where he had left it lying on the floor. He unscrewed the top and drank slowly, feeling the fizz bring life back to his tongue and throat. He opened one eye experimentally, shut it, then tried again. He put the top back on the Perrier bottle and checked his watch. Nine-thirty. Sometime after his meeting with O'Neill he had remembered to book a flight home at eleven from Dublin airport. He had time either to shower or to eat breakfast, but not both. It was no contest. He could not eat anyway. He sat on the side of the bed and decided he had better ring Crawshaw's office for an appointment. Jean-the-Hippo secretary answered the phone in her sing-song voice.

'Mister Craw-shaw's o-ffice.' The charm evaporated when she realised it was no one important. Crawshaw had not yet arrived, but she promised to tell him Mr Morgan had called. Marvellous. Mr Morgan was very grateful.

Bearing in mind the amount of Guinness he had drunk the night before, Morgan did not feel too bad. Even his stomach seemed more under control than usual, perhaps because he had not been drinking whiskey as well. He stood in the shower and washed his hair with one of the Shelbourne's fancy bottles of shampoo, enjoying the force of the water beating upon him. It helped him to wake up and to think.

The meeting with P J O'Neill had gone better than he expected, largely, Morgan thought, because O'Neill was of senior enough rank to make his own decisions. That was the trouble with Anderson in Belfast – not important enough to take the initiative, yet full of his own importance so he could screw you around. O'Neill, on the other hand, seemed to regard talking to a journalist

87

as more than the usual exercise in political propaganda. Maybe after all those years in the Maze it was something of a novelty.

'I don't trust the establishment media,' O'Neill said, like an echo of Martin Anderson. 'But I've always argued within the Movement that it is there to be used to get our message across. It would be inconsistent of me to tell other people to help radio – and television in particular – report on our struggle and try to get round the broadcasting ban, and then not agree to meet you. How far we go after this meeting is another matter.'

O'Neill seemed relaxed and spoke as if they were old friends. He wore a new Donegal tweed jacket and smart trousers with expensive brown brogues, looking more like a provincial teacher or a prosperous farmer's son than a terrorist. That was the problem. No horns. No pointed tail. No sign of the blood on the hands. Pity. Morgan was not clear how best to play the meeting. He knew they would discuss the kinds of questions he would want to ask in the interview, and maybe go into detail about how the satellite operation was supposed to bend the law. The problem was to decide how much O'Neill might open up to him now and provide him with enough information to make the whole thing work. O'Neill had to be persuaded to talk about overall strategy and the new structure of the organisation rather than just the routine stuff about British wickedness and the ritual incantation of republican themes.

'You don't choose to be a republican because you like the hours, or see the career prospects,' O'Neill was saying. 'In that context, life on the run now is just another one of the risks of the job. Republicans accept it. Like prison, or death. Except that it is more useful to the Movement than either of those things.'

'How have you been spending your time since you broke out of the Maze?'

'You don't expect me to tell you the answer to that,' O'Neill said politely.

That much was true, but you had to try. Morgan looked at O'Neill's thoughtful eyes. He was engaging and seemed honest even when he was being evasive. Maybe he had been schooled by the Jesuits. Emily had told Morgan that O'Neill had once begun to train as a priest, and had somehow lost his vocation. That, at least, was his reputation in West Belfast – thoughtful and studious, until he decided his republicanism was stronger than his Catholicism. Or maybe he thought there was no shortage of priests and a gap in the market for bombers. Morgan had dug out an old clipping from

Republican News which confirmed that O'Neill had given up the idea of a life in priesthood to 'join the armed struggle against the occupation forces in the Six Counties'. O'Neill was answering his question.

'All I will say about my time on the run is that I have never ceased to be on active service for the Irish Republican Army since the moment of my escape. And during that time I have been happy and safe among my own people in the twenty-six counties and in the Six Counties.'

'Both sides of the border?'

'Correct.'

O'Neill had shaved off the beard that featured in all the 'Wanted' posters issued since his escape. His hair was cut short and his face was capable of such a range of expressions that Morgan could not see how anyone could ever identify the scowling criminal of the posters with the animated face speaking to him now.

'It is said you are on the Army Council of the Provisional IRA,' Morgan said.

'Is it? I should be flattered.'

'It is said you are Director of External Operations.'

'Any republican would be delighted by such an honour, but equally delighted to serve the Movement in any way which presented itself.'

Definitely Jesuits, Morgan thought. Jesuits or the British Civil Service. Same kind of helpful answers. Same kind of delight in speaking yet saying nothing.

'Are you planning to bomb England?' In a way, the dumb questions were always the best.

O'Neill laughed and threw his arms wide in emphasis. 'Listen, Mr Morgan, you above all people should know we are *always* planning to bomb England. Always. Whether we succeed or not is another matter.' O'Neill clearly thought this a great joke, and began to warm to Morgan. He explained how bombing or not bombing England was a question not of changing IRA strategy, but of different tactical abilities.

'England is always a target. It is just that we cannot always manage to hit it and guarantee the safety of our volunteers. It is hostile country and presents us with all kinds of logistical problems.'

Morgan watched O'Neill carefully as he spoke. His eyes danced with animation and he frequently gestured with his hands to emphasise a particular point. It was becoming obvious that however well Morgan handled the recorded interview and however nasty the questions, O'Neill was never going to allow himself to be caught on any hook. He had considerable flexibility of mind beyond the usual maunderings of the Provo repertory company, and there was a risk that Crawshaw might have to realise that he had made a dreadful mistake. People, ordinary British people who loathed the IRA, might actually *like* P J O'Neill. There was no doubt the man had charm, even if what he actually said turned the flesh cold.

O'Neill had changed the subject and was in a more familiar gear. The British security forces, he was saying, had to be lucky all the time, while the IRA had shown with the Brighton bombing and other activities that they needed to be lucky only occasionally.

'Were you involved in the Brighton bombing?'

'There is no point in you asking me about specific incidents either now or when we do the interview, because if you do I will just refuse to say anything. Operational matters are out.'

He said 'when'. When we do the interview, not if we do it. Morgan thought it meant he was almost certainly home and dry, but he had become so absorbed in this piece of strategic thinking he was not keeping up with the tactical skirmishes in the conversation. O'Neill had said something about a war of attrition, the Long War against the British, and Morgan knew he had missed his cue to respond. O'Neill continued anyway.

'We in the Republican Movement are well aware, after twenty years of the current struggle, of the revolutionary possibilities of a single major guerrilla act,' O'Neill was saying, again emphasising the words by waving his hand at Morgan. 'The political apparatus of a revolutionary movement has to be there to capitalise on the action otherwise it is mere terrorism, but a single blow can change the course of history.'

'What exactly do you mean by that?' It was Morgan's standard question when he had not been listening properly. He felt it indicated the correct degree of enthusiasm ('Please tell me more') while ensuring that there would be further explanation of whatever it was the interviewee had just said. It always worked. Even with a failed Jesuit like O'Neill, though one day someone would reply 'I mean exactly what I have just said,' and leave Morgan stranded. Not O'Neill, not this time.

'I mean simply that when the Serbs killed the Arch-Duke Franz

Ferdinand in 1914 they brought about the First World War. They changed the course of history, even though their relative political weakness in comparison to the forces they unleashed meant they could do nothing to exploit the situation they had created. When the IRA tried to blow up half the British Cabinet at Brighton the British told the world they would stand up to terror, and yet within months they signed the Anglo-Irish treaty with the Irish government. Do not mistake me. I don't think the treaty is worth much. But do you really think any British government would ever give a foreign government – Ireland – a say in what it believes are British affairs if it had not been for the violence of the IRA, and in particular the morning when Mrs Thatcher woke up to find her hotel suite no longer included a bathroom?'

O'Neill's eyes were burning now with enthusiasm. He was so unlike the dead face in the beard on the 'Wanted' posters that Morgan knew no one could have recognised him. He was going to be an extraordinary interviewee, if Crawshaw did not change his mind about the whole project. Morgan turned the conversation to the rumours of a new political direction of the IRA, before returning to the question of whether O'Neill would do the interview or not. O'Neill said he was prepared to do it, but for his own security would have to lay down certain conditions. Morgan would be their only point of contact. No producers, directors or researchers were to make any arrangements, just Morgan. O'Neill recognised that others would have to be involved at a later stage, and when that time came Morgan was to tell Sinn Fein as soon as possible how many people were needed from the television team. The fewer the better. They were to check into Jury's hotel, and would be contacted about the precise date and location for the interview. They would have to allow a week in Ireland because O'Neill said he might have to call everything off at the last moment if he felt either his security or that of the people protecting him was at risk.

'Just remember,' O'Neill said, 'that while we accept your personal good faith, we are suspicious of all outside journalists and broadcasting organisations. We know the pressures you are now under from the British government, and we would be foolish to trust you.'

Morgan attempted some mild form of protest about the ethics of the new European journalism they were trying to create on satellite television.

'I'm not getting at you,' O'Neill said with a generous sweep of his hand. 'It is just that I recognise that all organisations betray the people who work for them. Not every day, but eventually they do so. And the better the organisation, the bigger the betrayal. I have enough problems without worrying who in your organisation I can trust and who I can't. So I take the short cut, and trust no one. Nothing personal.'

O'Neill stood up. The discussions were at an end. He shook Morgan's hand. 'Anyway,' he concluded, 'you have had a successful day. You came here to persuade me to do an interview for you, and I am now persuaded. We will meet again. Goodbye.'

Morgan stepped out of the shower and dried himself. He switched on the kettle in the hotel room to make tea before setting off for the airport. It had gone surprisingly well – O'Neill had seemed quite friendly at the end, before telling the pudgy Dubliner to show Morgan out by another circuitous route through the tenements towards St Stephen's Green. The Dubliner took his time – presumably yet another security precaution – staying with Morgan and delaying him until O'Neill had disappeared from the maisonette in some other direction. Morgan had forgotten how efficient the Provisionals could be in these matters, but then they had plenty of practice.

Morgan sipped his black tea and called a taxi to Dublin airport. On the journey through the centre of the city he watched the shoppers in O'Connell Street, grey crowds snaking past the General Post Office, the Irish tricolour flying stiffly in the breeze. There were three grim-faced newspaper sellers holding up that week's edition of *Republican News*, as the crowds slipped by. The taxi driver was keen to talk about the weather and how as an Englishman Morgan found the prices in Dublin. Morgan responded listlessly. He was pleased with himself, but was sure the real battle was just beginning. Dealing with the IRA was nothing compared to dealing with Capital Television, Crawshaw, the advertisers and, God help us, the government.

'Yes, the prices are steep,' he said. 'A lot worse than in London.'

'Wicked, just wicked,' the taxi driver agreed.

Morgan was especially impressed by one thing that O'Neill had said – that all organisations eventually betray those who work for them. At first it struck him as the argument of a man who had rejected the Catholic Church, recognising that the Church's unspoken primary duty was not to save souls but to save itself for future generations. The organisation had to continue even if some of the people who served it had to be sacrificed. Perhaps it also meant that O'Neill was fighting some unknown and labyrinthine battle against enemies within the IRA. If that was true – and there were always rumours of splits and disagreements – it would be very difficult to get at in time for the interview. Morgan would try.

O'Neill's observation was an acute comment on Morgan's own position. The truly venomous battles in Capital Satellite Television were fought against internal enemies not those supposed opponents on the outside. For example, Crawshaw may have changed his mind totally about the interview, leaving Morgan in an impossible position with O'Neill and the IRA. He may have even called in Donald Harris or Sheila Mortensen to give their expert opinions and supervise the P J O'Neill filming – which would equally be a funeral rite. And when Crawshaw realised that O'Neill was no vampire, no terrorist monster with a bolt through his neck, just a smartly dressed Irishman with a quiet, thoughtful manner who could smile easily and answer questions intelligently, then maybe Crawshaw might see all kinds of problems. The real fight was now going to start. Morgan was sure of it.

'And the price of a pint of stout,' he said to the taxi driver. 'It's unbelievable the cost now.'

'Surely,' the man agreed. 'And getting worse.'

Morgan flew Aer Lingus Executive class with, he assumed, the cream of Irish business sitting alongside him. He wondered how they might react to the news that he had been spending the last two weeks tracking down and finally meeting one of their country's leading subversives. He assumed that taking any one of them at random – say the one in the seat across the aircraft aisle with the blue suit and reading the *Financial Times*, or the one stuffing his cooked breakfast down his throat with astonishing speed, any of them would do – that they would not give a damn about Northern Ireland or the IRA provided that their own lives prospered and were largely unaffected by the violence. Ordinary Irish people were about as interested in what Morgan was doing as the people on the tube to Clapham. It was the paradox of the job. Neither the English nor the Irish wanted to know any more about an apparently insoluble problem which ground on from generation to generation. And yet here was Morgan – and now apparently

93

Crawshaw – telling people like the man in the blue suit that CTV knew what was best for them. Satellited subversives on the box. Just the prescription. Exactly what these good folk and thirty million like them needed. Jesus. Morgan thought it was unbelievable that he spent so much of his time producing stories which, if they went wrong, would lead to being fired from his job, and which if they went right no one would give a shit about anyway.

'Now that's showbiz,' he said to himself. 'Not business values.'

They were beginning the final approach to Heathrow, flying somewhere near Windsor. He could see the Thames like a glass snake coiling through the green fields, then sweeping by the castle with its stubby turrets and Union Jack on the uppermost, stretching out in the wind to the east. They were so low Morgan could see a military band practising in the castle grounds. One day, he thought, Mr O'Neill and his well-armed friends are going to drop in, here or over at Buckingham Palace just to say hello. Whatever O'Neill said about the supposed hardships of the struggle, it could not be all that difficult to hit soft civilian targets, even prestigious ones, in an open democracy in peacetime. Would any of that be the single act which would change Irish history? Morgan doubted it. The Provisionals never had a Kamikaze wing and never would have. Suicide was not a strong strand in Irish culture even if terrorism was. Anything the IRA planned would be designed to give maximum chance of escape for their own people, because despite all the nonsense about 'brigades' and 'active service units' Morgan guessed there were only a few dozen people at the heart of the organisation good enough to keep it going. They would plan and organise meticulously, have their big bang and then disappear, normally even before the bomb exploded.

That was the new technique. It was safer for the bombers, although it reduced the number of soft targets considerably, to ones important enough to spend so much time and effort on. Targets like the Prime Minister at Brighton, but maybe not Windsor Castle. The problem was, no one could ever be sure. The initiative always lay with the IRA. It was their call. Yet no matter who they shot or where they bombed, Morgan was sure that no single act in Britain could change the course of history to their advantage in the way O'Neill suggested. Any terrorism had always been counter-productive because no government could be seen to give in to gangsters and murderers, wasn't that it? Therefore the greater the IRA's military success the greater their political failure. That had to be the logic.

Morgan walked through the Special Branch check at Heathrow airport and wondered if they would spot O'Neill if he were travelling beside him in the queue. He doubted it. O'Neill would simply smile, and if they stopped him, produce papers to show he was a teacher or social worker over to study disadvantaged children in Hackney. They would smile back and let him pass.

'Thank you, sir.'

'Thank you, officer.'

At the CTV studios Morgan flashed his identity card and was waved through by the security staff with barely a casual glance. If O'Neill did have difficulty at Heathrow, Morgan was certain he would be able to saunter through into offices like those of CTV even if he wore a mask and carried a box marked 'Bomb'. The geriatrics at the security gate were not the sort to notice. Maybe, Morgan thought as he rose in the lift, I should suggest to Crawshaw that instead of videoing O'Neill in Ireland we bring him over for a live studio interview. If Crawshaw really does want extra publicity for our current affairs programmes, sticking one of Ireland's top terrorists live in front of millions of people might just do the trick. Or maybe we should have a phone-in to let the public talk to him directly the way they talk to government ministers at election time? 'Ask a Bomber,' that kind of thing. 'Kalashnikov Call – Your Satellite Hot Line to the Freedom Fighters.' It would certainly make news, if that was Crawshaw's intention.

'Morning Tony,' Donald Harris said, as Morgan reached the newsroom. He was reading Press Association copy, smoking a cigarette and watching one of his desk-top monitors. 'How are things?'

'Fine.'

At least Harris did not tax the imagination by starting up an original conversation. Morgan was grateful. Harris always asked how things were, and you always replied that they were fine. Any other response meant a real discussion, which neither of them wanted. Morgan began to move towards the coffee maker. He had an Irish coin to get rid of, and so was prepared to pay this time. But, remarkably, Harris appeared to be interested in moving beyond ritual grunts.

'What have you been up to?' he asked pleasantly. The tone was a warning signal. Morgan realised that he almost had Harris's undivided attention. Harris was still smoking and occasionally glancing at one of the television screens, but he was neither on the telephone nor reading incoming news stories. Something was wrong.

'Oh, just a little trip to Ireland,' Morgan said.

'Anything special – more revolting loyalists?'

'Ah, no, not this time. Is Crawshaw in?'

Harris said he had not seen him yet, though he assumed that he was. For a second Morgan thought Harris looked hurt. There were two possible explanations. Either the whole O'Neill project was coming unglued, in which case Morgan was probably in deepest shit. Or Harris had somehow guessed that something important was going on, but that he was not in on it. Maybe, Morgan thought, he believes Sheila Mortensen knows about the story and he is the only senior editorial figure to be excluded. That would drive him crazy. There was a way to find out.

'Is Sheila in?' Morgan said, innocently.

Harris looked as if he had been stabbed – which was probably appropriate if he believed he had been cut out of the loop on the Irish project. If Mortensen had been told about some sensitive story and Harris had not, then Crawshaw had gutted him. Neatly.

'I don't know. It's supposed to be a planning day for her,' Harris replied sourly. 'But I haven't seen her either. Anything I can help you with?'

'No. It's okay.'

Morgan loved it. Harris reacted as if a pail of ice-cold water had been thrown in his face, and he deserved it for making Morgan's days so miserable in the past. Gotcha!

Crawshaw had left a message that he wished to see Morgan as soon as he arrived in the office. Morgan made his excuses to Harris, and walked towards the executive office suite. It occurred to him on the way that he had exchanged more words with Crawshaw in the past two weeks than in the previous two years. He felt good, almost in the mood to celebrate. Even if Crawshaw cancelled the project now, Morgan had successfully completed his part.

'He has someone with him,' Jean-the-Hippo said sweetly from behind her desk. 'They won't be long. Would you like a coffee while you're waiting?'

Maybe she was not as stuck up as Morgan had thought. The

other matching secretary continued to type on her word processor, listening to recorded Crawshaw through her earphones. No doubt a moving experience.

'Yes,' he said. 'If it is not too much trouble.'

'No trouble at all,' Jean replied, and poured him a cup from the coffee maker.

This time, Morgan thought, I'll be properly prepared. He checked off a list of items he wanted to raise with Crawshaw: a memo defining his precise instructions; who the producer was; the problem about O'Neill's overall plausibility which might make the Satellite Broadcasting Authority even more anxious – an articulate terrorist who could create the impression that terrorism was attractive. He also wanted to check with Crawshaw that they could call the programme 'The Patriot Game'. It seemed the right title for O'Neill's bizarre life, since one way of dressing up the whole thing would be to use library film of various terrorist incidents and the Maze break-out, events O'Neill had been involved in. Selling it as an analysis of the kind of people who join the IRA might help them persuade the viewers that the implicit defiance of the British government was worth it, that the subject was being treated seriously and was not just a sensationalist stunt. O'Neill's sometimes cynical humour in speech would point up the idea of the historical game played out over the centuries between the British and Irish. Terrific.

'Know thine enemy,' he could hear Crawshaw say in his CBI-talk voice. 'That's the nature of the Patriot Game. Understand them so we can defeat them. That's the ticket. Responsible journalism, *par excellence*, for the switched-on audience in Europe. Well done, Morgan. How about a massive increase in your salary?'

Morgan's enthusiasm was brimming over now he could see how the film might go – maybe a history of the whole twenty-year campaign through O'Neill's eyes: the civil rights marches, the early violence, internment, imprisonment and escape, and now a life on the run. All Irish life is here. All in thirty minutes. Wonderful. A buzzer on Jean's desk sounded. She picked up the phone and talked to Crawshaw.

'He's ready,' she said. 'You can go through now.'

As he opened the door Morgan saw across the prairie of carpet that Crawshaw's visitor had not yet left. Crawshaw sat back in his chair, erect in his smart pinstripe suit. In front of him were two chairs, one empty. From the other a man, a few years younger and a great deal fitter looking than Morgan, stood up and held out his right hand.

'Tony,' Crawshaw said in a voice full of bonhomie. 'I'd like you to meet your producer for the trip. He is new to satellite television but he's an Ulsterman with a great deal of television experience in Northern Ireland. I think you two will make a formidable team.'

The Ulsterman shook Morgan's hand strongly.

'Pleased to meet you, Tony,' he said. 'My name is Harry Dunlop.'

Chapter Nine

Dublin

As soon as the pudgy Dubliner led Morgan away towards St Stephen's Green, P J O'Neill gave the old lady a ten pound note and his thanks. He slipped out from the maisonette to where his car was waiting. It was raining gently, the beads forming on the hairs of O'Neill's Donegal tweed jacket. He had left his two minders in the car during the meeting with Morgan, partly because there was no reason for Morgan to see more of the organisation than was absolutely necessary, but mainly to make sure the car was still there when O'Neill left. Once before he had come out from a high security meeting in the old lady's flat – a meeting with Sean Doherty, the Chief of Staff, to get the final clearance on the Durrant kidnap – and when he emerged his car had gone, stolen by the joyriders. It was the same all over Dublin. At least in the North a republican knew his car was likely to be safe. The consequences of stealing an IRA car in West Belfast were such that no one in full possession of their sanity would do it. Here, people had no respect. It was not just the North that had suffered from the division of the country. Around him in Dublin, O'Neill could see nothing but crime and decay, a society which did not have the stomach to tackle its own problems. The old woman had asked him about the heroin addicts shooting up in the stairways to her flat.

'I wish youse could do something about that, son,' she told him, pointing at the broken needles and the debris of the drug takers. 'This wasn't the State my family fought and died for.'

Her two brothers had been Republican Volunteers during the Tan War and were killed by Free State forces during the Civil War. She reminded O'Neill of his own grandmother, tough as nails, who had lived through the same period and lost virtually all the men in her family in one sort of Troubles or another. O'Neill put his hand on her shoulder and explained that if the modern Irish state with all

99

its resources could not tackle the problem then there was no way the Republican Movement could do so. She looked crestfallen.

'Until the creation of a socialist united Ireland,' he said, and she began to cheer up. 'Once the National Question is settled then we can begin to sort out other things. Until then, the struggle in the North has to be our one priority.'

He sometimes wondered if all that was true. When he talked to his comrades it was obvious to him they were united in what they were fighting against, but they were not so clear what they were fighting for. The divisions could be hidden under the usual slogans, and there was no point dwelling on the problems of victory when he had the problems of failure on his mind. All the time he spent thinking and planning to get the British out, O'Neill's essential belief that in the end the IRA would win, was tempered by deeper thoughts which had troubled him since his time in the Maze prison. There, day after day, he and the other republican prisoners had gone through a constantly evolving discussion of the ideas for a new Ireland. That discussion now found its way into all the speeches of Sinn Fein candidates in elections in the North. He knew their weakness had been in saying 'Brits Out' and stopping at that, rather than describing the vision of the New Ireland that would follow, the kind of New Ireland that would appeal to people like the old woman.

The new slogans were right, he was sure of it: for socialism, for a thirty-two-county-republic, for freedom of worship and freedom of conscience. It was all there. It gave them a target, a goal. But in his blackest moments O'Neill would look around at the material he had to deal with and wonder how even an entrenched republican government could push forward to make this new Ireland work.

'More likely we'll do the dirty work, get the Brits out, and the Free Staters will take the credit for it,' Billy McKeever had once said. O'Neill had disagreed, but McKeever's words had the ring of truth. If they ever did get the British out, then the real struggle for survival would begin. The Irish government would move to crush them, before the Republican Movement developed enough political force to appear a threat. They would be lined up against the same walls as the republicans of the Civil War, and meet the same fate. Maybe. But history was not repeatable. The slogans were more than just slogans. They were the only hope.

O'Neill climbed into the car and told the driver to head for the safe house in Howth. The 'Unsafe Safe House,' he called it. He was sure it was no longer secure, though he liked it too much to give it up willingly. It was the sort of place he dreamed of while in prison and never really believed he would see again – a large Victorian mansion on the seashore north of Dublin. It was at the end of a long drive, hidden from the road by a hawthorn hedge and a mass of rhododendrons that were now in full bloom. When he stayed there – maybe six or seven nights a month – he would walk for hours on the beach, listening to the waves and the seagulls shriek as they were swept up by the wind. It was everything that in prison had been denied him: the open spaces, the restlessness of the sea, a chance to be truly alone. O'Neill found that more than anywhere else, he could think things through in the solitude of the house, sitting among the ferns in the conservatory at the back or strolling round the grounds and watching the beating of the sea.

The trouble with trying to build a mass political movement from a tightly-knit guerrilla army, he thought, was that everybody spent all their time talking and debating. No one spent any time thinking. In prison when people lived on top of one another, political debates were not only permissible, they were the main source of education and entertainment. Everyone had a point of view; everyone wanted to discuss everything with the greatest degree of pedantic precision because it filled the time. Now, outside jail, with so much to do and no leisurely hours to spend in long and dreary debates, O'Neill simply wanted to be alone to make his decisions as quickly as possible. The 'Unsafe Safe House' bought him the time he needed.

The car crossed the Liffey and turned through the backstreets towards the GAA ground at Croke Park, before doubling back towards the coast. No one was following. O'Neill was amazed at the variety of routes his driver could invent to take him to the same place. There must be some mathematical formula to express the limit on the number, but it seemed infinite. If they were to be picked up by the police it would most likely be as a result of bad luck – stumbling into a roadblock meant for someone else – rather than a smart piece of detective work by the Gardai or a tip-off. O'Neill could not think of anyone seeking directly to betray him. His enemies in the Movement could not be so desperate to be rid of him. Even so, and despite his reluctance, he was preparing to abandon the house at Howth and find somewhere else. There would come a time when the police were bound to find out about it, a careless word, a hint passed on to the wrong man, a joke which reached the ears of an informer. The biggest risk about the house now was what had once been its greatest advantage: the fact that it was in a prosperous middle-class area. Ever since the kidnapping of the Lawford heiress by Dublin gangsters the previous year, the Gardai had increased their patrols significantly in the better suburbs. O'Neill thought it would be a fine irony if he were captured by an anti-robbery patrol, but it was an irony he could live without.

When there was time, or when they had the men, O'Neill would send a car ahead of his own to the house, or to wherever he was staying. The scout would telephone or use the short wave and tell O'Neill everything was all right. Today, there was no possibility of that, and O'Neill noticed his driver was slightly on edge. He kept to the speed limit, driving like a trained police driver, but grinding his teeth and flexing his jaw muscles with tension. O'Neill was glad he was nervous. It was most likely the routine things of daily life that would get them caught, not one grand error. Just a moment's care-lessness because the task being performed had become routine.

'Eamonn,' O'Neill said, as they reached the outskirts of Howth. 'I'm going north tonight. To Donegal. I want you and Sean just to look after the house. I'll be back in a few days.'

'Fine,' the driver said. 'No problem.'

Ever since he escaped from the Maze, O'Neill had thrown himself into the re-organisation of the Movement, trying to push it to re-define the balance between its military and political strategies. It had taken all his time, every waking hour that he could remember. Now he was going to think of himself, take two days off for some-thing that he had planned and thought about for years in prison. There were risks, but now was the time for a kind of pilgrimage. There was a short gap in the demands upon him, after the Durrant kidnapping and before the next part of the work in progress. The plans were complete. All that was necessary was to push the button to begin. He could afford the days to be spent in Donegal. There were repairs to be made to friendships, and maybe some apologies, before such things became irredeemable. This was the time to go, and then he would push the button.

Eamonn pulled the car into the gravel driveway, and approached the house with caution. There was no sign of life. It looked exactly as they had left it, the venetian blinds shut tight. Eamonn turned the car so it was pointing back out the driveway, and kept the engine running while Sean quickly checked the house. 'Okay,' he said.

O'Neill stepped out and opened the garage. He brought his own car – a five-year-old Datsun – outside.

'I'll phone in,' he said. 'Usual times. In case there's anything I should know about. If not, see you next week. I'll stop off in Dundalk on the way down.'

Eamonn and Sean nodded in farewell and returned to the house. O'Neill sped down the driveway too fast, excited and anxious about the trip ahead. There was much that he wanted to explain once he reached Donegal, to prove to himself as much as to anyone else, that the Movement had not dehumanised him, that he could re-establish the friendships from the past. He remembered the line from Yeats about too long a sacrifice making a stone of the heart. Well, he had sacrificed, but only because his heart was no stone. It was as open and as human as it had always been.

O'Neill took the Malahide road, sticking to the coast. Though it was longer, he preferred to be near the moving sea. He rolled the window down and felt the salt air stick in his hair and on his face. His driving had hardly improved since he escaped – not enough practice, since normally he was driven by Eamonn or someone else. But what would have once seemed a chore, the long road to the North, was now wholly a pleasure. O'Neill was free to enjoy it.

He had most of the route fixed in his mind – Navan to Kells and then on to Cavan, Ballyshannon and Donegal town, before turning straight northwards. He knew the end of the route so well, but not from this direction. For years, when he had been in Belfast, he would go to Burtonport and the Rosses at weekends when he could. They joked with him about it in the Movement: the middle-class boy whose parents had a country cottage in Donegal and who occasionally demanded weekends off from the armed struggle. The part-time Provo. He never apologised for it.

'The Donegal Gaeltacht,' O'Neill used to say. 'That's part of the Ireland that we're fighting for. The way the Dublin government treats Irish speaking, our language will be dead in a few more years. If I can't keep it alive, then at least I want to visit it on its sickbed. And that's as much a part of our country as anything we might fight for in Belfast.'

The meeting with Morgan reminded O'Neill how years before he had heard with embarrassment a Sinn Fein leader being asked by journalists at a news conference to describe the New Ireland and what it would involve. The man was clear in his mind that this 'New Ireland' would have no British troops in it and no links with the Westminster parliament, but beyond that, his was a pathetic display of ignorance and stupidity. O'Neill was not going to be like that. Never. If he finally did do the interview for English television – and he thought it likely – he would be able to give a fresh vision of an Ireland that worked as a proper community. None of the street fighting of Belfast and Derry, none of the crime and the drugs of Dublin and Cork. Even if the Donegal he remembered was not still alive, except in his dreams. He wanted to see it again now, to re-define what might become the future after the armed struggle succeeded.

While his marriage to Sheelagh had lasted, Donegal had been a special place for O'Neill. When he looked at the map to plan his route to the north, seeing the names again made a lump rise in his throat . . . Gweedore, Falcarragh, Portnoo, Lettermacaward, Dooish and Slieve Snaght. The sounds conjured up a fantasy world to which he once belonged, but which was now lost, a dream in which he had enjoyed a kind of happiness that would never return. There had been a time when he and Sheelagh had been staying at the family cottage at Bunbeg, not long after they were married. He had taken her to climb the peak of Errigal as his father had done with him years before, and as he wanted his own children to do with him. It had been one of those days when the wind off the Atlantic whipped the high clouds across the country but there was no rain. From the pointed summit, clutching each other in the wind's blast, Sheelagh and O'Neill could see clear across the hills to Derry and Northern Ireland.

'What's the difference,' O'Neill remembered his father asking him, on that very same peak years before. 'What's the difference between this country on which we are now standing, and that country whose smoke we see drifting above the mills of Derry?'

O'Neill was unsure what answer to give. 'I don't know, Da,' he said. 'I don't see where one ends and the other begins.'

It had been the right answer. His father said there was no difference, nor would there be again. From here on the peak of Errigal you saw one country, though not one state, a vision of Ireland's past and future, stretching out in a green patchwork to the horizon. On the same peak with Sheelagh, all those years later, he had told her the story and she laughed.

'I thought it was your mother who was the republican in the family.'

'She is,' O'Neill said. 'But I think the thin air must have got to the Da's head.'

The road towards Navan was full of farm traffic. Dirt-covered tractors spilled wet mud on the road, rough farm boys standing on the plate at the back behind the driver, watching him as he approached. He wondered what they would do if they recognised him. How many would turn him in? Fifty per cent? No, less. He was sure of it. Ten per cent, more likely. Certainly that many. The rest might not like him much, but at least they would understand. They would tolerate what he was about, even if they could not join in. There was safety in that tolerance.

It was starting to rain again, a fine drizzle hardly worth exciting the windscreen wipers to work for. The fields were green and rich and full of growing barley. The country was prospering. He passed through the villages towards Kells watching the ordinary folk of Ireland go about their business, half envious that they could sit down for tea at their own fireside with their own wife and children, not worrying about the next knock at the door. O'Neill slipped into third gear and accelerated away.

He felt a sense of nervousness in his stomach about what was to come. It had been a long time since he had last been in Donegal, three or four months before he ended up in prison. Years ago. Centuries. In another life. Whatever the risks he was now taking, in terms of the security forces being active on the southern side of the border, he was sure they were worth it. He would have taken them for Sheelagh if she had still been prepared to wait. As it was, he had married the Republican Movement now, in the way a nun marries the Church. He had made his choice of a life which precluded sitting in front of a television set in the evenings, drowning in the boredom of contentment and family relationships. If all that was no longer possible, it was important to stay in touch with the real world outside the cloister of republicanism. Donegal would be part of that. There was no stone. He had a normal heart.

The drizzle had stopped by the time he reached Ballyshannon and started on the winding roads through Donegal town and the short-cut through Frosses towards Burtonport. Up on the moors he could see the piles of blue plastic bags covering the newly-dug turf in the peat bogs, the sides of the bogs cut smooth by the spade. He remembered as a child asking his father how it was that people could leave valuable cut turf lying stacked in open country. Why did nobody steal it?

'Because this is Donegal, Patrick,' his father said, as if that were explanation enough. 'It is not Belfast. Here, no man would steal another man's turf, the fire from another man's grate. To do that would be lower than vermin.'

'But the people who would do it in Belfast. Are they vermin, Da?'

'No,' he remembered his father saying. 'Not vermin. Just victims.'

O'Neill wondered how his father, God rest his soul, would think of him now. In the early days of the Troubles his father's whole background – Master Sean O'Neill, history teacher at the Christian Brothers on the Stewartstown Road – had led to the worst rows at home O'Neill could ever recall. At first the old man had walked with the rest of them in the Civil Rights marches. O'Neill remembered that when the British Army arrived in Belfast in 1969 his father refused to join the immediate sense of general relief that they would keep the Protestants from attacking Catholic areas. He had said to his family that this was not the end of the violence, just the beginning of the real fight – not because he was a republican, but because he knew what the history of the island meant.

'Things are turning, Patrick. And you are witnessing history on the turn.'

The rows had come when it became clear O'Neill was not content to be a witness. He wanted to take part. When he joined the Republican Movement it seemed his father's whole attitude changed. He threatened to throw O'Neill into the street if he did not give up the IRA, and was persuaded otherwise only after repeated and tearful pleas from O'Neill's mother.

'He is a man now, Sean. He can take a man's decisions about how he should proceed with his life.'

'Well, if that's the way it is, then there's maybe no room for two men under this self-same roof. One of us will have to go.'

Sean O'Neill calmed down eventually, but specific incidents would set him off again. O'Neill remembered his father's disgust at the shooting of three off-duty Scottish soldiers by the IRA in North Belfast.

'Murder,' Sean O'Neill had said. 'Just cold-blooded murder.'

P J yelled back that if they weren't over here, then it wouldn't have happened to them. 'They had it coming, the murdering bastards. Do you know what they did . . .'

His father interrupted. 'I don't care what anyone did. The way to get the British out of this country is not to go around murdering working-class lads of your own age who happen to have joined their army because there was nothing else for them to do.'

'Then what is the way to get the British out?' O'Neill asked. 'Is it to read books, recite Irish history and pray that they go, like you do? Why is it you seem to think every struggle for independence in the past – the Fenians, 1916, everything – was a just struggle, yet the struggle we're having now you think immoral? You're just like the bloody Bishops, a bunch of hypocrites. Why is it that for all of you those who fought against the British in the past are heroes, and those who fight in the present are terrorists? To hell with the lot of you.'

O'Neill smiled as he recalled the fury between the teenage son and the middle-aged parent, and how his father had lifted his hand and hit him hard on the face. His pride had been wounded – a Volunteer being beaten by his own da – yet now he was sure it was the same fury all over the world, different generations in conflict over what was to be done. He remembered that later, after his arrest, he had read in the Maze something from Oscar Wilde saying that children always judge their parents; seldom if ever do they forgive them. In the end they had forgiven each other, father and son, but not without a struggle. O'Neill's mother had been scandalised by the row, partly by his own sudden contempt for religion after the years when he appeared to have longed to become a priest, and mostly, he now thought, because to her meal times were a kind of family sacrament. The rows between father and son ruined all that, like an argument during Mass.

'How is it,' his father had said, 'that you spend years telling your mother and me that you want to become a priest, and I spend years trying to talk you out of it. And now what have you become? Some vocation. I daren't think what you get up to and where you go at night. But if I ever found out you were involved in something like that murder of those soldiers, I'd never speak to you again. I swear it. You'd never any more be a son of mine. I'd rather be father to that friend of yours who has now gone off to Maynooth to do the thing I thought you wanted to do: become a priest and help your community. How it helps your community by murdering ordinary working-class Scotchmen, I don't know!'

Go to Maynooth like Jo-Jo McGuinn? Maybe. O'Neill could imagine it having happened, but his life would now be beyond comprehension. If he had chosen the priesthood he would also have chosen to work in the Third World, in the Philippines or Central America, where the Church stood with the people, not in Northern Ireland where it always ranked itself with the establishment. At the time, all he had wanted to do was to shock his father, to tell him with the most outrageous cheek he could muster that he himself would hardly have been involved in the killing of the three soldiers since it was obviously a North Belfast operation, not one by his own West Belfast battalion area. He thought better of it. As to Jo-Jo McGuinn becoming a priest when there was work to be done here, well that was up to him. The war would go well enough without him. O'Neill said nothing.

His car was now passing Gweebarra bay. The clouds had begun to shift to the east. Over the Atlantic the sky was clearing and blue was showing on the horizon. To his right, O'Neill could see the beginnings of the Derryveagh mountains, but Errigal and Dooish and Slieve Snaght were lost in the clouds. There was a chance that before he left he might manage to climb Errigal again, maybe once more take the air on the peak and gaze into the North. A chance. More likely, despite the break in the weather to the west, it would continue wet and grim and he would spend most of his time indoors. The Rosses were now less than ten miles away, and O'Neill felt uncontrollably nervous. It was like being on a job with a car load of arms and explosives, desperate to get it over with, yet proud to be there. O'Neill genuinely believed he could face his own death with equanimity. He had rehearsed the part so often in his mind, in his daydreams and nightmares. It would be either the bomb under the car from a loyalist assassin, or a machine-gun bullet in the back as he tried to run a roadblock filled with police and troops. There was an alternative and less glorious scene, the moment of his arrest. This was the early morning knock on the door, when he would ask for time to dress and shave rather than be dragged out as an undignified bundle to court, but they would refuse and manacle him as he stood, naked and unkempt. He had rehearsed it all in his mind, down to the blows on his face and head, the stomping of boots in his ribs, the coldness of the handcuffs. He was sure it would come, one way or the other, and the more he thought about it, the less it worried him. His nervousness now was of a different order. It was fear, but not for his personal safety. It was almost the fear of being spurned. Today's meeting he had not – could not have – rehearsed. It was an almost whimsical decision to place the telephone call and hope it would be received the way he longed it to be after all these years. He thought he had outgrown sentimentality, but O'Neill was feeling maudlin now.

He could see the small town, not much more than a village in the fading sunlight, on the far side of the bay. As he came closer, the church appeared to his right, stubby and grey on a raised plot near

108

the edge of the water. The fields were full of large rocks and poor sour-grass that the sheep could barely get a feed from. Some grazed on the seaweed thrown up by the last of the early summer storms, poking among the sand and the rock pools for whatever was left. Others trotted along the road in front of him, disturbed at their feeding on the verges. To his left, O'Neill could see some of the small islands out past the curve of the headland. The sea was calm, as if the Atlantic had decided to take a rest from the beating on the Bloody Foreland shore. The sun was almost ready to set, slipping slowly towards the water on the horizon, clear through the gap in the clouds and turning the sea gold and orange in a long swathe towards him.

O'Neill turned the Datsun into the churchyard and parked beside the graveyard wall. He paused for a moment to look at the priest's house, of solid grey stone. There was only one other car in the car park, the priest's own, he supposed; a blue Volkswagen, parked by the front door.

P J O'Neill took a small overnight bag from the boot of the Datsun and rang the bell, shuffling his feet nervously on the doorstep. A few minutes later a man of his own age in priest's garb opened the door. The two men stared at each other in silence.

He had put on weight, O'Neill thought. There was a plumpness round the cheeks he could not recall. The straggly beard of their teenage years had gone. The face was clean-shaven and smooth, red-jowled now, prosperous looking. There was no greying of the hair, but it was far shorter than O'Neill could ever recall – except maybe for their earliest schooldays, when they both had short back and sides, stuck fast to their heads with Brylcreem. They studied each other's faces without any words, as if seeking a sign long hidden. Suddenly the priest opened his arms wide, laughing, and embraced him.

'P J,' he chuckled. 'It is good to see you. I cannot tell you how I have waited for this time.'

O'Neill pushed him back, breaking the bear hug to look at him again. He smiled wide, his eyes twinkling with joy.

'Jo-Jo,' he said warmly. 'Or do I now call you Father Joseph? Words cannot say how I feel seeing you at last.'

Chapter Ten

London

Morgan had decided to make a special effort. Normally when he returned home after a trip he was exhausted, wanted a good meal and a drink and then to go to bed. This time he promised himself he would try to talk properly to Emily, to prove he was better than just the part-time father and occasional husband she told him he was. He wanted to wash the smell of the Irish trip off his body, to throw all his clothes in the washing-machine and clean himself, ready for the return visit whenever it came. He knew she would want to talk to him about all the little things that had happened with David and Louise in the week he had been away and he would force himself not to be bored by the slightest detail. In the past Emily always hungered for his return. It was not surprising that she found the company of the other mothers so tedious. The constant talk about other people's babies drove him demented. She would want to hear what he had been doing, and for reasons he could still not fully understand, she seemed more interested in Ireland than even he was. He wondered how she would take the news that he had actually met O'Neill and he had agreed to the project.

The children were eating when he arrived. Emily had placed fish fingers and beans before them, not because she approved of eating those things, but David was going through a period of fads, and his sister followed him in those as with everything else. The trade-off was that if she gave them fish fingers and beans, they would also eat the salad that went with it. Or at least part of it. Emily did not feel like arguing. Morgan kissed them all. When she talked to him it was matter-of-factly, a few pleasantries, nothing much more. He was surprised, expecting something better, and almost taken aback at the palpable tension between them. It was true that things were always difficult if he had been away for a long time, as they sought tentatively to re-establish their relationship. But this seemed much

111

more serious, as if she had been brooding and might explode at any opportunity.

Morgan knew he could say nothing of substance with the children present, neither about the trip nor more especially about the abortion. He wondered whether Emily had kept her word, or what he took to be her word, and had not done something silly. He thought he saw a slight flush on her cheek. Of embarrassment? Maybe she had gone ahead, despite him, or rather to spite him, and had had the abortion? No. The flush could have been the effort of looking after the children. It was difficult to judge.

Morgan sat down and began munching at a cake, sipping tea. He and Emily would eat a proper meal later. He was never hungry when he returned from a trip. The travelling, the long days, the airline food, something would always upset his stomach, and he wanted tea for now and something better later.

'How did it go?' Emily said eventually. 'Your trip.'

'Fine. Or at least better than I expected. I managed to meet him.'

'Who.'

'P J O'Neill.'

She looked at him, surprised. 'P J O'Neill?' she said, not sure if she was thinking of the same man. 'The Maze escaper?'

'Yes. I mentioned it to you before I left.'

Emily vaguely remembered.

'Things were a bit fraught,' she said. 'I had other things on my mind then.' Morgan looked alarmed.

'And now?' he asked.

'Well, I still have the same thing on my mind, but I suppose I am a bit calmer.'

Morgan said he was pleased to hear it. His wife pushed a stray brown hair behind her ear, and looked thoughtful.

'Didn't I say I thought I met some of his family in Belfast?'

Morgan replied that he thought she had mentioned something about O'Neill having had a vocation as a priest which he abandoned in order to join the IRA.

'Did you write of the family somewhere in one of your articles?'

'Not exactly,' Emily said. 'I think I did write . . .'

She broke off to stop her son pulling at Louise's plate. 'Any more of that, David, and you'll go straight off to bed.' He looked back, sullen. Unrepentant.

They decided that instead of cooking, she would put the children to bed and Morgan would fetch food from a Chinese takeaway.

112

When he returned, the children were already upstairs. Emily put a row of hot plates on the table and Morgan began spooning out the rice. He always bought too much, because he liked to try everything. Emily knew half of it would be left over, and she would re-heat it the following day for herself.

'You didn't do anything,' he said.

'Anything what?'

'Anything about the doctor.'

'The abortion,' she said, splashing some hot sauce on her plate. 'Oh, that. Not yet. I told you I wouldn't till you came back, but I haven't changed my mind. I went back to the doctor and have made arrangements. I go in ten days time. He said I shouldn't leave it any longer. There will be no fuss.'

'Is there no arguing with you?' Morgan said. 'Have you delayed for nearly two weeks just to tell me that I have no part to play?'

'There was going to be a delay anyway while I made the arrangements. And anyway, what part is there for you to play? You've done your bit up to now. What more is there for you? The part of oft-forgotten father?'

She looked at him sadly, as if she felt sorry she had gone quite so far. Morgan's face was flushed, and she could see he was hurt. Emily began patiently to rehearse the argument of two weeks before, the reasons why she wanted to go back to work, the fact that she knew she could not have it all – husband, family, career – and that she was tired of sacrificing her career for children.

'We do not need any more children,' she sighed. 'It is just like that. I am fulfilled – isn't that the word they use in those dreadful magazines – fulfilled enough as a mother without having to go through it all again. I have had the supposedly wonderful experience of childbirth twice, and I continue to have the experience every day in some different way. It doesn't mean I love you less, or love David less, or Louise. It just means I have had enough.'

He must have looked utterly dejected. She put her arm on his and smiled.

'Truly,' she said. 'I think it is the best for us. Not just for me, but for all of us.'

She paused for a moment. He absently pushed a fork load of beansprouts into his mouth.

'I don't understand,' she went on, 'why you are so cut up about it. What has got into you?'

'I didn't think you could do it,' Morgan said softly. 'I mean, it's

113

all very well to talk about abortions in theory as we used to at university – the "what if you got pregnant now, or raped, or the baby was handicapped debate". But this is no debate. This time it's a real child. And it is part of me as well as part of you, and I don't want to kill it.'

Emily wanted to change the subject and told him so. Morgan sat sulky and quiet. Emily murmured that if he really wanted to, they could talk about it one last time in the morning. He was always grizzly when he returned from a week away, and there would be more sense to it when he was less tired. She was glad to see him back, and did not want a fight. It made no difference – Morgan stayed sulky.

'Tell me more about Ireland,' she said cheerfully. 'And P J O'Neill.'

Morgan began to talk, telling her the details as he remembered them, and how things in the Republican Movement's offices in Belfast had changed, or not changed. He told her Anderson was still the same, as unpleasant as before and twice as arrogant. She laughed.

'I remember him years ago,' she said. 'Always reading some great Marxist tract and wanting to discuss it with me or anyone else he met. He was the only one of them all who had no sense of humour. And every time I wrote something about them he would phone me up and accuse me of bias. Every time, almost as a routine complaint to prove he distanced himself from me and everything I meant.'

Emily laughed at the thought, then asked again about O'Neill. Morgan told her of the meeting and of what had been agreed. She said she was surprised that Capital Satellite Television was prepared to take the risks associated with the project and told him so. Morgan thought they had discussed some of this before, but maybe she had been too preoccupied thinking about the abortion.

'I wonder what has come over Crawshaw,' she wondered. 'Even if he really does want to make the news rather than simply report it, he is taking quite a gamble that all his friends in the City or wherever don't suddenly desert him. Doesn't seem like the Crawshaw you've been describing to me all these months.'

'Maybe it is a bit like Richard Nixon,' Morgan said. 'Only a far out right-winger like Nixon could restore proper relations with China. Only a right-winger like De Gaulle could get the French out of Algeria. And only a complete fascist like Crawshaw could think

of doing a proper programme on the Provisionals, because his patriotism is not in question, and he is hardly some kind of closet Irish
republican. I think he might well get away with it.'

Emily laughed at the thought of Crawshaw the closet Provo, and
he loved her like this. It felt a bit like the way it once had been – the
two of them, half-committed to some view, half-cynical about what
it might imply, discussing politics until late over coffee in his college
rooms, then making love through the rest of the night. That was how
he remembered it anyway, and he felt a twist of nostalgia for the freedom and simplicity of what they once had, before the children were
born. Why had they allowed things to become so complicated?

'O'Neill came from a very religious background,' Emily said. 'I
remember that part of it well enough. His mother and father lived up
the Glen Road in Andersonstown, one of the big detached red brick
houses on the edge of the city. Middle-class, really. I don't remember
the father, but the mother was the one with the republican background. Wanted him to be a priest, but was content enough that he
chose the other line of business.'

'You remember him that well?' Morgan said. 'Do you think there
would be anything about him or his family in any of your articles at
the time?'

'I really don't think so. There were so many mothers like that, so
many of them I don't think O'Neill's mother got a look in. The ones I
concentrated on in the "Women Behind the Men Behind the Wire"
were all the best-known cases. O'Neill was nobody important then,
except that he was middle-class, and so a little different from the
ordinary. I tended to stick to the cases which really had made the
headlines. You remember the McNallys?'

Morgan vaguely recalled the name, not the story. Emily began to
talk of a whole family from Carrickmore in County Tyrone, five
brothers and one sister. Two brothers were dead, one killed by the
British Army, the other by his own bomb. One was in jail. One
brother and the sister were on the run. The mother was left with one
teenage son at home, and though she never said so, Emily was sure at
the time he was in the IRA.

'Proud she was of them all too,' Emily said. 'Proud of what they
had done and what they would do, even if they were killed in the
attempt.'

Morgan remembered the story now, even down to the fact that the
brother in jail had gone on hunger strike to demand political status.

'Irish republicanism,' he said, putting on his most pompous

115

voice, 'is like a genetic disease. And all too often the mother is the carrier.'

Emily laughed again.

'I remember that. Conor Cruise O'Brien in *The Observer* years ago. He was probably right. About the mother being the carrier, I mean, not about it being a genetic disease.'

'You know what?' Morgan said. 'The thing that most impressed me this time was that nothing at all has changed. You haven't been back in Belfast since before David was born – eight years, nine years?'

'Something like that.'

'And in all that time maybe Martin Anderson has got a few white hairs more in his beard and P J O'Neill who was in prison is out. And maybe the McNally boy who was out is now in. It doesn't much matter. It is the same old stuff. The same old boring stuff, after twenty years of dead bodies.'

'Well, if it's so boring why do you want to go there?' Emily asked. 'Why don't you stay behind here and look after the kids, and I'll go and talk to O'Neill. It won't bore me.'

It was meant as a serious offer, and he smiled. He said that he might take her up on it, except that she sounded too committed to make a go of things on television, especially super-independent, deregulated, business-values Euro-satellited TV for the twenty-first century.

'It's not the *New Statesman*, you know,' he said with a smirk. 'You can't get away with three paragraphs of fact and thirty of any old politically-biased toss like you used to.'

'Oh, I know how to be objective too,' she said. 'I can take the usual television and radio stance and pretend that provided you have a Conservative and a Labour Party spokesman on Northern Ireland both saying the same things, you are being balanced.'

'They don't say the same things.'

'True,' Emily said smiling. 'The Conservatives say Northern Ireland should remain a part of the United Kingdom until a majority want it otherwise. The Labour Party say they would like a united Ireland – but not until there's a majority in favour of it. Both hate the Provos. Breathtakingly different positions, I would say.'

'Hold on a minute,' Morgan responded. 'I never realised that you were a secret republican too. Crawshaw comes out of the closet as a Provo lover, and now you. It is all too much for a simple hack like me. I may have to have a glass of scotch to help me recover.'

She asked for one too, very weak, filled up with soda. They left the dirty plates and takeaway cartons on the dining table, and walked into the sitting-room. He threw himself down on the sofa, she on a large cushion on the floor. For a few moments they sat facing each other across the room in silence, sipping their drinks. Morgan thought again how like the old days it all was. Of course this time he owned the house, and he had fathered the kids, and if they wanted to they could go out and have a decent and expensive French meal instead of the cheap curries of their student days. But some things had not changed in their relationship, and one of those was her stubbornness when she had made up her mind.

He knew that he would have to get round to the question of the abortion again, but he could take his time. It need not be tonight, as she said. Maybe tomorrow. It would take a few days to sort out the filming and travel back to Dublin. There was no point in hurrying, and he had perhaps a total of ten days to make her change her mind. Not forcing the issue was his best tactic. No direct assault, just a series of skirmishes. Maybe he would fail, but he thought he could persuade her that their marriage was still working as it had in the past. He would tell her he intended to try harder at being the proper father she thought the children lacked. He was at least a half-decent husband. He did not cheat on her, as others did. Well, not much, and not regularly. If the O'Neill story helped kick-start his career again, it was possible that she might feel less of a need to go back to work, and he might be more fun to live with.

He had stopped telling her what he had been doing on Capital Satellite Reports mainly because he had been ashamed of the nonsense he was expected to produce. How could he come home and tell a wife as intelligent as Emily that he was pursuing an extremely challenging career when he had spent the day making a film about the new school Prince William was due to attend, or a one-and-a-half minute report about a children's ailment which was giving doctors in Gloucestershire cause for concern? It was chewing-gum for the European mind. He hated it, and half despised himself for putting up with it. If the O'Neill interview worked, it would put him back in the mainstream of proper journalism again. It would restore his self-respect, and that would rub off on their marriage.

'A nationalist,' she said. 'If you really want to know, I am an Irish nationalist, not a Republican. I believe that Ireland should be united, though preferably not by the Provos. That's simple enough, isn't it? I thought everybody in England with half a brain was an Irish nationalist too – including you.'

She took another sip of her weak whisky. She hardly ever drank alcohol any more. She was no longer interested in it, but it was an act of defiance during the pregnancy. She had tried not to nag him about his drinking, but Emily believed it was a sign of his perverse immaturity. If Morgan had lost the idealism of their university days, she could not understand why he had not also lost the other irritating young man's habit of demanding to get drunk. Why could he not keep the idealism and lose the booze?

Maybe, Emily thought, it was envy on her part. She recognised that despite the children, Morgan could remain as free of responsibilities as he had ever been. She was the one who had to remain sober for emergencies. But tonight she was enjoying the whisky, and that rather surprised her. It was as if the talk of Ireland had awakened an old craving within her, and part of that craving was for the hot Irish whiskeys she used to drink in dubious bars up and down the country while out chasing stories. Yet even though she wanted the abortion, she would not have drunk to excess, or taken a strong scotch in case it did harm to the foetus. It was heavily diluted, but the taste was still there.

'Homoeopathic alcohol,' she thought. 'Cure for all ills.'

She wanted to tell Morgan the joke, but thought better of it. It would be safer to stick to theoretical positions on Ireland than opening up taboo subjects – her pregnancy or his drinking.

Morgan said he did not like the word 'nationalist' when applied to people in Britain, so he did not see how he could be happy with the word when applied to foreigners. 'Nationalism' was something that two world wars this century had stamped out of most Europeans. He no longer cared whether Ireland was united or not. The future of five million people on an off-shore island did not seem now to be one of the world's great questions.

'In this I am utterly in tune with my audience,' he said. 'Or at least the British section of it. If you force most of them to state an opinion they would probably say they would like Ireland to be united. But that is only because they do not care at all about the subject, regarding all of Ireland like a dull toothache. They hope for a united Ireland because they think that will make the toothache go away, not because they have any enthusiasm for it. That's how most of them feel, and I'm beginning to agree with them.'

'You?' Emily said. 'When did you start to lose all interest?'

'Me? I haven't lost all interest, but I have begun to lose patience with it all over the last year or two, and this visit put the seal on it. I have never tasted the hopelessness of it all like this before. I've got older and more wrinkled and maybe more of a pain in the neck, but at least I have changed over twenty years. I am different now. Over there, nothing changes. Nothing important, anyway.'

Emily was beginning to get cold. The house was rambling and Victorian, and they had fitted a gas fire that looked as if it was burning real coal, into the original fireplace in the sitting-room. The coal was false and so was the supposed heat. She shuddered a little and turned the gas full on.

'It is only hopeless for you,' she said, 'because you don't have to put up with everything Irish people have to. It is not just on abortion that you've changed your mind. What happened to the student I used to know who led the University Union debate on civil rights for the Catholic people of Northern Ireland? What happened to the man who wanted to be posted to Belfast as a journalist so he could explain to people precisely what was going on?'

Morgan smiled. She was enjoying herself, playing with him. She knelt by the fire, warming her hands, her back to him, but her face turned his way as she made her arguments. He wanted to get down on the floor beside her and put his arms round her, but he hesitated too long and she sat back on her cushion again.

'What happened to him?' Morgan repeated. 'He went to Ireland. That's what happened to him. And he decided life was a little more complicated than a proposition in a university debate. That's what happened to him. And more recently what happened to him was that he went back and found that all his half suspicions had come true. The people over there don't want peace because their poxy little war is all that keeps them from terminal boredom. While they are shooting each other they can pretend that they are somehow important, that when Belfast belches the world sits up and takes notice. Well, it just isn't the case. And I'm going to ask O'Neill why the hell he doesn't give up and start living a life instead of chasing the little pot of republican gold at the end of the rainbow. Their Long War is just a twenty-year-old Long Yawn for the rest of us, British or Irish.'

Emily held hands up in mock outrage and said she was amazed at him for condemning a whole generation of Ulster people for relishing the Troubles. It was like condemning an animal for bellowing because it was caught in a trap.

'And anyway,' she said. 'If you really do believe that the most important medium of popular communication – television – can't make people interested in all the killing and death, then what the hell are you doing still working in it? Why don't you get yourself a real job?'

'I would,' he said, taking what she said with total seriousness as if she had struck him a surprise blow. 'Only I can't find one. I'm a bit late to train as a doctor or a lawyer. If I could re-train, then I might just do it. At least as a doctor I'd be doing something useful.'

She was taken aback by the grimness of his tone, as if he truly had been brooding on it for a while instead of just playing a verbal game with her. It had been going along like old times, with one of them striking a half-serious pose, so the other one could attack it. She had been so worried about avoiding mentioning the abortion, she had forgotten his unhappiness at work.

'I thought,' she said, trying to be emollient. 'I thought you were enjoying doing this story.'

Morgan explained that he was happy to be doing an important story, but he had ceased to believe that his job was important. That was the difference. Emily looked at him quizzically.

'That's not what you used to say,' she said. 'I remember you at dinner party after dinner party explaining to various bores and estate agents and chartered accountants and lawyers why journalism was not just a true profession, but the most important profession there was.'

'Maybe I did. But I don't feel that way now.'

'You did, though I am beginning to think you might have been saying it just to annoy them. You used to argue that without free and proper journalism there could be no democracy because democracy depended on the popular vote, and the people had to be properly informed in order to exercise their democratic choice. The only way to do that was through a responsible and active free press, radio and television. Something like that. You could be incredibly pompous when you said it, and what was remarkable was that they all used to take you seriously.'

Morgan smiled. He had not argued any such thing for years. He thought the idea of journalism being a profession was now vaguely ridiculous. It was barely a craft, with a level of skill somewhere between bricklaying and basket weaving, though perhaps not so useful. He remembered some of the words of his old arguments, but the reasons for saying them seemed remote.

'I think I can recall how that particular after dinner speech used to end,' he said. 'It was something about a free press being at the core of a free society. Therefore without *The Sun* newspaper we would all end up being run by a dictator.'

Emily laughed aloud. She said the ending was usually even worse than that. Depending on who it was around the dinner table Morgan most wanted to annoy, he would end by saying 'and so you see, unlike America which is a *proper* democracy with a Freedom of Information Act and a robust professional press, the United Kingdom remains an elective tyranny with no right to information, where we are banned from interviewing representatives of political organisations like Sinn Fein – even though they have almost sixty local councillors in Northern Ireland and one Westminster Member of Parliament. We are now a joke democracy, somewhere between a third world country and the new Soviet Union of Mikhail Gorbachev.'

Morgan filled himself another glass of scotch, and offered her one. Emily said she still had plenty in her glass. They talked a little of the kinds of people he had most annoyed round dinner tables with that kind of speech. Sometimes he would change course totally and argue that instead of tolerating an acceptable level of violence in Northern Ireland the British government should simply set up assassination squads to 'take out the ringleaders'. It never failed to surprise him how often this course of action, if advocated with sufficient degrees of spurious enthusiasm, would always lead to one or two dinner party guests admitting they thought it was a damn good idea, state assassination squads.

'But isn't murder, murder, as Mrs Thatcher would say?' he would interject at the right moment, taking precisely the opposite position. 'Surely we cannot kill people in the name of democracy? Surely everyone deserves the right of a fair trial, even terrorists. We can't just go out and sanction state murder?'

It was an old game, and he had stopped playing it. Morgan had noticed some three or four years back that people began reacting less and less when he said such things. At first he thought it was because most of his friends knew he liked to shock and annoy people in this way, but it was more than that. People genuinely were not interested any more. The whole subject had become a bore, and the conversation would turn to more interesting matters like house prices or foreign holidays, or the perils of the air traffic controllers' strike. Northern Ireland would just drive them home to their beds.

'The most potent medium of our times,' Morgan said, looking straight at Emily, and remembering something he forgot to challenge. 'Or whatever it was you called television, cannot make the tedious interesting. We cannot explain things to people who do not want to hear.'

Emily hitched her skirt up a little over her knees, now beginning to enjoy the warmth from the fire. It was probably the least efficient means of heating ever invented, but she liked watching the flames licking through the artificial coal.

'Then why is it,' she said, 'that the medium has failed? Why is it your satellite broadcasting is just a high-tech pap factory, and the idea of any serious, in-depth coverage of Northern Ireland seems like an aberration? Isn't it because people like you constantly try to balance two sets of arguments which simply cannot be balanced. You cannot pretend to "balance" one man who knows he is Irish with the views of another man who knows he is British. It just doesn't make sense. So your other trick was to try to pretend that you could explain Northern Ireland by looking back in its history – forgetting that most British people know so little about their own history that they are hardly likely to be interested in three-hundred-year-old struggles in a part of the country they regard as "abroad". Now television has given up completely, half brow-beaten by the British government, half surrendering because you want an easy life. It is not the medium that has failed. It's the people working in it.'

Morgan sighed. 'Well, what's your answer, Emily? Stop covering Northern Ireland altogether? Just not even try, because we are so poor at it? Or maybe satellite viewers would find your kind of journalism so fascinating we should increase coverage to eight hours of Ulster news a day?'

'No. Just stop trying to impose British ideas of fairness and balance. Be opinionated. Instead of grilling P J O'Neill as you probably will about all the innocent men he has murdered, let him present for the first time in an uncensored way his hopes for a united Ireland. Let the man speak directly to Britain and the people of Europe. Make it like a party political broadcast so we can judge him by it. What are you afraid of?'

Morgan replied that he might be tired of the Ireland story, but that wasn't going to make him into the propaganda mouthpiece for a bunch of murderers. They were making a strong enough statement of CTV's support for freedom of speech, without handing the airwaves over to a terrorist. P J O'Neill might have something interesting to say, but he was not going to get away with the usual pretence that he spoke for all of Ireland, the sham that the IRA was so popular people would even vote them into power. If he wanted to change Ireland, why didn't he do what people in civilised countries all over the world did: why didn't he get himself elected?

'Not O'Neill,' Emily said. 'But there are plenty of other Sinn Fein elected representatives. Why have you never tried to challenge the government before on coverage of their activities? You are only doing it with O'Neill because there is something sensational about interviewing a man on the run.'

Morgan was getting fed up with all this, and he did not like being lectured. There came a point when you just had to decide whether you were going to take these people at the value they set upon themselves – freedom fighters, men of the people – or as terrorists.

'Even knowing that we are not covered by the strict terms of the government ban, we would not want to put them on air very often because the audience has a right to know who and what it is listening to. The viewer has a right to understand the provenance of the material he or she is expected to take in.'

'What do you mean by that?' Emily asked, her eyes bright with the argument.

'I mean that Sinn Fein is not like the Liberal Party, or the Green Party, or any other democratic outfit on the fringes of real party politics, since Sinn Fein is just the legal flag of convenience for the IRA.'

'Well if you believe that then it sounds like you support the British government ban anyway. What's the point of interviewing O'Neill at all if you think he's like the head of the Mafia, rather than a political leader?'

Morgan was beginning to become exasperated.

'Look,' he said. 'They are like the Mafia in their methods, even if their aims are political. I know that some of the Sinn Fein representatives are little better than murderers – for whatever cause – but I can't introduce them as that on television, as criminals, murderers or whatever, because I can't prove it, even though everyone knows it is true. It's not just the British government which screws the broadcasters. Sinn Fein's own lawyers would begin libel actions against us if we hinted individuals were really criminals. We're in an impossible situation, and since I could not tell even the most basic truths about Sinn Fein, I'd be conning people. With P J O'Neill that difficulty goes because I can properly describe him as an IRA terrorist on the run. There would be no con.'

'I see,' Emily said coldly. 'So in your view you would be unable to interview any Conservative government minister on – say – the cutting of child benefit, if you happened to know that minister was an adulterer, or had fathered children out of wedlock. In that case you would feel advised to warn satellite viewers of this relevant fact before transmitting the interview, so they could – what was your phrase – know the provenance of what they were hearing?'

Morgan pointed out that there was a difference between adultery and murder, and an even greater difference between a minister in a government which had been elected to office, and a bunch of organised hoodlums in Belfast who consistently failed to get elected to anything. She started to argue, and his mind went soft. She was in full flood, telling him that he was just trying to make excuses so he would not be faced with the hard choices he really had to make. How could he pretend this nonsense to himself when everyone in the country knew who Sinn Fein were and what they stood for? Morgan was sure there was a good argument against her, but he could not be bothered to think of it. He was even more bored with Ireland than he'd thought. Perhaps she was right, that he should stay at home and mind the kids, or find some other job to do if he had so little interest in what he was supposed to be doing. She was still talking.

'The rage of Caliban seeing his face in the mirror,' she said.

He looked surprised. 'What is? Me?'

'No, dummy. The complaints of those who would rather forget about Northern Ireland totally, or any other bad news for that matter. The ones who whinge whenever anyone appears on television that they don't like. The people who were quite content with all the abuses suffered during the years of Unionist rule, so long as the problem did not surface in any way to annoy them. If you do *not* interview people like O'Neill from time to time then the bombs are going to go off every year in Brighton or in Oxford Street or the Bull Ring in Birmingham and kill dozens of ordinary people, and the Calibans are going to be jumping up and down wondering why.'

'Putting P J O'Neill on Capital Satellite Television is not going to stop the bombing.'

'Maybe not. But people at least will understand why it's happening.'

'Who cares why it's happening? It's how to stop it that people are interested in.'

Emily had finished her drink and put the glass on the edge of the fireplace. Maybe things had changed, and she had not been aware of it all. Emily began to think that like Martin Anderson and P J O'Neill and everything that was going on in Ireland, she had remained the same person she had been ten or even fifteen years before. Looking after the children had kept her from the changes she saw in Morgan, and perhaps that was not so bad.

'I didn't realise you had become such a big fan of Margaret Thatcher,' she said. 'I didn't realise you were one of the New Tories in favour of censorship of opinion on Northern Ireland.'

He thought it was such a silly comment, he should say nothing. The argument had run its course, and there was little else he wanted to add. He had enjoyed most of it, but now it was finished. Morgan picked up a newspaper lying on the floor next to the sofa and found the television page.

'I suppose we could watch the news.'

'If you like,' Emily mumbled. 'But I want an early night.'

He put the paper to one side and looked at her. Her legs were as good as ever they had been, her face pretty even without make up – attractive after a long day with David and Louise. She was looking into the flames, but could feel his gaze on her cheek. She pushed back the hair from the side of her face and looked at him.

'I still love you, you know,' he said softly. 'After all this time. I couldn't think of life with anyone else.'

She paused, and then looked back at the fire. There was something between them now, and he did not know what it was. It was not the argument about Ireland. She would not take those things so seriously, though he knew she could occasionally brood for days on something he had said and quote phrases from his arguments at some surprising moment as evidence of his failings. He had told her he loved her, and she had missed her cue to respond.

'What's the matter?' he said gently. 'What have I done? Do you really not love me any more?'

She remained where she was, staring into the fire. For a long time Morgan thought she was not going to speak at all, or perhaps simply say the word 'no' which would have cut him apart. After a short time, she shifted position on the cushion, rearranged her skirt, and continued staring at the fire as if hypnotised by the dancing yellow and orange.

'Speak,' he pleaded. 'Emily, speak to me.'

She turned towards him, still in a dream. When she began to

speak, the words came out slowly and quietly. She said that she thought she did love him, but she was confused. Everything seemed to have changed in the past few years. She had remained in a state of suspended animation, looking after the children and absorbed in being at home. Maybe he was right about what people cared about and did not care about. But if so, it was a far more brutal and unpleasant world than the one she had worked in before David was born. It was a world she wanted to find out about again.

'I think I do love you,' she said. 'But I loved what you were before better. You have become . . . Oh, I don't know what you've become. Or what we've become. But it is different now. I am sure of that.'

She looked vulnerable as he watched her speak. He wanted to do something and this time he slipped down from the sofa and moved over beside her. There was barely room on the cushion for two of them, but he pulled himself alongside and put his arm around her. She moved a little to accommodate him, but did not take her eyes away from the flames and the glowing coals. Morgan could smell a gentle touch of perfume on her neck. He kissed her twice under the chin, and she did not react. Then she pushed him away a little so she could talk.

'I think,' she said slowly. 'I think we have to decide.'

'What?' Morgan asked softly. 'What do we have to decide?'

'I think . . .' She began, and then there was a long pause, which Morgan let hang in the air, until Emily began speaking again. 'I think that one way or the other we have grown apart a great deal in the past couple of years. Neither of us has particularly noticed it. You've been unhappy at work, and I have been content, or exhausted, it's much the same thing, with what I have had to do at home. Now both of us have begun to realise we have to change again. And we can either change together, or we can change apart. Nothing can stay still.'

She stopped speaking for a moment. Morgan stroked her hair, and leaned his chin on her shoulder. He said nothing.

'If we have grown apart, then it is possible for us to grow back together again,' she said. 'I'm not sure. But I think so. Anyway, sometime in the next couple of months we have got to sort out our lives. I can't go on the way we have been for the past year.'

She apologised for not making herself clear, but Morgan understood. He felt it was an ultimatum. She turned from the fire and looked into his eyes, inches from her own.

'If it is, then it is an ultimatum for us both. We have both got to decide how to go on, and if we want to go on. You have either got to learn to be miserable in your job, or find some kind of job that makes you happy, because I'm not strong enough to carry this family when you are the way you have been. And I have to decide how I am going to cope with going back to work when everything you tell me makes me believe I am out of step with the times, and I would be better hiding here in my kitchen and behind my super-market shopping trolley.'

Morgan thought for a moment whether he should raise the question of the abortion again. It would have been wrong, tonight, and he did not want to end the evening with a row or with tears. He asked her what she wanted him to do, since she knew his present job paid the bills, and things had every appearance of getting better.

'I'm in no hurry,' she said. 'I don't want anything sudden or drastic to happen. But if you really have so little stomach for what you are doing, then maybe you should quit. There is just something empty in you, and I don't know why that should be. That emptiness is affecting me too. I don't know how to put it into words, but when you drink heavily, it's not the drinking that is the problem. It is this other thing – this vacuum, this dryness.'

She started to shake her head, as if annoyed with her own inability to find the right words. Morgan asked her if they should go to bed, and she nodded. Emily leaned over to the switch and turned off the gas, killing the flames immediately. The room was suddenly cold. She picked up the two whisky glasses and walked out to the kitchen. Morgan switched off the light and waited for her to return.

He wanted to walk up the stairs with her, arms round each other, like they used to do. He waited for five minutes and then heard the sound of running water. She would be a long time. Emily was having a bath.

Chapter Eleven

Donegal

P J O'Neill could not remember the last time he had been inside a priest's house. He thought perhaps it had been after the death of his father. One thing he could recall, they all had the same kind of smell: an indefinable mixture of mothballs, furniture polish and maybe violets – perhaps a special spray devised by Rome to be given to the housekeepers of the clergy in the same way as the priests themselves were given cassocks. Remarkably, even the house of Father Jo-Jo smelled the same, an odour handed down to him on graduation from Maynooth. The priest took O'Neill's overnight bag from his shoulder and led him in through the mustard-coloured hallway to the sitting-room at the back.

'It is simple,' he said. 'But it is home.'

O'Neill could see why the house had been built where it stood. It had the best position in the small town. The sitting-room window looked due west over the sea to where the sun, now a deeper red, had streaked across the calmness of the ocean. From a side window he could see the sweep of the main road through the town itself. O'Neill turned and looked round the room. There was an old, dark dresser with a whiskey decanter and glasses on top and a large Celtic cross propped up beside it. The Pope's picture was at the centre of the room above the peat fire, and the fire was lit even though the evening was warm. Above it, a large silver crucifix was hanging on the chimney breast, dominating the room. The priest stood by him at the window.

'Let me have a look at you, boy,' Father McGuinn said. 'Lord, you have changed. Gone is the beard and all that, the flared denim jeans and such things.' He started to laugh.

'You needn't laugh, Jo-Jo,' O'Neill said, laughing too. 'If you think I have changed, what about you? Put on a few pounds here and there. Mostly here.' He pointed to the priest's belly where it bulged a little at the waist. The priest laughed again.

'And anyway,' O'Neill continued, 'what should a man call you? Father, I suppose. Though Father Jo-Jo doesn't sound quite right. What do they call you round here? Father McGuinn?'

The priest's comfortable jowls began to shake with good humour.

'Round here the God-fearing souls call me Father Joseph,' he said. 'And the others call me that oul' bastard McGuinn. But you had better call me Jo-Jo like the old days, and I'll call you P J like I always did.'

He motioned O'Neill to sit down and asked if he wanted anything – tea, a bite to eat, whatever.

'The housekeeper is away for the weekend,' he said. 'So you'll have to make do with my cooking. Do you want to eat now or later?'

'Later would do fine, Jo-Jo,' O'Neill answered, smiling. 'Right now, the only thing I'd like is a breath of fresh air after that drive. I'm not used to sitting in a car for so long. I'd like a stretch of the legs. How about a walk on the strand before it gets dark?'

The priest stood up. 'Aye,' he said. 'It's a fine evening. We shouldn't miss it. Besides, it'll take the sun a while to set properly. Let's go.'

Outside the air was still, with the smell of wet heather after the rain. They walked down the tarmac path by the church. O'Neill could see the town stretching round the bay to his right. A few fishing boats were tied up and bobbing in the harbour. He could smell the smoke from the peat fires newly lit as the men returned from the sea or the fields. The priest led him down across the dry sand to the point, almost at the water's edge, where it was most firm. They began strolling round the bay, at first in silence.

'I have many things to tell you,' the priest said. 'Many things from the North, about old friends and family. Although I suppose you keep in touch through your own ways.'

'I do,' O'Neill nodded. 'Although I miss so much of it. I have not been able to go back to Belfast since my escape, and it is not the same sending other people as seeing with your own eyes and or using your own ears.'

A curlew which had been feeding near the water's edge by a small creek issuing out into the sea, flew off wheeling and crying in alarm at their approach. There was no traffic on the road, no one else walking on the beach, nothing out at sea. It was as if the world had disappeared, leaving them to patrol the strand alone.

'I hope I have caused you no embarrassment,' O'Neill said cautiously. 'Telephoning like that and asking to come to stay.'

'None,' the priest replied. 'In fact I was surprised at first to hear from you, and then flattered. I have followed what you have done as well as I could, with much interest. After everything, that you should trust me enough to come here, meant that our friendship was unchanged, and I was pleased.'

'It is unchanged,' O'Neill said. 'And in some ways I trust you more because you are not part of the Movement.'

The priest smiled. It had been eight years since they last met in Belfast, when he was a curate for a parish on the Antrim Road. They had been neighbours and friends right through infant school, skipping Mass on Sundays, playing football or handball instead and saving the sixpence that should have gone into the church collection to buy ice creams. There was a strangeness in their meeting now because they had led such close and intimate lives in the past, and suddenly they had so many years without any shared experiences.

'Why?' McGuinn asked. 'There are no problems in that regard are there?'

'On security?' O'Neill replied. 'No, I don't think so. I just meant that people inside an organisation are apt to say things to please me because of my position of leadership. Sometimes, for the truth, we should turn to people outside.'

He looked across at McGuinn's face, surprised at how old it now looked, and thinking that the priest was perhaps equally shocked by the changes in O'Neill himself. There was still a hesitancy in what they were saying, and O'Neill knew if he did not move quickly a kind of false politeness could spoil their weekend.

'We had better clear the air,' O'Neill said, and coughed a little as if to make a speech.

'There's no need to say anything,' McGuinn murmured in response. 'To tell me anything you do not want to. I should just be glad to have a house guest for the weekend, that's all.'

'Is that why you sent the housekeeper away?' O'Neill said, then regretted his lack of tact. The priest coloured a little, but before he could say anything, O'Neill continued. 'I am sorry to have been so abrupt. But I represent a danger to you just by being here. There could be problems if I am recognised. I wanted to come to see you, not to cause you any embarrassment or problems, but because since we decided to go our separate ways I have felt guilty about not treating you properly, the way our friendship deserved. I want you to know that I recognise how far the choices I have made about my life have cut me off from things and people that I love. Even if I can do little about it, it is important for me that my friends know I am not so unfeeling or uncaring as to wish it this way. It is just necessary for my own security and that of people like you that I keep distant.'

McGuinn watched him closely during the short speech. It was in many ways the same old P J – the eyes burning with enthusiasm and intelligence, the gestures animated, and yet the sense of it all revolving round O'Neill's own needs and feelings, his desire to be thought well of. Still, McGuinn was pleased to see him, intrigued and charmed again by his company. With P J things had never been dull in the past.

'You have been busy,' the priest said. 'And if we are to speak frankly, then you must realise I do know something of the pressures that must now be upon you. I recognise why you have cut yourself off from so many things and people you once knew. And I don't want to return to our old arguments, but I would like you to tell me now that you understand why I took my decisions, why I refused to go the way you wanted me to and join you in the Movement. We have had the argument before when we were younger and more passionate. I still have to condemn all the things you do, or your comrades do, or whatever. But tonight you are just P J O'Neill, an old friend, whom I love to see and think about often. I ask you to understand my position.'

O'Neill was surprised at McGuinn's directness. The old Jo-Jo that he remembered would have skirted round the subject and avoided everything that might have caused a row or even a disagreement. In the past it was always O'Neill who got to the heart of their differences, who believed that by provoking the most open discussion you could move forward to a new understanding.

'I understand, Jo-Jo,' he said. 'And I am glad we can clear the air.'

On the horizon the sun was now only a small red lip on the edge of the water, like a fire on the rim of the world. The light on the strand was tinged with pink and orange, bringing warmth to their faces. A rough tractor was taking the shore road and spluttering its way towards the town. It had been the first vehicle O'Neill had noticed since he arrived, its hoarse diesel rattle splitting the air.

132

Between the two men as they walked side by side, there was a sudden silence. O'Neill remembered how it had been – the times when he thought he had a vocation, right through the sixties, encouraged by his mother to persevere with the Latin and Greek and try for a place at Maynooth and a life in the priesthood. She had wanted that career for him ever since he showed such an aptitude for study, but his father had tried to push him another way. Any other way. At the age of fourteen his father told O'Neill that in the priesthood he might serve God but there were other ways to do so. He would inevitably isolate himself from other people and miss out so much on life.

'Life?' O'Neill thought at the time. 'The ould fella means sex.'

The fact that it was Jo-Jo McGuinn who entered the priesthood in the end surprised them all and disappointed O'Neill's mother the most. McGuinn's exam grades had not been as good as O'Neill's but he had the gift of perseverance.

'Do you remember,' O'Neill said, squeezing the priest by the arm. 'The day I saw you off for the Dublin train? Down at Great Victoria Street station – the day you set off for Maynooth?'

'I do,' McGuinn responded, chuckling. 'It was that long summer of 1970, and we were all sweating under the weight of everything my mother had packed for me. Two full suitcases stuffed with winter underwear in case I caught my death in the draughty corridors of the theological college. More heavy pullovers than a man could wear in ten years.'

'We parted as friends,' O'Neill said. 'Though I was getting involved in the Movement even by that time.'

McGuinn looked at him. 'I had already guessed so, although you never told me. It was not until later – until I returned, I think, to the Antrim Road parish – that things started to fall apart. It was then I realised how far we had separated in every way.'

'You still had your straggly beard then, mind. You were still trying to be an Irishman!'

The priest laughed. He found it easier to be in O'Neill's company than he had expected. It was not that the fight had gone out of him, but he knew he could no longer change O'Neill and O'Neill knew likewise. They had fallen out over what McGuinn called terrorism and what O'Neill had defended as the armed struggle. The words were bitter, as only they could be between friends. Now they were just adults who had stopped being disappointed in one another.

'Three years at Maynooth,' O'Neill had said at the time. 'And

133

you come back a stranger to your friends, your family and your people. I had never realised that when people said the Church would always be against us, they might mean you, Jo-Jo.'

McGuinn knew he had been as bitter in return. They were difficult times. Internment was still continuing. They had gone through the worst of the rioting but the bombing remained unchecked. The British Army imposed night-time curfews and random house searches. There were firefights every night in the backstreets off the Falls Road. McGuinn could have rehearsed the arguments in front of O'Neill again now on the beach, and received the same justifications in return. He knew they would be heard without animosity. It had been a long time healing, but McGuinn thought they had reached the point of forgiveness.

'We were still happy then,' O'Neill said, kicking aimlessly at a piece of washed-up seaweed. 'Because that was before the choices we made in our lives came back to haunt us.'

'Are you haunted now?'

O'Neill indicated he did not mean it in that way and shrugged his shoulders. He would not change a thing, not one decision. He knew what he was doing when he joined the Movement, and he knew what it would lead to. No one presented him with any different picture, any sales pitch to join. The irony was that his father had helped talk him out of the priesthood because it would isolate him from the mainstream of Irish life, and that decision eased him into the Republican Movement instead.

'How do you think I feel now, Jo-Jo,' O'Neill said. 'I am as cut off from things as you ever are, the loneliness of the priest without its compensations.'

McGuinn was surprised at O'Neill's frankness. It was almost a confession, made face to face on the beach not in the privacy of the church confessional. It demanded sympathy rather than forgiveness. The priest understood.

'If you had stayed in Belfast another year, Jo-Jo, you would have joined up too. It is just another priesthood.'

'Maybe,' McGuinn sighed, but his voice meant the opposite. 'But you know I could not kill anyone. Not plan it, or even consider it. I'm not a moral coward, but that's just the way I am. I am here to save souls, not to destroy human beings. There is no priesthood in that.'

'Nobody would accuse you of being a coward,' O'Neill said firmly. 'After what you used to do on those nights of rioting in the

New Lodge. We all knew about you. Out at midnight trying to encourage the lads to go home. Up till four in the morning attempting to get them released from the police stations. Telling the Brits to lay off on the tear gas because it was harming the old folk. You did your bit. Everybody knew it.'

They were reaching the end of the beach where the cliffs began in rocky outcrops then jutted deep into the bay. The sun had gone and in the deepening twilight there were sounds from the sheep and cattle in the fields in the distance, settling down for the night. They turned and began strolling back, still side by side. After the initial rows, they had tried to patch up their relationship but it was not easy. When McGuinn returned to the Falls to see his parents, they might meet for an hour or so, but O'Neill felt utterly constricted in what he could say, and McGuinn the same about what he could ask.

'It is better that you tell me nothing,' McGuinn had once said to him. 'Firstly because I do not want to know. Secondly because we should only argue, and thirdly because if anything goes wrong, you will not be able to blame me. If you are fighting your war, then fight it. My job is to give comfort as best I can and ease the people's suffering.'

After a time O'Neill had tried to avoid such meetings. There had seemed nothing left for them to say to each other. Now there was so much.

'Have you heard from Sheelagh?' O'Neill asked. The beach was suddenly very quiet. All he could hear was the sound of their feet on the sand and shingle. Even the lapping of the wavelets had been silenced. The priest looked at him.

'Not for some time,' he said slowly. 'Not since she went to Buffalo.'

'Ah,' O'Neill said. 'I knew she had gone somewhere in New York State. Buffalo is it.'

'Found a job through some friend of her uncle. Secretarial, I think, that kind of thing. The last letter I received said she was happy.'

'I'm glad of that,' O'Neill said. 'Did she explain how we broke up?'

'I suppose she did,' McGuinn replied sadly. 'I saw her after she wrote to you in the Maze. She explained it all to me then. She was very, very hurt by it, and for a time – God forgive me – I believed she might do herself harm. But she pulled through, thanks be to God. She is a fine woman.'

'O'Neill looked out to sea. The surface of the water was almost purple now, the colour draining gently towards the night. The lights of the town, such as they were, blinked in the darkness. He noticed that the last street light ended at the edge of town, precisely where the church stood on its small hill. Some previous priest had clearly done a good job with the District Council.

'I was broken up too,' O'Neill said, quietly. 'It came just a few months before we got out. We had been planning it all the time, though of course no one could be told. Not even her. I just thought she might hold on . . .'

O'Neill realised that the priest had stopped walking, and he stopped too.

'You're not bitter then,' McGuinn said. 'Bitter with her?'

'O'Neill shook his head. 'How could I be? She put up with so much. It was hardly a marriage at all. I was never there, especially towards the end when I knew they wanted to lift me and I started to go on the run. She had to take a decision, and I think she made the right one. For both of us. What kind of life could I have promised her? I'm still sad, very sad. But not bitter, no.'

The priest started to walk again. They were almost back at the house. He thanked God there had been no child, then he asked O'Neill if he would not think of joining Sheelagh in America, seeing whether they might get together again.

'I'm sure it could be arranged,' he said eagerly. 'You would know it better than me. But I suppose there are ways of fixing you up with another identity. You must have thought of it yourself – leaving all this and starting again with a clean sheet?'

O'Neill was surprised by the idea and replied that he honestly had not even considered it. He knew where his future lay, and it was here, in Ireland, however much he thought of Sheelagh. He could understand why she had wanted a complete break from it all and a new start, but there was to be no new beginning for him.

'This is me, Jo-Jo,' he said. 'This is me, and my life, and my choices. I'll live with them. There is no new start. No confession and forgiveness, sin and redemption. There is just the struggle.'

The priest moved beside him in silence, his features hidden in the darkness of the night. When they returned to the parish house McGuinn switched on the lights. O'Neill noticed for the first time that the priest had not locked the door. It was as his father had said. There was an Ireland where people could trust one another, where things did not disappear in the hands of someone else. This was that trusting Ireland and it had been in retreat for centuries. Maybe there was a way, somehow, of reversing the retreat and turning that Ireland loose to reconquer the rest of the land, a crusade from the Gaeltacht, not just of language and culture, but of moral force and identity.

McGuinn led him to the kitchen, took off his jacket and put on an apron.

He laughed.

'It looks stupid, doesn't it, to see a priest like this? Never mind. If we want to eat, then we have to start peeling things. And you're right P J. I did send the housekeeper away because you were coming. Not because I am embarrassed by you, but because I know how these people talk. The less that is known, the less risk to yourself.'

O'Neill smiled. 'Ach, we could have turned you into a freedom fighter after all,' he said. 'You're sleekit enough. You know principle number one – trust nobody. If you'd played your cards right, you could have been one of the Block Commanders inside the Maze by now.'

'What makes you think I would have got caught? Hell, P J, you near enough always beat me in marks at school, but I am the one who got the education from Jesuits. No RUC man would ever crack me under interrogation after the stuff those guys tried on us at Maynooth. I'd have them converted to the true Church before I left.'

They prepared the meal together, and ate in the kitchen, swapping stories of their childhood, of their parents and their school teachers. For both it was safe ground. When they finished eating they returned to the front room. The priest produced a pipe and a pouch from the cupboard next to the bookcase.

'A forgivable sin,' he said, grinning. 'The last of my vices. And even then I ration it to one pipe in the evenings after dinner.'

'You don't drink at all?'

'Not any more,' McGuinn said, nodding at the whiskey decanter. 'But don't let that stop you. That's what it's there for. Visitors.'

O'Neill declined.

'I have even fewer vices,' he said. 'I rarely touch a drop, and I don't smoke. And as for women . . .'

'As for women what?'

It was now O'Neill's turn to feel embarrassed. 'Is this Jo-Jo being curious, or Father Joseph?' he asked.

McGuinn laughed. He pulled the pipe from his mouth and blew a stream of smoke into the air.

'Father Joseph has also gone away with the housekeeper this weekend. He will return for Mass on Sunday. The question was asked by Jo-Jo.'

Now O'Neill laughed. He said he had not had much time for priests since he escaped from the Maze, and would not be going to confession any time in the near future. The question from McGuinn had seemed too like the kinds of questions he remembered in the confessional, and he would find his own salvation, or otherwise.

'But as for women,' he said. 'Well, there have been one or two. But I could not even think of something permanent after Sheelagh. Besides, the life I lead. The kind of women I meet now are all in the Movement. Those outside would be too dangerous. And those inside are part of the structure, and it's no good for morale for people to know that I have favourites.'

'Are you that important?'

McGuinn knew his question was on the edge of what was permissible, but he asked it anyway. He had heard rumours that O'Neill was now something very big – Chief of Staff, maybe. Who really knows? It was not the sort of rumour you heard in Donegal, but back in Belfast the families who had known P J were proud of him, as if he had just become a Bishop. Most of them were proud, anyway. O'Neill nodded.

'Important enough,' he said. 'Not irreplaceable. Not arrogant or full of pride. But I have an important job now, and am well regarded.'

The priest sucked at his pipe and thought for a moment.

'What will you do tomorrow?' he asked. 'In the morning I have some visits to make – to see a widow and to go to a farm where they are planning a wedding. The usual stuff round here. Nothing dramatic, like in Belfast, but I like the quiet and I like the chance to read. I'll be free come the afternoon. What will you do?'

O'Neill had not really thought in any detail. He had wanted to escape from Dublin and from everything the England team had brought him for one long weekend, before the pressure to mount the operation really began. When it started he would be on fully active service, and this was his last chance to act like an ordinary man. But now that he was here, he had no plans, except to keep out of the town as much as possible.

'Errigal,' he said, suddenly thinking what he might do. 'I want to climb it again like I did years ago. I suppose it hasn't changed?'

'Changed?' McGuinn echoed his tone. 'No. It's still as wet as Sin all the way up and as slippery as Hell all the way down, but you'll probably manage. And you return to Dublin when?'

'Probably on Sunday morning. Before you go to first Mass, I'll be off. People will see my car, but I don't want them to see me, just in case.'

'That's all right, P J,' McGuinn said. 'The only trouble is that round here they'll think I've sent the housekeeper away so I can get a woman in for the weekend.'

'They'll say that?' O'Neill asked, amused.

'Surely. But it'll do no harm. It'll probably boost my standing in the Rosses considerably.'

The house was starting to get cold. McGuinn had allowed the fire to die in the grate and raked the peat ashes until they formed a heap below. O'Neill began to feel very tired. It had been a long day, after all that business with the television reporter and the drive north. He would be glad to go to bed, as soon as it seemed polite to do so. McGuinn was puffing again at his pipe, reflectively.

'It's lonely here,' he said, in a solemn voice as if he was now beginning his own confession. 'Damned lonely. They are decent enough folk, but none of them have much of an education, or have been very far away except maybe the odd time to Dublin or to Glasgow to find a bit of work. It's not Belfast, and I miss the city and all it means.'

There was a sadness in McGuinn's voice which surprised O'Neill. It was as if he had been longing for the moment when he could tell someone this great secret which had been burdening him for so long. He could speak to O'Neill not only because he was an old friend, but also because there was no one to whom O'Neill could pass on the story.

'I came here out of some kind of idealism,' McGuinn went on. 'Because I had taken up the Gaelic at Maynooth, and because I wanted to do something to help improve the life of the nation. We'd been here as lads, staying at your parents' cottage in Bunbeg. We used to talk about keeping the Gaelic language alive and the beauty of this place, remember?'

O'Neill nodded. He remembered.

'Then I get here and find it is not like that at all. The people don't want to speak the Gaelic – or many of them don't. The girls want to move away to become secretaries in Dublin, and the men, or half of them, die for loneliness knowing all the best girls have gone off to become the wives of men in the city. And with the exception of the

139

doctor – who's half an alcoholic – and the chemist, who I don't trust to keep a confidence for more than five minutes, there's hardly a decent educated person here among us.'

The room seemed particularly gloomy, and Morgan realised the light bulb must have been of very low power. There was a separate reading light over the priest's shoulder, and he obviously used that in the evenings when he had no company. The room smelled of the peat fire and polish.

'All they want is to listen to television programmes about Dallas and California – anywhere but here. And they see the swimming-pools and the big cars, and some of them start to want that too. The unhappiness of it, of the envy and the materialism we have helped to create.'

O'Neill felt his eyelids begin to pinch with tiredness, as the smoke from the pipe started to get to him. This was not why he had travelled to Donegal. This was not what he had expected. The heavily jowled face was still talking, pouring out some of its misery to him, but while he nodded sympathetically, O'Neill wished it would end. The room went quiet and the sadness of the priest seemed to hang with the smoke, stale in the air. Father Joseph was looking straight at him.

'I am glad you came,' he said. 'You have answered two prayers of mine at once. To be properly reconciled with you before one of us dies, and to have some decent adult conversation with a man I can trust, and whose horizons go further than the end of the town pier.'

O'Neill rubbed the stubble on his jaw with the back of his hand. He smiled a forced sort of smile, and nodded at the priest. There was an emptiness here he had not expected. He thought that perhaps, somewhere, there would be the sense of certainty and purpose behind McGuinn's life or that of the community in the Rosses which would compensate for all the sacrifices he himself was forced to make. He was not sure what exactly he had been expecting. A link with the past and all that he was now cut off from, certainly. But also something more. To see how he himself might have developed if he had followed McGuinn's path to the priesthood. That was part of it too. But above all, a sense of Ireland was what he wanted. A sense of what the island had been and could become if good men and women were prepared to fight and die for it. He could not define it in words. He would know what it was once he found it, but tonight he was looking in the wrong place. O'Neill stood up.

140

'I think I should go to bed now,' he said. 'It's been a long day for me, and I expect for you too. We'll talk again in the morning.'

'Goodnight, P J,' the priest said, sadly, without rising. 'I'll just stay for a moment or two more and catch up with the reading. See you in the morning.'

'Goodnight.'

As O'Neill turned to leave he heard McGuinn switch on the reading light and slide a magazine from the coffee table onto his lap. Another match was struck and he re-lit his pipe. O'Neill was disappointed, though he could not exactly say why. As he walked up the stairs, the still tableau of the priest with his pipe sitting alone in the strange-smelling room was etched on his mind. It was the picture of a missionary, alone in a hostile land; a missionary who has grasped the awful truth that in the end his mission is without hope.

Chapter Twelve

Donegal

The air on Errigal was cold. It blew in gusts, clear and fresh from the west, flattening the heather to the hillside. O'Neill had parked his car at a bend in the road near the dirt track which began the ascent. The track widened through a rocky field, then narrowed again to nothing much better than a sheep path. The fine day promised by the previous evening's sunset had more or less come to pass. There were not many days without rain in Donegal, but this looked as if it could be one. The heather was still wet from the overnight dew, and O'Neill was grateful for the boots Jo-Jo had given him. He struck out purposefully, choosing the steepest of the tracks with the most direct route to the summit. The sudden effort made him pant hard, and he began to enjoy the touch of sweat on the back of his shirt. He realised how unfit he had let himself become.

'It's the bad food and the long days without air,' he said to himself, fighting for breath. 'It is worse now than ever it was in the Maze. At least there we were forced to take regular exercise.'

Ahead O'Neill could see the black and white of a hooded crow hopping across the moss and heather, looking for eggs to steal, and tossing him a suspicious glance. O'Neill had woken early, unable to sleep properly in the priest's old and sagging guest-room bed. Sometime after six he got up and made himself tea, standing in the front room looking at the early morning on the bay to the west. The sea was silver and calm out as far as his eyes could travel. Whatever had happened with McGuinn the night before – the strange mixture of nostalgia and disappointment at their meeting after all that time – whatever it was, just the sight of Ireland waking up was enough for him. There was something here to stir a man's heart. An Irishman that did not feel a sense of national pride on the Atlantic shore of Donegal, did not deserve to live. O'Neill swallowed a mouthful of hot tea.

143

When McGuinn awoke he passed the priest another mug of tea and the two of them talked in a desultory fashion. The novelty of his arrival had worn off for both of them. The initial burst of frankness had cleared the air of past hurts, but there was now a new gulf between them, one that O'Neill thought might be impossible to bridge. He wondered if it was simply that he and McGuinn had grown so far apart they could no longer really count each other as friends. There was no reason why two boys who had enjoyed football and fighting and a long childhood together should stay as friends now they were men, especially after the decisions they had taken on how to run the rest of their lives. Anyway, wasn't this supposed to be the disposable age? Fast food, paper plates, paper sheets, disposable razors, used for a time and thrown away. It could just as easily be the age of the disposable friend, used for a time and then abandoned.

On Errigal the slope upwards was becoming steeper, but O'Neill deliberately did not check his pace, forcing himself to climb energetically as if in a race against an invisible competitor. He did not want to look at any view until he came to the top, in case he was disappointed and felt it was not worth the trouble to plod on and up. The important thing was to keep going. He pushed his head down until his chest almost touched his knees and forced him to take the next rhythmical step. The backs of his calves ached with the dull hurt that comes from a sleeping muscle suddenly kicked into unexpected effort. In places the heather was so thick it wet his knees above the level of the priest's boots. His breath gushed out in a stream of warm air. He enjoyed listening to the effort of it. Onward.

McGuinn had said they would meet again in the afternoon, but O'Neill was not sure how much more he could take in Donegal. He knew Jo-Jo would never betray him, and so the risk here was no worse, and probably a good deal less, than anywhere else. But there was something about the meeting which filled him with sadness, as if one of the dreams he had nurtured in prison – or more precisely, one of the dreams which had nurtured *him* in prison – was proving simply to be that: just a dream, a vision without substance. O'Neill had promised himself in the Maze that if ever he had the chance, however bad and irreparable his relationship with Sheelagh might be, there would always be a way of rebuilding his old friendship with Jo-Jo, and through that rebuilding, he would remind himself he was still part of the human race. Like the rows

144

with his own father, the differences with Jo-Jo over the armed struggle were differences almost adolescent in character. Now both of them had the maturity to respect the other's choices in life. He had been sure of it. It wasn't much to ask.

When McGuinn found he was determined to climb Errigal, he offered O'Neill his own walking boots and a stiff canvas coat. O'Neill gratefully accepted, though he would have walked up naked and barefoot if there had been no other way. If the weather would let him, he was determined to see the view from the peak once again, before the Durrant affair and all that it implied took up his life for weeks without respite. If the operation was successful, the blow against the British would be so hard there would be no rest for any of them for months.

McGuinn had prepared to set off for his rounds. 'See you this afternoon, P J,' he called. 'About four.'

'See you then, Jo-Jo.'

The priest had paused in the door and then returned into the kitchen.

'I have prayed for you often, P J,' he said. 'From my time in Maynooth, and then again at the Antrim Road presbytery, to my time here. No matter what our differences have been and the strangeness that came for a time between us, I always mention you in my prayers.'

O'Neill did not know what to say. It had been a long time since anyone had ever spoken to him like that. The last person to do so was, he thought, a maiden aunt. From Jo-Jo, priest or not, he found the whole thing embarrassing, insufferable. He stuttered something in reply.

'And I . . . think of you. Often. Right through the time in the Maze, and since. That's why I contacted you again.'

Suddenly the priest was sitting down beside him, looking at him with his round, cheerful face and sad eyes.

'I'm glad, P J, that you did not forget me.' Then he added: 'Do you ever pray, P J?'

O'Neill sat back and took a heavy breath. 'No,' he said. 'Not any more.'

'Why not?'

O'Neill wanted McGuinn to go, or to find some excuse and run from the room himself, get in the car and drive until he reached Dublin. There were some things that were his, and his alone, to do and to think about. This was something he did not intend to share. He looked from the priest's face to the window and over the bay. A small fishing boat was heading out southwards to search for the whiting shoals off Aran Island or on the edge of Gweebarra Bay.

'It is a long story,' O'Neill said lethargically, trying to give the impression that the subject bored rather than offended him. 'Of how I came to lose my vocation or supposed vocation and you found yours. God will call people to things they are most suited in doing. I have been called to this.'

'But that doesn't explain why you do not pray. If you believe in God, how else can you talk to him?'

O'Neill looked at his own hands, and rubbed them together.

'I have nothing to say to him, for the moment. Nor he to me. The Church . . .'

McGuinn interrupted. 'I didn't ask you about the Church. I know your views on that, and though I might like to think they were different, I can understand what you think of the Church. It's your relationship with God I don't understand.'

O'Neill resented it, and despite himself, he showed the irritation. He did not see what right anyone had to pry into something so private, priest or friend. Neither had easy access to what a man believed.

'You are beginning to sound like a Protestant,' O'Neill said with a fixed smile. 'Not interested in why I despise the Church, only in why I do not talk to God. Next you will tell me you assent to the proposition of the priesthood of all believers.'

To O'Neill's surprise McGuinn laughed.

'Well,' he said. 'Maybe I do in some ways. There are things about the Calvinist spirit that I admire. And anyone in a large group or organisation finds problems with authority. For me the Church authority can be particularly irksome, but I get by. I swallow it up, and do my job. But it is you I am concerned about. I just thought that if you believe in God, there was no sense in ignoring him. There is comfort in prayer.'

O'Neill shrugged his shoulders, and refused to be drawn. He knew the comfort of prayer, and the hypocrisy of it, too. If he did pray, in his own fashion, he was certainly not going to discuss it with anyone. Maybe he had learned some Protestant ways too. The Church was not truly to be trusted, even the Church with a smile as wide as Jo-Jo McGuinn's. After thirty seconds of what became a tense silence, McGuinn ended the interrogation by standing to leave again.

'We can discuss it later,' he said, buttoning his jacket. 'This afternoon if you like. Or we can skip it. For now, I must be off. Enjoy Errigal.'

O'Neill's chest was tight with the effort of the climb. He wanted to try to make it to the peak without a break but it was not going to be possible. He stopped and pulled off the priest's canvas coat and spread it on the ground, sitting upon it with a thump and breathing hard. In front of him he could see the view that he had hoped to save for the top – the panorama over Lough Nacung and the road westwards towards Bunbeg and the sea. He felt his heart race at the beauty of the land. His lips were dry and he wished he had brought something to drink. He looked again down the Lough at the calm and blue of the water against the green fields by the loughside. Along the shore whin bushes were beginning to turn a full yellow in the warming early summer air.

O'Neill waited until his breathing had settled again into a normal pattern, then with an effort he stood up, determined to wait until the very top before spending any time looking at the countryside. He felt the sweat on his back cooling in the wind through his pullover, put the coat back on and started uphill again. As he began the first strides, he smiled to himself, knowing he had come not just to admire the view but to think in the clear air, to think through all those things which were unclear or insoluble when he was in Dublin. It was a strange feeling, to be so completely alone, not another soul on the hillside, no one for miles except the turf cutters in the bogland to the south. There were decisions to be taken, and he would take them. Now. Today.

O'Neill wondered what it was that he and his Movement of Belfast and Derry and Dublin could do for this piece of land where the heather had grown and the sheep had grazed for centuries. It seemed almost impertinent that he should believe his generation would bring about the changes to catapult Ireland into a new existence, free at last. Even after all these years of the British being here, he could not believe that the land of Ireland had changed much. The people, perhaps, their culture attacked, their language destroyed, their self-respect and self-confidence undermined. But the country? It would remain as it had remained despite the arrivals of the Danes and the English and the Lowland Scots and all the baggage they brought with them.

It had been almost a year since his escape, and a full nine months since he had begun to lead the England team. In that time, after the first few weeks in County Mayo trying to recuperate and find out what life outside prison might be like, O'Neill had grown wearier than he ever thought possible. At first when he broke out he simply wanted to go back to the North, pick up where he had left off, until he was killed or captured. Then he was persuaded that he was too valuable to be lost as a foot-soldier or battalion commander. There was work to be done reorganising the Movement, and his duty was to keep out of harm's way. Or so they said. The line-up on the Army Council of the IRA was such that the men from the North – Doherty, Martin Anderson, Ivan Murray and the others – wanted one of their own in charge of a new England team. Francie Coffey, the old commander and a Dubliner, had never much excited their imaginations. Sean Hughes, the quartermaster and a veteran of the fifties campaign, was the only other Dubliner on the Army Council, a friend and ally of Coffey, but even he thought it was time for him to go. O'Neill had been told they wanted him for the job, and said he would be happy to accept. All he had to do, Sean Doherty assured him, was to appear before the Army Council and explain what he would do in that position. It was important that they all endorse his appointment. A unanimous vote would keep to a minimum any bitterness against him as an upstart from the North who had pushed Francie Coffey aside.

'A job interview,' O'Neill said.

'Something like that,' Doherty replied.

Two weeks later they had met in Dun Laoghaire and called him in. He made a short speech which ended up criticising the seaside bombing campaign that Coffey had planned, as strategically and politically unsound.

'It would not have changed the course of history,' he said, 'in the way the Brighton bomb might have done if we had killed Margaret Thatcher or some senior members of the Cabinet. It is clear to me that one single act, provided it is directed against the British ruling classes, carries far more prestige than anything like the seaside bombings. It proves that our targets are within the British establishment not in the working classes, that the war is against the centres of power and not with the ordinary British people.'

It was a speech O'Neill thought his father might have been proud of. It proved he understood or had learned the historical context of things as Master Sean O'Neill had always wanted, and he had learned that ordinary working-class folk were not the real targets.

'What do you mean?' Sean Doherty said in his slow Derry accent.

'What one single act?'

'Well there are other targets comparable to the Brighton bombing,' O'Neill said with a smile. 'I could go into details now, but I think you might want us to discuss this in a smaller group. I think you could take it that hitting the British Royal Family would provoke a response even greater than hitting the British Cabinet, and certainly greater than a campaign in a few seaside towns.'

There was complete silence. O'Neill was aware that everyone in the room was looking directly at him.

'Easy enough to say, ould hand,' Doherty murmured, with a smile. 'Not so easy to do. Unless you have something more specific in mind.'

At that point O'Neill revealed the idea for the Durrant kidnap and what it was supposed to achieve. The result was breathtaking. Thirty seconds after he finished his exposition, Doherty moved that he be confirmed as Director of Operations. It was unanimous.

Now on the hillside the heather had thinned giving way to bog, moss and rocks. O'Neill stepped carefully, trying to keep to the sheep track, knowing that the moss could be treacherously deep and wet. He was almost at the top, and the fresh wind touched his face and felt cold. He pulled up the collar of the canvas coat.

Taking the job was one thing. Making it work had been different. The success of the Durrant kidnapping meant that he was, for now at least, totally secure in his post. No one would dare move against him. He had even been given two of Martin Anderson's people from Belfast to act as a reconnaissance team for what he was planning. Men and equipment would be directed towards him in whatever amounts he demanded – Sean Hughes had insisted upon it. It was all going his way, and yet he felt gnawed by the tension. He breathed hard and tried to think things through in order.

One: he had to ensure that Larry Kennedy – and perhaps Billy McKeever too – would speed ahead with their sea-diving lessons in Cork. There was time enough for all that, but he wanted to be sure Kennedy could do the job.

Two: he had to decide what to do with the Durrants when it was all over. Larry Kennedy wanted them shot. They were a security risk. Durrant knew all the faces well. The alternative was to release them, knowing that once they told their full story to the British media the propaganda impact would be unsurpassable. The effect on British morale when Durrant explained what he had lectured the IRA about, and revealed what had been stolen by the IRA team, would be the equivalent of another Brighton bomb. Maybe. But it could also backfire on McKeever and Kelly, Kennedy and O'Hagan. O'Neill had told them they need not wear masks during the time with the Durrants because the execution of the two would guarantee their security, and anyway their faces had been seen – however fleetingly – on the night of the kidnap itself. Now O'Neill had perhaps changed his mind. He had to decide. Soon.

Three: the interview with the television people. He would do it. He was sure it was the right thing. Martin Anderson had said it would work either way – if transmitted, a propaganda first for the Movement; if not transmitted, a major row about hypocritical British journalists being forced to concede to Conservative government pressure. As long as he could be sure about his own security, he would do it. He'd get Eamonn and some of the Dublin boys to make the arrangements. The 'Unsafe Safe House' in Howth might be the best location. It would guarantee that he could never use it again, and that was perhaps for the best. He was beginning to get bad feelings about the place.

O'Neill had almost reached the summit, and the path flattened slightly. He accelerated towards the top, then the way tightened and grew steep again, but he continued to force the pace. The problems he had to face demanded more precise thought, but up here at least he could order them with some clarity. He smiled. He had become almost like some kind of manager on a business training programme, a subversive with 'Out' and 'In' trays in his mind. Maybe he should get a secretary and a Filofax? He snorted hard with the effort of the final few yards.

On the top of Errigal the wind swept in straight from the Atlantic. He could see to the west the clouds were beginning to form over the sea, but above and around him now there was nothing but blue sky and a few wisps of white. He looked to the east, and at the end of the Derryveagh mountains he could see the cut in the land and the water of Lough Swilly. Derry city was there, somewhere in the distance, though he could not be sure that was what he saw. It was less exact than he remembered from his childhood.

Immediately below, the surface of Lough Nacung was still. He could see no one there, not a single car on the Lough road, nothing. It was like standing on top of the world, a world which had gone quiet because no one was awake but him. He stepped down a few paces from the top into the lee of the summit. He took off the canvas coat again and spread it down on the heather. There was some shelter here and his legs ached with the effort of the climb.

O'Neill thought for a moment of the priest, his round, cleanly-shaved face and wide smile. He knew what had been unspoken. The questions about prayer were only the start. Jo-Jo McGuinn would begin again in the afternoon in the same vein until he pulled O'Neill into the argument he did not want to have, the argument about the morality of the killings in the North as part of the armed struggle. O'Neill did not want to be drawn, and might simply make an excuse to leave early. There was nothing much left for him here. Sheelagh had never properly understood either, otherwise she would have waited for him to get out. She had made her decision, and there was no turning back and no bitterness either, at least not from him. She had a life to lead.

Father McGuinn was the same. There was a gulf which had begun more than a decade before. He knew McGuinn would say he shared the aims of the Republican Movement, but its methods were wrong. O'Neill knew McGuinn would say that because Irish priests always said that from the outside. Always said it because they did not recognise that the end of the rebellion was impossible without the means. There had to be blood, because only the blood sacrifice could make men free. It was an alternative Eucharist which he knew to be the only way. He knew it was a blasphemy, but without the blood there would be nothing, no Resurrection of Ireland without a Crucifixion.

'And he expects me to pray!' O'Neill shouted aloud to the wind. 'To pray, steeped in that blasphemy!'

The people he could trust were no longer there. Not Sheelagh, who had betrayed him in her way. Understandable but a betrayal. Not Jo-Jo McGuinn. Not his parents, God have mercy on their souls. Not even the others in the Movement, because they had their weaknesses and their favourites. Their dedication had to be to the organisation in which they operated, not to the individuals within it. It had to be the only loyalty, to keep the Irish Republican Army in existence for the continuation of the Long War, whatever the cost in the blood sacrifice of the troops in that army. O'Neill sighed deeply. Even if people were fickle, the land of

Ireland could not betray him. It was as it had always been, and always would be.

He took another deep breath and lay backwards on the coat, shutting his eyes and grabbing at the heather with tight fists. With his eyes closed, he could imagine the spinning of the earth beneath him on a slow gyre around the sun, turning and turning in the gentle evolution of the planets, as he held on to the soil of Ireland for support.

Chapter Thirteen

Donegal

P J O'Neill started the car and swung it around in the parking space by the church. He saluted a farewell at the priest standing in the doorway of the Parish House, waving slowly. The journey was not going to be long, maybe three hours, and he was happy to be back in the solitude of the car again. He could feel as he sat in the driver's seat that his legs were stiffening from the climb up Errigal. If anything, the descent had been the worst part, trying to keep his balance as the borrowed priest's boots slid on the wet heather.

Father McGuinn had been there waiting for him on his return. O'Neill decided he would escape as soon as possible, with as much politeness as he could muster. In the event, it was not as bad as he had feared. The opening rounds where they fenced with each other passed without any more references to prayer. McGuinn made some fried eggs and bread and tea, and they sat facing each other over the kitchen table telling more stories of the old days, safe in the past.

'He ended up in the Maze,' O'Neill said. 'And the brother too. Whole family of them joined the IRA. It nearly destroyed the mother, when she saw the British picking them up one after the other and putting them inside, brothers and sisters.'

'I did the honours at the wedding,' McGuinn said. 'Married some farmer from out near Desertmartin. A whole tribe of them pitched up from the country to the church. Some family. I never thought they would stay together, and I was right. Sad really, but you can't expect a girl from West Belfast to be happy out in the country.'

'Ah, that one was an old friend of Sheelagh's. I never could stand him. Two-faced. Did you hear, he tried to move to England and set up a business, but it went bust?'

And so it went, to O'Neill's relief. McGuinn had decided to play

153

things gently, perhaps recognising that he had pushed too far. O'Neill ate, talked, had his bath and paid some ritual compliments to McGuinn on his hospitality. He said he would like to stay until early the following morning, but there was work for him to do in County Louth on the way back to Dublin. He hoped Jo-Jo understood. The priest said he did. They even hugged one another again on the doorstep, and O'Neill promised to return, for longer next time.

'Provided you don't try to convert me to Christianity,' he said.

The priest laughed.

'Ach,' he said. 'I know when I'm dealing with a full-blooded pagan. I would never try to preach the Gospel among the truly heathen savages. I'm just sorry you won't stay another night.'

'Not this time, Jo-Jo. Next time, perhaps.'

It had been better than O'Neill hoped. He decided that he really might return, some day – not so much to see McGuinn as to relive the old places in Donegal that he did not have time to go to now. He wanted to look again at the cottage in Bunbeg. They had sold it after his father's death, and he wondered what the new owners had made of it. Then there was also Slieve Snaght to climb again, and maybe even a turn round the Bloody Foreland and the Atlantic drive with the Singing Pub, which he had not seen for years.

'Till the next time, Jo-Jo.'

'Till the next time, P J,' the priest replied. 'Take care of yourself. Keep safe now.'

'I'll try.'

As he started on the road round the bay he could see in his mirror that McGuinn had moved to the edge of the house to watch the car disappear southwards. He began to feel a slight guilt at his hurry to escape and the derision he felt at Jo-Jo's cries of loneliness, but the moment passed. There would never be feelings of guilt, he had promised himself. There was no time to waste on the luxury of regret. Where the journey north had been an adventure, the return south as darkness began to fall, was a chore. The second time in as many days travelling back on the same road could hardly compete with the first time in more than a decade driving up to Donegal. O'Neill was glad when he came to the sweep of Ravensdale forest and could see the lights of Dundalk in the distance. On the right at the edge of a field, the bungalow sat back from the road. The lights were already burning behind the curtains in the front room and in the kitchen to the side. The gates were open and he drove in, braking hard on the loose gravel on the driveway. Suddenly O'Neill saw McKeever at the window. Alerted by the noise, his hand was at his waistband, and he was staring intently from behind the curtain.

'Good lad,' O'Neill thought. 'At least one of them is awake.'

Siobhan O'Hagan opened the door.

'*Cead Mile Failte!*' she said. 'I hear you've been in the Gaeltacht.'

'It is good to see you, Siobhan,' O'Neill replied with a smile.

Billy McKeever stepped out from the main room and shook his hand.

'Welcome to the front-line, P J,' he said. 'You've come at just the right time. Durrant has been showing us a new party trick. We're in the garage.'

'I'm always ready to learn new tricks,' O'Neill smiled. 'Hold on a minute.' He took a black balaclava from the pocket of his tweed jacket and pulled it over his head.

In the garage, Larry Kennedy and Brendan Kelly sat at either end of the workbench. Gordon Durrant was in the middle, scraping a small quantity of white powder from a piece of filter paper on to a metal block. When he saw the eyes of the newcomer staring at him from behind the black balaclava, he stood up, startled, as if he had suddenly been struck a blow.

'Continue,' O'Neill said. 'I hear you have something to show me.'

Durrant did not move. Larry Kennedy rasped at him to sit down and get on with it.

'You heard the Boss. Move it.'

Durrant nervously took his seat. He paused for a moment and then began methodically, letting the white powder drop onto the metal until he had a small pile, much less than a half of a teaspoonful in volume. He raised an ordinary hammer slowly above the pile, then let it drop in an arc onto the block. There was an astonishingly loud bang.

'Detonators,' Larry Kennedy said, his thin face suffused with triumph. 'It's the powder at the heart of detonators. And he has just shown us how to make it from hydrochloric acid, acetone and a few other bits and pieces.'

'You're a genius, prof,' McKeever said with genuine enthusiasm.

Durrant looked back at their smiling faces, feeling both happy and ashamed. He swept the remaining powder from the filter paper into a jam jar and secured the lid. The Thin Man was talking to the Boss in an animated way, as if his own genius had been responsible for what had happened, not Durrant's. Durrant noticed the Boss had changed tack, turning the conversation away from Kennedy's praise for his own smartness, to more matter-of-fact questions about what they had learned so far.

'Has he shown you what you need to know about the magnetic explosives?'

Durrant looked over at the Boss as he stood at the door which connected the garage to the rest of the house. He was an incongruous sight, wearing what was obviously a well cut and expensive tweed jacket, and the black balaclava, like a caricature of the world's best dressed terrorist.

'Not yet,' the Thin Man said. 'We decided we wanted to hear things that would be of constant benefit to the Movement first, things we can pass on, like being able to make detonators. Bearing in mind we thought there was no particular rush on the magnetic. That's the next thing, though. Isn't that right, prof?'

Durrant hated the Thin Man more when he was attempting to sound affable. At least when he was unpleasant it was predictable and acceptable. Being patronised or praised was harder to take.

'That's right,' Durrant agreed. 'Just as you say. The properties of the magnetic explosives next.'

'We shall need that quite soon, perhaps sooner than you thought,' the Boss said, his lips moist and poking through the edge of the balaclava. Durrant tried to work out whether he had a beard. It looked as if he was clean shaven, but you could not really tell. Kennedy was nodding; McKeever frowning and wrinkling his forehead. Durrant still could not decide precisely the chain of command, the relationship between these people.

'We were thinking of spending a day learning how to make a shaped charge so it cuts metal,' McKeever said. 'The way to make the most out of an explosion's energy, first. As a sort of preamble to the main thing. Wasn't that it, prof?'

'Well,' Durrant said morosely. 'You cannot really understand how the magnetic explosive works until you understand how shaped charges work. It all depends whether you want only to learn how to use these things or if you want to understand something about their properties. It is possible to do it either way, depending on how much time you've got.'

There was some kind of general discussion between them, which drew to a close when the Boss pointed out that there was enough time to understand the processes as well as simply find out how to use the explosives. McKeever said they did not really need to know why things happened as long as they could make them happen. Then the Girl butted in, saying she would like to know as much as Durrant could tell them. For his part, as Durrant listened to them, he thought of an unruly and poorly organised university seminar group deciding how they wanted to be taught in the weeks ahead. Still, it was not his discussion, and he had other things to do. He finished clearing up in the garage and the Thin Man said he had to be locked up in his room. The Boxer put his hand on Durrant's sleeve as if to lead him away, but the professor stood rigidly in place. He decided it might be his last chance to talk to the Boss and he had to use it, even if the Thin Man made him pay for it afterwards.

'When will you let me go?' he said, in a calm, clear voice. It was like a pistol shot in the middle of their conversation, as if a servant had violently interrupted the business of his masters. The eyes in the balaclava stared back at him. The Thin Man said something about not asking any questions and get him out of here but the Boss said to leave him be.

'When we are ready,' he nodded at Durrant. 'Not a second before. When we have finished with you. That will be time enough.'

'And when will that be?' Durrant shot back. 'Why should I continue to help you when things you have promised me, like seeing my wife again, have not happened? Why shouldn't I refuse to help you any more?'

Durrant could smell that the Boss had been out in the rain. The wet wool from the Donegal tweed gave off a gentle, damp smell. Suddenly he felt a thrill of fear as the Boss stared at him and said nothing. It was something almost physical, as if a spasm passed through his bowels. Durrant knew they could kill him now, without a second thought.

'Listen,' the Boss said quietly. 'I don't have to make any deals with you at all. Not at all. You will co-operate with us because you have no other choice. We have been as decent to you as we can, but if you start making waves, your wife dies. Simple as that.'

He paused for a moment, weighing his words with care.

'However, maybe we should try to cheer you up. It might make you work better. You can see your wife as soon as you have explained the magnetic explosives to the volunteers here. When they are satisfied they know as much as they need to know about it, we will bring her to you. We are not inhuman. We know what you are going through. But volunteers in this movement are going through far worse things every day of their lives in the prisons of the North, and you will just have to put up with it until we decide to let you go. This is not a bargain I'm striking with you. It is the way things are going to be.'

The rat had entered Durrant's skull. He just could not understand why the Boss took such precautions to keep his own identity concealed and the others faced him without wearing balaclavas. Durrant knew that in this inconsistency there was danger. Somehow he sensed that they would never release him alive.

'So you will let me go in the end will you?' he asked. 'Why shouldn't I just think you are going to kill Margaret and me whatever I do?'

'You can believe whatever you like,' the Boss retorted, losing patience. 'But if you want to cheer yourself up you might think that we would believe that in letting you go at the right time when you can no longer jeopardise current operations, by letting you go then, we might be doing ourselves a favour. It would become a major propaganda victory for us, when you start telling your story. Anyway, I'm not here to argue with the likes of you or to cheer you up. You've heard as much as I'm going to say. Get him out of here.'

The Boxer's grip on Durrant's forearm had not been relaxed during the conversation. Now it became uncomfortably tight. The man's strength could not be ignored. Half pulled by the Boxer, Durrant walked back to his room. A stiff push from behind propelled him inside. He fell on the bed and lay there, listening to the click of the key in the door lock.

In the garage, as soon as Durrant left, O'Neill pulled off his balaclava.

'Jesus,' he gasped, looking at McKeever. 'What a sweat you have in one of these. Let's go out and get some air. The back garden's safe is it?'

'Safe enough,' McKeever grunted. 'There's no one within miles of here. No one overlooking us at all at the back. Besides, it's almost dark now.'

'Fine. Let's walk, Billy.'

To Larry Kennedy and Siobhan O'Hagan, O'Neill said he

would like a cup of tea in a few moments. He explained that he just wanted some fresh air and a turn round the garden. Kennedy and the girl looked at each other, curious to know why he wanted to speak to McKeever alone.

'Old time friendship,' Siobhan O'Hagan said wryly. 'From the Maze prison days.'

'Perhaps,' Larry Kennedy replied, half lost in thought. 'Or perhaps he's checking up on the way I've been running things. You never know with O'Neill. He doesn't trust anybody.'

The two of them walked into the garden, where McKeever had made an attempt to cut the grass with a rusty lawnmower he found in the shed. Middle-class virtues like gardening did not come easily to him, and O'Neill noticed even in the deepening twilight bunched leaves of ground elder and buttercups choking the rose bed. It felt almost like summer, warmer than it had been in Donegal. The air smelled of flowers and a new growth of grass. They walked to the far end of the garden in silence.

'Larry Kennedy will be going off soon to Cork to his diving lessons,' O'Neill said, stopping the stroll beside the oak tree. 'He should take two weeks at it, which will give us plenty of time to complete the "Work in Progress". He'll even earn a certificate from the British Sub Aqua Club. Some deal, eh? To get acknowledgement of your diving skills from the Brits.'

McKeever smiled and looked at O'Neill's face. It was a face of character, he thought, and intelligence. The years in Long Kesh had not aged him, but the past months on the run, the sleeping every night in a different bed, the not knowing which of your comrades might betray you, had left O'Neill with deepening lines round his eyes and hair flecked with grey. McKeever wondered whether it was as simple as that, or whether O'Neill's ambitions had also taken their toll. McKeever could not understand what a life might be like not being involved in the armed struggle against the British. It was all he had ever wanted to do, the thing which gave him respect in the New Lodge road area where he had been raised, the thing which gave his life a sense of purpose. It was the kind of respect he thought O'Neill himself might have got in the priesthood, yet he chose a different way. They all knew about his background and his supposed vocation which he had abandoned for the armed struggle. McKeever never understood why such a choice, which had not been open to him, had been so easily

159

rejected by O'Neill. Would he not have served Ireland just as well as part of its church? Whatever the reasons, there was in the man, McKeever now recognised, a strange sense of ambition which shone through everything he turned to. It was as if O'Neill was not content with doing what he did, but wanted to go down in the history books as the best ever, the man who really did change the world. It was the kind of naked ambition McKeever saw in Brendan Kelly, and did not like.

McKeever smiled upon O'Neill's manoeuvrings to advance himself within the Republican Movement, happy to see an old friend prosper. At the same time he was uneasy, sensing the strain of the internal politics – the moves which replaced Coffey as Director of External Operations, and the constant political battle to keep Hughes and the other Coffey allies off his back – that had aged O'Neill. McKeever was sure of it.

It was for the very same reason that O'Neill liked to talk openly to McKeever. His lack of personal ambition made him the perfect foot-soldier, loyal to the Movement and not constantly searching out the main chance as Larry Kennedy always did. 'Cool Kennedy', the man who could get the job done, and who might just one day end up replacing O'Neill himself on the Army Council. Kennedy knew O'Neill's suspicions, and would not take kindly to his role of making tea while McKeever and O'Neill talked privately in the garden. He resented the way O'Neill planned everything himself, and sprang the details on the rest of them at the last moment when there was little they could contribute to the overall strategy. O'Neill's natural secretiveness meant he always referred to the job as 'Work in Progress', which infuriated Kennedy.

'What do you mean, "Work in Progress",' Kennedy had said, when O'Neill first started to unveil the plans to kidnap Durrant. 'How come you tell us who we are to kidnap only at the last moment, and then tell me I have to take diving lessons, but you don't tell us the final reason for all this. What kind of games are you playing P J – and why don't you trust your own team to help plan the operation we're to get involved with?'

'Larry,' O'Neill had said in his most indulgent manner. 'You know the score. Security, not games. I criticised Coffey for keeping too loose a rein on the last England team. I can hardly make the same mistake again. Everyone gets to know what they need to know, at the last possible moment they need to know it. That's it. I can't tell you more just yet. It might risk the whole operation.

That's the way we're working from now on. I trust all of you. All I'm asking is for you to trust me in return.'

McKeever thought at the time that O'Neill was interested in keeping the operation secret not only from the security forces but also from Coffey, Hughes and the others. Larry Kennedy might tell them. There were factions within factions at work here and McKeever for one didn't want to know anything about it, though O'Neill seemed to regard some of the others in the Movement as being about as dangerous to him as the British. The result was that no one, maybe with the exception of the Chief of Staff and O'Neill himself, knew either the target or the real reasoning behind the Durrant kidnap.

'All I'm trying to say,' Kennedy had replied, 'is that you have me as officer commanding the active service unit, you're putting me through stupid diving courses down in Cork, and all you tell me about it is that it is "Work in Fucking Progress" – it's not going to be easy to work with you, P J.'

O'Neill saw his chance. He said slowly: 'Well, if the work doesn't suit you, you could always be of service to the Movement back in East Tyrone. Billy can do the diving course, and I'll get another volunteer drafted in from Martin Anderson. There's no problem.'

That was the end of it, at least publicly. Kennedy had complained no more and prepared to go off cheerfully enough to his diving course, whenever it came and whatever it was for.

It was now almost completely dark and the lights of Dundalk shed an orange glow on the sky. The air was still, waiting for the next shower to blow in from the west. McKeever realised O'Neill was speaking to him again, rehearsing a series of orders as if reading from a list.

'Remember, Durrant must explain in detail everything about the Magnex. Everything. You seem to have him well enough trained so that he obeys everything you say, but it is more important than ever now. On other matters it was at least possible that we could check what he has been saying. On the magnetic explosives, since he invented the bloody gear and has published so little on it, there will be no way of checking until we come to use it on "Work in Progress". It has to be right first time. You have to make sure he is now sufficiently terrified of you – or of Kennedy – to tell it all. And remember . . .'

McKeever knew what he was going to say since he had said it to them a thousand times. He mentally repeated it in time with O'Neill's words.

'. . insist that he tells you how to make the time and power units fully waterproof against sea water.'

'We will, P J. Sure we will.'

'How has Kennedy been?'

'The usual, P J. Much the same as before. He scares the shit out of the prof, and Brendan and me try to keep him cheerful. It seems to work, though sometimes he goes over the top and I think he's actually going to beat the old guy up.'

'If he does, you stop him. You hear me? You won't get the best out of a man like Durrant with beatings. He'll turn in on himself and harden. Keep him confused, off-balance. That's the way. Understood?'

'Understood,' McKeever repeated.

O'Neill looked both agitated and as if he was operating on auto-pilot, the words a speech he had planned to deliver a long time ago but which had been postponed. McKeever was to hear it all now, as he rattled through it.

'The target ship will arrive in Glasgow in a month's time, on the 25th of June. It will be there for three days, and then it's due to set sail for the Outer Hebrides and the Western Highlands of Scotland. The only possible time for "Work in Progress" to be a success is the 26th or 27th of June, and I have planned for the 26th. I will meet Kennedy in Dublin on his way back here from the diving course and will brief him properly, but I wanted you to know the timetable we are working to. You must not tell anyone here – neither Kelly nor Siobhan O'Hagan. Let Kennedy break the news when he gets back from the diving course, otherwise he will just get offended and say I have broken usual army procedure by informing his active service unit before he gets the chance.'

McKeever nodded and O'Neill continued in a breathless rush.

'When he asks you what we have been talking about out here, tell him I wanted to know how he was behaving. It's the truth, anyway and the more he thinks I'm checking on him, the easier he is for me to deal with. I don't want him getting out of hand.'

McKeever nodded again. They were standing at the edge of the garden by the farthest hawthorn hedge where it jutted onto the farmland. It was a bizarre scene, the two men whispering in the darkness, engrossed in each other's company. McKeever thought he caught a glimpse of Kennedy's face looking at them from one of the rear bedroom windows, but he wasn't sure. O'Neill was still talking.

'The ship is some four thousand tons, but I'll check that and the draught as soon as I get back to Dublin. It is important you ask Durrant's advice for the way to attack a target of that size. If the figures are wrong I will telephone you from Dublin tomorrow and tell you the new sizes for "Work in Progress". You can tell Kennedy that too. I will supply him with the plans which are supposed to be available to me now in Dublin. The important thing is to be sure in your own minds that Durrant explains the best method of rapid and complete destruction. At the final stage, Kennedy might have to show Durrant the plans to check where best to fix the Magnex. We'll have to judge how to play that, but if that's what we have to do then he should leave it to the latest possible time. At no stage is Durrant to be told the name of "Work in Progress". He can read about it in the newspapers, if he lives that long. Travel arrangements will be for two of you on the Preston route – it's a coal boat this time, so they might make you work for your sail – and two through Stranraer. You'll have to go on separate days and there will be no contact with our local auxiliaries in Scotland for obvious reasons. We've arranged two safe houses in Glasgow. One for three of you. The other for Siobhan and the gear. Okay?'

'Okay so far.'

'I will tell you the rest nearer the time, and I will repeat it all to Kennedy if he survives the diving course in Cork. If he's no good, then we might have to send you.'

'Me? You're kidding me, P J. I prefer sticking to the land.'

O'Neill laughed. 'Let's go back to the house, otherwise people will be wondering what two men can be finding so interesting to talk about down the end of their garden.'

A large moth, the first McKeever had seen that spring, flew from the mayflowers in the hawthorn on a dizzy path towards the lights of the bungalow. The two men followed it in silence. Then McKeever asked if Durrant was to be got rid of, and if so, when. O'Neill replied that he was not sure.

'I was going to put in another team, maybe the South Armagh boys, to guard him and his wife while you went over to Scotland and then have them dealt with, but now I don't know. These last couple of days made me think that there would be a propaganda coup from his release. The only catch would be that he can identify all of you.'

'I'm not so keen on that, P J. I mean, whatever you have in mind

163

for "Work in Progress" we'd be hunted from house to house in the South here just as much as in the North. We'd have to go abroad. America or something. It would be easier to stiff them. One look at the Special Branch files and we'd be done.'

O'Neill stopped his pace. They were ten yards from the house.

'You are probably right,' he said. 'Unless we made them blind or something.'

'How do you mean?' McKeever responded.

'Blind, you know. Put their eyes out. It could be done.'

McKeever was amazed. He had never heard a suggestion like it, and you never knew whether O'Neill was serious or not. One moment the charm and disciplined thought. The next moment, this.

'Ach, no, P J. It'd be real cruel, that. It'd make us look bad.'

O'Neill nodded, but said nothing. McKeever knew he was trying to work out which solution to the problem would make him look best. Dead Durrants or live Durrants; blind Durrants or Durrants that could help the police. It didn't much matter. O'Neill would decide and someone would be found to do the job. But not him. Not McKeever. He wasn't going to do any of that. The South Armagh boys might, but not him.

'What is imperative,' O'Neill said, 'and I will repeat it to Kennedy now inside, and you tell him it too, is that when we have finished with the Durrants we keep them together but not here. Move him to the house where we are keeping her. It is the best location if we decide to stiff them, nearer the forest. I'll put the South Armagh boys up there for a while until I've decided what to do. But I think it's best to move Durrant from here when you finish, so he is separated from the explosives.'

McKeever nodded in agreement. O'Neill started to walk towards the house again, but McKeever put a hand on his arm and stopped him. He decided to take a risk, to gauge exactly the level of 'Work in Progress', since if it really was as big as O'Neill said, it reflected directly on his own safety. A really big job probably meant it would become vital to make sure the Durrants were killed. The hunt for them would become insufferable after something as big as the Brighton bombing.

'You haven't told us, P J, what the name of this boat is,' McKeever said. 'Or do you just want to leave it that it's HMS "Work in Progress"? '

O'Neill looked at McKeever's worried face, the wrinkled

forehead stretching back to where his hair had receded. They would have to be told sooner or later. The Army Council already knew. He was wasting time keeping it a secret still.

'Ah, the name of the ship, Billy. Well, I suppose I could leave it for another few days until Larry has completed his course. But you might as well know. Maybe I should tell you all tonight.' O'Neill paused a little and smiled, his eyes alive with enthusiasm.

'It's the ''Britannia'', Billy,' he whispered. 'The Royal Yacht ''Britannia''.'

Chapter Fourteen

June, Dublin

The lounge bar in Jury's Hotel heaved with the evening's drinkers. There was a knot of Americans in striped blazers and tartan trousers complaining to each other that no one in Ireland could find them a copy of the *International Herald Tribune*. A blue-rinsed matron in her late sixties showed her overweight and bored husband an Irish lace table napkin she had bought in the hotel shop for twenty dollars, and which he thought you could buy in O'Connell Street for two – supposing you were in a mood to buy it at all, which he was not. A dozen or so youngish Dublin businessmen crammed together at the bar, full of Guinness and bonhomie and ready at any minute to break into a chorus of rugby songs. The barmen eyed them warily, knowing that if the singing did begin, the manager would insist on throwing them out.

Morgan sat at the far corner of the bar looking at the Americans with disdain, and the Dubliners with disgust. He sank a couple of mouthfuls of stout dejectedly. Dunlop was upstairs in his room unpacking. The rest of the crew were scheduled to arrive later. At all costs he wanted to avoid having dinner with the cameraman and sound recordist. That could really spoil the evening. Morgan believed there were only two kinds of camera crew – those that fended for themselves and were generally a pleasure to be with (because you hardly ever saw them), and those who expected the reporter and producer not only to set up the story but plan the entertainment and the dinner as well. Morgan had never worked with this crew before. They had been hired for the job on Dunlop's recommendation, and so he had no idea which category they fitted into, but he suspected the worst.

Morgan had not left London in a good mood. Emily had started to waver on the idea of having the abortion, but in the end he had been unable to extract from her a promise that she would not go

167

ahead. He had tried every argument he could think of, but there was nothing which marked out a clear victory. He thought he had allowed things in their marriage to deteriorate too far, and now he was going to pay the price. It was almost as if the marriage had only managed to hang together by a thread and the weight of the new child would be sufficient to break it apart. At one point they had fallen into turgid pro- and anti-abortion arguments, as if they were discussing a matter of public policy rather than the life of their own child.

'Foetus,' Emily had corrected him. 'Not child. Foetus.'

'Very well. Foetus, then.' Morgan had replied with bad grace, and the argument continued.

There had been some hope because she had recognised that there were changes in him, that the challenges of the O'Neill story were pulling him out of his depression about work. But Emily felt there was no point in her trying to make decisions about their life together in the future on the basis of Morgan's sudden cheerfulness.

'Does that mean the success of our marriage depends only upon your relationship with whoever happens to be your assignment editor?' she had asked, bitterly. 'If it does, it is hardly a basis for a great future.'

Emily argued that if he was beginning to cheer up at work, and if she went back to writing, and they got a nanny, their marriage might well survive. But all three of these things had to happen, and there had to be an abortion. Without that she could not hope to pull her own life together. There were to be no more arguments.

Morgan swallowed hard on his pint. It was always the same. He had the illusion that he could take decisions and influence events, but in reality the decisions which mattered were taken for him by other people, by Emily and Crawshaw, Harris and Mortensen. However hard he tried to swim against the tide, it was as much as Morgan thought he could do to keep afloat. At least the planned filming with O'Neill absorbed him in a way nothing had done for years. The work anaesthetised him against everything else in his life, and he thought he should be grateful.

On his return to Dublin, Morgan had called in at the Sinn Fein offices on Parnell Square to let them know when the film crew would arrive and that they would be ready for business from the following day. Their response was so non-committal that he was not entirely sure whether the interview was going to happen.

'It's still on, I hope?' he asked one of them.

'Nobody's told me it's off,' was the reply.

Morgan gave them the telephone number where he could be contacted – Jury's hotel, as O'Neill had demanded – and hoped for the best. He knew he might have to wait for as long as a week, but there was no choice. He wondered whether there was a time limit he ought to set, a date when he would decide to pull out if nothing had happened. It was best not to think of such things.

'Have patience,' Dunlop had said to him on the flight over.

Have patience, Morgan thought sulkily. In a hotel which costs ninety quid a night in a town where you can't tell anyone what you are up to, on a story with a producer you don't know, and working to a boss in London who inspires so much confidence it's like working for Rasputin. Patience my arse.

There was something about Dunlop that Morgan found unsettling, though he could not put his finger on it. Crawshaw had said there would be no problems with Dunlop's professionalism. He was an Ulsterman and therefore knew all the rules. He was streetwise enough to fit in with whatever happened in Ireland. Morgan had nodded in agreement, but he knew that several experienced Capital Television producers were lying around the office doing damn all, people with far more experience than Dunlop seemed to have, and whom Morgan already knew and trusted. Saying Dunlop would be best for a job in Ireland because he was an Ulsterman was an odd way of putting it. Did Crawshaw really believe you had to be an Eskimo to know what an igloo looked like? Maybe he did. But Morgan would have preferred any of the producers he knew well at his side if things got difficult. How would Dunlop handle it, for example, if Morgan started to ask difficult questions and O'Neill demanded that they give him the tape so he could destroy it? O'Neill was capable of anything, but what would Dunlop be capable of in a real crisis? Who was Dunlop anyway? What had he done? Crawshaw said he knew Dunlop's work from America and Australia, and that he had made documentaries in Belfast for Ulster TV and the BBC in Northern Ireland, though that was some years ago. Moreover, Dunlop wanted to operate with a crew which he had used for years all over the world. He said they would be perfect for the O'Neill interview because they were tough, experienced and could keep their mouths shut. That was all Crawshaw knew about them, the sum total of their recommendations for a job which could leave everybody covered in shit. There was worse to come. Dunlop was from Ballymena. Now that was novel. Picking a Ballymena Protestant to make a film about the IRA seemed to Morgan like taking an Israeli film crew to shoot a documentary on Colonel Gaddaffi. It was not the best idea of casting Morgan had ever come across. Super Ballymena Bigot meets Super IRA Terrorist. Encounter of the year. Jesus. Morgan took another deep pull at his Guinness.

The Dublin business crowd were just beginning to break into a chorus of 'An Engineer's Wife' when one of the hotel under-managers in a dinner jacket and bow tie stepped out from behind the bar and told them if they did not stop they would be on the street in five minutes.

'*Oh, Jesus . . .*'

'*Ach. C'mon now ould fella . . .*'

'*Wait here now . . .*'

Some of the Americans had decided to leave. It was almost eight o'clock and probably their bed time, Morgan thought, as he watched the men drink the dregs of their whiskey and the women finish their cokes. Middle-aged American tourists seemed to live on a time scale different from the rest of humanity, eating their main meal at six in the evening and disappearing when the rest of Dublin was just beginning to wake up. He was glad of that. It made more room in the bar.

Morgan began to try to put into words what it was about Dunlop that most disturbed him. He was not sure he could spell it out. It was not just something about not knowing him, his strengths and weaknesses. And it was not just the question of Dunlop being so obviously a Northern Ireland Protestant on a story about republicans. There was a vague unease, but he could not identify it. Dunlop was about six feet tall, well built, maybe early thirties. He had a clipped, almost unfriendly manner, and when Morgan asked him about his previous films or his assignments to America and Australia, he spoke as if it bored him.

'Lots of money,' he said. 'Good times. They pay well, but what they want is not demanding. Good fun while it lasted.'

He said he knew Crawshaw from years past, when he had been involved in making industrial and promotional videos for companies as a sideline. Crawshaw had given him a break, and he was grateful. For his part, Morgan thought Dunlop spoke more like a business manager than a film maker. He seemed to have no specific idea of how he wanted to shoot the O'Neill interview, and few ideas of how they could use pictures to enliven what would otherwise just be a man's head speaking for half an hour. Surely he did not think they could make a whole programme in which the only pictures were of O'Neill sitting in a chair answering questions? It might be the core of the programme, but there had to be something more.

Morgan had tried several times to find out about Dunlop's experience. He had said that after working for five years in Belfast he had gone to Central America and been filming in El Salvador as a freelance for CBS and NBC, using that as a route into the American networks. Then they had started laying off staff and he had gone to Australia, where he found it impossible to get a permanent work permit. He wanted to come home and settle down in Britain again, had been looking around for something, and had approached Crawshaw. The O'Neill project had come up, and Dunlop jumped at the chance. It was the best opportunity he could think of to make a name for himself again in Britain.

He was right about that. It would make his name. Morgan wondered whether Dunlop was one of those rare characters who found the past without interest, and lived only for the present day. He was no raconteur, unlike most producers or reporters who Morgan believed were at least capable of being adequate self-publicists. On the contrary, Morgan would have described Dunlop as shy, reticent. Partly out of curiosity, but also because he suspected it annoyed Dunlop, Morgan continued to prod, to extract any information he could. The reticence might have been a tight-lipped Ballymena habit, but other producers always had a fund of personal anecdotes which they told over dinner, or to impress interviewees. Morgan always used to think you had been working with a producer for too long when you knew his stories and anecdotes as well as he did, so you could get to the punchline first. That was never going to become a problem with Dunlop. There were no punchlines.

When they talked about the O'Neill interview, Dunlop repeated that since Morgan was the driving force behind the whole story, he would rely on Morgan's judgement in terms of areas for questioning. And as for pictures, or library film, or other sequences they might shoot, didn't that depend on how much O'Neill was prepared to say? Wouldn't they be better to wait until after the interview and then discuss how best to structure the whole film? Morgan thought there must be something original they could shoot.

'We can hardly ask the most wanted man in Ireland to be filmed walking down the road or anything like that,' Morgan said. 'Nor can we ask someone on the Army Council of the IRA to let us film him making the tea or tending the roses in the back garden. And I don't suppose he'd let us film him making a bomb or firing his Armalite. But we do need pictures of him doing something. Got any ideas?'

Dunlop said he would think about it, though his feeling was that the interview could run virtually by itself. O'Neill's own words were the story, not a whole load of illustrative material. To Morgan, Dunlop's replies seemed to show a reversal of roles. Normally as the reporter Morgan would be trying to talk the producer out of using too many pictures because they got in the way of the story. Now he was listening to a producer telling him that pictures were really not necessary. Maybe this was the way things worked in El Salvador and Australia. Morgan noticed that Dunlop did become more animated when they discussed O'Neill's character, and what Morgan's impressions of him had been. He also wanted to know what Morgan thought the arrangements for the interview would be like, how many people O'Neill would have with him and so on.

'Oh, I'd guess there would be three others apart from O'Neill,' Morgan said. 'Two or three others. But the thing you really must understand is that the personality of the man will shine through in the interview, which means we have to make it clear somehow that he is a murderer, responsible for all kinds of terrorist acts. If we do not do that, we really will lay ourselves open to the charge of editorial irresponsibility. You see, O'Neill is quite – I know the word is overused, but it's the best one I can think of – quite charismatic. He actually smiles a bit, not like the face on the wanted posters. He's well dressed. Clean shaven. Decent-looking man. Sense of humour. Good talker.'

And, Morgan thought as Dunlop continued to listen carefully to the description, in all of that quite unlike you, you dour Ballymena bastard.

Dunlop appeared at the door of Jury's bar and threaded his way through the group of now staggering and maudlin businessmen. He wore faded jeans, an open neck shirt and running shoes. He vaguely reminded Morgan of something or someone, but he could not think exactly what it was. The moment passed. Later that night, as he lay on his bed unable to sleep, Morgan remembered. Dunlop was like one of the Israeli security men who had taken Morgan's film crew's luggage to bits in Jerusalem a year before. Just like him. Informal.

Casual in his dress. Yet behind all the informality, there was something clinical and hard.

'I hope we get the summer weather you are clearly expecting,' Morgan said. 'You look as if you are dressed more for Australia than Dublin. Never mind, you'll soon cool down. Like a drink?'

'Why not,' Dunlop said. 'I'll take a wee Bush. And water.'

Morgan smiled. The Ulsterman drank his native liquor, Bushmill's whiskey. He probably refused to touch the stuff distilled in the Catholic Republic of Ireland. Dunlop took the glass and sipped gingerly while they waited for Morgan's next pint of Guinness to settle. He looked round the crowded bar and told Morgan he thought it would be difficult to talk freely. He suggested that while they wait for the crew to arrive, they take the drinks up to his room and speak in private. Morgan agreed. The barman slid the full pint of stout on to a beer mat, Morgan took a swig and then followed Dunlop as he wound his way back through the bar to the hotel lifts.

Dunlop's room was the usual large double-bedded pastel coloured affair that could have been a hotel anywhere between Dublin and Denver. He pointed Morgan in the direction of a pink and beige flower-covered sofa and told him to sit down. Dunlop perched, drink in hand, on the edge of the writing desk near the door.

'We have a problem,' Dunlop said.

'What do you mean?'

'Well, more specifically, Tony, *you* have a problem.'

'I don't get it. Has Crawshaw called the whole thing off?'

Dunlop sipped his whiskey and put the glass down on the table beside him. He put his fingers together and cracked the knuckles as if he were preparing for a fight. For the first time that Morgan could remember, Dunlop initiated a conversation.

'Crawshaw has not been entirely straight with you,' he said. 'He has his reasons, I suppose, and he's left it up to me to tell you what is going on. I am going to be totally straight, mainly because I find it too much of a strain to be otherwise. You are going to listen to what I have got to say right until the moment I have finished. You will not lose your temper or try to walk out of here. That would be a mistake. Understand?'

Morgan put down his pint in amazement. No one had ever talked to him like this before. Nobody he had ever worked with. Nobody.

'What the fuck's going on?'

Dunlop ignored the question. He moved his whiskey glass away from the edge of the writing desk, stood up and began pacing backwards and forwards, effectively blocking off the bedroom door.

'We are trying to find P J O'Neill,' he said. 'And by "we" I do not mean Capital Television.'

'Who do you mean then?'

'I will explain more quickly if you don't interrupt. I mean the forces of the British state. Call us that if you wish. The good guys. The people who keep us all from falling into chaos. You needn't know any more about titles or names of organisations, and I won't be telling you anything more except that what we are doing is for the benefit of the whole country. You do not even need to know precisely why we are trying to find O'Neill, beyond the fact that he is an escaped terrorist and a convicted murderer, and it would be better for everybody if a man like that was not on the loose. What you do need to know is that it is now extremely urgent that we locate him. And it is because it is so urgent we have used you, quite unashamedly, with Crawshaw's complicity, to get us within striking distance of O'Neill. You are someone they trust. No, that's going too far. You are someone PIRA is apparently prepared to do business with, because you television people deliver them the one thing they need to survive – publicity. We have depended upon that fact.'

Dunlop sat down on the desk again, and looked at the back of his knuckles. Morgan thought it was as if he was about to yawn. Like all his previous stories about filming in Central America or Australia, it seemed it was a bore for Dunlop to have to tell it, but he had no choice. Morgan, struck dumb, had forgotten about his Guinness. Dunlop was now staring at him.

'We want you to act just as normal when the telephone message comes from them for the rendezvous with O'Neill. It may, of course, not happen, in which case we will have to try other things. But we think it will. And when it does, we will all go along as planned and film the interview with him. I will – or more likely someone from my crew will – fit a device onto O'Neill's car. It will enable us to trace him, wherever he goes in Ireland. That is our mission.'

Dunlop remembered he had a whiskey and took another sip. Morgan leaned across and picked up his Guinness again. It was cold and thick on his tongue, and all the taste had gone out of it.

'I decided to tell you this now before they make contact with us, because I assume you are already suspicious of me from the way you keep pounding me with questions about my background. I can dodge them well enough, I suppose, but I figured you would become even more suspicious when you meet my crew. If we are stuck here for a week waiting for O'Neill to call, you would eventually get the message. You'd be dumb not to. I thought from the start it would have been better if Crawshaw had made sure you knew what was happening, that you were on-side. He said none of his people would be keen to get into this if they knew the full story. I suppose he is right. Anyway, the point is now that I thought if I told you the truth, I could explain precisely why I want you to help me. It is the logic of the old cliché that one volunteer is worth ten pressed men. I want you now to volunteer. What do you say?'

Morgan looked at Dunlop in a mixture of anger and disbelief. He knew that the actor in his own temperament – just that little bit of an actor which was sufficient to carry him through the business of television – would have loved a scene, a full-blown row with this pompous little turd in his open-necked shirt and training shoes. Something told him it would not be the right thing to do. The journalist in him fought the opposite way, the way to get the story without letting the bastard really see what you think of him.

'Who are you, Harry Dunlop? Is that your name? Are you really called Harry Dunlop?'

'As a name it's as good as any other,' Dunlop said, smiling. 'It's a Scots-Irish name. A Ballymena name. That's enough, isn't it?'

'But who do you represent? MI5? Six? Who? If you can't be trusted to tell me your name I suppose I shouldn't bother asking you who you work for.'

'No, you shouldn't bother, but you're on the right track. People like those you have mentioned would be in the right area, I suppose you could say. Some of those in government circles refer to us as "The Funnies". Make of that what you want. Maybe it means we have a special sense of humour.'

Dunlop laughed, an unusual enough occurrence for Morgan to notice. Then he paused abruptly.

'That's pretty much the story,' he said. 'Now will you agree to help us?'

Behind his straightforward irritation at what Dunlop was saying and now this justification for his instinctive repugnance towards him, Morgan also remembered his first news editor on the *South Wales Echo* telling him his job was to report news, not make it. The news editor, whose name escaped him now, though it could have been Jones or Hughes or something, was a fat slob of a drinking man, useless after lunch for anything other than singing Welsh rugby songs, but his judgement had always been right.

'Never become the story, boy,' he remembered Jones saying in his ringing Welsh tones. 'Never have to make your excuses and leave. Never become part of the action or you are done. You cannot report on it if you *are* it. You've got to choose.'

What Jones or Hughes or Whoever had been talking about was not getting involved in any kind of political activity, even local politics. It was one or the other, journalism or running for the city council. You could not do both properly, since one was supposed to be independent and the other had to show a commitment to something, even if it was only to make sure the drains were kept clean. Refusing to get involved fitted easily enough with Morgan's own temperament. He always used to think he was unbiased because he frequently changed his vote at different elections and despised almost all politicians equally. It was as good a definition of objectivity as he could think of, even if he also knew there was indecision and cynicism mixed in there somewhere. What the hell, it was better than the attitude of some of his colleagues. He knew there were those who used their journalism to suck up to the political parties in the hope of obtaining some soft parliamentary seat somewhere. Morgan loathed people like that. It wasn't just that they were forced to become bum-kissers with people Morgan would never normally want to socialise with. It was the fact that these sort of people were by nature Joiners and Belongers, people who felt they had to get involved and who defined themselves by what they were members of – trade unions, golf clubs, Rotary clubs, societies, political parties. Morgan would not join anything, any group, any club, any trade union, anything which somehow suggested a group of people should combine together for common action. He was his own man.

'I haven't volunteered to join anything since I left the Boy Scouts aged thirteen,' he said to Dunlop. 'Why should I join you?'

'Because it will save lives. Exactly whose lives I can't disclose. Because it will put a man in jail, a man who *should* be in jail. Because it will help your country. What more reasons do you need?'

It was either because Morgan felt there was a sneer too far in what Dunlop had said, or because the absurdity of the situation had finally got to him. Either way, Morgan found himself standing up and shouting, jabbing at Dunlop with an outstretched finger, stoking his anger in the hope it hid the thrill of fear he felt in his guts.

'Look you fuckwit, if I had wanted to become a policeman I would have joined a fucking police force. As it happens I decided not to bother. I'm supposed to be a journalist. If you are looking for an informer or some kind of tout to play your silly games, you had better look elsewhere. And if you really think the Provos are such a bunch of arseholes that they are going to let a film crew waltz in and fit a bug to the car of an Army Council member who is on the run, you don't want help from me. You want it from a psychiatrist. Or a grave digger. Best of luck, pal, but count me out.'

Through it all Dunlop was grinning, standing there in his open neck shirt, his jeans and running shoes, and smiling from ear to ear. Morgan wanted to hit him, to hear his fist crack open Dunlop's asinine nose and listen to the Ballymena accent cry in pain. Wipe the smile away forever. Bastard.

'I'm sure P J and the boys will like your grin. They might like it so much they'll probably tear your smug fucking head off so they can keep it as a souvenir.'

Dunlop continued smiling as if enjoying some secret joke. He snorted then moved back from the door and perched again on the table's edge. He swigged down the rest of his whiskey.

'I am grinning because I told Crawshaw you'd be like this. And it is nice to get it right. I can see why you're a reporter. Nice turn of phrase, grave diggers and all that. But I suppose I'm also smiling because I know so much about you it would make you blush. About your marriage, your drinking too much, your little bits on the side. Your office politics. You name it. How much you fiddle on your expenses. All that sort of stuff.'

It was Morgan's turn to smile. 'What are you going to do? Blackmail me over a first class return I had on the train to Leeds when I only went second class? Or that I claimed I bought P J O'Neill dinner one night when I ate by myself? Grow up, Dunlop.'

'No, that's not what I meant. I don't play childish games. I told you that I want you to want to help us, to volunteer. I could have kept you completely in the dark. That was what Crawshaw wanted. He said you would be so busy worrying about the interview and whether your career would go down the toilet if you made a mess of it, that you would not notice anything strange going on. I thought he was wrong, though looking at your file I can see why he thought like that. Anyway, I decided that your ignorance could conceivably wreck the entire operation. The chances of something going wrong are, as you say, an important calculation, and I wanted to make sure that you are not one extra thing that might go wrong.'

Morgan could not control the raw anger in his voice.

'Well if you know so much about me, you'll also know how much I loathe people who bleed for causes. Life's too short to spend your time screwed up and making sacrifices for abstractions, for some better communist or capitalist land where there's jam tomorrow and maybe there was jam yesterday. I want my jam today, and I'm not going to allow you to rope me in to some squalid conspiracy. If you want to capture the freedom fighters, you'll have to do it all by yourself, Rambo. I quit.'

Dunlop stared at him. There was no humour in his voice now. It was like a man reading Morgan's obituary.

'You don't seem to understand, Tony. I know you do not regard the IRA as freedom fighters any more than I do. You regard them as the murdering gangsters that they are and the rest of the British population believes them to be. You left behind that liberal English left-wing crap about the poor Irish guerrillas a long time ago when you found out about their scams and their protection rackets.'

Morgan interrupted. 'No. It wasn't then. It was years before. It was on Bloody Friday when I saw the bodies of ordinary folk being swept into plastic bags at Belfast's Oxford Street bus station when the IRA let off all those no-warning bombs. That was when it was.'

'Well, whenever. We know you are just as happy as any of us to see them behind bars.'

'Providing they are put there legally and fairly – and by someone else, not me,' Morgan said. 'I'm not playing in your game, Dunlop, so for Christ's sake don't think you can talk me into this or stir up my conscience. It really isn't possible. The conscience died a long time ago. You are right about one thing, I was beginning to get suspicious about you, and if I had found out a bit more I would probably have blown this whole thing out of the water. I am glad at least you told me what has been going on, unlike that duplicitous bastard Crawshaw. But just because you have told me about your schemes doesn't make me want to become part of them. I am not playing. End of story.'

Dunlop sighed with exasperation. He folded his arms and looked at the floor. It was almost as if he believed that someone making an informed choice would be mad not to do as he wanted.

'Let me explain this again in words of one syllable,' he said slowly. 'So you can catch up. O'Neill is part of a gang who have kidnapped two very important people. The news has been kept secret, but believe me, it is true. If we find O'Neill we stand a good chance of saving their lives, and those of a very large number of other people as well. Now, this project is being attacked by several different characters in several different ways. The way I'm working on seems the most likely to produce results. We're pretty sure they have bitten at your offer for the interview. Clear so far?'

Morgan said nothing. He remembered his drink again, reached for the Guinness, and took a long pull. He could not believe this was happening to him. It was all a joke.

'From now on one of us will stay in your room to take the call from the Provos when it comes. If you do not co-operate we will just say that you stepped out for a moment. I will identify myself as your producer and make the arrangements, and we will hope for the best. It will make life difficult since they said all dealings have to be made through you, but we might have to take the chance. The result will be that if you do not appear at the rendezvous, our chances of being caught are the greater and the chance of us saving at least two lives could be lost. We may have to take a different tack in dealing with O'Neill, and it might all be too late. For you it will be disastrous. Whatever happens, the IRA will believe you have betrayed them. Things will go wrong, you were the contact, it will be your fault.'

Dunlop took a deep breath, as if the concentrated effort of so much speaking all at once was too much for him. He let out the breath in a long sigh. Morgan looked at his face, not much younger than his own. He wondered what sort of man this could possibly be. How could any human being act like this? Dunlop continued talking.

'You should think about that, because whatever your arguments about not joining things, you are a part of this now. There is no escape route and no way out except to co-operate. Any other course of action and I would put your life expectancy at around a few weeks, and that is just my natural optimism. It would more likely be days.'

Dunlop paused again, apparently collecting his thoughts for the next part of his argument. He ran a hand through the front of his light brown hair and pushed it back over his scalp. Morgan supposed that what he hated most about the man was not just what he was saying, but his complete control of the proceedings. It was as if he had scripted every one of Morgan's possible rebuttals in advance and was now moving to box him in. It was like one of those rehearsed sales pitches which, however you respond, end up with you buying encyclopedias. Morgan did not want any. There was enough of the renegade in him to refuse whatever logic Dunlop was selling. He could go to the Dublin newspapers and blow the story away. He still had friends who would believe him and print that. He could pretend to go along with it and then at the last moment try to warn the Provos off. There were many possibilities. Dunlop had started talking again.

'There's another part to this. You have not shut your ears, and I have told you very sensitive information. Anything you do to destroy the operation now that you have been fully informed about it would mean that you have taken a conscious decision to be in collusion with terrorists – with those at the very centre of the IRA. Under those circumstances, however hard you bleat about journalistic ethics, I think you might find it very difficult ever to work again in British television, or newspapers, unless you feel you might fit in on the *Socialist Worker* and *Morning Star*.'

If nothing else, Morgan thought, he did not want to be on the same side as this slimeball. Anything Dunlop was fighting for, it would be better to be against. He found it difficult even to listen to the words of what now seemed like a lecture.

'If you do help us – since the moral and patriotic arguments don't seem to wash with you – if you do help us there will be rewards.'

'What kind of rewards?' Morgan shot back. 'A state funeral?'

'Not exactly,' Dunlop said with a grin. 'Though I'm sure it could be arranged. No, it appears your Mr Crawshaw is looking for someone to front a three year film project on life in South America. You get it if you play along. Based in Rio de Janeiro, or Buenos Aires or somewhere. Lots of money.'

Dunlop laughed. 'You see, there is a carrot here as well as a stick. Though personally, I shouldn't discount the size of the stick.'

In his anger with Dunlop, Morgan had rather forgotten Crawshaw again.

'He knows about it all does he?'

'Of course.'

'From the start?'

'Naturally. He's a close personal friend of one of my bosses. So I understand, anyway. We asked him to help. He agreed straight away.'

'What does he get out of it? A knighthood?'

180

Dunlop smiled again. He could not make out whether Morgan's jokes were a sign that despite his words he might yet become a volunteer, or whether they were purely defensive, masking the trouble he might cause later. In a sense it did not really matter. Provided the Provos were serious about taking part, Morgan's help was almost irrelevant, given the true nature of the plan.

'More likely a peerage and an extension of the Capital Television satellite franchise into the twenty-first century. But you are getting off the point. Help us and you get a decent assignment for three years on full expenses, which might help you put together things for a far better life – you and your family. Don't help us and we'll go ahead anyway. Crawshaw will fire you, and you'll have to spend the rest of your short life wondering when and how the Boys are going to come for you. You'll be unemployable. How could you continue to be a reporter when the moment you appear on screen, the Provos will know where you are and will come looking? How far can you run on no money? One night wherever you are hiding, the Boys'll turn up and blow you away. Probably one in the back of the head after a few hours with them in the Romper Room, seeing what they can beat out of you. Not much of a choice I'd say. Maybe you see it differently, but I need an answer now. What is it?'

Dunlop seemed to have relaxed a little. Maybe the whiskey had done its work, or perhaps he could feel Morgan squirm in front of him. Morgan felt his face flush with heat and anger and humiliation. He wanted to tell Dunlop just to go screw himself, if only because no one should ever be treated in the way he was being treated now. The whole thing stank. He had never felt he had any great guiding principles, and the idea of not getting involved had served him all right up to now. He was not going to be trapped into taking sides by someone like Dunlop. It was true that he did not like the Provos and they did not particularly like him, but business was business, and they had an adequate working relationship. Both sides knew that. Now he was supposed to be in a new business. Treachery. There was nothing Morgan could think of to say. There was no logic he could bring to bear to persuade someone with the blindness of Dunlop's conviction that he was not going to play his game, that it was not right. He knew his face was red with the effort of thought and the exasperation of being forced to listen. There was sweat on his brow, and he felt sticky and weak. He wanted to get out into the fresh Dublin air and let the wind clear his head of this nonsense. Then he noticed Dunlop had picked up the telephone and was dialling an outside number.

'Yes, it's me. Yes. Yes, I've told him what he needs to know. And I've told him about South America if he co-operates. No, if he decides he is not going to, we will go ahead anyway. I've told him that too. And he has already mentioned to the Boys that just in case he is not in his hotel room when they call, they should ask for me. So I can make the arrangements anyway. It will be all right. Yes. Yes.'

Dunlop turned to Morgan and handed him the telephone.

'Crawshaw,' he said. 'He wants to speak to you.'

The voice at the other end of the line was smooth, charming, familiar.

'Dear boy, congratulations,' Crawshaw intoned. 'You are just about to be selected for our major satellite documentary contribution for the next three years about the building of South America and its new frontiers, in a joint venture with Australia-Cable and Canada Channel Five. Well done.'

Morgan could think of nothing to say. He made a non-committal noise to show he was still on the line.

'Sorry to spring all this on to you so suddenly, but I am sure you understand. It was the way we thought best. And now it really must all work out. You must co-operate in every way with your producer. I am sure you will see that, and all that it means. Have a good trip, think about the South American assignment, and good luck.'

There was a click at the other end of the line. Morgan looked over at Dunlop, relaxed, his hands stuffed in the pockets of his jeans. He could feel the sweat stippled on his own forehead, and a sudden wave of loathing. The telephone receiver was moist in his hands, like some animal that had died. He stared at it for a second, then slipped it back on its cradle.

Chapter Fifteen

Dublin

Morgan lay on his bed and smoked. He was fully dressed and slightly drunk, but only slightly. The light from the Dublin street lamps made his room glow orange. He could hear the music throbbing in Jury's hotel disco and the dull pounding of a thousand feet beating out a masturbatory rhythm on the sprung floor. Somewhere across the road towards Ballsbridge a police siren was wailing in the empty night. A drunk yelled an obscenity across the hotel car park that Morgan could not quite catch. It was past midnight. There had been no calls and no messages. When Morgan finished the cigarette he lit another one from its butt, as he had been doing for the past half hour. He remembered one of the more refined women producers at Capital Television telling him it was a 'common' habit, and he should not do it. From then on he did it all the time she was within irritation range. For a while he had thought he might give up smoking totally, then something would happen and he would start again. He needed cigarettes to think. First it was the abortion. Now this. He blew the smoke carefully skywards, watching it disperse in the half-light from the window.

Morgan's anger at Dunlop, and most of the humiliation and resentment he had felt at the way he had been manipulated by Crawshaw, had gone. He felt cold, neutral, as if what was happening was a story he had learned about someone else. It was a curious sensation. He had in front of him the kind of job he always dreamed about. All he had to do was reach across and touch it. He would be sent to South America, run his own life, schedule his own hours, make his own mistakes without the direct intervention of a Harris or a Mortensen or a Crawshaw. It was there, before him like a banquet of splendidly prepared and delicious smelling foods, a massive trough in which he could gorge himself if he would only bend his neck a little. Yet he had no appetite. He could not even

183

claim to feel scared. There had been times when he had felt terrified: once in Uganda when a boy soldier no more than twelve years old discharged the entire magazine from his Kalashnikov into the ground in front of Morgan's feet. They had stared at each other in mutual loathing, and he knew his life was hanging by its fingertips, but the moment passed. There was the time in Belfast when a dozen loyalists in leather jackets had lined him up against a wall and threatened to beat him to death in some shabby backstreet off the Shankill Road.

'Fenian loving bastards,' one of them had yelled in his face. 'Reporters are scum.'

That time he had been sure he was going to be beaten to a blood puree, but somehow after a lot of threats and talk, they decided to let him go without even striking him. They appeared content with his terror.

Tonight there was no fear or anguish. There was nothing at all. He was sure the threats from Dunlop had to be taken seriously, but that was only another way of saying Dunlop meant every word he said. There was a carrot as well as a stick, and the stick was large. He would be aborted like a foetus, a bundle of cells, by O'Neill and his people if they found out. Or he would be aborted one way or the other by Dunlop too. The only thing was to act like a foetus, not to be a human being with fears and desires and ambitions. To be the bundle of meat they had reduced him to.

When he thought it through, there was nothing in his life that seemed so important to make him regret leaving it. A heart attack, a car crash, a bullet in the neck from the Provos, one was as good as the other. They would all do the job, and somewhere between the ages of forty-six or, say, seventy-six, it would all be over anyway. He was not going to grovel to them about it. He wasn't in control at the moment he was conceived. He had limited control over what happened next, his birth and the life that followed it. Why should he expect to have any say in the moment of his death?

Morgan lit another cigarette. He did not remember having smoked so many at one time since the hours before David was born, pacing the corridors like the caricature of an expectant father, wincing with the screams of the mothers giving birth. He watched Louise being born, but not David. Emily said his nervousness would upset her. She would rather proceed alone. The cigarettes seemed to have no taste. He was smoking air.

There was something which niggled at him, now he had decided it was not fear that would keep him alive. That something was curiosity. He wanted to know more about Dunlop and O'Neill and whoever it was that had disappeared and was the point of Dunlop's quest. There was something here which, despite himself, excited Morgan. He wondered whether there might be a book in it, now or in the future – a book that he could write blowing the lid off some shabby British dirty tricks operation, conceived by whoever Crawshaw's dodgy friends were and executed by the dreadful Dunlop. Or perhaps it was a different book, one detailing his own extraordinary personal heroism as he helped the forces of Light triumph over those of Darkness. Or was it the other way round. How could he tell?

There was a story here, and he could feel it. It caused a prickle of excitement behind his eyes, a sensation he had not felt for a couple of years, the belief that he was on the edge of finding out something truly important. It was a story worth pursuing, not worth dying for, but maybe worth staying alive for. For a moment Morgan felt almost as he used to when he was a child playing cowboys and Indians in the woods near his home. It was a game the precise end of which did not matter, but playing it was always fun. The excitement was to work out which side would leap out from the ferns or the bushes and surprise the other. This might be the same, the game worth playing, but you had to be on one side or the other. There were cowboys and Indians, but no neutrals.

'Just think of us as the good guys,' Dunlop had said. 'Or you could call us "The Funnies". '

It did not really matter whether they were the good guys or not. Who was to say? And when the other members of Dunlop's supposed film crew arrived, they didn't seem so 'Funny' after all. Morgan could understand why Dunlop had to tell him the whole story. Fifteen minutes with the 'film crew' and he would have smelled a rat.

There were three of them, all in their mid-thirties and all with strong Ulster accents. A few minutes after Morgan spoke to Crawshaw in London, the crew called Dunlop's room on the hotel internal telephone. Dunlop told them to unload the cars and then come up to the room to meet Morgan. They lumbered in, all three with the same look that Morgan had noticed on Dunlop, the look of the Israeli security men: small, tough, casual, hard. The worn jeans and training shoes. The Lacoste tee-shirts which in Israel were always finished off with the ultimate in male jewellery and fashionable accessories: an Uzi sub-machine gun, or an M1 carbine. The three introduced themselves as Mike Dickinson, the cameraman, his sound recordist Charlie Barwood, and Dave Hinkley on lights. Since Dunlop immediately told them he had briefed Morgan fully about what he called the 'nature of our mission', Morgan thought the pretence that they really could perform the functions of a film crew was laughable. Maybe they wanted to persuade each other of their roles, even if they could not persuade him. The introductions proved to be the total of their conversation with Morgan. They shook his hand in turn and then sat down.

'Any problem with the gear?' Dunlop asked.

'None,' Dickinson said. 'Irish Customs said the usual "have you any goods on", we handed them the carnet and that was that. We picked up the rest in the safe house here. No problems.'

'Have you stowed it all in the rooms?'

'In my room. There's nothing left in the cars.'

Dunlop laughed. He said he was just a wee bit nervous that some of their stuff might find its way into the hands of the Dublin joyriders. The other three seemed to think this was a good joke. Dickinson said life in the Dublin slums could get a lot more interesting in the weeks ahead if the yobs had managed to pick up the gear they had on board. Everyone except Morgan laughed again with the easy comradeship of men who have often worked together. Dunlop continued to give them a short briefing, talking to the other three as if Morgan was not there.

Out in the Dublin night there was a squeal of tyres as a driver, probably drunk, tried to accelerate fast away from the hotel. The dance floor was no longer pounding. They had switched to slow songs, a mournful beat from black American soul singers. Morgan could imagine the dancers propped against each other, slowly circumnavigating the hall. Someone said a few words in a guttural grunt from the car park. A car door slammed.

Morgan knew Crawshaw's bribe was as good as anything he could ever have asked for, perfectly pitched to make it the kind of thing Crawshaw believed Morgan really wanted. They would have established from his file how he had repeatedly asked to make a proper documentary series and had always been turned down. They would know from the Capital television doctor and from office gossip about his drinking, and they would have guessed fairly easily about the stresses on his marriage. It would not have been so difficult. Maybe they even knew about the abortion? He could not believe that. No. If they did, they would have found some way of using that against him too. They did not know. For a moment Morgan wanted to call Emily and ask her advice, but it was almost two in the morning. Anyway, what could he tell her? That this one trip that he thought might put him back on course again was going to end up with him dead in some foreign ditch? That he could not make it work? That he was to be rewarded and go off to Brazil to make a series of documentaries? What was it – a promotion or a death sentence?

He stubbed out the remains of the cigarette and decided to hold off having another one. He knew he would smell like an ashtray and feel ill in the morning. What the hell. Feeling sick was the least of his problems. There were times when he had joked about going through a mid-life crisis, trying to adjust to the limits of his blunted ambition. He was never going to be a big television star with his own chat show and a fan club. Nor was he going to become a new Woodward and Bernstein uncovering the political scandal of the century. Morgan was, he was sure of it, a competent and experienced hack who knew a good story when he saw one and knew how to tell it. He could cope with the new triviality expected of him on satellite television and still earn enough money to keep the building society off his back, get pissed and fed and if he was lucky, keep his family together too. He loved his wife. He loved his children. They loved him, and Emily loved him sometimes. It was not so bad, yet it was not so wonderful he would be desperate to defend it from any major jolts which could move it in another direction. Three years in South America. It would show he was being taken seriously again. It could be the big break he had wanted for so long.

The only thing which did not entirely compute was the bizarre appeal from Dunlop to his moral sense and his patriotism. If he knew Morgan's character from the files, why was he trying that sort of stuff? Whatever information they had on him was not particularly acute, or maybe they saw the world in such a fixed way that they assumed everyone was like them, ready to fight and die for Queen and country if only they could be lucky enough to be given the chance. Surely they must have known – if they knew he drank too much – that he was not going to buy that kind of argument?

In the past, when Morgan had drunk too much and stood around the bar arguing with the others at CTV about the ethical dilemmas of their profession, he had always told them he thought he could avoid all political attachments because he was a journalist,

187

someone who might report on other people's wars but certainly was not going to bleed in them. When he was trying to be particularly impressive he would say that when he used to read Malraux and Camus and Sartre and other literature of commitment it was as if it were written by intelligent aliens from another planet.

'Who would volunteer to fight in the Spanish Civil war now, on either side?' he remembered saying. 'Would you go? You? To defend the beaches of Benidorm from fascist tyranny?'

He had swayed and gestured loudly, pointing to each one in the bar in turn, asking them if they would sign up for Franco or the International Brigade.

'Idealism,' he shouted. 'Horse shit. Not any more. That's what we've done. Television. We've created the Ironic Age where nobody takes anyone seriously any more. We know that Andy Warhol was right. Everyone is famous for fifteen minutes and ten minutes after that they are in disgrace. It's exactly the same with all the world's great causes. Nobody thinks they look so great any more.'

Nobody had contradicted Morgan at the time, either because they agreed or because they were all as drunk as he was. Somebody said not even Jesus would survive twenty minutes on 'Panorama' with Sir Robin Day.

'But he'd have to come on,' another voice added. 'He couldn't get Christianity started without coming on television. Not now.'

Everybody laughed, except Morgan. They had missed the point. Dunlop, Barwood, Hinkley and Dickinson; O'Neill, Martin Anderson and all the others were men who fought because they wanted to fight, for causes they wanted to succeed. They had somehow missed out on the fact it was an Ironic Age. They were completely out of tune with the times. Morgan was right. The people on the Clapham tube thought like him. They did not much care who inherited Ireland, the terrorist bombers with their beards and blank eyes and lying propaganda, or Crawshaw's friends with their starched cuffs and well-pressed suits. The people on the Clapham tube were not going to inherit anything. Neither was he. Neither, if he but knew it, was Dunlop or Dickinson, Hinkley and Barwood. They were just the new cavemen of the Ironic Age.

Morgan cheered up at the thought that, however it worked out, there might just be a book in it after all. When the heat was off he could explain in print how he was sucked in by one side to betray the other. He might be able to write it from the relative safety of Rio de

Janeiro or whichever exotic hole they were prepared to find for him to make his documentary series. He might get himself killed in the process. He lit another cigarette and lay back on the pillows, puffing hard. He might be killed anyway. Crossing the road. Choking on his beer. From cancer. The method did not much matter. The time would not be of his choosing. Once you recognised that, you had to relax.

What drove Dunlop? Hinkley and the others were goons. If they were not doing this they'd be robbing banks or climbing mountains. But Dunlop was intelligent. Maybe he really was a Ballymena bigot with a few old scores to settle with the IRA. Who knows what these crazy Northern Protestants think? It had to be some kind of tribal hatred or desire for revenge that drove him. How else could you explain what was a real enthusiasm for what he was doing? Action Man soldier, maybe in the SAS, maybe the real James Bond. Who knows? Morgan admitted that he was partially impressed by Dunlop's apparent moral certainties, the assurance with which he could say he was with the 'good guys'. There was something quite likeable about him, his decisiveness, his energy. What Morgan distrusted was the idea that here was a man with a mission – he'd even used the word – 'their mission'. What kind of talk was that? Morgan had heard too much of it already in Northern Ireland. What having a mission meant was the ability to confuse energy with morality, or self-righteousness with doing the right thing. Just because Dunlop was an enthusiast did not mean his cause was worthwhile. Just because P J O'Neill was a good talker and would come over well on television did not make him any less of a murderer. Morgan had seen it all before in the 'Summer Crusades' on the Antrim coast when Protestant preachers in large marquees would rant before audiences about sin and salvation, and bring lost souls back to Jesus. Dunlop was on some other crusade, but the hymn tunes were the same. Hitting the Godless terrorists, the children of Rome, the Whore of Babylon smitten with Calvinist zeal. Dunlop had tried to make Morgan's choice of whether or not to help him sound like the choice between the Kingdom of God and aiding Satan.

'No man can serve two masters,' he remembered one of the County Antrim preachers yelling at his congregation. 'No man can serve both the Devil and the Lord. Choose. All children of the Lord must choose, and in so doing choose the difference between Eternal Life and Everlasting Damnation.'

At the time Morgan had chosen. He had chosen to get out of the tent and leave the evangelist preaching to the morons who were unable to think for themselves. What kind of choice was that? Of course he was against sin and loved motherhood and apple pie. So what? Morgan knew he had the luxury of thought, he could reason things through, however difficult. The trouble was that Dunlop was no hick preacher on a summer crusade, and Morgan could not run out of the tent. He was trapped in its folds. He lit yet another cigarette from the butt of the last.

It was now shortly before two o'clock in the morning. The effects of the Guinness had almost completely worn off. He felt clear-headed and sober, wide awake. Something came into his mind from two or three hours before, the moment when Dunlop had strayed from whatever script he had written for their encounter. Morgan had said something about betraying people being against every professional judgement, every ethic of his job. He would never work again if he did it, and deservedly no one would employ someone with a track record of treachery as a journalist.

'I'm not supposed to reveal my sources,' Morgan said ironically. 'Never mind actually betray them to the other side. How could I look at my face in the mirror in the mornings if I did what you are suggesting.'

Dunlop had hissed at him with genuine passion, his Ballymena accent strongest now he was angry.

'Journalists' professional ethics,' he spat out with contempt. 'Like a hoor's morals. Lives are at risk and you tell me this about ethics. Christ, man. Can you not see what kind of a hypocrite it is that you are?'

In the orange glow of the hotel room some three hours later, with the drink dying in him and the coldness and the loneliness of it all upon him, Morgan could not recall how strongly he had agreed to go through with what Dunlop wanted. It was not as if he had been convinced by any kind of argument. It was more that he had grown tired of being lectured, tired of sitting with Dunlop and the three virtually silent members of the film crew. There came a point when he had said yes to Dunlop. Yes. *Yes*. Whatever you want, Harry. Yes, Harry. Certainly, Harry. All with sufficient sincerity to allow Dunlop to draw the discussions to a close, but at the same time to leave the question of whether Morgan could be trusted in some doubt.

Dunlop had advised Morgan to go to bed. He was happy to

oblige, to get away from them and to sleep. He was not sure they really believed his acceptance of the role they had created for him. He was not sure he believed his own words either. He had the feeling that he was taking the line of least resistance rather than choosing which side to settle on. To have said 'No' would have meant a strong decision. He would have had to work out whether to betray them to the Provos or the Press, or just to walk out and get the next flight back to London. To say 'Yes' meant doing what the prevailing wind was doing, to bend like a reed in the gusts. It was the sensible thing to do. His only real fears were less about what he had eventually agreed to than about his own dignity. He wondered whether he should have put up a better fight against Dunlop before surrendering. What the hell. The battle was lost.

There were only two cigarettes left in the packet. The music had stopped in the disco. The dancers had paired off and the drunks were being cast out into the Dublin night. He could hear the banging of car doors and the clatter of unsteady high heels across the car park. There was nothing heroic to be done. There was no grand sacrifice. The clamps were coming for the foetus and it would surrender with ease.

'Goodnight now. 'Night. Night, then. T'anks a lot now. Night.'

That was it. The choice had been made. The choice was not to choose any more. He would have to lie back and think of England. Or Ireland. Or South America.

Chapter Sixteen

County Louth

Gordon Durrant rose early and listened. Sometimes if they had a heavy night he could hear the Boxer or the Skull snoring, but now the house was quiet, like a church before the morning's first service. He rubbed his eyes with the back of his hands and stretched himself. He pulled back the blankets and stood naked on a patch of carpet, staring at the window. On an impulse, he took a pace forward and began gently easing a corner of the curtain away from the window. Inch by inch he unpicked the dusty smelling cloth from the nails until he had uncovered half the glass. He stopped and listened again. There was still no sound, except for his own breathing. He rubbed his forehead with the back of his hand and noticed he was sweating. Then he pressed his head tightly to the glass. It was wonderfully cool to the touch. Looking downwards he could see through the slats in the shutters what was obviously a concrete path round the outside of the house. He closed his eyes and smiled. It was his first and only glimpse of the outside world in days that now seemed like months. Or years. This dull patch of grey concrete a few feet from his nose was freedom, a different world from the patch of colourless room in which he now stood.

Durrant stared at the concrete again, and the early morning light made him feel like yelling out in triumph. He wanted to rip back the curtain properly from the window and bathe in the light, but it would have been a futile and passing ecstasy. There was work to be done. He began to examine the window frame with great care. The shutters had a makeshift appearance, screwed to the wooden frame rather than bolted properly on to the brick work. There was what looked like a heavy metal rod or rods strapped across the front of them, the bars on his cell which ensured he could not force his way out. It was a poor man's prison, but one from which he could not escape without tools or explosives. Durrant had repeatedly turned

193

over in his mind all the different strategies for escape. There was only one plan which made sense, and he would have only one chance to make it work. If he tried and failed they would either shoot him or make his life so impossible that death would be preferable. He was sure their attempts at humanity were based on the assurance of his cowardice and broken spirit, and once he had demonstrated that he was like any prisoner of war, a man whose main duty was to escape, their whole attitude would change. They would probably keep him shackled and blindfolded, except when he had to work. He knew it would drive him towards insanity. He clenched his fists, and took a deep breath. One chance, which had to succeed.

Durrant had listened carefully every time the Boxer went out to buy food or collect equipment. By the sound of the car he appeared to turn left at the end of the drive. Left, Durrant was sure of it. Time after time. The Boss had arrived at least once from that direction too. So did the Girl and the Thin Man, regularly. The only sensible inference was that the nearest town lay in that direction. Or the main road, or whatever tokens there were round here of a greater civilisation than the bungalow. After the escape, Durrant would run in that direction, though he questioned how far his fitness had degenerated. If he did not kill them all during the escape, they would catch him again. No mercy.

He had tried timing their shopping trips. When the Boxer forgot to buy something and was forced by the Skull to go back again, he sometimes took as little as twenty-five minutes to reach the shops and return. Durrant assumed it might take fifteen minutes to park and queue in a shop and buy whatever it was had been forgotten, which meant it took just ten minutes to drive into town, five minutes each way. At an average speed, maybe thirty miles an hour, then the town was two or three miles away at most. Allowing for traffic . . . even less. A month ago Durrant would have regarded that as a short run, but at his age fitness disappeared quickly and returned slowly. He had not been able to take any real exercise since his kidnap. It was not that it had been forbidden, just that there was so little space and he had been too demoralised to bother. Now that he had decided on the escape plan, Durrant's morale improved. He used all his free time to go through the series of Canadian Air Force exercises he remembered from years before, to stretch and bend his legs and keep his body as supple as he could. Still, the most important thing now was timing. If he hit them during the evening when the Boxer and the Skull were alone and half pickled on whiskey, then he need not worry about how well he could run. He could beat a corpse.

Durrant smiled and took one last look at the sunlight on the concrete. He began pushing the curtain back on to the window frame, hooking the threads on the nails. He fussed over it until it hung as if it had not been touched. Then he sat at the end of the bed and looked at the shapes on the wallpaper, turning the plan over in his mind. At first Durrant had thought that the garage would have been the easiest place to escape from. Only a flimsy metal door separated him from the outside world, and he had a certain degree of access to all the equipment. But he was never allowed to be there unsupervised, and despite the pleasure it would give him to create a demonstration which would blow up in the Thin Man's face, he could not think how it might be done without injuring himself. The only place where he could work unsupervised – apart from the toilet which was too small and depended on him being led there by one of them – was the bedroom itself. The problem was how to get sufficient explosives and other gear from the garage to the bedroom without being caught. He knew that when he began boring them during a heavily theoretical session their attention started to wander. By around half past eleven every morning they were also less than attentive, thinking of lunch, tired after two hours of talk. He had already managed to bring out some detonating powder from under their noses, and some wire.

The worst problem was Margaret. It was fine in the beginning, when Durrant had been too depressed to think of escape or anything like it. There were no choices open to him and his demoralisation had been complete. Then there was a short period when Durrant had been so grateful to be alive, and so thankful that they had not killed Margaret, that he believed everything they said. Be good, and you and your wife will be released. Become a problem, and your wife is dead. Yes sir. No sir.

It took some time before he realised that they could kill Margaret only once. It was a dreadful thing to think, but he knew that their threats were a sign of weakness, not strength. If they killed her, he would not work for them again. If they killed him, they would get no further information. He had, therefore, some cards to play, though he was not entirely sure how best to play them. Mostly he alternated between what he thought of as his soft and hard days. His soft days were those in which Durrant tended to believe them – when it seemed logical as well as humane that they would let him meet Margaret soon, that they would both be released at the end of the training sessions, that it would all end like some fairy tale, happily ever after. On the hard days he was sure that neither of them would ever be freed. It would not make sense to release two potential witnesses who could describe their captors and would stand up in court and ensure that they went to jail. That meant he had to escape, and if they killed Margaret as a result, well, they would have killed her anyway. More likely there would be little point in killing her once he had gone, and they would release her immediately. Unlike him, she had not been giving lessons and so would not be able to identify her captors. She was probably being kept blindfolded all the time . . .

Durrant bit his lips hard until it hurt. He stood up and began his exercises, touching his toes in a series of long stretches. Breathing came easily at first, but he was still not sure how he would stand up to a hard run in the dark, in a state of panic.

'She's a negative asset,' he said to himself. 'They can use her as a brake on me doing anything silly while I'm here, but once I am gone she is of no value to them. There would be no point in killing her.'

He almost believed the logic of that, but had been with the Skull and the Thin Man long enough to know that they operated on a plane quite different from his own. It did not matter. He had to escape, with Margaret or without.

'She's dead anyway,' he thought. 'Why should I believe she is still alive? And why should I be held back here by a person who is no longer alive.'

Durrant pulled the top cover off the bed and laid it on the floor. He hooked his legs under the bed and began his sit-ups, slowly at first and then gathering pace. He felt the first aches on his stomach muscles and continued until the pain seemed to numb itself, then he fell back full-length on the blanket and looked at the ceiling.

'Such hatred,' he mused bitterly. 'I've never felt anything like it before, stronger than any love I have for Margaret. I hate them and it will kill me unless I get out of here. They are eating me up, like a cancer of the mind and spirit.'

He pushed some of his hair back from his forehead and rubbed his jaw. He needed a haircut, needed a shave, needed a long bath – everything. He began the series of knee-bends and felt his left knee creak and complain. He tried to regularise his breathing until it came in a proper rhythm. Then he went through the rest of the exercises in order, repeating the sit-ups and the knee-bends until his body ran with sweat, finally throwing himself on the bed, glistening. He ran his hand down his stomach muscles. They were beginning to feel hard.

When Durrant had first slipped some of the detonator powder into his pocket in rolled up filter papers, he had no clear idea what to do with it. There had to be an escape, and a plan would come to him, but for the moment he would take what he needed when the opportunity arose. Then he remembered that they had bought him – at his insistence – a cheap Parker pen which used plastic ink cartridges. He hid the powder in his room until he had time to squeeze the ink down the toilet and wash the cartridges thoroughly. When they were dry he half-filled each with the powder. The squat plastic shapes felt good between his fingers. They even looked like detonators. Durrant smiled again. He wondered if the Thin Man would think of such a thing for his home-made efforts. He doubted it.

What Durrant most needed was explosives. Everything else would be simple. Without explosives he could do nothing. A quantity sufficient to get him out and prevent pursuit was bound to be bulky. They were extremely careful not to let him near any of the explosives in the garage. Under instructions from the Thin Man they had separated his equipment into three piles. All the commercially made detonators and most of the gelignite had gone completely. For all Durrant knew, they were already in bombs exploding in Northern Ireland.

The second pile included the few remaining sticks of gelignite, the Magnex magnetic explosives and plastic explosives which were locked away in an old metal safe in the corner of the garage. Durrant was not allowed to take anything from it. When he wanted to show them something which demanded his handling of PETN or RDX they would take it from the safe and bring it to him at the table. One of them would always stand back, hand on the gun in his waistband, as if to show Durrant that one mistaken move would be his last. It would be impossible to steal anything.

The third pile, however, was more promising. They had left in the tea chests in the garage all those bits and pieces which they had decided were not dangerous: the unmarked aerosol cans; the batteries, wires, connectors; a few plugs and crocodile clips; his notes and various pieces of junk. Some of Durrant's chemicals were in the tea chest. Other bottles, including one of hydrochloric acid and another of hydrogen peroxide, were sitting on the garage shelves. The unmarked aerosol cans contained Foamex – foamed explosive – which was not especially powerful but had its uses. None of them had expressed any curiosity about the cans. If they did ask, Durrant had decided to tell them the cans contained an inert fixative for holding detonators in place, which sounded plausible and could not be disproved. Foamex looked like shaving cream, but was made from stabilised plastic explosive which was completely inert until sprayed from the can and mixed with the propellant gases. Its relative lack of punch meant that for any serious military operations it was little more than a curiosity.

'But in the hands of a terrorist,' he used to say, on occasional demonstrations to NATO Special Forces groups, 'this versatility could make it an extremely useful weapon.'

Durrant stood up and began to dress, slowly and deliberately. His body had cooled after the exercises, but fastening each button on his shirt took an effort of will, as if he were preparing himself for the day ahead. He shook his head and muttered aloud, arguing with his inner voice. The weapons of terrorism were what he needed. He had never set out deliberately to kill anyone before. It was a different feeling. He had decided to lose his virginity.

'Perhaps I should ask the Skull and the Boxer,' he thought, 'whether I will feel different afterwards. I might want to smoke.'

Nails, Durrant suddenly remembered. Nails and screws and any other odd pieces of metal. He must have them, they were vital. He pulled on his trousers and tied his shoes. Nails. He had forgotten. He would get them as soon as he could.

Durrant heard a sound in the house which startled him like sudden gunfire. A door creaked open and someone padded down the hallway. His heart pounded as if he were a burglar caught with his loot. He heard the toilet flush, and footsteps again in the hall. A fist rapped loudly on his door. The Boxer.

'Good morning now, prof,' he yelled cheerily. 'Time to get up. Rise and shine!'

Durrant stood bolt upright, full of guilt and fear as if the Boxer had disturbed him with his thoughts spread out on the bed. His breath came in nervous bursts, but he controlled it and tried to make his voice sound relaxed.

'Morning. I'm already up.'

'Breakfast in ten minutes. Busy day ahead.'

It was slightly optimistic. Half-an-hour later, when Brendan Kelly brought in the tray with cornflakes, tea and toast, he asked Durrant if he wanted to pee. He shook his head. The Boxer locked the door in silence. Durrant munched his cold toast without enthusiasm and swilled down the tea. It was the worst moment of the day. It was like the hour before an examination when you sit waiting to receive the paper, wondering if you have revised the right questions. There would be the first encounter with the Thin Man which could set the tone for the whole day. For more than a week he had disappeared, and then the day before he had turned up again looking fit and relaxed, as if he had taken a short holiday. His mood seemed much the better for it. Then he had taken the sulks – something the Skull had told him, Durrant surmised. He had heard their raised voices during the lunchbreak when he himself had been kept in his room until almost three o'clock. Whatever they had been arguing about, it left a gulf between the four of them. For the two hours or so which remained of the work, the Thin Man had been at his charmless best, taking out his spite on Durrant. The Girl (who seemed more like the Thin Man's lover as Durrant watched them in each other's company), the Girl too, had given him a hard time. She was like the Tomboy who wants the men to realise she is tougher than anything they could pretend to be. Durrant had often wanted to say that to her face, but was too afraid. When the Girl and the Thin Man had gone home at the end of the day's work, Durrant had taken a chance. He made the comment about the Girl to the Skull as they offered him a glass of whiskey in consolation for all the troubles he had endured during the day.

'Ach, her,' the Skull scoffed, wrinkling his wide forehead. 'She's only an ould bitch. Permanently the bad time of the month with her. Don't pay it any mind.'

That night it seemed the row between the Skull and the Thin Man had created a peculiar comradeship with Durrant. Nothing was said, but the Skull appeared to harbour some kind of guilt that Durrant might suffer the Thin Man's cruelty as a result of his own conflict. Durrant said, experimentally, that he felt a bit like the dog who was mistreated by his master because his master had been having problems with his boss.

'Could be righter than you know on that score, prof,' the Boxer had responded. The Skull nodded silently. Neither of them explained any further what the argument had been about.

Durrant finished his breakfast and heard a car draw up the gravel driveway. It approached as usual, from the left. He heard the voices of the Thin Man and the Girl. They seemed to be friendly enough. Durrant pushed the breakfast tray to the middle of the bed, his body tensing for the knock on the door. He stood up and stretched.

'Another day, another dollar,' he muttered aloud.

The Boxer came for him, rolling back the locks and standing in the doorframe. 'Yes, you guessed, prof. It's that time again.'

Durrant complained that it was like being a worker on the Ford production line – getting up at dawn, bolting his bits and pieces together, returning home exhausted.

'Only I'm not on piece work,' he added.

'Ach, we don't get overtime either, prof. C'mon now.'

The Boxer walked behind Durrant through the kitchen, down the connecting passage and into the garage. The others were already sitting round the table like schoolchildren waiting for their first chemistry lesson. The Thin Man looked at Durrant and said a sombre good morning. The Girl, as usual, said nothing. On the workbench in front of them, Durrant noticed a coil of magnetic explosive which they had taken out of the safe. It was like a flat brown snake. Kelly closed the door behind him.

The Thin Man spoke again. 'Right, prof. Magnetic explosives today. Lesson one. The big time.'

All four of them were now facing him. Durrant could sit at the bench if he wished, but he chose to stand. He looked from face to face and guessed that they were in a better mood. They seemed slightly on edge, but it was more with an air of anticipation than of threats or nervousness. The two tea chests were in their usual position, just to one side of the workbench. Durrant began by picking up the coil of Magnex and stroking it gently, like a barber rubbing a favourite leather strop.

'Magnetic explosives,' Durrant announced in his best lecture room voice.

'One of the most significant developments in explosive technology since the Second World War. Magnex for short.'

He began pacing up and down as he always did when he was at his most engrossed, delivering a favourite lecture.

'You will remember that I have described how to shape a charge to direct the blast, that one kilogramme of charge used in the correct way is better than ten kilogrammes where the force of the explosion is allowed to dissipate. Magnex, in essence, does the shaping for you. The explosives you people are now using in Northern Ireland are part of a technology first developed a hundred years ago. Even the military plastic explosives I have described to you are rooted in developments which date from the Second World War. Since then, there have been very few major advances. I do not claim that Magnex is a quantum leap, but what it does is to use the chemistry of Second World War explosives with the blast theory of modern day physics. The result is a charge which an idiot with one hour's basic training could use to peel apart a twenty centimetre thick steel plate.'

Their faces were all upturned towards him, listening intently. Durrant put the Magnex on the bench with a theatrical flourish.

'This,' he said, 'is the explosive equivalent of a hot knife through butter.'

He began pacing again, watching them carefully. Though they had all seen the Magnex a dozen times before, they were staring at it rather than at him, transfixed by its potential. The Girl put a hand to the coil and ran her fingers along it. It felt like dull plastic but with no hint of stickiness.

'You will notice,' Durrant explained, peering into the tea chests, 'that there are two very different sides to the Magnex strips. The explosive itself is the brown side, thick and pliant. On the other side is a thin black speckled strip.'

The four moved closer together. The Thin Man turned the strip over like a schoolchild invited to stroke his first rabbit. Durrant could see the two cans of Foamex sitting on top of the junk in the right-hand chest.

'The black speckled strip is made up of metallic particles suspended in the explosive mixture. They are magnetic and, as a result, the strip can easily be bent around large metal objects – typically round the base of something like an oil platform which is no longer wanted. The small groove which runs along the side of the strip is a method of channelling the shock waves from the blast to produce, in simple terms, a cutting edge about five millimetres thick and as long as the length of the charge itself.'

Durrant was sure he could pick up one of the cans. He could do it now, if he dared. But perhaps now was too early since he would have to hide it for longer in his room. He would collect the other stuff first. He was sure that was right.

'You asked me before if Magnex will detonate effectively under water. Indeed, it was one of the first questions you asked me shortly after my . . . arrival here.'

They were looking at him again. The spell had been broken for a second. It was as well he had left the can alone. Timing was everything.

'As I explained to you then, underwater detonation is one of the principal reasons for the invention of Magnex. The fact that it does have this property, and that when spun off the production line it is possible to produce varying thicknesses, lengths and strengths of charge, makes it ideal for use under water. Oil platforms, wrecked ships, even cutting up a ship for salvage. There are no particular problems with any of that. It will blow a hole as neat as you please in the side of a wreck, open it out like a tin of sardines and not require hours of work as oxy-acetylene equipment does.'

The Thin Man was about to interrupt, Durrant could sense it. This time Kennedy was polite and apologised for the interruption. He had two questions which he said he had put before but wanted to hear the answers again. It was the same old story. Ask, listen. Repeat, check. Ask again.

'What are the most difficult problems when detonating under water?' the Thin Man asked. 'And can Magnex be detected by the same security equipment as is used for gelignite?'

Durrant answered carefully, as if dealing with a peculiarly persistent but not very bright student. Detonation under water, he reminded them, was almost as simple as detonation in the atmosphere but there were two caveats. The timing devices had to be different because the time and power units had to be sealed properly. Wave action could cause problems in certain circumstances.

'As to the second point, I thought I had explained repeatedly that the so called "bomb sniffers" employed at most airports can only detect the least sophisticated explosives. Gelignite will set them off, but then gelignite will set off a good dog. Plastic explosives are much more difficult to detect because they do not vaporise. Until the various governments responsible for their manufacture insert a vaporising agent to aid detection when the material goes astray, they are virtually impossible to pick up on most of the available screening equipment. Clear?'

The Thin Man appeared to accept the point, despite Durrant's exasperated and nagging tone. Durrant enjoyed these tiny triumphs, and had learned how far he could push them, so that his four pupils remained humbled rather than angry. In petty victories his dignity returned. In such circumstances he could feel that he was better than their slave, a man of free will who could make them feel foolish for their naive questions and ignorance. A few days before, while the Thin Man was away, the Skull had confessed that they had serious problems with their radio controlled bombs. Even the Girl had taken up the conversation and had more or less admitted that random radio signal sweeps by the security forces in Northern Ireland had meant there had been half a dozen 'own goals', with IRA men being blown apart by their own bombs. They were convinced that army and police Landrovers had scanners which could detonate bombs several hundred metres ahead.

'There was one I was on near Newry,' the Girl added. 'We had it set up in a culvert and were watching from the County Louth side of the border. We could see a car coming along the road with the Brits about two hundred yards behind. We were ready to set it off and it blew up ahead of time, blew some other civilian car fifty feet into the air. There was nothing left of it, and the Brits got offside.'

'Must have a scanner,' the Skull nodded, his forehead furrowed. 'Couldn't be any other way.'

Durrant knew of at least two simple ways in which they could have made their radio controlled bombs more effective. He had almost wanted to impress them with his easy knowledge, to make them see that even if they had the guns, he had the intellect. He kept silent, and the moment passed. Now he was talking, but something had caught his eye. There was a nail-, nut-, bolt- and screw-holder resting on a shelf by his right arm. Dozens of screws lay carelessly on the shelf in what his captors obviously thought was the secure area of the garage. Durrant leaned casually on the shelf.

'There are details of the time and power units we could discuss later,' he said. 'But first I think we should continue with the precise properties of the explosive itself. Let me give you some figures.'

He picked up a couple of screws and began fiddling with them in full view of the four grouped around the workbench.

'Notice the width of the groove,' he said dramatically, gesturing towards the Magnex on the bench with his left hand while gently pushing a couple of screws into his right trouser pocket.

'The groove is really a channel to force the shock waves from the blast onto the target material in an ordered fashion, producing a surgical cut. It is therefore crucial to the performance and yield of the explosives. Your car bombs in Belfast are probably the greatest

203

waste of explosives and the most inefficient use of material that I have ever heard about. All over the place. By contrast, Magnex is the most efficient directed charge ever to come into production.'

Two more screws and a large nail. It was far easier than he had supposed. Maybe enough for one day. A little more in the afternoon and the Foamex either when he knew Margaret was on her way, or when he despaired of her arrival. He would do it yet. He would do it soon. The Girl asked how the Magnex compared pound weight for pound weight with Semtex H and the other kinds of military plastic. He began to explain with enthusiasm, – it was an intelligent question. He rattled off more figures, looking at the Girl and noticing again how feminine she could look. She was careful in her make-up, and spent time fussing with her appearance, her hair especially. It was in long, soft brown curls, resting on her shoulders and falling in her eyes as she studied the Magnex. From time to time she pushed a stray curl behind her ear, or threw her head backwards and pulled a handful of hair away from her face. It was odd for him to remember what a woman might look like, even to think of her as a woman at all. He wondered what it would be like if she smiled. Maybe she never did.

'And so given the dilution of the explosives necessary in the manufacturing process,' he heard himself saying, 'it is not wholly surprising to find that kilo for kilo traditional military plastic is more powerful. But given the ease-of-use characteristics of Magnex, you will find . . .'

It was then that he realised how to do it. It came upon him so suddenly, as if there was a Muse which produced inspiration in such circumstances. There was a sense of warmth which spread in intensity all over his body to such an extent that he worried he was blushing. At that moment all the different parts of an escape plan cohered. The Foamex, the bits and pieces for the shrapnel, the detonators and odds and ends he had already taken – they all made sense. He knew his lips were moving and his lecture voice was filling the garage, but his eyes and mind were now on precisely how his plan could be carried out, and how he could effect maximum damage on them and still escape.

Durrant rubbed his forehead with the back of his hand and felt it sweating again. He was glad he had not tried for the Foamex, since the sweat might look like guilt and he would have been caught. They were being polite to him now. They were listening with care: The Skull was frowning; the Boxer was rocking on the rear legs of his chair; the Thin Man stared at him unblinkingly; the Girl looked at the Magnex. Durrant paced up and down, trying to cool off. He would show them now. There was a way. Intellect was what mattered, not the simple energy of activists. He could match skill against fanaticism, his doubts against their certainties and still win. He was like a shaped charge, a cut of magnetic explosive. They were the dull weight of one of their car bombs, packed with home-made explosives and blasting out in all directions. He smiled at the thought, and he felt his words singing off his tongue.

'It does not make sense, however, to fail to complete a loop of Magnex, because the system will only function properly when a shaped charge is used to cut right round a pedestal or tear a large sheet from the side of a hull.'

Talking meant he did not have to listen to them. It put him in control for a while. Every time he was forced to listen to their bleating and whingeing, he found a lost cause. It was this that offended him as much as anything. It wasn't just the idea of the kidnap, the threats against him and his wife, the use of his explosives to kill and maim other people. It was the futility of it all, a fact which to him seemed so obvious and to them was a hidden secret. Durrant had become prisoner to a lost cause. Twenty years after they had begun their campaign, they had achieved nothing. The best they could hope for was to be recognised as a heroic failure, their violence a refusal to be pushed gently into historical oblivion. Durrant remembered the Skull showing him the little finger of his left hand, reduced to a tiny stump.

'Detonator,' he said, sucking at his whiskey. 'We had a wee problem with a batch of them. Near took my hand off.'

There was a pause. The Skull had thought for a moment, as if wondering whether he should tell Durrant a family secret. Then he said that one of the wee problems with the detonators resulted in his brother being killed. Durrant shook his head in genuine sadness. It had been one of his soft days.

'For what?' Durrant asked quietly, almost to himself. The Skull looked at him as if he had posed the question of a madman.

'For the Struggle,' he spat out. 'For the Movement.' And then with growing intensity. 'For Ireland.'

'For an Ireland he will never see,' Durrant murmured, wondering at the bizarre trinity: Struggle, Movement, Ireland. The repeated tone of grief in his own voice seemed to calm the Skull. When he spoke again it was far softer, at an almost ruminative pace.

'For a United Ireland that maybe none of us will ever see. But that doesn't mean it's not worth fighting for.'

The gloom had descended on the evening as they all stared at their whiskeys. Then the Boxer had chipped in with his usual justification.

'We fight, prof, because we have no choice. We can't do nothing else.'

'*Ich kann nichts anderes.*'

'What?'

'Oh, nothing,' Durrant said impatiently. 'Just something a German was supposed to have said years ago. It's pretty much the same as you have been saying to me. "I can do no other." '

They let the moment pass in silence. Durrant had taken up his whiskey glass and gone to bed. As he had gulped the last mouthful he had wondered what kind of rational world meant these Catholic 'Sons of Ulster' could use the same justification for murder as Martin Luther had used to protest against the excesses of Catholicism. Necessity, he thought, was truly the last refuge of the scoundrel, when even patriotism would not do. If they felt they had no choice, what choice had they left him? To escape or not. The only difference was that he was not Irish. He did not want to be part of a glorious failure. He would settle for a success, however grubby. He wanted only to win.

Now in the garage the Thin Man was looking at him curiously. Durrant was winding up his general introduction to Magnex. He would move on to practical problems of application, and then to difficulties under water. When he caught the Thin Man's eye a shudder of fear ran through him, though he could not understand why. There was something in the look which he could not fathom. The Thin Man's dry skin looked better today, but he had a quickness about him which alarmed Durrant. It was as if Durrant's time with them was at an end, and the Thin Man wanted to hurry it up. Maybe the Magnex was to be the last lesson and he would be killed as soon as it was completed. He was Scheherazade, running out of stories. Durrant took a deep breath.

'Any questions on this general part,' he asked, 'before I start on the specific problems of detonation.'

There was silence. He looked at their faces, turned towards him. He pushed the hair back from his eyes and prepared to continue. It would have to be soon, Margaret or no Margaret. He could do it without any worries. He would kill them all if he could. Even the

206

Girl, with her carefully tossed hair and unsmiling lips. Especially the Girl. He could enjoy any of it. He would gloat in their blood, in the death of the losers. It would have to be soon.

'Right,' he said, catching the Thin Man's gaze. 'We move on.'

As he spoke and paced up and down, through the lining of his trouser pocket, Gordon Durrant could feel the prickle of metal. More than a dozen nails and screws chafed through the cloth. He smiled with delight as their points scratched on his thigh.

Chapter Seventeen

Dublin

It was seven in the morning and the telephone shrieked beside Morgan's left ear. He was already awake. He had dozed a little through the night, lying on the bed fully dressed in his crumpled clothes. For a moment he thought it must be his wake-up call, but he had not ordered one.

'Morgan,' a man's voice rasped. It had a Dublin accent.

'Yes.'

'Are you fixed for today?'

'Today?' At first he did not understand. Then he sat upright in the bed. He saw Charlie Barwood sitting on the couch, motionless, watching him. He remembered.

'For today, yes. It's today is it?'

The Dublin accent did not respond.

'Leave the hotel at ten o'clock this morning. All of you in two cars only. Drive to Phoenix Park, to the Wellington monument. Park at the roadside and leave the crew sitting in the cars. You and the producer walk up to the monument. Be there by ten-thirty. You'll be met eventually. Got it?'

'Wellington monument at ten-thirty.'

The Dublin accent hung up without any more talk. The sun was streaming through a gap in the curtains. Morgan swung his feet off the bed and sat on the edge, shaking himself awake, rubbing his jaw with the palm of his hand. He walked over to the window and pulled the curtains back, staring east and south towards the Wicklow hills and the blue sky beyond. It looked like it was going to be a perfect day for filming. He took a deep breath. Barwood, without saying a word, stirred from the couch and picked up the telephone.

'Harry? It's Charlie. It's go for today. Phoenix Park by ten-thirty this morning. No. Yes. No, he did okay. You want me to come in for a talk? Okay.'

Barwood turned towards Morgan and told him he was going to see Dunlop.

'Meet at breakfast in half an hour,' he said, and then as an afterthought, 'you did all right, fella.'

As soon as Barwood left, Morgan filled the basin in the bathroom to the brim with cold water and ducked his face underneath, splashing the floor. It had to be today. They would want to get it over with. O'Neill's whole career had been built on his decisiveness, seizing the chances that were offered to him. Now he had decided to do it, and to do it as soon as he could. Well.

In the glow of the shaving light and by the tints of the mirror Morgan thought he did not look bad, or at least as bad as he felt. He prodded the lines round his eyes and the bags underneath. It made him think of something he had not remembered for years, the morning after he first slept with a girl, almost thirty years before. He had peered into a mirror in his parents' house in Cardiff and wondered whether he looked any different, whether there was some outward sign of the new inner turmoil. They always said at his school that you could tell whether a girl was a virgin or not just by looking at her. Maybe they were right. Maybe in Phoenix Park in a few hours time someone would notice the lost innocence and begin asking questions. If so, he was dead.

Morgan pulled off his bathrobe and dropped it in the puddle on the floor, turned on the shower and stepped into the scalding blast. He pressed his head under the shower until it ached from the sting of the water. When he stepped out he began to feel better. He liked the freshness of the white towels on his body, wrapped himself in three of them and shaved with some care. He chose his shirt and tie with almost as much attention as he used when he presented programmes from the studio. He smiled at the thought of the performance he was about to give, a live performance without the benefit of a properly written and fully rehearsed script. The joke was that he had never formally agreed to do anything. Neither Dunlop nor anyone else could say he had truly said yes to being part of their plans, but it was obvious that he acted and thought as if he was now inextricably bound up with them. He had volunteered, and they were taking him for granted, apparently trusting him enough to leave him alone without the benefit of Barwood's company. The result, now that Barwood had gone, was that Morgan could pick up the telephone, call Sinn Fein's offices in Parnell Square and confess all.

Morgan knotted his tie hard on his throat. He wondered why he had not said anything to the Dubliner on the telephone. That would have been even easier. He could simply have said 'It's all off', or 'We're being watched', or any of a hundred different excuses which would have blown the whole project out of the water. In that half-awake moment he had chosen the line of least resistance following Dunlop's principles to the letter: agree, don't explain or apologise; just say yes. It was hardly a sign of his commitment. Trying to phone them now would be to take a truly active part in betraying Dunlop and the others. He combed his hair back from his face and rubbed his cheeks until they began to show red.

Normally Morgan rehearsed major television interviews with great care, playing both parts simultaneously, trying to guess where the interviewee would move in response to his questions. At such a time he always rose early, before the crew, breakfasting alone with his notebook. He would do the same today, playing the game to the last letter of perfection. Morgan pulled the notebook from his brown leather bag, selected a couple of pens and tried to think how he could interview O'Neill under the new circumstances. How should he begin? Question One: 'Mr O'Neill – you see that big Ballymena man behind the camera, says his name is Dunlop? He is actually a Brit spy. You didn't know? Well, how interesting. Do you mind telling me how you feel about that? Your initial reaction?'

Morgan adjusted his tie again in the bathroom mirror and went downstairs. He sat in Jury's coffee shop drinking orange juice and eating through a traditional fried breakfast. It was what film crews always called the Irish heart-attack-on-a-plate: two fried eggs, bacon, sausages, black pudding, fried bread, potato bread and soda scones. Morgan did not feel hungry, but knew he could be about to spend the rest of the day chasing half way across Ireland in pursuit of a chimera. The supposed meeting might just be another one of their tests. It had happened like that to him before, changing cars, shifting camera equipment in and out, driving from Belfast to Derry to Donegal to Sligo and back again to Belfast without ever finding the IRA men he was supposed to be meeting. This time with O'Neill, Morgan had the impression that there would be no messing about. Either he would have said no at an early stage, or he would go ahead promptly to get it out of the way – and that appeared to be the option he had chosen. Besides, Morgan thought, pushing another rasher of bacon to the back of his mouth, he would not have felt truly back in Ireland without the impossible breakfasts and the bitter, weak coffee.

When Dunlop arrived he was objectionably cheerful. He loped across the coffee shop in yet another of his casual shirts, with the same jeans and sneakers. He offered a too-hearty good morning and then made some small talk to Morgan about the Ulster fry looking good.

'It may be an Ulster fry where you come from,' Morgan retorted, 'but down here it's just a fried breakfast.'

'Ach, we're being political early this morning.'

'Just a bit. I've got an interview to work on before we go. Unless you have any objections and would prefer to call the whole thing off?'

'Not at the moment,' Dunlop said. 'Anyway, I hear from Charlie that you handled things all right on the phone.'

Morgan shrugged.

'Then welcome on board, Tony.'

There was a silence while Morgan pretended to be thinking of his next question for O'Neill. He looked up again from his papers and asked why Dunlop had been so sure he would not strangle Barwood in his sleep and run off in the night. Dunlop smiled and helped himself to coffee from Morgan's pot.

'May I?' he asked, after pouring it. 'Ah, well, I suppose I had faith in your good judgement, and I believed in your word when you told us in the end that you were prepared to help us. And I suppose above all there was my profound belief that you have very little choice. You would finally come round to it. I was just hoping you would come round to it soon, before O'Neill made his move.'

'It's curiosity,' Morgan said.

'What is?'

'Why I stayed. I think it's that anyway. It must be the only reason. That, or the sort of sluggishness which means I'm not prepared to stand up and be strong enough against what other people expect of me. Maybe I'm a conformist after all. I hadn't expected that, but I am. I like to please people. I thought never taking part in things was a way of staying above people, but I guess I have no choice now. Like nearly everyone else, and despite what I've always believed, I'm a servant not a master.'

The waitress produced a tray loaded with Dunlop's breakfast and placed it neatly in front of him. The coffee shop was filling up with the early morning Americans and a few businessmen who sat alone at the bar, munching their toast and reading the *Irish Times*. Dunlop had expected, in the end, a degree of complicity from Morgan, but not this. It was a surrender. He cut one of his eggs open and it spilled orange across the plate.

'I should have thought that was the only recognisable journalistic ethic, anyway,' Dunlop said. 'Curiosity. All the rest is bullshit.'

Morgan smiled into his coffee. 'How are we travelling?'

Dunlop dipped his toast into the egg yolk. He explained that he had already briefed the crew and they were preparing two cars, one for Morgan, Barwood and himself. Dickinson and Hinkley would follow.

'That's not normal practice,' Morgan said, surprised. 'Cameraman and sound always travel together. Lights separate. Looks funny.'

Dunlop nodded, and agreed that if it seemed wrong he would change it. He had a mouthful of black pudding and was racing through his breakfast as if he had not eaten for weeks. His metabolism always seemed to speed up when there was a prospect of some kind of action. He was also a little worried by Morgan's help. He had expected a surly compliance. Enthusiasm he could do without. It could be a bluff, yet what was the point? If Morgan had been about to betray them he would surely have done so by now. The longer he co-operated, the more impossible it would be for him to escape from the project. Dunlop had to believe that Morgan was rational enough to realise that there was no sensible alternative. Unless Morgan actually turned crazy, it was likely that he really would co-operate. Morgan was leaning towards him with an air of confidentiality, as if they were about to discuss some business secret or a piece of office gossip.

'Tell me something, Dunlop. Two things actually. What is your real name? It cannot be Dunlop, I just don't believe it. And secondly, can any of those goons you have got working with us actually operate the camera equipment? If they are going to botch the whole thing, I'd rather know now.'

Dunlop smiled, pushed his breakfast away from him and wiped the corners of his mouth with a paper napkin.

'The answer to the first question is yes, of course it is my real name. But then I would hardly say any different would I? There are plenty of Dunlops in the Ballymena telephone directory and at least one will remember me as his favourite nephew. I am sure of it. Unfortunately both my parents died young. As to the second question, the answer is also yes. We are dealing here with a fully accredited ACTT camera crew who can shoot on three quarter inch, although today I have asked for Betacam for improved clarity. The interview, which I am pleased to see you are working on so assiduously, will be beautifully framed. So will the cut-away questions. It will all be produced to the highest technical standards. Besides which, as you must know, and despite all the craft union bullshit talked by the ACTT, any five-year-old child could work a Sony Betacam.'

'Maybe,' Morgan nodded, 'but O'Neill is an intelligent man, and if you or any of your people start behaving like a five-year-old with the camera he will notice and we're done for. Got that?'

Morgan was beginning to feel the peculiar nervousness in his stomach that he always felt before a big interview, as if his whole career would be judged on the results of the one hour talk that would follow sometime this morning. Dunlop had learned all the right television terms. Maybe he had spent a day or so looking at how a camera worked. It would probably be good enough to get past O'Neill. Probably. Morgan worried equally about his own professionalism. Would there be something in his voice or manner that would give it all away? More than anything he wanted to be sure that he would give the performance of his life. He wanted to be thought of as doing well, and despite his strongest feelings that everything was wrong, everything corrupted, he felt pangs of excitement twist within him. He wanted to know how the story would end.

Morgan went back to his room to collect his coat and briefcase. He decided there was one more thing he had to do before setting off; he had to telephone Emily. He paused, wondering whether it was wise, then dialled the number.

'You're up early,' she yawned.

'Oh, I'm sorry. I hope I didn't wake you.'

'No, I'm up anyway.'

'Ah, good,' he responded. 'We should be filming our main interview this morning.'

'Oh, good luck. I hope it goes well.'

'Have you decided about the other thing, or thought any more about it?'

Emily said nothing at first. She could not handle the idea of an early morning row. Morgan's constant attempts to change her mind on the abortion surprised her. It had been years since she had found

214

him with such deep feelings for or against anything, and now his tenacity was remarkable. That, and some of the other things he had been saying about a change of career, had almost persuaded her to give in, to have the baby, to employ the nanny that they needed and get back to work whenever she had recovered from the pregnancy. It would also mean that on the matter of her conscience, as he put it, bearing the whole burden of the destruction of the child, she could feel so much better.

'I have thought more about it,' she said. 'But not differently about it, if that is what you mean. Or not decisively so. You are very persistent.'

She was not sure what to do. She knew her own decisiveness was something false, put on to try to shame Morgan into pulling himself together. Why did some men become like that, losing their motivation and all the energy that made them worth marrying or being with in the first place? When she was honest with herself, the idea of a new child did not matter to her at all. She had made the appointment and would go in to have the abortion in two days time. Or maybe, before then, she would change her mind. Emily knew what she really wanted was to find a way to bring back the husband that she had gradually lost over the previous five years, the husband who once saw how the world could be changed to smooth out all the bumps and hard places, and who now seemed happy enough to change himself to fit in with the bumps. Emily admitted that since the Ireland project started, Morgan had begun to regain his self-respect, even if he had become more cynical about Ireland itself. It was as if work had the capacity to redeem him from himself.

'No arguments,' Morgan said, 'if you have definitely made up your mind. If you haven't, and there is anything I can say, I'd like to say it now.'

He paused, waiting for her to interrupt. She said nothing, which he took as a hopeful sign, and continued.

'I just wanted to say two things to you. One: there is now a possibility of me being transferred to South America to make a series of documentaries over the next three years. If you fancied living in Rio, or Miami, or Buenos Aires or wherever, I think it could be arranged. We'll talk about it when I get back.'

Still she kept quiet.

'And two,' Morgan continued, 'whatever you decide, and how-ever bad I feel about it, I still love you very much, and I'll continue to love you very much even if you go ahead with the abortion.'

He stopped talking and there was a long silence on the telephone. It was so long that for a moment Morgan felt he had been cut off, he was pouring his heart out on a line which had already been disconnected.

'Emily? You still there?'

'Yes,' she said in a soft voice. 'I'm still here, Tony.'

'Forgive me for it all,' he pleaded gently. 'All the stupidities.'

He could hear her sighing into the phone.

'I still have a few qualities,' he went on. 'I can see that if you could love me once and then I changed, if I change back maybe you will love me again the way I love you.'

He could hear her voice at the other end, tense and soft, breathing the words gently into his ear.

'I love you, Tony,' she said, her voice suddenly caught with emotion. 'Be careful, won't you?'

Chapter Eighteen

Dublin

Dunlop and Morgan met in the lobby shortly before ten o'clock.
A group of American tourists waited by the door for a bus trip
to Glendalough and the Wicklow Hills. The Irish Development
Agency was about to hold a seminar for local businesses on how to
attract risk capital from abroad. Two IDA hostesses in shamrock-
green skirts and decorated linen blouses stood in the hotel entrance
directing businessmen towards the conference room, smiling
widely.

Morgan followed Dunlop through the crush. Outside the front
door the crew had parked two Hertz Rent-a-Car Ford Sierras, fully
laden with equipment. Dunlop instructed Morgan to drive the lead
car, and climbed into the front seat beside him. Dave Hinkley, the
lighting man, was already sitting in the back seat. At ten o'clock
Morgan started to move out of the front gates of the hotel car park
into the brightness of the morning. He looked to see if there were
any obvious Provos checking their departure, or anyone from the
Gardai Special Branch. The street was quiet except for half a dozen
taxi drivers standing by their cars at the rank on the corner, joking
and laughing in the sunshine.

They drove past the American Embassy and then through one of
the red-brick Georgian squares near St Stephen's Green. The
Grafton Street end of Dublin was alive and prosperous, as Ireland's
middle-classes went shopping, dodging in and out of expensive
boutiques and antique crystal and silver shops. They turned the cars
towards the Liffey. The sun was glinting on the river's surface as it
pushed like green oil towards the sea. A rag-and-bone merchant
whipped his horse past the entrance to the Four Courts, cursing as
the animal, flanks heaving, strained to make speed along the river
side. Morgan ensured that the other Sierra was behind him at each
set of traffic lights. Dunlop adjusted the mirror at his window to see

217

whether they were being followed. For the moment, he was more worried about the Irish police than about the Provisionals, but there was no sign of anyone in pursuit. He used the portable radio to make sure that the other car could hear them.

'Okay and clear,' Dickinson said.

Morgan glanced from the road and looked at Dunlop. He noticed for the first time that Dunlop was wearing a bulky and expensive leather jacket over his tee-shirt. It was too good to resist.

'Did they tell you to dress like that?' Morgan asked. 'Or are you doing it for a dare?'

'What do you mean?'

'Well, it's just that in your leather and jeans and training shoes you look like a caricature of every film director I've ever worked with. Pity they forgot the gold medallion, and the pen round the neck. I suppose you've got a clipboard too?'

Dunlop did not reply, and Morgan looked in the mirror to catch any reaction from Hinkley's face, but there was none. Morgan had cheered up. The telephone call to Emily had been painless, almost pleasant. It had been a long time since she had last told him she loved him. He was totally sincere about wanting to save the baby if he could. he thought it might just be possible, but even if he failed, in a curious way all this talk about saving life had somehow pulled him together. It had made him wonder about his own depression, and if it mattered whether he worked well or his career prospered, whether he filmed terrorists in Ireland or some dreary report on the Royal Family in London. It was all the same. If there was a purpose to it, then the life he led would have to be its own goal – just being alive was enough, even if you were destined to be as expendable as a foetus in someone else's plans for the future.

Dunlop's silence contributed to Morgan's cheerfulness. He assumed that Dunlop was feeling nervous. He showed all the signs. Morgan felt completely calm and thought he might even try to work off some of the humiliations of the night before and get himself into a combative mood for the interview by annoying Dunlop and Hinkley as much as possible. If they were determined to force him to volunteer, then the bastards would have to pay for it.

At the edge of Phoenix Park, Morgan turned right up the hill. The tip of the Wellington monument could be seen stretching above the trees, a harsh granite. At that distance it looked of little size or significance. It was shortly after 10.15 am.

'A great soldier, the Duke of Wellington,' Morgan said. 'For an

Irishman. I suppose you are familiar with him, Harry. As a great soldier and an Irishman yourself.'

'I'm familiar enough with him,' Dunlop responded, unimpressed. 'On five pound notes. We have made good time. Drive round the ring road once more.'

A police squad car was coming towards them with the words 'Garda Siochana' in large blue letters on its side. The two officers inside were so busy talking they paid the Sierra scant attention. There were a few cars dotted around the park. A man was throwing sticks for a doberman, which bounded like a demented deer wasting its energy in a futile game. Two boys on BMX bikes were slaloming through a ring of trees, bouncing hard on the rough track. A teenage boy and girl, hand in hand, walked on the edge of the grass, oblivious to everything but each other's company. Dunlop told Morgan to park on the north side of the monument. They got out of the car together leaving Hinkley, motionless and impassive, in the back. The other two had parked the second crew car about thirty yards behind him.

Dickinson and Barwood produced copies of tabloid newspapers and were reading them, looking relaxed and more like a film crew than Morgan would have supposed possible. Dunlop motioned him to start towards the monument. They walked briskly, side by side in silence. The pinnacle of the monument on the flat podium of granite stairs looked vast now that they were closing on it. Morgan had forgotten how huge it really was, erected by a grateful country in memory of an Irish soldier who had saved the United Kingdom in its hour of need. Was Wellington Irish in any way that made sense? Was Oscar Wilde? George Bernard Shaw? The Irish could not choose which Anglos they wanted as part of their heritage, Morgan thought, and which they would rather forget. They could not choose George Bernard Shaw and W.B. Yeats while denying Wellington. If they wanted the British to get out of Ireland, as they kept telling everybody, would they give up all claim to those who were British first, then Irish? Oscar Wilde? Maria Edgeworth? Shaw? Yeats? Lady Gregory?

Dunlop seemed calm enough, but Morgan noticed his speech was quicker and more clipped than before. He wanted to get on with the job, but if there was to be a long wait, Morgan wondered how he might cope. Would he crack if the Provisionals delayed the meeting, sending them round Ireland from corner to corner? They circled the monument, looking around to see that no one

219

had arrived before them, then sat down in the sunshine facing eastwards.

'It's not as impressive, of course, as the lion at the site of Waterloo,' Morgan said. 'As a monument that is. But then you probably know that. Or do Ballymena folk lose interest in battles fought after 1690?'

Dunlop was neither offended nor amused.

'Do you always treat your producers in this way, Tony? A little rough, a little sarcasm?'

'Keeps them on their toes,' Morgan replied. 'And anyway, it helps you remember that I'm smarter and more articulate than you are, which boosts my self-respect. It's not a huge intellectual triumph, but I need all I can get at the moment. Besides, it is also good practice before a big interview to feel aggressive. I mean verbally, of course, not any aggression of the sort you might appreciate.'

Dunlop was barely listening. He was watching a rusty blue Datsun car with two men inside, driving on the ring road around the monument, past their parked Sierras. It did not stop, and from all he could tell at such a distance the men inside showed no interest either in him or in the crew.

Morgan looked at his watch. 10.45. Never on time, the Irish. Not Catholics at least. Prods like Dunlop, hell, *he'd* be on time for his own execution. He'd had the discipline of good time-keeping beaten into him from infancy, never mind what happened to him in the Army. If he really was from Ballymena, he'd probably find basic training a light relief after a Presbyterian childhood. Morgan smiled. That was the difference. Dunlop was trained to think. Morgan was educated to think. It was a neat phrase, and he'd wait for the right opportunity to hit him with it. He pulled his cigarettes from his pocket and offered Dunlop one before remembering that he didn't smoke.

'In the interview,' Dunlop said, 'are you really going to give him a hard time?'

'Does it matter?'

'Of course it matters. He'll be expecting it. If you're soft, he'll be surprised. He's a terrorist. And anyway, Crawshaw said to remind you to give him a hard time. Do your job properly. If you're up to it.'

Morgan said he would give O'Neill a hard time because nothing else was possible. It was rule number one of television. You could invite any bastard on to the screen to peddle his ludicrous propaganda, as long as you were able to show your disdain by being rude to them. He struck a match on the granite base of the monument.

'It is called objectivity.'

'And you have to practise being rude to people in order to beef up your capacity to be objective?'

Morgan laughed. 'No, the rudeness is just a gift. But I like to keep in shape. I like to train in that way. You lift heavy weights or pull the wings off butterflies or do whatever it is you have to do to make yourself such a shit. Me, I just cultivate being rude. Besides which, I did not sleep very well last night. You gave me nightmares, you and the talkative Mr Barwood. And I've discovered after years in the job that when I get tired I don't perform badly. I perform equally as well, but I get grumpy.'

Dunlop said nothing. They sat in silence for a while, as Morgan blew smoke rings into the clear air. It was the kind of day when Ireland can be beautiful and even Morgan could not get enough of it. He wished for an idle moment that they would be whisked off to the Ring of Kerry or the Blasket Islands to do the interview, where Ireland was alive and as unspoiled as it had always been, not in this urban toilet they had for a capital.

Morgan smoked his cigarette down to a butt and stubbed it out on the stone. It was past eleven o'clock and Dunlop's nervousness was growing more pronounced. He stood up and started to walk to the other side of the monument to check the angles he could not see from where they sat. Nothing. After completing a full circle of the base, he returned to where Morgan squatted, hovering close, hesitating between standing and sitting down beside him. Dunlop shuffled his feet and then walked to the corner of the monument a second time. This time he saw the rusty blue Datsun again turn behind the trees and come along the straight section of road on the north side. It stopped, and one of the two men inside got out. He wore a denim jacket and old jeans. The man looked around him, stretched his arms in a lazy sort of way and ambled towards the two parked crew cars.

Dunlop began walking towards Morgan, watching the man constantly. He passed the rear crew car and casually looked in, then he walked to the front car, and did the same again. A few yards after he passed it, he took a sharp right-hand turn across the grass, striding out purposefully to where Morgan sat.

'Morgan,' Dunlop called. 'I think we've got company.'

The new arrival was thick-set and thickly bearded. He could have been the brother of the pudgy Dubliner who had led Morgan to the first meeting with O'Neill, but he was slimmer and taller, with calm eyes. He wore heavy duty work boots with thick rubber soles, and kept his hands in his pockets while he walked. He was chewing gum. When he arrived at the monument he looked at Morgan, sitting on the step and Dunlop standing over him. After a few seconds he nodded.

'Which one's Morgan?'

'Me.'

'How many of youse?'

'Five in all. Two cars. The Sierras over there that you walked past.'

'Who's this?'

'I'm Harry Dunlop. The producer.'

'You from the North?'

'Yes.'

'Sounds like it.'

The Dubliner seemed uninterested. He spat out his gum, and looked around him. The young couple had gone, the man with the doberman had disappeared. The boys in the woods were still running their bike race in the distance. Otherwise the park was empty and warm in the green summer glare.

'You're to follow me in the cars. Tell them in the second car to keep together, because I won't be waiting for anyone who gets lost. Got it?'

Without waiting for a reply, he turned on his heel and strode back towards his car, leaving Dunlop and Morgan ten yards adrift in his wake. When they reached the cars Dunlop told the crew in the second Sierra to stay close, and they set off. The Datsun moved first in the direction of Dublin city centre, and then when it reached the edge of the park turned back the opposite way towards Maynooth. Morgan checked his mirror. Behind the Sierra there had been a coal lorry and a coach, a couple of cars which had turned off, and now nothing. Nothing. He was sure, or as sure as he could be, that no one was following them.

About five miles further west the Datsun turned left past a battered sign for Marychurch. There were a few golfers on a course which had seen better days, pulling their carts up the fairway. On another tee, two women were getting ready to drive off. The Datsun accelerated up a hill and turned left down a narrow track through the trees. At the top there was a wide unsurfaced car park and a ramshackle building four storeys high with wide brown cracks in its white walls. A dull, black-painted sign announced, 'Marychurch Hotel and Country Club'. The Dubliner got out of the Datsun. Morgan could see the other man in the passenger seat, but he did not move. The Dubliner told them to park, leave all their gear in the cars and go inside. They were expected. Even before they could get inside the building, the Dubliner climbed back into the Datsun, turned it round and then drove off. Neither he nor his partner gave them a second glance.

From the brightness and warmth of the day, entering the Country Club was like going into a burrow. It had a dark hallway with a worn chocolate-coloured carpet. The air felt damp, with a vague and indefinable smell which Morgan thought might have been boiled cabbage. Dunlop called out 'hello' twice, but there was no answer. The crew fanned out in different directions down the hallway, and then disappeared into side rooms. Dunlop stayed with Morgan by the reception desk. There was an old and grimy brass bell. Dunlop rang it loudly. Nothing happened. Then he noticed a small dining-room set for about twenty people for lunch. At the end of the room there was a pair of dirty looking swing doors and a young woman pushed through. She was dressed in a black top and skirt with a clean white apron, as if she had inherited her outfit from some long gone but tidy grandmother. She carried a large silver tray filled with cups and plates of biscuits. A cloud of steam and cooking smells followed her from the kitchen.

'Here youse are, gentlemen,' she said, walking over to a table by the window which overlooked the car park. 'Coffee and biscuits. I'll have to go back and get the scones.'

The crew arrived from wherever they had been prowling, as if waiting for the cue. They sat down and Morgan poured cups of coffee for all of them. They shared the silence of non-believers in a shrine, not exactly sure what was expected of them yet afraid to make any noise in case it caused offence. The waitress returned with scones still hot from the baking, pushed them into the open space in the middle of the table and left without a further word. Dunlop refused the coffee and the scones.

'You on a diet, Harry?' Morgan asked, mouth full of warm scone and butter. 'If you don't eat you'll never grow up to be a big boy like Charlie Barwood here.'

No one smiled. Morgan's own stomach was acting a little strangely too. It wasn't just the lack of sleep. He needed to be more careful about what he ate. Maybe he was getting an ulcer. He had refused to go to the doctor, figuring that it would be just another way to force him to stop drinking. He might go and see a doctor eventually. If he was determined to break out into a new life, maybe a full check-up would not be so bad. The time passed so slowly in the silence and gloom that Morgan wanted to sit outside in the sunshine. It was nearly one o'clock and he wondered when the golfers would be coming in for lunch. He was on his fourth cigarette and the coffee had long gone cold when the girl came to collect the plates.

'We were expecting company,' Dunlop explained. 'Any idea when our friends might arrive? The ones who ordered the coffee?'

She had no idea. They did not say.

'Will youse be wanting lunch?'

'Ah, that depends. We'd better wait a bit and see.'

'Only we start to serve it at one and finish at two. So if youse want, just let me know by half past if that's all right.'

There was a noise in the car park and he could see a couple of groups of golfers parking their caddy cars at the door. They went to their cars and changed into ordinary shoes, then came into the building.

'Bar first,' one of them said. 'Then eat.'

'I could murder a pint.'

'Me too.'

'Just try me.'

'You're in the chair, Sean. After missing that last putt.'

Morgan was about to reach for another cigarette. He had it half out of the packet when he heard the sound of a car engine. They all looked up and saw the Datsun return, still with two men in it. The gum chewer in denims got out, the other man was now driving and he remained in the car.

'Right, lads,' the gum chewer said. 'Time to go. Again it's not far, but don't lose us. We'll stop this time if we see anyone caught by the traffic lights. Okay? Right.'

Morgan stuffed the cigarette back into the packet and stood up. Somehow he believed it was now really going to happen. There was an urgency about the gum chewer, as if he had looked over them over and satisfied himself they were not being followed, then contacted O'Neill. Morgan could not be sure, but it seemed less like the wild goose chase he had been expecting. Once, in Belfast, his crew had literally been hijacked and taken to where the IRA were firing a volley of shots in a back alley off the Falls Road. They were told to film it, and make it fast. Today he had that same feeling. For the first time he really believed the Provisionals were going to put up O'Neill and do so without delay. He felt the pulse of excitement beat through his chest.

This time Dunlop said he would drive, and Morgan cheerfully handed him the keys. He did not want to have to think about traffic at a moment like this. He did not want to think about what Dunlop was going to do either. He only wanted to think about the interview, and to hope that Barwood or Hinkley or Dickinson or whoever was going to bug the car was competent enough not to get caught.

The Datsun took the road back to Dublin, all the way they had come before, past Phoenix Park and the monument and along the quays. For a moment Morgan thought they were going to go back to Jury's hotel where the Dubliner would thank them for their interest and suggest they might find it more profitable to interview the Irish Development Agency on the problems of inward investment. Then they were swinging north again, and Morgan recognised what that might mean – the Belfast road and two hours driving into bandit country near the Irish border, an interview in some dirty barn near Camlough or Crossmaglen. Instead they turned east and picked up the Howth Road.

'I told you these guys were cautious, Harry,' Morgan said. 'They let us stew for a while. Then it's round and round Dublin, now it's a trip to the seaside. And maybe another long wait. Think you can handle the pressure?'

Dunlop smiled, concentrating on his driving.

'I can handle it, Tony. And I'm glad to see you're so cheerful. I hope the interview is going to be good.'

'Oh, it'll be good all right. You might even learn something. You never know.'

They lost the working-class houses of the north Dublin council estates and passed into the open countryside near Howth. The houses were large and secluded, tucked behind trees and sand dunes. It was golf club country, and Morgan wondered if that was the key to the new IRA – a developing interest in the middle-class game. Up till now he had assumed their only sporting enthusiasm had been to blow up golf clubhouses in the North. And now they were taking them here. Morgan was about to tell his latest theory to Dunlop, but paused when they were passed by a couple of Garda squad cars on routine patrol. The Gardai sped past and turned off down a side road. The Datsun continued at a steady thirty-five miles an hour.

Morgan could see the strand now, stretching for miles into the distance. The tide was out and thousands of gulls and wading birds were walking along the shore. A few spun above the gentle waves in wide arcs, their flight disappearing in the brightness of the sky. The Datsun took a sharp right down a lane and along a row of fir trees. There was a large house about a hundred yards away, half hidden by rhododendron bushes. Two cars already stood on the gravel outside, a Toyota and a Cavalier. With the Datsun and the Sierras, that made five altogether. Quite a little party.

Morgan could see some movement in a conservatory at the side of the house, but it was so overgrown with foliage that he could not quite make out what was going on. A face perhaps, a man watching. Then nothing. They halted with a crunch on the gravel, and quickly got out of the car. Morgan felt the chill blast of sea air, a surprise in the sunshine. He buttoned the front of his jacket and stuffed his tie inside. He looked round the front of the house and saw, half a mile away, a solitary figure by the water's edge, a man, hands in his pockets staring at the waves.

'You've to set up the camera and lights in the front room,' the gum chewer said. 'He'll be along shortly.'

Dickinson and Hinkley began carrying gear inside. Barwood brought in lights and all three looked sufficiently like a professional crew for Morgan to cease paying them any attention. The gum chewer left and sent another Provo into the room to watch over them, a slim, hard-looking case with a short, well-trimmed moustache. He rested back on the settee, grim and silent. Morgan sat down in the interviewer's chair and began reading through his notes for the questions. He heard Dunlop asking for the toilet, which he assumed was just another way of looking around the house. There seemed to be people moving about everywhere – Hinkley now with a couple of lights, Dickinson or maybe Barwood playing with a tripod, Dunlop moving in and out with Hinkley. In the chaos of having a film crew with them, even the Provos would get a little confused about who precisely was doing what and where.

Morgan looked round the front room. It was rather grand, lined with leather-bound books and what appeared to be Victorian period oil and watercolour landscapes. A large antique map of the four traditional provinces of Ireland hung above the fireplace. On the opposite wall there was another of similar vintage showing the ancient place names of Leinster. A shiny upright piano stood in the corner. It was the house of an Irish banker or maybe a doctor or university lecturer, with a certain taste and discrimination.

It was not the place to film a terrorist because here he would look like everything he was not supposed to be. Respectable, decent and solid. Maybe even well read. Like a Cabinet Minister. A bank manager. Morgan was sure Hinkley had been assigned to keep an eye on him, and he was bored with waiting for O'Neill. There was no sign of Dunlop, so Morgan decided to make an excuse about having to pick up his notebook, and go out to the car to see what was going on. The hard-faced Provo guard didn't seem to care. Hinkley and Dickinson said nothing. Outside, the gum chewing Provo and his driver were leaning on their Datsun watching Barwood pull boxes from the back of one of the Sierras. Morgan wondered if Dunlop really believed he could plant a device here, right under their noses. He could not be so stupid. Either the whole thing was off, or Dunlop would have to come up with some kind of incident to pull all the Provos into the house. Anyway, which was O'Neill's car – the Cavalier or the Toyota? How would Dunlop find out? Supposing he swopped and took the beat-up old Datsun? Supposing he was not even here, he had decided at the last minute that the Garda patrol just up the road was too close for comfort and disappeared. It could happen. Why not? Still, it was not Morgan's problem if they bugged the wrong vehicle or the whole thing fell apart. He had his own job to worry about, and it would keep him busy enough. He opened the front door of the first Sierra and took out his notebook.

'We'll be ready for him in five minutes,' he yelled to the gum chewer. 'In fact we're almost completely set up now.'

'No problem. You take your time,' the man yelled back and continued his conversation with his driver.

Morgan turned to go into the house when he noticed the man on the beach was walking towards them. He was stocky and smartly dressed, with a thick Donegal tweed jacket buttoned at the waist, his tie tucked inside carefully so it did not flap in the breeze.

It was O'Neill himself, looking as Morgan had assumed he would: respectable, middle-class, yet slightly different from the last time they met. He had grown his beard again. It had yet to thicken fully, but behind what there was, he was beginning to look as he did on the 'wanted' posters. P J O'Neill was going to live up to his image.

'Good afternoon, Mr Morgan,' O'Neill began, stretching out his hand in greeting. 'I hope you have many questions for me today. Good ones – and I hope I have the answers to match.'

Morgan shook his hand and looked him full in the eyes. O'Neill waved to Morgan to go inside the house, a warm smile lighting up his face from edge to edge.

Chapter Nineteen

County Louth

Durrant had been promised a day off. They'd all said they were pleased with him, even the Thin Man. The Magnex lesson had opened their eyes to some new possibilities that Durrant could only guess at.

'It's the tool for the job,' the Thin Man had said, nodding his head enthusiastically. 'No doubt about it.'

What the job was, none of them revealed. Maybe they did not even know. The Skull and the Boxer had told him repeatedly that security was so important within the Movement, that no one asked questions, that you would be told what you needed to know and when you needed to know it. Durrant could not care less. He had done what they asked him, and accomplished it all in a professional manner. Now there was talk of a reward, and that was all that interested him. The Thin Man had suggested it, and the Skull said they would fix it up: a meeting with Margaret as soon as possible. Durrant tried not to become excited. It would either happen or it would not. There was no point in worrying about it or planning for it. They had promised it before and it had never happened. Why should it happen this time?

Durrant had become peculiarly attached to the Skull and the Boxer, and it made him feel embarrassed. There were a dozen small ways in which they could have behaved badly towards him but instead they had gone out of their way to try to make his life more bearable. When they failed to keep him cheerful and he dropped into one of his black days, they would shrug their shoulders and complain with him, as if they were all equally victims of an inhumane system that no one could be blamed for. Despite Durrant warming to those two, the Girl and the Thin Man remained strangers, terrorists and captors and barely human beings. He was sure that if any of them were to kill him, it would be one of these two.

229

The Girl would toss her hair back from her face, curl up a soft and reddened lip, and fire into the back of his head. The Thin Man would do it without thinking, an automaton who would be as pleased to murder as to eat his breakfast. Yet somehow Durrant was sure that the Skull and the Boxer would not be able to kill him now, unless he did something stupid. Like try to escape.

'I didn't know you accepted women in the IRA,' Durrant had said one night to the Skull and Boxer over a whiskey. The Skull had wrinkled his forehead and muttered a few words half to himself.

'She's not a woman. She's a soldier.'

'Well, maybe,' Durrant agreed, 'and maybe I'm getting old and out of touch with things. But why isn't a woman like that married and bringing up a family?'

The Boxer helped himself to another drink and pushed the bottle towards Durrant. For some days he had been accorded the privilege of pouring his own whiskey. If he did not think too hard about the day's work or the loneliness of his bedroom he could almost imagine himself on holiday in a friend's Irish cottage.

'Sometimes,' the Boxer said, laconically, 'talking to you, prof, is like talking to someone from another planet. She's from West Belfast. Her boyfriend got shot by the Brits a few years ago. Tried to ambush a foot patrol when the magazine fell out of his Armalite. They heard the clatter of the metal on the pavement – and bye bye boyfriend. She was already in the Movement then, like, but it helped make up her mind for her that there was no point bringing up children in a country like that.'

It all made sense of a sort to Durrant, or at least it was coherent. But night after night he began to think he was watching the rehearsals of a Provisional IRA Repertory Company. The men would tell him stories. Some were probably true, others false. Many he could not decide. All of them were spun out with verve and emotion and Durrant was sure that, during the moment of the telling at least, each story was believed by the Skull and the Boxer themselves. Each little tale pointed inexorably towards propaganda, with the result that Durrant thought more and more of his old history lessons about the first year of the First World War. He could recall all those stories of babies being bayoneted by advancing German troops in Belgium, the rape of the poor neutral country which had encouraged young men to volunteer for service in the front line. But there was something about the Skull's stories which had an even more haunting quality, something beyond propaganda, like a myth or some sort of religious truth enshrined in the text.

'Provisionals' Parables,' he once said to himself. 'Like the tales of a new religion, recited as part of the Creed.'

The Thin Man continued to make Durrant nervous. It was partly because he seemed so ill at ease with himself, as if he spent his whole life believing it was an examination, as if one mistake or a stray laugh could result in failure. His staccato questions cut the air in the garage like pistol shots.

'How big a detonator for that charge?' Durrant would begin to answer. 'Do I need a booster charge or not?' Durrant would begin again.'How do I join the Magnex together to be sure of cutting in a circle?' And again. 'If the target ship could make twenty knots, could the charge come loose?'

It was this last question which appeared to interest the Thin Man most, since he asked it frequently. In the garage, throughout the previous day's session, there had been incessant questions on detonation under water; whether one large charge would be more effective than two small ones; whether a simultaneous detonation was preferable or two separated by half a second. If the vessel moved, would it make a difference? Did the water temperature matter? Would the charge stay fixed in rough seas? Force six? Seven? Right?

If they asked, Durrant answered. If they did not ask, well, he was too tired to think of the questions they should have been asking anyway. That was their business, and so was the secret of the target. Durrant had ceased to be curious. Maybe one day he would read about it all in the newspapers. In the meantime he would get on with the business of surviving.

In their interrogations, he thought they did not miss very much. The Thin Man was by far the brightest, the quickest at taking lateral leaps and seeing how a new or different use could be found for a certain piece of equipment. Durrant could say honestly that he hated the Thin Man, hated and feared him in equal measure, but he would admit that he had been wrong to be patronising towards his abilities. They were not fools, none of them, whatever their other failings. He remembered a phrase from television, when politician after politician would stand up to condemn 'mindless terrorism'. It made him laugh now. If they really believed it was 'mindless' then that perhaps explained why, twenty years on, they had so singularly failed to come to grips with it. If they did not believe it was 'mind-less' then they were treating the British public like children. It was precisely *because* the IRA people were so thoughtful that it made them so evil, Durrant was sure of it.

He enjoyed forcing them to dodge his own enquiries, a petty game which cheered him up. He would respond to their questions with such answers as: 'It depends what sort of ship you have in mind. How big is it?' The Thin Man would duck the question and then hurriedly attempt to change the subject. Durrant was by now sure that the Thin Man knew what target they were about to attack, even if the other three had not been told. That, and the fact that he had very little left to tell them, meant Durrant was sure that the attack was imminent, and that his own fate would soon be decided. If the promises about a visit from Margaret proved true, then it could be a prelude to their release. Or execution.

There had been one bonus as a result of their joy at the Magnex lessons. At the end of the main lesson when he had gone through all the basic craft necessary to use the explosives, the Thin Man, the Skull and the Girl all left the garage at the same time. Durrant could hear them discussing something in hushed voices punctuated by occasional laughter, as if they could not believe the properties of the explosives under their control. The Boxer stood in the garage on guard with Durrant. He stuck his hands deep into his pockets and yawned. Durrant moved towards the Magnex, but the Boxer turned him away.

'You know the rules, prof. You tidy up the wires and all the bits, but stay away from the explosives. I'll sort them out.'

Reluctantly, the Boxer brought his hands from his pockets and began winding the Magnex coils together. Durrant tidied the wires and clips, carefully putting them together. The Boxer locked the cabinet containing the explosives and slipped the key into his jeans pocket. He picked up a copy of the *Irish Independent*.

'I'll get you a cup of tea in a minute, prof,' he muttered and opened the paper, relaxed now that the explosives had been safely tidied away.

Durrant carefully cleaned the work bench, rolling the remaining clingfilm back into its pack, placing all the wires in their box. He saw one of the cans of Foamex sitting on the top and his chest began to thump. He thought the Boxer must be able to hear his breath catch and deepen, but there was no response and the pages of the *Independent* continued to turn. Durrant put the remaining clips into the box and slid his hand on to the Foamex can. He pulled it from the box and stuck it under his pullover, stuffed securely into

232

the waistband of his trousers. The metal touched his bare skin at a gap in his shirt, chilled like the side of a knife blade. He was sure that this time the Boxer would notice his sudden intake of breath. The Boxer looked up from his paper.

'You all finished, prof?' he asked with no real curiosity. 'If you're all set I'll take you inside and get you cleaned up. I'm dying for a taste of tea.'

Durrant was led to the bathroom where he washed perfunctorily, wanting only to get back to his room. Once there, the Boxer locked the door and returned to the kitchen to brew the tea. Durrant hesitated at first, then pulled the can of Foamex from his waistband and pushed it under the mattress at the head of the bed. The slight raising of the mattress was hidden by the pillows. He sat back and breathed heavily. Durrant knew he had to move quickly now. He had everything in place, and the sensible thing would be to make his move that same night, except that the promises about Margaret weighed heavily with him. He would not forgive himself if he acted one day too soon, if he escaped and she was killed. He would wait another twenty-four hours. Maximum. It was their last chance to keep their word. As soon as they brought Margaret to him he would make his move. If they did not bring her, he would move anyway. That evening they said they were prepared to celebrate with him by letting him eat with them for the first time. It was hardly a major concession, but Durrant was grateful to the Boxer for breaking the monotony of the bedroom, where he would just think and worry. They broke open a new bottle of Power's and began drinking deeply as soon as the dinner of fried egg, bacon and sausage had been eaten.

'I phoned the Boss last night, prof,' the Skull said, as if he had forgotten to tell Durrant something which might or might not interest him. The Skull poured a splash of water into his whiskey and took a sip before continuing. 'Meant to say to you earlier. I told him how well you had done, and that we were near the end of what you could tell us. He said that you could see your wife now. He just left it to us to fix it.'

Durrant almost spluttered into his whiskey. It seemed as if they might be serious this time.

'When?' he asked.

'We'll just have to see. We have our own operational factors to consider. The Boss wanted you moved to where she is. Says it'll be better for security. But our friends looking after her want to bring her here, so they can use the garage the way we've done. We'll have to see. It could be as soon as tomorrow. Might not be for a few days. But probably tomorrow.'

That was it. Just a simple statement, as if they were discussing cutting the hedge or having fish and chips for lunch. Durrant's brain was in such turmoil he was sure he must have been abysmal company for the rest of the night. He did not want to talk. He wanted to think. If they moved him now, his whole plan could be in pieces. It would be difficult to bring all the stuff with him, though he could try. There was too much to think about. When, mercifully, it was late enough for him to escape to his bedroom, the whiskey and the excitement made it impossible to think properly and after an hour of twisting and tossing under the sheets, Durrant turned over and slept deeply.

The following day they made breakfast and repeated to him that it was a day off. He could stay in his room and read, they said, though it was an order rather than a suggestion. They were doing something and he was not to get involved. He heard the door slam and assumed one of them had gone out. From the other room he could hear the sound of RTE pop radio. That would mean it was the Boxer who stayed in, and the Skull who had gone out. He was sure of it.

Durrant pulled the can of Foamex from behind the mattress. He weighed it in his hands and checked it was full. It looked like any other aerosol can without the label. He shook it, then took off the top and squeezed gently. A small spray, the consistency of shaving foam though with a metallic sheen like aluminium foil spun out from the can. Durrant wiped the small gobbets of foam from his hands onto the carpet, rubbing them in until they disappeared. Then he replaced the can under the mattress. From the inside of his jacket, hanging on the back of a chair, Durrant pulled out his fountain pen case and checked the makeshift detonators inside. He put them back carefully.

Durrant stood at the washbasin and brushed his teeth hard. He opened his washing bag and pulled out the small plastic pouch now filled with nails and screws, half a pound in weight or even more. Plenty. Everything was ready, except Durrant himself. He kept thinking that they were using Margaret as they had done from the beginning, simply to keep him under control, unable to make decisions in a state of emotional flux. He could wait for her forever. What if they did not move him, and she did not arrive? If everything he needed was in the room, then why not try tonight, with her or without? Durrant shook his head and began pacing the length of the room, four strides one way, four strides back. He thought of it as his caged tiger routine, up and down up and down getting nowhere, but the movement helped him think – the way long walks cleared his mind when he was in Norfolk. He lit a cigarette, and continued pacing.

When he had smoked the cigarette down to its butt, Durrant stubbed it out and again sat on the bed. He stared at the shapes on the wallpaper for the hundredth time, trying to make sense of the forms. He had come to recognise patterns without logic or sense. There was no helping it. That was the way it was. He had tried to impose his notions of order upon it all, on what had happened to him, on what they told him about Ireland, on his plans for escape, but nothing had worked. All he could do was escape from it – there was to be no more agonising.

He lit another cigarette, absent-mindedly. He had made his decision, for better or worse. He rolled back on the bed again, re-set the pillows and closed his eyes. Sleep was impossible, but he needed to rest, happy that the comforting lump of the Foamex can was prodding through the mattress into the small of his back.

Chapter Twenty

Howth

When Morgan and O'Neill entered the hallway they met Dunlop coming down the stairs, drying his hands on a handkerchief.

'No towel,' he said. 'In the toilet.'

Morgan introduced him, and he and O'Neill shook hands.

'Dunlop,' O'Neill said thoughtfully. 'And you're County Antrim by the sound of you.'

'County Antrim is right,' Dunlop agreed. 'Ballymena.'

'Ah,' O'Neill laughed. 'I've often heard it said that Ballymena is a great place to be *from*.'

'You could say so,' Dunlop responded warmly, staring at O'Neill's re-grown beard. 'Anyway, I'm living in London now.'

'A city I like very much,' O'Neill said. 'Only for some reason they have taken against me there. I was served with an exclusion order ten years ago under the Prevention of Terrorism Act.'

'Oh I don't know,' Morgan butted in. 'I'm sure if you made your plans to visit London well known in advance you could be assured a warm enough welcome.'

O'Neill said they were about to have a cup of tea and discuss the interview. Did Dunlop want to join them?

'No, you go ahead. I want to make sure the crew are setting up properly. We don't want to keep you any longer than necessary, P J.'

There was another Provo in the kitchen, which made four of them, plus O'Neill himself. Morgan turned round and noticed Hinkley had followed him.

'Harry said there might be a chance of a cup of tea,' Hinkley said. 'I've done my bit. We're just waiting for the others, then everything'll be ready.'

The Provo passed over three full mugs. Morgan looked to see if any of O'Neill's men were armed, but if they were, the weapons

237

were well concealed. He could not believe that the team guarding P J would not have at least a couple of shorts, but they were being cool and discreet. For now.

He assumed O'Neill had decided to grow back his beard for television, and would remove it immediately after the interview. He would need a better disguise than a mere shave after the publicity the interview would give him. Also the beard was not a complete success – thinner and lighter than the one in the 'wanted' posters, but it did the trick. It made him look more like an Irish terrorist from central casting.

O'Neill asked Morgan to run through a few of the questions. Morgan said he would inform him of the areas he was interested in, but the precise questions would depend on how clear the responses were. He mentioned a couple of the most obvious questions and paused for O'Neill to comment, but he said nothing. O'Neill stroked his beard once or twice, either in thought, or because the newness of it after his time with a completely clean face caused him some discomfort.

'I take it, Tony,' O'Neill began, 'that you will shout at me and be rude during the interview so your viewers know how tough you really are.'

'Maybe,' Morgan admitted, slightly embarrassed at O'Neill's directness.

'There's no "maybes" in it,' he said bluntly. 'I'm not criticising you for it. All I want is your word that whatever histrionics you have to go through to prove how much you are distanced from all of us evil men in the IRA, you do not cut my words about.'

'We have to reserve the right to edit answers,' Morgan explained. 'You can't expect me to surrender editorial control to you.'

'No?' O'Neill responded, matter-of-factly. 'Well, I can insist that you use whole answers, not chop up bits of them.'

Morgan was beginning to feel irritated. Hinkley shifted from foot to foot, taking a deep swig of his tea. The other Provo leaned on the sink, arms crossed as if totally uninterested.

'Look,' Morgan tried again. 'I will do my best to use only whole answers, provided that you keep the average length of an answer down to about thirty seconds. I promise I will not cut you about or distort the sense of what you have to say. It would be in no one's interest to do so. I cannot make you inarticulate or stupid because you are neither. Nor can I make you say things you do not want to say. But I may have to cut bits, and that is that.'

O'Neill's face looked like thunder. For a moment Morgan thought he might pull out of the interview, though he could not think why this sticking point should arise so late and with such vehemence. When O'Neill spoke again he was calm and without rancour. He said he had made up his mind to give the interview, and just wanted it to be handled honestly.

'When will they transmit it, Tony?' he asked amicably. 'If they transmit it?'

Morgan smiled. He said that no date had been set, but he expected they would not want to sit on something like this for more than a week or two. News organisations were so leaky, someone would get word of the interview, and if there was a campaign in the press before transmission, the pressure not to transmit would be strong. O'Neill listened attentively, nodding and asking a few supplementary questions of his own. He seemed to have relaxed, and to be happy to wait for the interview itself to hear the rest of Morgan's questions. Then he stood up and said he was sure they would be ready for them in the other room.

The television lights were full and bright, the room already warm and stuffy. Dunlop stood by the door, Dickinson and Barwood sat together on the sofa. The hard-looking Provo leaned against the piano and was joined by the one who had made them tea.

'You have got to realise that the Republican Movement has every reason to be suspicious of you and your company. I don't mean you personally,' O'Neill said to Morgan, as if carrying on their conversation.

'I know what you mean.'

'The British media have done us few favours in the past. We will watch this film of yours with great interest. If it does not appear within, say, two weeks we will assume that you have been censored more than usual. In that unhappy event we will run a major story in *Republican News*, telling our people what has happened, how we were asked for an interview and how it never appeared.'

Morgan had guessed as much. It was the usual IRA game of heads we win, tails we cannot lose. Since Morgan had played that game in order to get the interview in the first place, he could hardly complain.

'In that context,' O'Neill continued, 'there is one condition for the interview which I forgot to mention earlier, and had better tell you about now. I do not see that it will cause you any problems. I shall record the interview in full on this pocket cassette recorder. A

239

full transcript will be published in our regular edition of *Republican News* two weeks from Thursday. The timing will, I'm sure, give your people plenty of time to edit the programme. From our point of view what we run in *Republican News* will either be a straightforward story plus the transcript or it will be a special "Censorship Edition" explaining how the Republican Movement attempted to give the British media one last chance to play fair but that we were betrayed yet again. As well as the full recording of the interview for transcription purposes, let me introduce to you a comrade of mine in the corner who takes photographs for *Republican News*, Gerry Branagan. Gerry will just take a few black and white snaps of the proceedings when we are all settled down in the interview positions.'

Morgan began to protest about not wanting to be used for political propaganda purposes, but O'Neill silenced him. This time there was steel in his voice.

'Those are the conditions for the interview. They are not for negotiation. If they cause you any grief then that can only be because you already know the interview will never be transmitted, and if you really believe that, you should leave here now without wasting my time.'

Before Morgan could say anything further, Dunlop began speaking. He said it was most irregular to try to hold them to ransom like that, but he appreciated the problems O'Neill faced. If that was a precondition of the interview then they would have to abide by it, though he wished O'Neill had informed them earlier.

'We've got to operate in some kind of atmosphere of trust,' he said. 'I just wish you had let us know your full range of demands before we began so that we could clear things back in London.'

'Don't worry,' O'Neill responded, turning to Dunlop. 'You have my word of honour that no pictures of any of you will be printed in *Republican News* if the film is transmitted.' Dunlop nodded as if satisfied.

'It takes an Ulsterman,' O'Neill continued, looking at Dunlop, 'to recognise reality when it stares him in the face. Let's get on with it.'

The photographer took a few shots of Dickinson lining up his camera on O'Neill, and a few more of Morgan and O'Neill sitting together.

'Please don't take any face-on shots of the crew,' Dunlop asked. 'It's not that we're shy, but Tony gets paid to be a reporter and have his face seen on screen. The film crew do not, and you can make the kind of point you would want to make without readily identifying them. I'm sure you can understand that.'

O'Neill nodded. He was no longer worried about the details. He told the photographer just to take shots of him with Morgan, and a couple of wide shots showing the television camera in place and the back of the cameraman's head. That would do. O'Neill stroked his beard again, adjusted his position on a cream-coloured easy chair, and put his tape recorder on the table.

'Ready?' he asked, and started it rolling.

Morgan began. O'Neill was hesitant at first, nervously seeking for reasons why he might have joined the Republican Movement in 1969, and why he had moved with the Provisionals when they split from the Official IRA.

'Rusty Guns,' he threw out. 'That's what the people called the Official IRA. The men who were great at talking about fighting when they were in the bars on a Saturday night, but who were never able to do anything when their time came. "IRA – the I Ran Away Army" or that's what people were saying about them, and the people were right. There was only one way, for something to be born out of the ashes of those first loyalist pogroms against our people. And that something was the Provisionals.'

O'Neill started to warm up. He admitted that the early Provisionals had no real 'ideology' except to get the British out of Ireland.

'That was ideology enough, or so it appeared in the early seventies. Then we grew in sophistication. Some of us were thrown into jail and we began to read and talk and argue.'

'What did you read?'

'Everything we could lay our hands on. James Connolly, Padraig Pearse, Sean O'Casey.'

'Marx?'

'Him too. And Lenin. And Guevara. And George Bernard Shaw. And Irish history books. Everything we could get our hands on, and a lot of things we were not supposed to get our hands on.'

O'Neill was beginning to sweat slightly under the strong lights, but he was so absorbed in the interview that it did not matter. Morgan, too, had forgotten everything but the interview itself. There were only two people left in the world, and he wanted to extract from O'Neill the points of faith which separated him from all other men, to challenge him at the roots of his belief. They began talking about the violence, and O'Neill parried easily by justifying the 'armed struggle' and the rights of any oppressed people to throw off the oppressor.

'And don't *you* oppress?' Morgan asked. 'Isn't the IRA's boot on the neck of the civilian population in Northern Ireland from whom you extort money, upon whom you prey?'

'If that was anything other than a bit of typical British propaganda, I would answer it at length. But if what you say is true, then why does the IRA have the clear support of the civilian population – support which it has to have in order to survive?'

'Which civilians? What's clear about it? The sixteen dog breeders murdered when the IRA planted a firebomb at the annual Collie Club dinner in the La Mon House Hotel? Did they support you? Did they have a choice?'

O'Neill hit back with the usual litany of British wrongdoing, from Bloody Sunday to internment and the shooting of a twelve-year-old girl by paratroops in South Armagh. Why don't you condemn that? If murder is murder then why isn't it murder if the British forces do it? And so it went. Every time Morgan pushed him on terrorism he replied that it was a war of national liberation and if Morgan wanted to call it terrorism that was fine. But didn't the British now sit down with all sorts of people who were formerly regarded as terrorists? The Israeli government? The successors of the Mau Mau in Kenya? Wasn't George Washington regarded as little more than a terrorist when he freed America from British rule? Not quite. It was the 'whataboutery' Morgan knew he could expect. Every time he made a point about what the IRA were responsible for, O'Neill would dodge the question and say 'what about' something else which the British or the Protestants had done. Round and round the Irish mulberry bush. But whatabout . . .

Then they finished the first tape, and O'Neill asked for water. Barwood went to fetch a glass and Dunlop offered to get a replacement tape from the car. He suggested the man from *Republican News* might want to take a few more photographs now.

'It is going very well,' Morgan said to O'Neill. 'Very well indeed. You look just a little bit hot. Why not mop your forehead.'

Barwood returned with a pitcher of water and two glasses. Dunlop passed a fresh tape to Dickinson and they were ready to begin again. From where he was sitting facing O'Neill, Morgan could not see precisely what the crew were doing and he did not want to turn round and look. He was sure Barwood and Dunlop had slipped out of the room again.

'Running,' Dickinson said. 'Go in five. Quiet please.'

The man from *Republican News* and the other Provo stood still against the piano. There was the sound of a seagull's cry from outside, and perhaps the sound of a car boot springing open. Morgan could not be sure. O'Neill licked his lips and Morgan began again.

'Murder is murder,' he heard himself saying to O'Neill. 'Whether you claim a political motive or not. And you cannot justify acts of IRA barbarity on the grounds that other people act like monsters too.'

'But the British themselves recognise we are a special case, that we are not common criminals or people who can be dismissed with the word "murderer". They recognise that we would not commit crimes but for the political forces around us. That is why they pass special anti-terrorism laws. That is why they have special jails and for a time we were given special category status in prison . . .'

Morgan could see O'Neill was building up to talk of the Hunger Strike now. He knew the rehearsed thought processes and the words before they came. The Hunger Strike it was.

'. . and that came about because the British then tried to stop the special privileges they had given us for so long . . . British hypocrisy . . . human rights . . . martyrs for freedom . . .'

It was all there. Everything O'Neill spoke about had capital letters. Hunger Strike. The Famine. The Easter Rising. Big issues. Big letters. It was time for Morgan to put the boot in again.

'If your actions are justified why does the vast majority of Irish people reject everything you stand for at the ballot box? They reject . . .'

O'Neill's face was tense and alert, listening to every nuance of the question and looking for the weak spot. He was ready for Morgan to pause so that he could seize the chance to answer straight away, for the benefit of the readers of the transcript in *Republican News* if not for the viewers of Capital Television. Before Morgan had finished the question he heard the door behind him swing open. He was ready to yell 'cut' in his irritation, but he saw the surprise on O'Neill's face and he turned towards the door.

Dunlop and Hinkley were standing a few feet apart. Both had Heckler and Koch MP5 sub-machine guns. Dunlop's was pointing directly at O'Neill's chest, Barwood's at the man from *Republican News* and the other Provo. Those two were now pressing their bodies hard against the upright piano as if somehow they might manage to escape through the wood behind, their faces taut with shock and fear. The room was suddenly silent. Dickinson and Barwood moved away from the camera, switched off the strong lights and turned to go into the hall.

'Clear up outside,' Dunlop shouted over his shoulder towards them. 'Bring what's left of them inside and stick it in the kitchen.'

He continued to stare straight at O'Neill whose face was now ashen. There was sweat sticking to the bottom of his beard. Dunlop ordered the two by the piano to sit on the floor with their hands on the tops of their heads, fingers clasped.

'Your two friends outside are dead now, P J,' Dunlop said, flatly. Morgan noticed all his earlier tension had gone. 'I'll show you them in a minute if you like. Better still' – he jabbed the muzzle of the gun so it pointed towards the man from *Republican News* – 'better still, I'll show you what will happen to the man from Ireland's liveliest tabloid unless you decide to help us. It's a simple little question, requiring much less thought than any of the brain power you have just been witnessing from Morgan here. Are you ready?'

O'Neill did not respond. He was holding the arms of his chair tightly with his hands. The knuckles were white. He looked like a man on the dentist's couch who knows he is about to feel the drill. They could hear from the hallway the sound of bodies being dragged towards the kitchen. Dickinson was grunting. Dunlop began to speak slowly and clearly.

'Where have you hidden Durrant and his wife?'

There was a long pause. Morgan thought O'Neill was unable rather than just unwilling to talk. Then in a hoarse little voice cracked with fear, he said:

'Who's he? Never heard the name.'

'You disappoint me, Paddy,' Dunlop spat out. 'I thought you could do better than that.'

He nodded at Hinkley who interpreted the sign and took half a pace forward to kick the *Republican News* photographer full in the face. The man's nose exploded blood red across his mouth and he fell groaning towards the carpet. The other Provo by the piano started to move to help him, then saw Dunlop's gun pointing directly at him. The photographer groaned, alone in his pain.

'You bastard,' Morgan shouted, standing up from his armchair. 'You pack of bastards!'

'Shut up, Morgan,' Dunlop cut in. 'The same could easily happen to you. Sit down.'

244

Morgan obeyed. Dunlop walked over to the table, picked up O'Neill's tape recorder and handed it to Hinkley.

'It's been running long enough, Tony, to get the gist of how helpful you have been in setting up Paddy here. If O'Neill should decide not to help us now, well that's too bad for him and too bad for you too. I'm sure one way or the other *Republican News* would be interested in the text of the interview and the events which followed. So just keep out of it for now.'

The photographer was still groaning. Morgan put his hands over his face and tried not to look at P J O'Neill. Dunlop turned back towards O'Neill.

'Well, Paddy. This is it. Time's up. I have infinite patience, but my colleague here, Mr Hinkley, is quite frankly a bit of a bastard. You can either tell us right now where Durrant and his wife are being held, or you will tell us within an hour or two and that short period of delay will be the most unpleasant of your life. I promise. Now where are they?'

Dickinson and Barwood came back into the room. 'We've sorted them out and turned round the cars.'

'Okay. Start carrying some gear out – and don't forget chummy's camera and this tape recorder. When that's all done, stay at the front and keep watch. Barwood, you stay here.'

The *Republican News* photographer had recovered from the blow and was trying to sit back against the piano, holding his nose together. One of the Provos assumed he could help him. Hinkley picked up the photographer's camera and smashed it hard on the crown of his head.

Dunlop watched, unmoved. He told Hinkley he had a question for him.

'What was that technique that always worked? I've forgotten.'

'In Dhofar, sir?' Hinkley asked, opening up the back of the camera and exposing the pictures. 'The technique from Dhofar?'

'The one from Dhofar,' Dunlop agreed. 'Yes, that's it. Explain it to Mr O'Neill will you.'

'Well,' Hinkley said, speaking slowly as if searching for the correct words. 'It's like this. We discovered that the Dhofari rebels were a bunch of hard bastards, and there was bugger all you could do to loosen their tongues. Life was so awful there in the middle of the desert that the odd smack on the head didn't seem to worry them. Then one of their own type – doctor, he was, I think – one of their own, anyway, told our lads that the most sensitive area on the human body was the skin on the belly. Lots of nerve endings close to the surface or something. He said that in the middle ages their own rulers found the one way they could loosen tongues was to start pulling that skin off with a knife. "Flaying alive" he called it.'

'Ever tried it on an Irishman?' Dunlop queried.

'Not yet. But it worked a treat on the Dhofaris.'

Morgan had had enough. He stood up and demanded that they stop. They had said they intended to follow O'Neill, to put a bug in his car. Nobody had mentioned anything about shootings and killings and torture.

'Sit down, Morgan,' Dunlop yelled. 'This is your last chance. I'm just as happy to shoot you as any of these other bastards. You're only useless luggage to us now anyway. So sit down!'

Morgan looked at him, now completely adrift. Whatever choice he had made, or whatever choices he had refused to make, had led to this. There was nothing he could do. He could not defeat their guns with words, their violence with reason. They were two groups fighting out incomprehensible battles, and he could only just keep out of the crossfire. He crumpled, and slumped back into the chair.

'What these fellas do,' Dunlop said, indicating O'Neill, but for Morgan's benefit, 'is much more subtle than anything we might have picked up from the Dhofaris. If the IRA want information from you they take you out and start dropping breeze-blocks on the backs of your hands until they've broken every bone. Then they do it on your feet, then your legs, then your arms. Then you want them to kill you, but they don't. They just leave you for hours, a paraplegic in the jelly of your own body, not able to stand or move, just a mess of pain. Then maybe, if you're lucky, one of them will end it by putting a bullet in the back of your head. That's the way these guys play it. And this time, after a lot of thought, we've decided to play by their rules instead of ours.'

He turned back to O'Neill. 'You know what that means, Paddy. Last chance, coming up. Then it's our equivalent of the breeze-blocks. You'll talk one way or the other. Now, where are they?'

O'Neill had regained a little of his composure. His hands were still tight on the arms of the chair, but the initial shock had passed.

'I don't know what you are talking about.'

Dunlop nodded to Barwood who fired a short burst from the Heckler and Koch into the face of the photographer. His head opened like a tomato under a hammer, spraying the piano and the Provo beside him with blood. The Provo cried out hysterically, frantically trying to wipe the blood from his face and clothes.

'Where did you say, Paddy?'

Morgan saw O'Neill swallowing hard. His fear made Morgan's own more bearable. He could feel the rush of events sweeping down on him like a flood from the future. He took a deep breath, hoping O'Neill would answer. Any answer.

'Where did you say they are?' Dunlop repeated.

O'Neill's voice had almost gone. He licked his lips slowly with his tongue and opened his mouth a little as if to speak, but the words would not come. Morgan had never seen a man so frightened and yet struggling for control. O'Neill licked his lips a second time and began to speak in the cracked voice of a broken man.

'Between Drogheda and Dundalk. Small cottage near Ardee off the Slane road. Near McGillivray's farm.'

It was half panic, half a calculated move, and the best O'Neill could think of. The chances were the Durrants were now away from the bungalow. Maybe a few of the South Armagh boys would be holed up there. It was difficult to tell. If Kennedy had done as he was supposed to, they would be operating from the other house. O'Neill began to tremble. He had not ordered Kennedy to move the Durrants, only advised him. Kennedy would do as he damn well liked. It might all come apart, but he had no room for manoeuvre. This Dunlop was a madman.

Dunlop seemed unmoved. He looked at O'Neill's face for a full ten seconds, studying every line as if making up his mind whether the man could be trusted.

'It had better be right for your sake,' Dunlop said harshly. 'I'm not best known for my patience.'

Dunlop ordered handcuffs for O'Neill while Hinkley took care of the remaining Provo, who was still sprawled on the floor, the back of his head stained with blood. Dunlop put his hand on Morgan's shoulder and signalled to him to follow out to the front yard. Morgan did not move.

'Go fuck yourself, Dunlop. I've done enough. I'm a reporter not a mercenary.'

'It's not what you can do for us now, Tony,' Dunlop hissed. 'It's what we can do for you. Like keep you alive and out of an Irish jail for starters. Get in the car and sit in the back seat, while we finish off here.'

Morgan got up to move. Barwood had already cuffed O'Neill and was ready to put him in the car. There were two large patches of blood across the piano and the walls, and another on the floor. Dickinson reappeared with a gallon can of petrol and what could only be some kind of small bomb.

'Fitting, isn't it,' Dunlop grunted, 'that these incompetents from the IRA should blow themselves up in, say, two hours time while priming a bomb. Yet another own goal. How sad. It won't destroy all the evidence but the fire will help. From what I hear Irish forensic surgery is such a joke that they will find it difficult trying to work out whether what we have here are dead Provos or old library books. If we're lucky, there won't be enough of the bodies left for them to see that they were shot first. Anyway, that's not my problem.'

Morgan watched Dickinson and Hinkley bundle O'Neill into the first Sierra. Hinkley got in beside him. Morgan looked towards the sea and noticed that the tide was coming in. The wading birds had flown off somewhere else. There was only one solitary gull wheeling around the chimney stacks of the house, calling out tunelessly. Barwood came out of the house last. He muttered something to Dunlop which Morgan could not catch, then slammed the house door tight, and so hard it seemed the foundations shook. Morgan felt his eyes swim as he heard the crew start the car engines. He could see Hinkley's bull neck as he looked straight at O'Neill trussed beside him in the back seat. Hinkley found a travel rug and put it over his knees, covering the Heckler and Koch which was pointing at O'Neill's waist. The sunshine seemed to stretch out along the beach towards Dublin and southwards towards the Wicklow hills. The American tourists would have seen Glendalough by now, would have had enough of country roads and small green fields, and be bouncing back through Ballsbridge to Jury's Hotel. Morgan rubbed his hand over his face and looked into the lead Sierra. Dunlop, now in control, his nervousness utterly gone, was staring at him as if trying to decide whether to kill him too.

'Get in now Tony,' he yelled. 'For Christ's sake hurry up. We've got a long way to go.'

Morgan felt a sudden spasm in his belly. He leaned over the back of the car and vomited hard on the gravel.

Chapter Twenty-One

County Louth

When Gordon Durrant awoke it was early afternoon, and Kelly was hammering on the door.

'Wake up, prof. Can't sleep all day.'

He heard the key rattle in the lock and sat up with a start, terrified lest he had been careless and left something incriminating lying around, or in case the Boxer wanted to begin a surprise search of the room. As the door opened he could smell bacon frying. The Boxer was smiling.

'Good news, prof. Your wife will be here later today. We've made all the arrangements and the two of you'll be together while the rest of us are away on a wee job. We still have to look after you for a while, for reasons of operational security. Some of our comrades will hold on to you for a bit. But you'll definitely be together. Better for you, and easier for us. How's that suit you?'

Durrant did not know how to react. He smiled and said something about it being terrific news, really terrific. He wanted to stay calm and pretend it was of no consequence, so he would not look a fool if it really did not happen, but the rush of information made his body fill with blood. He knew he had gone red and was sweating. For a moment he thought he might cry, or just yell out something for the sake of yelling, but he controlled himself. He reached over sideways for a cigarette and pulled one from the packet, trembling.

'Maybe you want to fix yourself up, prof,' the Boxer said. 'Clean up and have a shave.'

Durrant nodded. He picked up his washing bag and moved into the hallway. He was still shaking. He felt so ludicrously grateful that he wanted to hug the Boxer, though he could see from the man's eyes refusing to catch his own, that the Boxer was openly embarrassed, presumably at the pitiful figure Durrant now cut. He opened the bathroom door and looked at himself in the mirror. A cloud of cigarette smoke partly obscured his face, and he took the cigarette from his lips, placing it on the side of the toilet cistern. He looked again at himself in the mirror. There were slow tears rolling from his eyes, despite his determination to show no emotion. He wiped them away, and realised why the Boxer had looked so embarrassed. Durrant stood back to take a wider view of the mirror.

'An old, grey man,' he said quietly to his reflection. 'Old and grey. Nearly sucked dry.'

The first thing he noticed, though it must have been true for days and it had escaped his attention, was that his hair was far too long. It flopped in his eyes and down over his collar. He needed a proper shave and there were long wiry hairs growing untrimmed from his nostrils. He had been happy to be half madman, half beggar, when the only people who saw him were the people who caused his suffering. Now he had to look smarter, to pretend to be a man again. He began to shave carefully, and then bathe and wash his hair. He would not smoke until she arrived – she nagged him a little about smoking and said kissing him could be like kissing an ashtray. He would not smell like an ashtray today. He took the still-lit cigarette and threw it into the toilet. Then he scrubbed his teeth and replaced the toothbrush and paste in his washing bag. He caught sight of the plastic bag containing the nails and screws that were to become his shrapnel. For a moment he wondered if the Boxer had simply used the story of the visit to get him out of the room and search for the can of Foamex.

'You there?' he shouted through the bathroom door into the hallway.

'Sure, prof. I'm here.'

Good. Durrant asked if he could take a bath. The Boxer agreed and when Durrant returned to his room he changed his shirt. It had not been ironed, but it was at least clean. Nothing was ever ironed. They had a washing-machine in the house, but either did not have an iron, did not want to use it, or did not want to give him access to it. Somehow Durrant could not imagine all these staff captains and battalion commanders (or whatever it was they called themselves) smoothing out the creases in their shirts, but then he supposed someone had to do it. He could hear something from the kitchen. Above the cooking and sizzling sounds, the Skull was singing along in his nasal voice with some sentimental ballad on the radio. It was the sort of thing which Durrant knew would start a row, because the

Boxer hated country and western and the Skull refused to listen to pop music.

'That's enough of that ould rubbish,' he would say and switch the dials. It was sometimes comical to listen to them, this Belfast Odd Couple. If Durrant ever did get out and gave a statement to the police, they would not believe half of it.

'And they rowed constantly, you say Mr Durrant?'

'Yes, Inspector.'

'About what, mainly? The "Armed Struggle"? Republican politics? Specific targets?'

'No. Dolly Parton, mainly. Sometimes Slim Whitman and Big Tom and the Mainliners.'

They would never believe him. He hardly believed himself.

'And you drank whiskey with them?'

'Frequently. Not in the first week, but frequently thereafter.'

'What did you talk about?'

'Well, all kinds of things really. But I suppose mostly they tried to persuade me to vote Sinn Fein. I guess that was it. A sort of long drawn-out party political broadcast.'

It was hopeless. If ever he did escape, he would simply go away somewhere and bury himself, talking to no one about anything. Not even Margaret. They could discuss Norse sagas or football or something, but what had happened in the bungalow was a twisted dream which no one could explain or make sense of, and therefore no one should hear. Suddenly there were voices calling his name. Voices from the hallway.

'Come on prof, or it'll get cold,' the Boxer said as the door swung open.

Durrant rubbed his eyes. He hoped he had not been crying again without noticing it.

'Come on, feeding time at the zoo.'

Durrant pulled himself up from the bed and walked unsteadily towards the kitchen. McKeever had placed his bacon and eggs on a plate under the grill to keep warm. He was cooking more fried bread. He dug another chunk of lard from the pack and dropped it into the pan. It smoked and skated round the edges.

'Make the tea will you, prof? Six cups, I'd guess. Your wife should be here any minute. They phoned before they left, and it doesn't take long, where they're coming from.'

Durrant heard the words but could barely take them in. If he kept telling himself this was only another part of their psychological

251

torture to build him up and knock him down, then he would not be so disappointed when Margaret did not arrive. He propped himself against the sink, unsmiling, and filled the kettle.

'He doesn't seem too happy about it,' the Boxer said to the Skull with a laugh, his mouth full of fried bread. 'Maybe she nags him at home.'

'No, I *am* happy,' Durrant said, pulling the tea from the cupboard. 'Of course I'm happy. But I won't believe it until it happens. that's all. You can understand that, can't you?'

'Just remember that we keep our side of bargains, prof,' the Skull said, without humour. 'We told you you would get to see her if you co-operated, and we've kept our word. Okay?'

'True enough,' Durrant accepted. It was always easy to agree. Agree to anything. 'True as you say. You kept your word.'

'And the Boss said he'll be up here over the next day or so. He wants to see you both. I expect he'll want to tell you himself, but there's no reason why I can't. He'll want to talk to you about your release and how we intend to handle it.'

Durrant poured the boiling water over the tea and stuck the lid on the pot. He prepared the six mugs and set them to one side. After a few minutes the Boxer told him there was no point in waiting for the others to arrive.

'Pour three now,' he instructed. Durrant obeyed.

The other three empty mugs sat staring at him reproachfully. He sipped his tea and waited. He could hear the Boxer slurp from his mug. The Skull pulled out a morning newspaper and read it in a desultory fashion. Durrant looked at the Boxer, mournfully chewing a piece of bread, and the Skull, with the maimed fingers of his left hand across the front page of the *Irish Press*. Could it be? Margaret would arrive. Really? Durrant turned to his tea.

He heard a car in the driveway, approaching from the left. It had to be the Girl and the Thin Man. It was their car, certainly, by the sound. He stood up. His legs felt unsteady, as if he had just been ill and was only now beginning to recover. He leaned against the sink. Kelly went to the door, leaving McKeever to watch Durrant.

'It's okay, prof,' the Skull said, calmly. 'It's okay. Just relax.'

The Girl came into the kitchen first, pulling someone behind her by the hand. The someone was Margaret, blindfolded but not otherwise tied, holding tightly to the Girl. She nudged her onto a chair at the kitchen table, then the Boxer took off the blindfold. Margaret Durrant blinked in the light, looked straight ahead at her husband, unable to focus her eyes properly. Durrant ran forward and took her in his arms, pulling her up from the chair, hugging and kissing her. He could feel her shake at his touch, and then begin to cry. He held her for what seemed like the most precious minutes of his life, held her until McKeever tapped him on the shoulder, opened the door and pointed to Durrant's bedroom.

'Will youse go in there,' he said in an exasperated voice. 'Some of us are trying to eat.'

By the time – some half an hour later – that McKeever called them again and asked if they too wanted to eat, they had composed themselves. Margaret Durrant had a black smear round her eyes. The mascara given to her by the Girl to cheer up an otherwise chalk-white complexion had been a waste, carried down her cheeks with the first tears, staining her husband's face as they kissed. Durrant found it hard to accept that it was really her. She looked so different from the idea of his wife that he carried round in his memory. Her waist was thinner than he had remembered, or maybe she had become thin. Her hair was straight now, the ends ragged – too long a time without being cut. Her skin was softer than he could ever have imagined, soft and thin like a child's.

For a time they sat and held hands on the bed like a couple of adolescents on a first date. They each made an attempt at mumbling their happiness to the other. The door of the bedroom had been left unlocked and in response to McKeever's call to eat, they had tried to compose themselves, then walked into the kitchen hand in hand. The Girl, the Skull, the Boxer and the Thin Man sat round the kitchen table drinking mugs of tea. McKeever stood up and motioned at Margaret Durrant to sit down, while he fetched the food.

'Just tea,' she said, pushing back the hair from her forehead, embarrassed at the black smear down her cheeks. 'I'm not really hungry. Tea will be fine.'

'Ach,' said McKeever. 'You'll never grow up to be a big fine girl if you don't eat your fry.'

Durrant poured two mugs of tea, and handed one to his wife. He felt odd, as if Margaret had, for the first time, been brought to meet some business colleagues of his, some old friends in whose company he was easy but with whom she would feel strange. He almost wanted to make introductions, but assumed that Margaret had her own nicknames for the two she knew, the Thin Man and the Girl. Maybe Beowulf and his Monster, what was her name? Griselda or something. He couldn't remember. Beowulf looked uncharacter-istically cheerful, which made Durrant wary.

'We're all staying here tonight,' the Thin Man explained. 'Then that's it. An end to us being one big happy family. You will not be seeing us again.'

Thank Christ, thought Durrant.

'What will happen to us?' he said, quietly.

'The Boss will be here soon enough and he can tell you the details,' the Thin Man added. 'There'll be another team who will look after you for a while. You've been very helpful. Or at least you started being helpful after I explained things to you. We're going to hold on to you for some time yet, maybe two or three weeks. It's not up to me. The Boss wanted you moved by tonight, but I've decided to hold off until he arrives. I'd rather keep you here, since we won't be using this place again. The cover will be blown. Maybe you'll be moved eventually, maybe not. If everything goes well you'll soon be released.'

Durrant had never seen the Thin Man look so relaxed. It was as if he had bled Durrant of everything, or everything he thought was there. That task was finished and now there was no hostility, just coldness. He had moved on to other business, and Durrant was history. Durrant decided to push his luck, knowing that anything more than one question, however innocent, would irritate the Thin Man into a vicious rebuff.

'Will we be allowed to stay together?'

There was silence in the kitchen. The Thin Man took a swig of his tea, and looked Durrant coldly in the eyes. He paused, and then said without his usual malice:

'I guess so. That's what I understand. But it's not my decision. It's up to the Boss and whatever team he gets to look after you. You're off our hands from tomorrow. That's all I care about.'

Evidently. Durrant put his arms round his wife's neck as she sat at the table. She stroked his hand with hers.

'There is one thing,' the Thin Man said slowly. 'One small thing.' His mouth was slack in its normal sneer again. Durrant knew he was about to be stabbed. He looked at Margaret, hoping she would not be hurt too.

'What?' he asked.

'You will not be released until the four of us return from where we are going. That could take us two, maybe three weeks. We will not get back in one piece if you have told us anything false about

Magnex, or anything else for that matter. Your lives depend on ours. I want you to remember that.'

The air in the kitchen was suddenly cold. Durrant stared into the Thin Man's eyes. They were blue, unblinking. His rough voice was still in the air. Every time it hit Durrant it was like being gutted with a serrated knife. The blade was in his belly and the Thin Man began twisting it again.

'If there is anything you want to tell us, any little mistakes you might have made, or anything you overlooked and forgot or got wrong, now would be a good time.'

Durrant had nothing to say. He looked at the floor and then at Margaret.

'I've told you it all,' he said quietly. 'All I can, anyway. Since you won't tell me what you want the Magnex for, I can't advise you in detail. If you had told me what the target was, I could go further. You know that.'

The Thin Man smiled, and went back to drinking his tea. After ten minutes more in the kitchen, most of it in silence, the Thin Man announced that they had work to do. The Skull told Durrant that he and his wife would have to be locked in the bedroom again. He led them out, turned the key and checked the locks. Then McKeever returned to the kitchen.

'When do we leave for Scotland?' he asked Larry Kennedy.

'Probably Monday. There's no hurry. Headquarters have worked out three separate routes. I'll go with Siobhan. You and Brendan go by two different routes. We meet up at the safe house in Partick.'

McKeever decided that it was unwise to let Kennedy know just how much detail the Boss had already given him. He nodded, then asked how the gear was getting there.

'Two other couriers. The Boss will explain more tonight or tomorrow, whenever he turns up. I haven't been able to tell him that we decided to keep the Durrants here, so I've left Barney McGeogh and a couple of the South Armagh boys at the other place and they will come here with him when he turns up.'

'Are you sure,' McKeever asked, 'that we shouldn't have moved Durrant to the other house like the Boss said? He's very particular on keeping to exact locations.'

The Thin Man smiled. 'Well, I decided that he was wrong on this one. If he decides to release Durrant then this house is no good anyway. It'll be too hot. I'm still hoping to persuade him that we should stiff the pair of them. I talked it over with Barney McGeogh, and he's of the same mind. His boys'll do it once we're gone.'

'*If* you can persuade the Boss,' McKeever cautioned.

'If I can persuade the Boss,' Kennedy repeated. 'Anyway, the real problem is shifting all the gear. It will be taken to another safe house, somewhere near Anniesland. I don't even know the contact there. We've got a week to case the docks, try a dummy run and get ready.'

Brendan Kelly began to clear the tea cups. Siobhan O'Hagan tossed her hair behind her shoulder.

'Return to base will also be by three separate routes,' she said. 'The timing should work out so even the latest one is back sixteen hours before it goes off.'

'Diving equipment?' Kelly asked.

'All taken care of,' Kennedy replied with a smile. 'That's the only part of the gear already in place.'

'Shorts?'

'Ah, they're in place as well.' Siobhan O'Hagan smiled. 'We'll be using gear that's been in Glasgow for a while and is clean. As far as I know there's a stash in the second safe house. Half-a-dozen Webleys, couple of Star pistols, couple of Smith and Wessons. All we need. Nothing bigger. No point in moving AKs.'

Brendan Kelly could feel his heart beat at the thought of it. It was all right for the others, McKeever and Siobhan had both done time. Larry Kennedy was too smart to get caught. But how would he fare? Could he cope with it if he was caught? Life, with a minimum stip. Definitely. Twenty five years, could be more. Ach, jail or death. It did not much matter. One or other would catch up with him sooner or later. There might be the odd line in the history books, if they brought it off. In this case maybe even a poem. It would change history. His own history, McKeever's, British history definitely, and Irish history. He was sure of it.

'How many of the bastards are there going to be on board?' Kelly asked.

Larry Kennedy grinned. 'Enough,' he said.

'Which ones?'

'Elizabrit and Philip, and one or two flunkeys. It's the full Royal visit to the Highlands and Islands – or don't you keep up with the British Royal Family stories in *The Sun*?'

Kelly looked round the kitchen. There was silence, as if the full extent of what they were planning had only just sunk in. One

256

moment it was just a job like any other he had done, then when someone spelled it out in such clear words he could not help feeling scared. It had never been done before. Nothing like that. Not since – well not since any history he could remember. Even Guy Fawkes's Papish plot was a failure, and that was the only thing he could think of that even came close. He caught McKeever's eye, then McKeever looked away. Siobhan was looking at her finger-nails, saying nothing. Kennedy was staring straight at him, unblinking, expressionless.

'What a cool bastard,' Kelly thought. 'I've seen more emotion in a bucket of herring.'

He returned Kennedy's gaze. Siobhan O'Hagan stretched her arms wide. Kelly noticed the curve of her breasts and wondered whether there was ever any chance of getting a hand round them. Maybe one day. After Larry Kennedy's luck ran out. It wouldn't be easy, but she might. One day.

'P J doesn't want to decide what to do about the Durrants until after the operation,' Siobhan said. 'It's difficult to see which way it will go. If we succeed, there's straightaway a constitutional crisis in England, as well as a period of mourning and what P J calls a crumbling of national morale. There will be severe repression from the Brits in the Six Counties, but the people will handle that. Then the Brits'll have to decide whether the war in the North is worth all that it's cost them. They'll talk tough at first with the usual no surrender to terrorism stuff, and the immediate crisis will last several weeks after the mission itself. P J reckons that releasing the Durrants at that stage to tell their tale might just be the final push to discredit British security at all levels.'

'What do you think, Siobhan?' McKeever asked.

Siobhan O'Hagan smiled at him. 'I think we should get rid of them now. They're just going to tie down volunteers to guard them for three weeks. They know our identities so could testify against us. Christ knows what else they know. If we succeed in what we're doing, then one half-daft Brit scientist more or less telling the British newspapers how we did it, is not going to matter a damn.'

McKeever cut in. 'The Boss said to me he might even order them blinded so they wouldn't be able to identify us. I said I thought that was going too far. I don't suppose he was serious. Just thinking aloud.'

'So what,' Kennedy muttered. 'Dead or alive, blinded or seeing. It's not a matter of what we should do with them. Like Siobhan says, it's a matter of whether we should tie down more assets, when we could just stiff them before we go. Barney McGeogh was curious about what we'd got out of them. I couldn't tell him everything at once, but I'd guess that when we're gone he'll put Durrant through everything we have done, trying to pump him for information. That way looking after the Durrants'll sort of pay for itself. Barney'll get something in return.'

McKeever thought for a moment, then explained that it was hardly worth the trouble since the South Armagh boys would hear everything the prof had said eventually. They had already passed on all the information about making detonators and about shaping charges. Suddenly, McKeever realised he was getting the full laser stare from Kennedy.

'You seem as interested in the fate of the Durrants as in the fate of the mission,' Kennedy challenged.

'No . . . no . . . I just wondered.'

'You know, P J told me about this. He said there were two problems with a long kidnap. The first is you have to make contact with the authorities if you want a ransom, and that means you are going to get caught. Well, we got round that one. The second problem, he said, was that some people start getting attached to those they kidnapped.'

McKeever tried to protest. Kennedy ignored him.

'In fact it gets so bad that some volunteers have difficulty in obeying orders if the target has to be stiffed. The South Armagh boys will have no such problem, but if it was up to me I'd have them done tonight and I'd make you do it, McKeever.'

Siobhan O'Hagan stood up. 'We're wasting time,' she said. 'There's things to be done.'

She told Kelly and McKeever to make sure that all the gear was wrapped and ready for transportation. The Magnex was now in a brown plastic hold-all. The detonators were kept separately, and the time and power units were in a third bag, ready for the courier. Kennedy and Siobhan O'Hagan had arranged to travel over first, mainly because Kennedy wanted time to check the airtanks and seals on the equipment. They all stood up, and began to go through a list of what had yet to be done.

As the buzz of their conversation rose and fell, only the loudest of the arguments were audible in the bedroom. Durrant outlined to his wife in whispers his plans for escape. Margaret Durrant was too shocked by their sudden meeting to understand anything of what he was saying, and Durrant himself was too shocked to notice. He gabbled through his worries – whether they would be able to run fast enough to get clear; whether he could produce sufficient distractions in the way of explosions to hamper pursuit; whether he could find any civilisation round here; whether their kidnappers might just release them anyway; and whether the people in the next town might not hand him straight back to the IRA again. He went through it all, holding his wife's hands tightly in his own as he spoke, but the rattle of his words was too complicated. At first she could not work out whether he was arguing that they should escape, or that it was too difficult even to try. She nodded occasionally and hoped he would understand. After a while she began to speak, each word an effort of pronunciation.

'They kept me,' she said, 'in a room smaller than this. All the time. No window. Nothing. The one you call the Thin Man wanted me tied up all the time. The woman objected. Then I think there were two or three others. One anyway, a man – no a boy – a boy of no more than eighteen years old by the sound of his voice. He brought me my food. Never spoke to me. Ever. It was like he was on some test, never to speak like that. I don't know. They gave me a blindfold. Everytime any of them came in, I had to wear it. Every time. Today is the first time I have seen any of their faces. First time.'

She took a deep breath. Durrant listened to her words, knowing that when she finished he would have to go back over the entire plan again. He had not realised how bad she was. He would have to be patient.

'I heard them arguing once. The Thin Man and the Girl, and someone else. They were arguing about us. The Thin Man – you could tell it was him because of his awful hoarse voice – he said if you were released you would go back to re-join the "British War Machine". That's what he actually called it. He meant you'd go back to lecturing on explosives, I suppose. He wanted us both killed when you'd told them everything they wanted to hear. The other man was arguing, but I couldn't make out what he was saying. The Girl chipped in. She seemed to agree with the Thin Man.'

Margaret Durrant paused and gazed fixedly into the middle distance, her eyes focused on nothing. It was as if she was still held in a blindfold. Durrant asked gently if she had heard what they decided.

'No,' she said, shaking her head. 'I couldn't hear. But I don't trust them, Gordon. I don't think they want to let us go. And I don't think they intend to keep us together. I'm sure the only reason we're together tonight is because they need to be together to make their plans. When they split up tomorrow, they'll probably split us up, too.'

Durrant was amazed by his wife. She was speaking as coolly as she did when dissecting an Icelandic saga. He thought she was in a jumble, but her words were perfectly clear. There was no emotion, no tears. If she had not listened to what he had been saying about the escape, that was only because she was sorting all this in her own mind instead. She turned so she could look straight into his eyes.

'If there is a chance for us to get away tonight,' she went on, 'I want to take it. Even if we fail. I won't be separated from you again. Ever.'

Durrant kissed her gently. Then he pulled back.

'I've been lecturing people telling them how to do things for long enough. It is my turn now. Let's see whether I can really bring the house down.'

Chapter Twenty-Two

The Boyne Valley

The river Boyne was in full flood. Ever since they left Dublin it had been raining, a slow steady rain that looked as if it might fall forever. The cars wound north in a haphazard convoy through the suburbs and into the country, Dickinson and Barwood in front, some half a mile ahead. In Balbriggan, Dunlop used the radio to make sure Dickinson and Barwood were still within range. Morgan stared from his side window as the car sat at traffic lights, looking glumly at the faces of shoppers as they struggled through the sodden late afternoon with their plastic bags filled with groceries. Except for the radio message, no one spoke.

Hinkley sat in the back seat eyeing O'Neill. The car had central locking with child-proof locks. There was nowhere for O'Neill to go, unless he chose to somersault into the front seat and somehow escape out of the door beside Morgan or Dunlop himself. Morgan tried to keep his eyes on the road, frightened to turn round and catch O'Neill's eyes. Once he had half turned, just enough to see Hinkley, motionless, a tartan travelling rug and an old Barbour waxed jacket carelessly draped across his knees. He could have been a country squire but for the fact that Morgan noticed, between the Barbour and the rug, the muzzle of the Heckler and Koch sub-machine gun pointed at O'Neill's belly.

As they turned down the hill of the Slane road, pointing north in the direction of the signs for Belfast and Ardee, Morgan looked out over the Boyne river where it was swollen and brown, bursting from its banks into the meadows on either side of the plain. Here, or somewhere round here in 1690 he thought, King William and his armies had defeated the Catholic enemy and consolidated the Glorious Revolution, the victory of a Protestant King over the forces of the Anti-Christ. Or so they said in Northern Ireland. Only

261

there did anyone remember it, the battle which had launched a thousand pieces of graffiti.

'One King, One Crown. No Pope in this Town.'

Well, maybe. Morgan looked across to Dunlop, his face taut with the concentration of driving and whatever lay ahead. He wondered if Dunlop, or any other Ulster Protestant, knew that the neatness of the legend was not quite the same as the historical fact; that the Pope had actually supported the Protestant Williamite cause, seeking the defeat of the Catholic James in order to bring about a geo-political weakening of the French. Ireland and its petty quarrels were a side show. Then, as always. There was nothing here worth fighting for, or dying over. Morgan realised that even if Dunlop did know, he would not care. There was no doubt within him. He was like P J O'Neill, a martyr to his own certainties just as Morgan himself was destroyed by his sense of doubt. Morgan leaned his forehead on the car window, feeling the coolness, and then, surprisingly, Dunlop spoke.

'How does the song go, Paddy?' he asked, his first words in fifty miles. ' "And the Boyne shall run red with redundance of blood." Isn't that it? James Clarence Mangan.'

O'Neill said nothing. Dunlop changed gears at a low hairpin bend and began the slow climb into Slane town. There was hardly any traffic on the road. Ahead, climbing the hill to the left, they could see the tail lights of Dickinson and Barwood's Sierra. Dunlop began again.

'There was one thing I wanted to say to you, Paddy. And I want to make sure you're listening.' There was no reply from O'Neill. Dunlop continued.

'I just wanted to assure you that if, for any reason, you have picked the wrong direction in which to send us, or intend to pick the wrong house when we get there, or if there is any other error of judgement or fact that you're thinking of, then you better start talking about it now. Right now. I am in no mood for surprises, got that?'

There was a pause. Still no response from O'Neill.

'I'm not unreasonable,' Dunlop said, cheerfully. 'I'm capable of forgiveness. But I would have to hear a genuine confession followed by an act of contrition.'

There was a slight movement in the back seat from O'Neill and he appeared to clear his throat. Morgan could see Dunlop glance at him in the rear-view mirror.

'Wrong river,' O'Neill said, his voice thin and weak.

Dunlop took his foot off the accelerator and looked back at him. 'What the fuck do you mean wrong river?'

'Wrong river,' O'Neill repeated with a nervous laugh. 'The poem says "And the *Erne* shall run red with redundance of blood." Not the Boyne. James Clarence Mangan.'

Dunlop gunned the car again, and picked up the radio to tell the other Sierra they were still on course.

'Glad to see you're keeping a sense of humour, Paddy,' he said. 'Fucking glad.'

Morgan stared at the drenched patchwork fields, dull through the grey drizzle. This was the forty shades of green the Irish Tourist Board was always boasting about, grasses and sedges, hawthorn, oak and beech woods all grey in the rain, dissolving into vagueness. The only relief was the occasional white bungalow stark in the gloom, and starker still because at only five o'clock on what was supposed to be an early summer's day, some of them even had their lights on.

Morgan had the strange sensation that he was not just any passenger in the car, but a permanent passenger, hijacked by Dunlop and tied to a roller coaster that none of them could abandon. The important thing was to survive. He thought for a moment about Emily and the children, and whether they would miss him if he were to die. He had always supposed that it would not much matter. In the end, all things were the same. You lived carefully, ate health food, didn't smoke and were run over by a bus. You ate the wrong things, smoked and drank too much, and lived for years more. All the same.

Now that Morgan faced the real prospect of a bullet in the back from Hinkley, or maybe from one of O'Neill's friends, he had changed his mind. It would have been different if he had not lived, or if he was to be killed. It did make a difference to him whether Emily had a baby or an abortion. Maybe in the great scheme of things it was of no consequence – or no more consequence than who won the Battle of the Boyne all those years ago. But it really did make a difference to him, and despite not being able to put it into words or argue it in rational discussion, there were some things worth the struggle. Maybe he was against her having an abortion because he had come to realise that life was its own reward. That the purpose, the reason for living, was not clear to him as it was to O'Neill or Dunlop and all those others who lived and died for great

263

causes, but life itself was its own triumph against the odds, and taking life was the great sin.

Suddenly Morgan felt a controlled anger pass through his body, an anger at himself for becoming trapped and an anger against the others for exploiting him. He looked at Dunlop again, who took a second to turn away from the road and return his gaze. Then he pulled down the sun visor in front of him, and stared in the vanity mirror at Hinkley, who sat unblinking, alert. Morgan shifted his position a few inches to one side so he could see O'Neill's face. It was older and more grim than he remembered, now the face of the man from the 'Wanted' posters rather than the relaxed one Morgan had met in the Dublin tenement not long ago. O'Neill looked directly back into the mirror, and Morgan felt the reproach of his stare. He tucked the sun visor away again.

'I think you should tell us what we're in for,' Morgan said to Dunlop, pleasantly surprised that his own voice appeared strong where O'Neill's seemed so weak. 'O'Neill and I want to know what you are going to do, and more especially what you're going to do with us.'

Dunlop looked across at Morgan, wondering whether he had swapped sides again. When he began speaking it was softly and deliberately, in his most irritatingly didactic tone.

'It's like this, Tony,' he said. 'What happens next really depends on O'Neill here. Since you seem so concerned about him and want to link your fate to his, I'll spell it out for the benefit of both of you. If O'Neill's gang are where he says they are, then we will have to take steps to get the Durrants out, either straight away or tomorrow. We could hole up overnight, around here. O'Neill's people are not the only ones to have safe houses in the Irish Republic. We have a facility available to us near Dundalk, should we require it. But if all goes well, we'll slip over the border and maybe by midnight tonight we'll be having a party in Gough Barracks to celebrate. If it all goes badly, largely because O'Neill has decided to mess us about, then I suppose we'll have a little party down on this side of the border, but it will be one O'Neill will enjoy a lot less.'

'And me?' Morgan asked. 'What am I supposed to do?'

'You, Tony, are supposed to keep out the way until we sort all this out. This is one of those jobs when you either have to stand up or sit down. Wobble around in between as you like to do, and you risk getting your balls shot off. Clear?'

Morgan did not respond. He put his forehead back on the glass.

His breath stuck to the window pane, blotting out the grey and the drizzle. He had no doubt that Dunlop spoke the truth. He was now excess to requirements. There was no purpose in him being part of the scene. But for the inconvenience of him bleeding on the car seat, there was no particular reason why they should keep him alive either.

The car swung through Collon, pausing at a crossroads, to allow a tractor to back out fully into the road. The youth hanging on to the back footplate stared at them, expressionless, then waved a thankyou in the rain. Morgan wondered whether O'Neill might try to seize his chance to raise the alarm in a last desperate act of heroism, but he sat motionless and impassive.

Morgan was curious to know whether the interview with O'Neill would be broadcast. It was a thought apparently of the utmost irrelevance, yet if it were to be broadcast, then how could they explain O'Neill's sudden re-appearance north of the border to stand trial for his part in the jail escape? The idea was ludicrous. Maybe it always had been ludicrous, only he had been too obsessed with the mechanics of the story and the whole idea of telling it, to realise how dumb it had been from the moment Crawshaw had made his initial suggestion. Worse, whatever happened to O'Neill, the IRA would know he, Morgan, had set up the interview. Whatever happened now, he would be a wanted man, hunted by them until they caught up with him. He had fallen, and they would know. There would be a bullet in the back. The car set off again, and Dunlop put in another call to Dickinson and Barwood. Their voices were faint now, probably at the edge of the radio's range.

'We'll wait,' Dickinson said, 'until you catch up.'

'You are either on the side of justice, or you are against it,' Morgan said to himself with a smile. They were the words of Margaret Thatcher – or maybe the Prime Minister had said you are either on the side of terrorism or against it. It did not much matter. The sentiment was the same. There was no middle way. Either you fought with King William or King James, even if you knew the issues were more complicated than either of them pretended. It was hard to imagine being either on the side of Dunlop or O'Neill. Maybe he was on the side of Crawshaw and big expenses and family life and long trips to South America and a happy bank manager. He could not believe so. He always thought if he was on anyone's side it was that of decency and justice, fairness and truth, and all the words that seemed so vacuous now. God! What a mess. Morgan rubbed his eyes with his fingers, as if clearing the worst of the thoughts away. He remembered something.

'Who are the Durrants?' he asked.

'Well, now Tony,' Dunlop said, with good humour. 'There's a good question. Full marks for investigative reporting.'

Then Dunlop's voice dropped its air of banter and became suddenly cold. 'Tell him, O'Neill,' he snapped. 'Tell him who the Durrants are.'

Morgan could hear O'Neill shift a little in his seat. He turned slightly and saw Hinkley tensing beneath the Barbour and the tartan blanket. There was no answer. Morgan decided he could now bear to look O'Neill full in the face. He shifted in his seat, loosening the seat belt, and turned round. Face to face, the changes in O'Neill were even more stark than they had seemed in the vanity mirror. The man who had been arguing so coherently about the heroic sacrifices of the republican struggle and the dangers of the revolutionary path looked destroyed, a crumpled leaf. He was not going to answer.

'Who are the Durrants?' Morgan repeated, his face nine inches from O'Neill's own. O'Neill looked away, unable to keep his eyes on Morgan. Morgan thought he was going to continue with his stubborn refusal to speak, as if Morgan was just another interrogator. Then he began hoarsely.

'Gordon Durrant, former professor of chemistry at Trinity College, Cambridge. Explosives expert. Resident of the village of Steeple Morden near King's Lynn in Norfolk. Married. Wife some kind of literature expert, Norse sagas. He is an inventor of new explosives. Interesting man.'

O'Neill fell silent and continued looking out of the window. Morgan turned round in his seat to face the road ahead. The rain had slackened. The windscreen wipers screeched too much on the dry screen, and Dunlop switched them off.

'Paddy,' Dunlop said. 'Maybe now you are being so talkative you might explain to us all why you wanted to kidnap Professor Durrant and his wife. The answer is obvious, but it always sounds good coming from your lips.'

'We wanted her to lecture us in the old sagas,' O'Neill replied. 'We felt we were missing something in our culture without it.'

Dunlop smiled. He concentrated on overtaking a slow lorry before speaking again. 'I think when I next ask you that question you should maybe try to do a bit better, old son,' he said with a grin.

'You see, Sergeant Hinkley here really does have this theory about whether Catholics or Moslems make better martyrs to the cause, and he was intending to interest you in this discussion later this evening. But for the moment I'd like you to explain for the benefit of all of us – but particularly our journalist colleague – where you first laid eyes on Professor Durrant. Again, I know the answer, but I'd like to hear it from you.'

O'Neill leaned forward in his seat so that his face appeared between the headrests in the front of the car. Hinkley moved a little too, changing the angle for a better shot if he needed one.

'On television,' O'Neill spat out violently. 'Where else? That's where everything that matters takes place nowadays, isn't it?'

O'Neill began to laugh, a series of short, staccato noises that were little more than nervous cackles. He stopped abruptly, and spoke again, now serious.

'I remember it well. On a programme called "Science Today". Made, I think, by your company, Morgan, if memory serves me right.'

Now it was Dunlop's turn to make a sort of laughing noise, in his case almost a giggle. They slowed down for another bend and Morgan could see a group of fat milk cows chewing the cud, their backs to the west in preparation for more bursts of rain from the Atlantic.

'Is that supposed to make me feel responsible for something?' Morgan asked coldly. 'Responsible for killings and kidnappings, just because you saw something on television? Because you bastards would never have thought of killing each other before John Logie Baird invented TV? Jesus. I thought some of the people I meet are full of crap, but you two are the best ever.'

O'Neill withdrew his face from the front of the car, and sat back in his seat. Dunlop giggled again. They were now almost in Ardee. The signpost was old and white with black writing that looked like a relic of British days. Dunlop demanded directions to the house from O'Neill, who gave them immediately, as if determined to please. They began threading through the town and Dunlop radioed ahead to the other car.

'Slow down,' he said. 'Or pull over. We'll take the lead now.'

It was always going to be safer keeping O'Neill in the second car, but in the country roads west of Dundalk and Ardee, and in the rain, there was little chance of a roadblock from the Irish Army. They passed half a dozen large new bungalows, and O'Neill told them to turn right down a country lane. There were a few scattered houses, a gap, and some more.

'It's the next one on the left,' O'Neill pointed out. 'The one on its own, well set back from the road. Green-coloured garage door.'

Dunlop lowered his speed slightly and looked up the gravel path towards the house. He could see no signs of movement. The bungalow was large, in the Irish country ranch style, with a gently sloping roof and a picket fence at the end of the drive. The blinds were closed but there was a light shining in the front room, and a car at the top of the driveway parked hard up against the garage door. Green, as O'Neill had said. Dunlop continued to drive for another mile, then stopped the car on the sodden verge where it made a small lay-by next to a wood. The second Sierra pulled up behind. Barwood and Dickinson got out and as they approached, Dunlop ordered Hinkley to get out too.

'Morgan. O'Neill,' Dunlop said, stepping from the car. 'This message is for either or both of you. Don't try to get restless in the car. Either of you steps out, you both die. Got it?'

Hinkley opened the car boot and began removing pieces of equipment. Morgan pulled down the vanity mirror but could not see what was going on. He caught O'Neill's eye. O'Neill at first said nothing, and then he whispered Morgan's name.

'Morgan, listen. Don't turn round. Are you listening?'

'Yes,' Morgan whispered back.

'They will probably leave that bastard Hinkley to look after us. If I get half a chance, I'm going to run for it. And you're going to help me. Got that?'

Morgan kept silent. Hinkley slammed shut the boot of the car, and walked off with Dunlop to join Barwood and Dickinson at the second Sierra.

'I said, you are going to help me, Morgan. All you have to do is distract him for a minute, hold on to him, something to give me a chance of getting away into the woods. A few seconds, that's all. They won't shoot a fellow Brit like you, whatever they might say. It'd be too much hassle for them to explain it. But me, I'm already dead meat. It's the least you can do, Morgan, after betraying us all.'

Morgan looked again in the mirror. O'Neill's eyes were alive, as if he had been recharged with electricity. Morgan was about to point out that O'Neill himself was not above treachery. He had betrayed his own people, otherwise they would not be where they now were, but faced with O'Neill's sudden agitation, he decided not to say it. The thought of escape had resurrected the corpse.

'I'll think about it,' Morgan said.

O'Neill could not make out what his chances now were. The car in the driveway was not that of Barney McGeogh and the South Armagh boys. It belonged to Siobhan O'Hagan, he was sure of it. That meant – or probably meant – he had miscalculated. Kennedy had not followed his advice and had moved Mrs Durrant to be with her husband, rather than the other way around. He could not be sure. There was still a chance – fifty-fifty, maybe – that the Durrants had gone. Certainly the explosives would not be there. Or shouldn't be. Supposing Kennedy had defied him on that, too, and refused to send them with the scuba equipment? It was possible the whole plan would come apart, and yet there was nothing he could do. He had made his choices, as he told Jo-Jo McGuinn. He would have to live with them. Or die with them. It was much the same.

A few minutes later, Dunlop returned with Hinkley, still carrying the Heckler and Koch, but hidden this time in the ample folds of his Barbour jacket. Dunlop ordered O'Neill to sit still, and Morgan to move into the back seat alongside him. When they were in together, Dunlop opened the front door and addressed them like dull school-children.

'The car doors have child-proof locks,' he repeated. 'I am saying it again just so you get my meaning. Your only way out is through the front door, and any sign of gymnastics from either of you and you're dead. Hinkley will be staying with you, while the rest of us check out O'Neill's story. Hinkley will quite cheerfully shoot either of you, Tony, so don't think you can wave your Press Card and walk away from this one. And O'Neill, if you're fucking us about, this is your last chance to say so.'

O'Neill had nothing to say. Dunlop nodded at Hinkley who produced a short length of cord and expertly tied O'Neill's wrists and thumbs tightly together.

'Don't even think of it,' Hinkley warned.

It was the longest unprompted sentence Morgan could remember from his lips, but he decided not to say so. Being smart now might mean at least being tied up too. Hinkley slammed the car door, and turned the key in the central locking system.

Morgan felt strange. He had expected his biliousness to return as it always did in moments of stress and tension, but not this time. Maybe he did not have the duodenal ulcer he had been persuading himself was the cause of all his troubles. The strangeness was worse than that. It was almost as if all the hazy fragments of his life – the drinking, the marriage, the children, the work – were beginning to come together in sharp focus, just at the point when he might lose them. He was going to die. There was no other possibility. Soon they were going to kill him. Either it would be Dunlop's people or it would be O'Neill's people. Or he would be hit in the crossfire between them. It would not matter one way or the other. A bullet was a bullet, from whichever gun it came. He would be just as dead from a gun fired in a good cause as a bad one, even supposing there was a good cause. But that was not what made him feel strange. He was not frightened. If anything, looking at O'Neill, Morgan felt he was the cool one and O'Neill was beginning to go to pieces.

The strangeness was simply that each of those parts of his life was starting to make a little sense now it might soon be over. He knew there was no purpose in any of it, no usefulness. However he tried to delude himself, what passed for his career was just a way of filling in time and paying the bills. Having children was just something that had happened to him, like getting married. There had never seemed any point to it. There was no reason to have children rather than not. Yet he knew that of everything that was happening to him, all the events that spiralled around him out of his control, the one thing he most cared about was Emily's abortion. All the things that he thought about had, in their way, made him happy: the children, the marriage, sometimes the job, even the drinking. He was not able to be like these morons, the people with guns who were fighting for their various kinds of Promised Land which Morgan could see would never exist. But Morgan could have his own Promised Land. It was a fragmentary, unspectacular one. It was ten minutes of proper conversation with the children. It was making love to Emily. It was a decent meal with friends. In between, there was lots of boring stuff that he had to get through to make those little blips of pleasure possible, but the blips of pleasure were worth the trouble, just for themselves. There was a life, and it was worth a little effort. The realisation of it made him shiver in the darkness.

Morgan turned round to look out of the back window of the car. Dunlop, Dickinson and Barwood had walked off. Hinkley was standing by the driver's door of the second car, his hands buried deep in the folds of his waxed coat. The rain had stopped completely. It was going to be a fine night.

Not for Country, Morgan thought to himself. Not for God. Not for Idealism. Just Life for its own sake. None of the little cigarette butts of his own pleasures made anything grand. None of them spoke of heroism. But there were heroes a-plenty littering the cemeteries of the world. It would be enough for him to hear the first cries of Emily's new baby, if she would let him. It was a part in the world's glory which would outshine anything the others might do as bit players in the re-run of the Battle of the Boyne. For that, he would try to stay alive. It was not much, but it was enough.

Chapter Twenty-Three

County Louth

The barley was tall and straight, swaying gently in the wind. From his position at the edge of the field in the gathering dusk, Dunlop could see through a hawthorn hedge and into the bungalow's kitchen. The lights were on inside, the curtains fully open. He could see a crowd of people – three? four? five maybe? – shuffling around, chattering, drinking tea. He could not make out any faces, but from their exaggerated movements they seemed to be talking loudly. He noticed that the garage window was blocked off with sacking or old curtains, and there was a back bedroom which – unlike anything else in the house – was covered by a set of white shutters, bolted fast and with a metal rod keeping them tight to the wall. Even a County Louth farmer would find it hard to think of it as being good taste. Maybe O'Neill had not misled them.

The wetness from the barley soaked through Dunlop's trousers. He liked the sensation. He always liked the rain, it cleansed him of all his worries. Now it had stopped, he enjoyed the calm it brought, the sounds of the birds making a few last calls in the twilight. He needed the country air after the closeness of the car, and he breathed deeply a few times, clearing his lungs. Dunlop had sent Dickinson and Barwood to check the other side of the bungalow, and to call him if they saw anything unusual. Hinkley was on his own. There were only two radios, and besides, if anything happened there would not be time for any of them to help him. He knew what to do. Even if they had brought three radios, Hinkley was not such a great conversationalist. The only real problem would come if he had to shoot O'Neill and Morgan, and the sound of the gunfire carried towards the bungalow. Then Dunlop would have to move faster than he wanted to.

Dunlop heard Dickinson's voice crackling over the handset. They could see from the far side of the house that someone was

273

moving outside, crunching on the gravel path and putting something in one of the cars at the garage door. It was heavy equipment, Dickinson said, in large tote bags. The man doing the shifting was short and thick-set, with a bent nose. He carried the bags with effortless ease, but he had been careless.

'Pistol,' he hissed over the radio. 'In his trouser waistband. Defo. Confirmed pistol.'

That seemed to settle it. The house was hot. Whether the Durrants were inside was another matter. If they were, or if one of them was there, then Dunlop would bet they were being held either in the garage or in the room with the shutters. They seemed the most secure.

'Watch. Wait. Listen,' Dunlop instructed.

'Acknowledged.'

'I'm returning to the vehicles. Call on short wave as necessary.'

'Acknowledged.'

It was now almost completely dark, though the clouds had parted and the night would be fine. Dunlop had some decisions to make, and perhaps three hours in which to make them. O'Neill had led them to a safe house, he was sure of it, but whether it was the correct safe house would have to be a matter for his own judgement. It was not that it had been too easy. He really believed there were few in the IRA who had a martyr complex, and Dunlop was sure O'Neill had simply collapsed, saving his own skin and sacrificing the others. He had seen it before from them – heroes when things were going well, cowards when up against it. O'Neill would not have enjoyed what had happened in the house in Howth, and he would have realised that going back to the Maze where he might have a chance was better than anything Hinkley would do to him. Even so, Dunlop wanted to hear more from O'Neill. If this was the safe house, then O'Neill would be able to describe exactly where Durrant was held. If he could not do that, then he would be turned over to Hinkley.

And there were other problems. Any kind of rescue was not going to be easy. For all the times he had planned such things in training exercises, this one was the most difficult Dunlop had seen. It was going to prove messy and noisy, even though they were far enough from town and neighbours not to worry much about the sound of gunfire, especially from a Heckler and Koch. If the rain started again, that part of it would be even better. The question was whether to attempt something immediately or to take O'Neill to their own safe house and wait. They could interrogate him properly, make sure they had every detail of the lay-out in the bungalow, and then carry out the assault with the greatest degree of efficiency. But that meant delay, more travelling on hostile roads, more exposure to risk.

A new house like the bungalow was hardly the best choice from the kidnappers' point of view. There would be no cellar, and consequently there would always be a chance for the victims to escape, through windows or even through walls if they were able to work at them enough. That meant that the Provisionals might keep them tied or chained to a radiator or some other major fitting. Since there were two hostages, the likelihood was that they would be kept in separate houses. Dunlop's blood ran still at the thought. Maybe Durrant himself was not here – maybe only his wife? What then? Maybe P J O'Neill had lied to them after all.

Dunlop felt the wetness from the field soak through his trousers. His boots were clogged with mud. He did not know what to think. If they were moving gear into the car, the IRA active service unit must be on the move. In which case, he had no choice but to go in now. Shit. What a mess. He would begin to interrogate O'Neill in the car, and say he knew there was another house. Where was it? O'Neill had been too easy, even for a man who was sure he would be killed if he did not co-operate. If there was a second house, that meant using a second team and hitting them both simultaneously, and that was not really possible. There was a second team available, but not of Ulstermen. If Dunlop was right, the one reason he had been picked was for London to be able to deny the operation if something went wrong. There was no point in contacting Stormont or Gough barracks about the second team. None would be forthcoming. Dunlop could see the two cars sitting by the side of the road. He could make out the figure of Hinkley in the rear vehicle, and decided to move out from the field onto the road so he did not cause any surprises. Hinkley was not very good with surprises. Although their instructions had been precise, the methods they were to use were left vague.

'There is no point,' Paul Marlowe had said at his last meeting in Stormont, 'in me telling you how to do your job. All I will tell you is that we have one rule. You are not allowed to fire on any member of the Irish security forces under any circumstances. Beyond that, and within the yellow card rules of engagement, handle it your own way.'

Dunlop had told the rest of the team about the operational rules, and they had all nodded sagely, as if it would really matter in the end. As he looked at the faces of Barwood, Dickinson and Hinkley, Dunlop knew if the choice was to shoot a member of the Irish security forces or be captured in the south, the shooting would be done. He stepped well out from the hedge. Hinkley could see him clearly in the rear view mirror.

'Handle it your own way,' Marlowe had said. Except there was no 'own way'. He did not have one. It was like one of those advertisements for joining the army he used to see in the Sunday newspaper colour supplements: There's three of you and ten of them. You have two beer bottles, four planks of wood and a bit of string. You have to cross Grand Canyon then storm the fort. How do you do it? Hinkley stepped out from the car at his approach.

'I'm going to talk to O'Neill,' Dunlop explained. 'Stay in this car and keep watch.'

Dunlop handed him the radio. 'And check we have got enough stun and shrapnel grenades. Put them in the small rucksack. Separate pockets.'

Hinkley nodded. Dunlop handed him the Heckler and Koch. 'I'll pick it up in a minute. I'll make do with the Browning while I'm talking to O'Neill.'

'You want me to take Morgan out?' Hinkley said.

'No. He might learn something.'

Dunlop opened the front door of the first Sierra and sat in the seat, facing O'Neill and Morgan.

'We have a little time,' he said. 'And I want to talk to O'Neill. You, Morgan, will say nothing. It is a private conversation between two Ulstermen, to fill in the weary hours before we finish our business here.'

Morgan shrugged his shoulders. O'Neill stared at the headrest in front of him, impassive, silent.

'I want you to describe the bungalow, O'Neill.'

O'Neill said nothing.

Dunlop tried again. 'We have not got much time, and I'm an impatient man. We are at the side of a country road which is so quiet I think I have seen three cars on it since I parked here. You have brought us to a safe house and I want to know more about it. If you decide not to tell me in a civilised fashion, Hinkley will take you over that wall and into the forest and I guarantee within half an hour you will be begging to sell me your grandmother. Speak.'

O'Neill cleared his throat. Morgan thought he had regained some of his composure from earlier. His voice was stronger but still trembled.

'Green garage, three bedrooms, gravel path, kitchen. Toilet. What do you want to know?'

'Shutters?'

'What shutters?' O'Neill said.

'Tell me about the shutters.'

O'Neill paused and swallowed hard. He said there was a set of white shutters on one of the back bedrooms, and something similar over the toilet window. That was all he knew.

'Where does Durrant sleep?'

'How should I know?'

'Guess.'

'Look,' O'Neill said angrily, 'I'm not in the mood for games, Dunlop, or whatever you call yourself. I've brought you here and betrayed my people. That's as much as I'm doing. There are no more threats from you that mean anything to me, nor is there anything much you can offer me. The best I get now is life in the Maze prison. The worst is I get shot and maybe have to suffer a little from Hinkley, but there's very little for me to choose.'

Dunlop smiled. 'In another life I guess you and I could get on okay, O'Neill,' he said. 'There's bits of you I see in me and bits of me I see in you.'

'Is that supposed to be a compliment?'

'Not exactly, P J. It's not that you chose the wrong side. I could understand that. But you also chose the wrong way.'

O'Neill blinked a little. He had a premonition that he was going to be hit, and there was no way to avoid it. He tried to think of something else, of the way things could have been if he had chosen differently, of anything which could soften the blow to come. His mind wandered and he could see himself, standing on Errigal's peak in the sunlight, Sheelagh by his side, astride the rocks and heather. He tried to speak to her but the words stuck in his throat and as he coughed hard to release them, the whole scene vanished.

The darkness had now settled and Morgan could barely make out either man's face. He knew there would be a gun pointing at O'Neill, and that it would be hopeless for him even to think of escape. Besides, he could not believe he was capable of it. The stuffing had gone out of him. He could only surrender, with perhaps a few brave words.

277

'You mean we're decent Ulster brothers under the skin,' O'Neill said with an effort. 'Despite the fact that you're nothing but a British assassin hired out to do their dirty work.'

Dunlop felt the coolness of the Browning 9mm snug in his right hand. He was no assassin. He knew there was a difference between acting as the arm of a democracy facing a dire emergency, and acting as a terrorist who spoke for no one. He was sure of it even if O'Neill was not. There was something about the moment that burned Dunlop, that made him want to act out the role O'Neill had carved for him, the assassin who would plant two rounds in the middle of his smug face. Dunlop controlled himself. He began to realise for the first time that it was not Irish republicanism that he hated, but Irish republicans. The political theory might be bankrupt, but that was not what mattered. It was how people like O'Neill twisted the theory to justify anything. Dunlop could not rid the world of the theory, but he could remove some of the monsters it had allowed to flourish.

'Maybe we are decent Ulster brothers under the skin,' Dunlop said, coldly. 'And in another life maybe I could buy you a drink and you could buy me one and we could talk of old times. But right now all you need to understand is that I'm not doing this job for the British. I *am* the British. I'm doing this job for me.'

'You might think you're British,' O'Neill cut in sharply, as if winning the argument might make him free. 'But they don't see you that way. You're Irish in their eyes if not your own. They'll never accept you as one of themselves. You're like a black man saying you are no nigger, when that's how your white boss treats you.'

Morgan wanted to say something, but he had picked up the coldness in Dunlop's voice even if O'Neill had not. This was the argument between Cain and Abel, he thought, and there was no room for mediators. Dunlop leaned backwards, and tried to wedge himself comfortably against the steering wheel so he could look at O'Neill and think. He realised the argument bored him. There was nothing to be said. He wanted straight facts, whatever it took to extract them. It was not that he could not make the opposite case, it was that he did not have to. If you are born British and feel British you are British. If O'Neill did not like it, that was his problem. There was nothing more to discuss.

The only thing Dunlop found interesting was meeting the enemy face to face. He had heard Sinn Fein people speak on television and had read their documents, but there was never any chance to talk to the Provisionals directly. They kept saying they 'respected the Protestant tradition in Irish history' and all that hypocritical bullshit, but none of them ever bothered to talk to Protestants because they did not want to know what most of their fellow citizens thought or believed. The closest O'Neill had probably come to an ordinary Ulster Protestant was shooting one. Dunlop began to feel his anger recede. It was now simply a clinical matter. He would proceed with this conversation for another five minutes, until nine o'clock, and then one way or the other O'Neill would tell him what he wanted to hear.

'Tell me something, O'Neill,' Dunlop said. 'Morgan probably knows the answer to this, but I have never heard it from a Provo, and I would like to. When your people talk of a New Ireland, where will the Protestants be?'

O'Neill gave his nervous little laugh. 'Why?' he asked. 'Do you want to join us?'

'Maybe it depends on the answer,' Dunlop responded. 'Tell me what will happen to the Protestants like me?'

O'Neill cleared his throat again. It was obvious to Morgan that he dipped in and out of nervousness, swinging this way and that in response to Dunlop's questions. He might even collapse altogether, without Dunlop or Hinkley laying a hand upon him.

'Protestants can stay if they want to build a New Ireland,' O'Neill said seriously, as if the question had come up in Morgan's interview. He did not know what to make of the conversation. He could not believe Dunlop was just filling in time, but equally he could not see what he was getting at. He was sure the violence would come, and was surprised it was taking so long. In the meantime he slipped into the easy language he had used with Morgan.

'Once the British get out,' he went on, 'the whole situation will change. Working-class Protestants will realise they are closer to working-class Catholics than the kind of tribal loyalties the British have forced on us. Protestants will be perfectly at home in a thirty-two-county socialist republic.'

Dunlop heard the words in the gloom, and searched to see O'Neill's expression. 'Who are the British, O'Neill?' he queried. 'People like me?'

'If you like. Crown Forces.'

Dunlop turned away. He was physically uncomfortable now,

twisting to look at O'Neill in the back seat. He had thought as much, though he had never heard one of them explain it to him before. In a way it was a privilege to hear how little people like O'Neill really understood.

'There are twelve thousand or so regulars working in the police in Northern Ireland,' Dunlop said. 'All of whom consider themselves British and all of whom you consider to be legitimate targets. And there are about eleven thousand in the Ulster Defence Regiment. Then there are all those in the Territorial Army, and those in the regular army. Then there are the British civil servants. And then there are the families of all of those people I have just mentioned – maybe, if you include the widest possible family, you could multiply those figures by ten or twelve. Then there are the friends of these people, and then there is everybody who thinks he or she is British. How many do you think that makes?'

O'Neill was silent. Dunlop felt his anger return, though he was able to check the venom in his words. Morgan found it easy to sit in the corner and listen. They were like two children squabbling over the same toy, each convinced of their right of ownership. Morgan could not understand why each seemed to think the other might be persuadable by force of argument. It was absurd even to consider it, yet as he spoke Morgan was surprised to find that Dunlop was beginning to sound more human. Dunlop was speaking again. In a calm voice he told O'Neill that the figures added up almost to the entire Protestant community in Northern Ireland, and a sizeable section of the Catholic community there, too.

'And you speak for none of them, O'Neill,' he said with passion. 'None.'

O'Neill could feel the suppressed anger in Dunlop's voice. He could not quite understand what all this was about, why Dunlop was wasting time with him in this way, as if what he believed mattered. It was like Jo-Jo McGuinn trying to persuade him to pray. He would not be converted to whatever it was they were selling. Then O'Neill miscalculated. He assumed that the more Dunlop was provoked, and the more unreasonable or passionate he became, the greater the opportunity for escape, or at least the more likely he was to persuade Morgan to help him when the time came.

'I speak for everybody who has suffered under British colonial rule,' O'Neill affirmed, his voice now at full strength. He was going to add something about the past generations involved in the Struggle, but the words were strangled at birth. Somewhere from the darkness Dunlop pushed the butt of the Browning pistol straight forward until it struck O'Neill hard on the mouth. His gashed lip dripped blood, black in the gloom, in a sudden splash onto his tied arms. O'Neill let out a cry and pulled his hands back to protect his face.

'Now,' Dunlop said. 'The Civics class is over, O'Neill. I want some answers.'

Chapter Twenty-Four

County Louth

Morgan produced a packet of cigarettes, lit one and began to smoke. Then he remembered his manners, or rather remembered O'Neill's presence, and offered him one.

'I don't,' O'Neill hissed. A minute later he added that it was bad for the health. Morgan heard him chuckling in the darkness. O'Neill's mouth had stopped bleeding but was still swollen where Dunlop had jabbed it with the butt and then the muzzle of his pistol. O'Neill could feel little of the pain. He had numbed himself to it, but could not speak properly because his misshapen mouth, distended as after a visit to the dentist, hindered his effort to form words. Dunlop had left the car when the night fell as heavily as it was ever going to on such a summer's evening. He slammed the car door and spoke a few muffled words with Hinkley, who squatted outside, hidden by the grass, his back resting on a fence post.

'They are going to kill me,' O'Neill said, forcing the words to come. 'And maybe you too.'

Morgan did not reply. Death was not the problem. It was life that presented the difficulties.

'They are going to kill us both,' O'Neill repeated, but Morgan was not listening.

He was wondering whether Emily had gone through with the abortion after all. Despite their years of marriage so much of her remained a mystery. He knew she practised brinkmanship routinely in their affairs, forcing him to the edge of his patience and then calmly withdrawing. The abortion might be the same, a bluff, another test of the struggle of the two of them for control in their marriage. Or it might not.

'I said they will almost certainly kill you as well, Morgan.'

Morgan looked at O'Neill, or at the shape where O'Neill was, offended that his own thoughts should have been interrupted.

'My wife,' Morgan said, 'has been planning to have an abortion.'

O'Neill could hear a sharp intake of breath. 'What?' he said, meaning less the question about the abortion than why Morgan was talking about this now.

'Why?' O'Neill added, recognising that Morgan was his only hope. 'Does she never want children?'

'We already have two. It's not that. I don't really know what it is. It is something to do with revenge on the father for not being there enough. But the father doesn't want an innocent life to be lost for such a reason. It is not right.' Morgan shook his head and sank back again into his own thoughts.

O'Neill could think of nothing to add. 'It is not right,' he said eventually, echoing Morgan's words.

Morgan's detachment from what O'Neill genuinely thought was their joint predicament made things very difficult. O'Neill felt the tightness of the knots at his wrist and on his thumbs, and he tried to stretch and change his position. He thought again of Sheelagh and the prospect of having children of his own. New York State, Buffalo. That was it. Where Jo-Jo had wanted him to go. As if it was so easy, running away like that. He could not do it. Everything he had done had been for a reason, a good reason, a patriotic reason. All that he was guilty of was a misjudgement. He could see himself on Errigal again, but not with Sheelagh this time. He was with the priest and they were climbing side by side. He was walking up the lower slopes with Jo-Jo McGuinn, talking, laughing, until they could see the level of mist and low cloud ahead. As they were about to enter the mist McGuinn fell back leaving O'Neill to climb on all alone. He could see the priest's form fading as he himself continued upwards, pushing hard against the stones and the rough heather, groping his way onward until the clouds began to thin and the summit appeared in view, wreathed in a halo of bright summer sunshine. O'Neill closed his eyes to fix the reverie in his brain. He took a deep breath as if fighting off the effort of the climb. He could taste the cold air and see for miles in the sharp light above the clouds. There were things to be done.

'I am going to escape,' he said softly, but in a voice without a trace of doubt. 'And you, Morgan, are coming with me.'

Dunlop believed he had extracted everything possible from O'Neill in such a short time. He wondered whether a prolonged interrogation might reveal much more – names, dates, places. It was possible, but only a private interrogation. Once they got O'Neill north of the border the RUC would start screwing things up with their 'guidelines' and their closed-circuit television cameras, and their judges' rules. It would be hopeless. O'Neill would just scream for a lawyer and remain silent and the police, terrified of a lifetime's form filling, would do exactly what he wanted.

Dunlop looked in the rucksack. The training discipline said stun grenades on the left, shrapnel grenades on the right. He moved them carefully into his pockets. It would not be too sensible to mix them up. He was supposed to rescue the Durrants, not leave them in fragments. The trouble with continuing the O'Neill interrogation was that he probably did not know very much about the location of gear, and once news of his disappearance from Howth spread, all the units in which he had a direct interest would change names, addresses and MOs. There was no point worrying about it. The quicker Dunlop got O'Neill north to Gough barracks the better.

The plan – such as he had been able to form one – would have to be that he would not use any of the grenades unless he could help it. Whatever neighbours there were might not hear the sound of gunfire, especially if it was confined inside the house, but they certainly would wonder who was responsible for the fireworks when the grenades went off. Dunlop assumed the best method would be to move down in the darkness to the outside of the house and cover the kitchen himself. He would send Dickinson to the living-room and Barwood to the front door. Ringing the doorbell would be as dumb a move as he could think of, but if they got the timing right it might act like a thunderflash. It would draw those inside in one direction, giving him a split second to get into the kitchen. Dickinson could fire through the picture windows in the front. There was a chance Durrant would be in the front room, but he doubted it. He had finally beaten out of O'Neill the confirmation of his own suspicion that Durrant slept in the back bedroom, the one with the bolted shutters. That made life a little easier, unless O'Neill was lying.

'Your mission,' Marlowe had said to him at the last briefing, 'is to bring out the Durrants alive, with all the equipment stolen from his laboratory. If that is not possible, then an acceptable second best is to render everything unusable. You could detonate all the equipment to make sure it is destroyed.'

'And the Durrants themselves?'

'Alive of course. There is no second best. There is no "otherwise unusable" on human assets.'

285

The road towards the bungalow was completely quiet. Not a car had passed him, not a sound except the repeated bellowing of a cow in the distance. For a moment the moon shone brightly through a break in the clouds, but was covered again as the wind brought more heavy weather across from the west. Dunlop called Dickinson on the radio and told him to leave Barwood watching the front door, and to meet him at the top of the garden. It was now as dark as it was going to get. If they were lucky, the moon would keep itself hidden, but the conditions were not ideal.

When Dunlop reached the back of the garden he stood beside an oak tree which stuck through the hawthorn hedge, hoping to catch sight of Dickinson. He felt the excitement that always hit him just before an operation. He knew he was better than anything they could throw at him – better than O'Neill certainly, and better trained than anyone in the bungalow. Dunlop tensed his arm muscles and relaxed them two or three times, like a boxer in the ring before a prizefight.

'This time,' Dunlop said to himself. 'This time we decide the rules. This time we win one back.'

Larry Kennedy was lecturing the others on the need to take counter measures against being followed, especially when they arrived in Glasgow. They sat in the front room in a small group round the fire. McKeever had insisted on lighting it, though the others said the evening was not cold. McKeever was sure he recognised one of Kennedy's moods, the one where he would drone on for hours, demanding that they pay attention to minor details and consider problems that simply would not arise.

'Take the bus,' Kennedy instructed. 'Always take the bus. They can follow you in a car or a taxi, but they look damned stupid stopping at every bus stop. Then if you are being followed it's most likely someone who got on the bus with you. Change buses twice. Stand or sit near the entrance and watch who gets on after you. Just keep alert.'

'Yes, Larry,' McKeever said. He had heard the same things maybe fifty times before from people better qualified than Larry Kennedy.

'And remember – no looking up old friends in Glasgow. No drinking in bars in the town.'

Kelly produced a bottle of whiskey. 'That doesn't mean we can't have a taste now, Larry, does it?' he said.

McKeever nodded, and indicated that he wouldn't mind a drop. Siobhan O'Hagan shook her head, Larry Kennedy said he would take a wee one.

'Aye. I thought your throat must be dry, Larry,' Kelly laughed. 'With all the thinking you've been doing.' He began pouring the drinks. The Girl changed her mind. She would have a small one too, to drink to the success of the operation. It would bring them good luck. McKeever frowned. He said he was sure it would be a great triumph for the Movement when they pulled it off, a great day for Ireland.

'And a great day for P J O'Neill,' Kelly added. 'Don't let's forget. If we do the "Britannia", then O'Neill will be Chief of Staff within six months, mark my words. The Coffey–Hughes domination of this Movement will be at an end, and that will mean no more pissing around in local councils and daft politics. The Brits will ban Sinn Fein as a start of their repression. They'll even be forced to bring back internment. We will be in the home straight, because then they will have no other cards to play. And we can say ballocks to constitutional politics. Our mandate comes only from the Provisional Republic of 1916, and screw the lot of youse.'

Larry Kennedy didn't respond. He nodded slowly at the words. It was clear they all agreed with Kelly. This would be the most important action of the twenty-year campaign, a fitting twentieth anniversary. The glasses were filled, and each took one.

'O'Neill knows he's within a shout of the Chief's job already,' Kennedy said. 'Those of us who help him to the job will not be forgotten. Mark my words on that. Twenty years of fighting and this will be the final push, the one that will bring victory.'

He stood up and invited the rest of them to do the same. 'I want to drink a toast to the Republic declared in 1916 and not yet achieved. May we strike the blow that will bring that Thirty-Two County Socialist Republic into existence. *Slainte!*'

'*Slainte! Slainte! Slainte!*'

Chapter Twenty-Five

County Louth

The rain began to fall softly, as large, slow clouds drifted across the moon. Dunlop sat in his patch in the barley field and waited. He had given Dickinson and Barwood a time and a rough outline: eleven-thirty, beginning with the ring on the doorbell. He would confirm by radio, which gave him enough leeway for second thoughts. Any signs of movement and they had to tell him. If the targets became alarmed – maybe because someone had discovered what had happened in Howth – they would have to move in immediately.

Dunlop had doubts. At first he figured it might be best to wait until two in the morning, when whoever was in the bungalow would almost certainly be asleep. The problem was that what he would gain in surprise he would lose by noise. Two in the morning meant a forced entry, grenades of one kind or another, the works. At eleven-thirty, the ringing doorbell might produce a better response. There would be surprise and alarm, but it would draw them one way. If they co-ordinated things correctly, the doorbell really would be as good as a stun grenade. He was sure of it.

Hinkley occasionally got up from the grass verge and stretched his legs. He would walk round the Sierra, keeping his distance, staring at Morgan and O'Neill. He could hear them talking and wondered if he should shut them up, but except by sitting in the car there was no way he could prevent a few whispers. Besides, the locking system meant that, short of team gymnastics from the two of them, there was no way of escape. Hinkley was happy to note that Dunlop seemed to regard their survival as a matter of indifference.

'Alive if possible,' were his last words to Hinkley before setting off for the bungalow. 'Dead if necessary.'

Hinkley looked up and down the road, but there was no traffic.

He thought he had counted three cars in the previous hour, but it could have been four. He expected a few more after the pubs closed in Dundalk. He turned round the front of the Sierra, walking slowly and noiselessly, staring at the heads of O'Neill and Morgan. They were not talking now. Perhaps they were wondering whether he had been ordered to stiff them. Let them wonder. Doubt was best. He walked a few paces away and then turned back into the long wet grass. He settled down again silent and motionless, his back leaning against a fence post.

O'Neill and Morgan watched him circling, uneasy in their seats like fenced-in goats eyeing a hungry tiger. When they saw Hinkley resume his seat, O'Neill began to speak again. He asked Morgan to untie him.

'No,' Morgan said.

'It's my last chance. I've got to try something before the others get back, and I can't do it without your help. Untie me.'

Morgan refused. There had been half an hour of this, of alternating threats and wheedling from O'Neill. He had pointed out repeatedly that this was their last chance, that they might get away from Hinkley on his own but not if the others returned. Hinkley was going to kill them, it was only a matter of time. That last circling of the car proved it.

'You said you wanted to save life, didn't you?' O'Neill said desperately. 'That's what all this stuff on the abortion was all about. Well, you betrayed me. Now's your chance to make amends for that and save at least one life, even if it isn't the one your wife is carrying.'

Morgan took a deep breath. 'Give me your hands,' he whispered, and O'Neill jabbed them towards him. Morgan paused for a moment, then started to untie the knots. In the darkness and with the tightness of Hinkley's work, it was difficult. When he finished, O'Neill rubbed the feeling back into his wrists. The cord had bruised and rutted his skin. His thumbs began to ache as the blood returned.

'Now call Hinkley over. You've got to get him to open the door and distract him for a second. Tell him you want to go to the toilet or something.'

Morgan thought for a moment. He looked across to O'Neill but his face was lost in the darkness. Only the desperation in his voice cut through. Morgan knocked on the car window, and watched Hinkley stiffen. Outside there was just enough light to see him stand up, the lump under his Barbour jacket raised in the direction of the car.

'I need a piss,' Morgan yelled. Hinkley did not move. Morgan rolled down the window a little.

'I need a piss,' he repeated. 'You'll have to let me out.'

Hinkley stood up. He looked both ways down the road. There was nothing in the area. He moved towards the car door, pulling the keys from his pocket.

'When I unlock it,' he said, 'you wait until I get back to the fence. Then you come out slowly. You piss right on the rear wheel of the car. You move more than one foot from the car and I'll shoot. Got it?'

Morgan nodded. Hinkley looked at O'Neill.

'And if you so much as blink, pal, I'll have you as well.'

Hinkley unlocked the doors with his left hand, keeping his right for the sub-machine gun. He stood back, then stepped away towards the fence. Morgan climbed out and stood next to the rear wheel of the car. He unzipped himself and made ready, but the water would not come. It was the gun pointing at his back, and his fear of what O'Neill might do. He stood impotent, flies undone, for a full minute which seemed to stretch like a long Sunday afternoon. Eventually he began to manage it and splashed the wheel as he had been told to do. O'Neill still did not move. Morgan finished. He had to ask Hinkley's permission to get back inside. He could not stand there forever, waiting for O'Neill to move.

'Okay,' Hinkley said. 'Do it slow, and shut the door properly.'

Morgan climbed back into the car, surprised and relieved that O'Neill had failed to seize the chance. He sat facing forward staring at the headrest of the seat in front. Morgan pulled the door shut and Hinkley came back towards them, using his left hand again to turn the key in the central locking system. When Hinkley was safely out of earshot, sitting back by the fence, Morgan turned to O'Neill.

'What was all that about?' he whispered. 'I thought you were going to try something?'

There was no reply. O'Neill continued staring at the headrest in front of him. His courage had risen in a wave and then broken at the one moment when he could have escaped. He was partly disgusted with himself, bereft of feeling as if he had spent so much of his fear on the trip up from Dublin that there was nothing left. Maybe his last order to Morgan to try to get the doors opened had been the final boost of adrenalin and now there was nothing left, just a sack of a man who had no more fight inside him. Morgan's questions hung in the stale air of the car. O'Neill rubbed his wrists again with his free hands and silently stared at the headrest.

Gordon Durrant was feeling so cheerful it was all he could do to stop himself whistling. He moved about the bedroom nimbly, tipping nearly a full bottle of whiskey into the metal waste paper basket, and placing it carefully by the door. His wife stared at him. The Skull had knocked on the bedroom door an hour earlier and brought in the whiskey bottle, a jug of water and two glasses.

'Thought you might like to celebrate,' he said. 'We don't run to champagne, but a bottle of Power's is good enough.'

Durrant took the bottle with a smile. Good enough, he thought. It's like Christmas.

'Thank you very much,' he grinned. 'What a nice idea.'

The Skull wished them a good night. 'See you in the morning.'

Durrant could not stop grinning. It was a piece of unbelievable luck which might help things along nicely. He was not sure quite how it would go – it was only whiskey, not petrol. But it would do. It would add to the surprise. The problem was to contain himself and relax until he was sure the Skull and the others were busy in their own conversations and would not come in again. After half an hour or so, the muffled rumble of their discussions appeared to have reached a point where the chance of any of them breaking away to check on him seemed remote. Durrant could not work out if they were arguing, but certainly all four voices were, at times, raised in unison. He tipped out the contents of the whiskey bottle into the metal waste paper basket, and then took the can of Foamex from under the mattress. He worked carefully, pulling the curtains away from the window frame so they did not rip entirely. He told his wife to sit on the bed and do nothing, then he began spraying the Foamex, gently at first but with increasing pressure into the gaps round the window frame.

Durrant used the end of a screwdriver to gouge enough space in one corner in which to insert a large lump of Foamex and the detonator. The blast, when it came, would be round most of the window frame but the pressure would be uneven, and so the whole thing should blow clear. Margaret Durrant got up from the bed and pressed her head to the door. She could hear the sound of glasses in the front room. It was not an argument. Toasts were being drunk, or someone was making a celebratory speech. It was almost a party.

Durrant carved out another space at the opposite end of the window frame, levered it open half an inch, and filled it with more foam. He stood back and admired his work, content. Then he moved from the window to the door. He filled the glass which had contained his toothbrush to the brim with Foamex. He had planned to stuff the glass with nails as well as a detonator, but he realised the water jug was better. He threw the water out, placed the toothbrush glass of Foamex inside the jug and surrounded it with nails. Then he popped a second detonator into the Foamex in the glass.

He had enough wiring left for two short electrical circuits, and he bared the wires to make contact across the door. He wrapped their ends carefully together so they passed a current except when the door was opened. Then he taped the end of the circuit to the mantel above the door, resting the jug of Foamex and shrapnel on the door ledge and sticking it securely. He began the laborious process of checking the circuits and lacing up the batteries. Durrant always told people to check each circuit twice before deciding it was ready. Method is everything, he used to say. Method, and routine. He'd better take his own advice.

'There's one other trick I think we have time for,' he said aloud to Margaret. She looked at her husband's strange smile and smiled back. He shook the remains of the can of Foamex. There was still a third of it left. Durrant took the empty whiskey bottle and filled it with the rest of the explosives, watching the aluminium-coloured foam slide into the glass. Then he stood the bottle behind the door, upright in the metal waste paper basket and surrounded by the whiskey. He used the remaining detonators and wire to link it to the booby trap circuit around the door.

'I don't know if all this will work,' he said cheerfully. 'I'm probably better teaching than doing. But we'll soon find out. The one which will definitely work is the window circuit. I reckon we'll have about ten seconds to get out of the window before they come in through the door. We'll have to move very fast at that point. If the door circuit doesn't work properly we could be in trouble. There's shrapnel in there and the whiskey should go up like a small petrol bomb. Whatever happens, when we get outside, follow me, and we'll just have to hope we head in the right direction.'

He said it all so confidently that Margaret Durrant simply

nodded back. Then Durrant signalled to her to pull the mattress off the bed and stand it on end so they could use it as a shield between them and the window.

'Cover your ears with your hands and don't think about anything other than getting out of that window. If there is anything left hanging – any glass or splinters round the frame – we will use the chair to knock it off or the pillow to push through. But don't waste time. As soon as the first bang happens, we have to get out before the booby trap circuit goes off.'

Margaret Durrant put an arm out to him. He kissed her fingers quickly, too intent on his plan, and pushed her hand away. He hoped he had crammed enough Foamex round the window frame to blow it, the shutters and metal bars clean away. He was sure he had got it right. There was probably enough in the whiskey bottle and the jug to demolish the back end of the bungalow, and them with it, if they were not already well down the garden before the Thin Man and the others came through the door. He prayed that the Skull and the Boxer would be so surprised that it would take them ten seconds or more to work out what was going on. Maybe they might think it was the garage going up, a fault in their storage system.

Durrant checked his watch. It was almost twenty-past eleven. He was certain that no one would come in now, not at this time. He could probably wait as long as he liked, maybe until after they had gone to bed. But tonight they were behaving strangely – the arrival of Margaret and the Thin Man and the Girl had upset the routine. Maybe they were to be moved out, or at least maybe their captors would decide to take Margaret away with them after a short visit. He wanted to check the circuits again to make sure he had done everything possible, and then he would go.

Outside, Dunlop began to move from the barley field into the garden. He crossed from his position behind the oak to crouch behind a stubby plum tree which was now almost in full bloom. The rain had stopped again, and there was a short break in the clouds, but the next shower would not be long in coming. It would be better in the rain. The sounds would not travel so well. He switched on his radio.

'Move into position now,' he said. They acknowledged. 'The doorbell to be at eleven-thirty, which is in precisely eight minutes. I will make one last check call with three minutes to go.'

Dunlop felt the peculiar tightness he always had before action, as if he wound himself up in concentration waiting for the moment to begin the release. He pushed the catch on the Heckler and Koch to automatic. He was a privileged man. Most of those who joined up were allowed to put on army fatigues and plod the streets of Ulster as targets for the IRA. He was one of the few to turn from hunted to hunter, and whatever happened in the next few minutes, he was going to do it for those who had suffered at the other end of the campaign. This one was for sanity and order, against the law of the jungle. He felt the coldness of the gun's muzzle with his fingertips. It would not remain cold for long.

Dunlop was going to allow himself a few more minutes in the garden and then move into position at the kitchen window. In one of the fields nearby he could hear the faint sound of a cow coughing. The hawthorn hedge rustled in the wind. The next shower could be only minutes away, and might come at the right time.

He looked at his watch, took one pace out from behind the tree, and was about to sprint across the lawn, when there was an enormous crash. The shuttered window exploded outwards like the top of a plastic bottle which has suddenly been squeezed. There was a short flash of red flame and a ball of grey smoke, billowing out into the garden. Dunlop rolled back round behind the tree in his surprise, pulling the Heckler and Koch into the firing position, believing he was coming under attack.

A woman's legs appeared where the window had been. Through the clearing smoke, Dunlop could see the metal bars on the outside had been blown away and the woman slid from the sill on to the ground and turned to look inside. A man followed her out – thin and wiry with long, grey hair falling in his eyes. He grabbed her hand, and they began running across the garden in the opposite direction to Dunlop, sprinting stiffly up the side of the hedge and towards the open fields. Dunlop was about to call Barwood and Dickinson on the radio to move in immediately, when he heard shouts from within the bungalow and what sounded like the breaking of wood.

Kelly was first through the bedroom door, followed by McKeever, both with Browning 9 mm automatic pistols in their hands. In their panic they could not find the key and Kelly kicked at the lock, cracking the door open and breaking the threaded wires. There was a flash, a bang, and half-a-dozen nails exploded into Kelly's skull. The waste paper basket detonated, shattering the door into a thousand pieces and sending glass, wood and metal shrapnel into McKeever's stomach and face. He fell on the floor, clutching at the worst of the wounds, bleeding heavily on the lifeless legs of Kelly. The remains of the whiskey burned with a clear flame on the charred carpet.

Dunlop forgot the radio and ran to the kitchen door instead. He smashed the glass with the butt of the Heckler and Koch. The key was in the lock on the inside, and he reached in to turn it. He heard a noise at the front and a bang that sounded like a pistol shot. Then he saw a girl in the hallway with a pistol at chest height, levelled in his direction. She tensed to squeeze the trigger but he fired first. The burst was short, so quiet after the blasts of the explosions that it could have been rain after thunder, and the girl seemed to fall into it, tipping on to the floor, her stomach and chest spilling blood.

Dunlop moved swiftly through the kitchen and crouched beside the girl's body. He fired twice, short bursts into her head, then he turned and looked into the shattered bedroom which stank of burned wood and plastic. There were two bodies covered in debris and a large stain of blood on the wall. He stepped past and walked into the main room, the Heckler and Koch tight at his waist. The room was empty, but Dunlop heard another pistol shot from in front of the house, and spun round. A car started and roared down the driveway, kicking up gravel, followed by the sudden rat-a-tat of one of their own weapons, and the sound of breaking glass.

'Dickinson,' he yelled. 'Barwood! Did you get the fucker?'

There was no answer. Then Dunlop heard a moan from outside. The front door was slightly open and he pushed it wide with his foot. He could see on the ground the source of the sound. It was Dickinson, clutching his belly. Beside him Barwood was face down in the gravel, motionless.

'One of them,' Dickinson said. 'Just one. Shot Barwood in the back of the head from almost point blank range and me in the guts. Must have doubled round behind us. We were just about ready to ring the bell when you set off those bangs and we knew something was up. You didn't say nothing about it being Guy Fawkes' night.'

Dunlop looked at Barwood's body and saw the black trickle of blood from a gaping wound in the back of his head into the stones. Dunlop turned him over gently, but the exit wound had left nothing of his face. He looked again at Dickinson. The wound was on the right side of his belly. A single shot there would not kill, unless by loss of blood. They had to move quickly. Dunlop went back into the house and had a final look around. The three inside were definitely dead. He returned to the front, picked up Barwood's Heckler and Koch and then unhitched Dickinson's from his shoulder.

'Think you can make it to the car,' he said, 'before the police arrive?'

Dickinson nodded. He stood up, bleeding through his fingers, and walked by Dunlop's side down the gravel.

Chapter Twenty-Six

Gough Barracks, County Armagh

The room had recently been painted in the colour of shiny puce, so that the light from a single strip in the ceiling rebounded off the walls and hurt the eyes. There were two bunk beds, a white wash-hand basin and some fresh towels. The only thing to break the monotony of the walls was a small cork notice board. It was empty, except for two drawing pins. The orderly told Morgan it was a room shared by two lieutenants who were now both on a training course back in England.

'Lucky devils,' he said. Morgan nodded.

There was a shower outside in the corridor, but Morgan had been told that if he wanted to leave the room for any reason, he had first to stick his head out of the door and alert the orderly. He was positioned at a desk at the end of the corridor reading a fat Harold Robbins novel. Morgan stripped to the waist and washed his face, and the top half of his body in the basin. He could smell the stale sweat where the shirt had stuck for hours. He rubbed the bristles on his chin and studied his face in the mirror. Some of the hairs were grey, but most were brown. He was not old yet, by Jesus. Or dead either. It was a start. The wash-basin was not good enough. Morgan decided he had better have a proper shower and stripped completely, winding a towel round his waist. He opened the door and yelled down the corridor to the orderly, explaining what he was about to do.

'And is there any chance you can get me a razor and some shampoo?'

'Not just at the moment, sir. I'm afraid I can't leave you alone here just yet. Captain's orders. Later I'll bring you a full kit.'

Morgan stepped into the shower and began to wash and scrub. He used the soap on his hair, though he knew it would bring him out in dandruff. He hadn't used soap like that since he was fifteen and

299

in the Boy Scouts. He rubbed and pulled at the hair to make sure it was clean. He towelled himself hard and then returned to the room. The orderly sat, unblinking, still turning the pages of his book. Morgan closed the door behind him and jumped on to the top bunk. He lay naked on his back, and lit a cigarette. There were only two left, and when he finished those the orderly better damn well go and get him some more.

Morgan felt he had spent hours as a spectator at an event which had failed to suck him in as one of the players. He re-lived bits of it from various angles. He looked at it again through his own eyes first. Then he tried to think what Dunlop must have thought, or how O'Neill had felt. He could be like a camera recording from the outside what had happened, filming himself struggling in the action. He could see it now, in slow motion replay, as if there were two Tony Morgans, the one who happened to be in a car near the Irish border with a wanted IRA terrorist and a British army gun-man, and a second Tony Morgan who was now about to script a commentary to make sense of the mess of real life.

First there had been a small bang in the distance, nothing that really sounded like an explosion. It was as though someone had thrown a large brick through a window, shattering it into a thousand pieces. Then there had been a pause, a few seconds at most, and a much louder bang, a sort of crump noise which Morgan had heard many times before in Belfast. It was the kind of noise which could only have been an explosion. When that happened he had felt O'Neill stiffen beside him as if he had recovered his courage again, or knew that the next in the series of bangs would be aimed at him. Outside in the darkness, Morgan could sense Hinkley was there somewhere, motionless, a malign shadow surrounding them. There might have been a couple of pops or bangs like guns going off, and then noth-ing. Nothing at all for five minutes or more until a car drove past them, speeding away from the house. It was hardly a police car; more like a drunk on his way back to his farm from a night out at the pub. The headlights, for a moment, lit up the inside of the Sierra, and picked out Hinkley, tense against the post, the gun raised under his coat like a grotesque erection. Morgan could see that O'Neill's hand was on the seat in front, but he sat rigid, appar-ently unable to move. Then just as the headlights swept past, in the split second of renewed darkness, Morgan could feel O'Neill rolling forward into the front seat. In the same movement, he opened the driver's door facing the road, illuminating the inside of the car with the dismal glow of the vanity light. Hinkley, dazzled by the glare of the headlights and trying to re-adjust his sight to the darkness, stood up when he heard the car door open and took two paces forward.

O'Neill began to sprint up the road, trying to keep the parked Sierra in Hinkley's field of fire. But like a dancer in a grim ballet, Hinkley took three quick steps to his right and fired a short burst into O'Neill's back. O'Neill checked, stood upright, as if he had suddenly decided not to continue running and was felled by a second burst from the sub-machine gun. Hinkley looked about carefully, and then with a relaxed walk towards the car, pressed his face against the side window of the Sierra, staring at Morgan. The face was distorted by its pressure on the glass, bent and malformed.

'Stay there you,' he yelled, his face grotesque with hatred. He jabbed the gun's muzzle towards the window and for a moment Morgan thought he was going to fire. Then Hinkley stood back from the car, pushed his gun into the folds of his Barbour coat, and walked towards where O'Neill lay. Morgan sat tight, watching as he stepped up to the body, kicked it once, then turned it belly up with his foot. He fired another short burst straight at O'Neill's face, then he put down the Heckler and Koch, pulled the corpse from the road, draped it over his shoulders and picked up the gun again. Morgan thought he was about to dump O'Neill's body beside him in the car, but Hinkley walked past the Sierra to the fence and threw O'Neill into the long grass.

Hinkley was now trying to work out what to do next. There was no sound in the night air. The car driver who had distracted Hinkley must have heard some of the sounds of explosions in the bungalow. The noise would have carried over the fields as well, and so someone would have called the police. Maybe the Gardai had heard the bangs as far away as Dundalk. It was obviously time to leave. Hinkley returned to the Sierra and opened the back door. The muzzle of his gun was pointed at Morgan's chest, and for a second time he thought he might be going to join O'Neill over the fence in the long grass.

'Out,' Hinkley ordered. Morgan obliged. He wanted to live now, and he would give Hinkley no excuse to kill him. Instead of the bullet in the back he was half expecting, Hinkley told him to get into the driver's seat, and climbed into the front beside him.

'Drive,' he shouted.

'Where to?'

'Back to the bungalow.'

301

Morgan started the motor and turned the car round. About fifty yards from the end of the bungalow's driveway they saw Dunlop and Dickinson. Dunlop had three sub-machine guns round his shoulder, tangled together like outsize medallions. Dickinson was limping, holding his belly. Morgan stopped beside them. They climbed in and Dunlop told Hinkley to swap sides with Morgan and drive himself.

'The Blayney road,' Dunlop said. 'If we take the Keady crossing we are guaranteed no problems, on the Northern side at least. If we're stopped the instructions are not to fire on members of the Irish security forces or on their Customs and Excise people. I propose to ignore that, Hinkley, if it comes to it. But you will make sure we are not stopped. Got that?'

'Yes sir.' Hinkley was swinging the car at seventy miles an hour round the country bends. The road ahead was empty.

'What happened to O'Neill?' Dunlop asked, as if he didn't really care.

'Tried to escape. Didn't make it. I threw him in the field.'

Dunlop thought for a moment. 'Well, I suppose it doesn't matter much now. Once we get north of the border they'd never let you use your Dhofari interrogation methods on him anyway.'

'I never used them on the Dhofaris either.'

Dunlop laughed. 'I know. But it did the job, didn't it?'

On the road through Castleblayney they saw one drunk, lighting a cigarette and staggering homewards, and one police car, sitting empty outside the Gardai station. Inside there was a light in a window. No army, no national cordon, no interest. Another night in a sleepy village. At the Keady border crossing, there was nothing except the routine sign telling drivers to stop for the Customs checkpoint. It was empty too, and Hinkley pushed the car through at seventy. On the northern side it was just as quiet. The security forces were either keeping away by design, or because it was too much like bandit country for them to feel comfortable. No RUC, no British Army. Dunlop began to relax. He felt his face flush hot as if he had taken a whiskey. He let out a long sigh, and looked at Dickinson who had remained silent since they had been picked up.

'How is it?'

'Bearable. It's better now we're off those Irish country roads.'

'Aye,' Dunlop said, in a broad Ballymena accent. 'Welcome back to British Ulster and Civilisation.'

They could see a gentle orange glow from the street lamps as they approached Armagh town. When they turned round the first of the security barriers, the rain began again. At Gough barracks Dunlop jumped out and rang the bell at the rear entrance. He shouted something into a security phone. The inner doors of the barracks swung open and three uniformed RUC men with flak jackets and rifles came out. Two stuck to the walls of the barracks, looking hard at the car and peering out into the darkness for signs of an attack. Then they shut the inner doors, and opened the outer caging to let the car in, sandwiched in a security cordon. They checked Dunlop's identification, and opened the inner doors.

'All weapons must be discharged at the pit before going inside,' one of them said to Dunlop.

'Never mind that,' Dunlop barked back, his hair wet on his forehead in the rain. 'Where are the medics? This man is badly wounded.'

The police constable did not know Dunlop, but he recognised the tone of command. He used his radio to call for assistance, and within minutes half a dozen soldiers in uniform ran to the car, followed by two men in plain clothes and more police. They bundled Dickinson onto a stretcher. Morgan was led off under escort to his room. As he went, he noticed Dunlop and Hinkley shaking hands with one of the men in plain clothes and walking into a Nissen hut in the yard.

Morgan was smoking his last cigarette, still naked, still lying on the bed. He puffed the rings skywards, trying to form them perfectly as he used to when he was a teenager, enjoying the novelty of smoking. He tried to remember the last time he had been in Gough barracks. It was years before – maybe ten years before – and he had been making a film about the police. They had let him film RUC patrols right up to the border through Camlough and Crossmaglen and all the other IRA strongholds that wound round that part of south Armagh and the southern end of County Down. 'The Front Line' he had called the film, on how to police without consent in the most embittered and hostile part of a divided community. Now that he remembered, it had been one of those trips which had changed him. He had started off as hostile as Emily was now to the RUC, the occupation police force in Catholic areas, the people who had terrorised Catholics at the start of the Troubles, all the usual prejudices. Making the film, he had begun to be impressed. It had been easier when he saw things as Emily did, black and white, with the

303

police pure black. Then things began to get complicated and messy. The bad guys started to act like good guys, and the supposed good guys turned out to be murderers.

The cigarette was finished and Morgan reached over to stub it out. He was going to call the orderly again and demand cigarettes, a razor and shampoo as soon as possible, but he stopped when he heard footsteps in the corridor. There was a knock, and before Morgan could say anything, Dunlop walked in with another man, the man whose hand he had been shaking in the rain. The newcomer was middle-aged, handsome, with neat grey hair. He wore a heavy Marks and Spencer pullover and slacks, though Morgan guessed he was more at home in pinstripes.

'This gentleman represents the British government, Tony,' Dunlop explained without enthusiasm. 'He wanted to meet you.'

'How do you do.' Morgan shook the proffered hand and pulled the towel round his waist. 'As you can see I'm not exactly in a fit state to receive visitors. But never mind, do come in.'

Dunlop moved over to the chair and sat down. Morgan thought he looked tired, deflated now that the action had finished. It reminded him of O'Neill, for a moment, like a balloon that was once puffed up and is now only wrinkled skin. The other man – Paul Marlowe – began to speak.

'I am afraid I cannot at this point tell you who I am,' he said stiffly. 'But as Captain Dunlop says, I am a civil servant responsible for the intelligence and political end of what has been going on.'

Morgan started to pull on his trousers. 'Well if this is an official visit from the colonial power, I'd better put on my best formal gear.'

Marlowe smiled. 'I am extremely glad that the unfortunate events of the last day or so have not blunted your sense of humour. Captain Dunlop has told me about it.'

'It's about all I have left,' Morgan muttered. 'Good humour.'

Dunlop interrupted. He was impatient to leave. 'Listen Tony. I have to go. Hear what this man tells you, and pay attention to it. I understand that tonight has been your last Irish story for some time. Crawshaw has confirmed you are to work on documentaries in South America. You will probably be paid more in a year than I'll earn in a lifetime. Your new base of operations is to be Rio de Janeiro. It's been fun working with you. When you get tired of Rio, no doubt we'll see you in Ballymena sometime. Goodbye.'

Dunlop stood up and held out his hand. Morgan shook it firmly, then Dunlop nodded at Marlowe and walked out of the room. As his footsteps faded down the corridor Morgan noticed the civil servant was breathing on his spectacles and wiping them clean with the hem of his pullover. The effort seemed to leave him without words, because he began to speak again only when the glasses were back on his nose.

'We owe you an explanation,' Marlowe said. 'A proper one. Please sit down.'

Morgan did as he was told, occupying the chair Dunlop had abandoned. Marlowe began pacing up and down the room trying to work out where to begin.

'The story, Mr Morgan, in full official terms, is this: in late April a British explosives expert, an academic called Gordon Durrant, was kidnapped with his wife and taken from his home in Norfolk to the Irish Republic. The kidnappers were part of a very important IRA cell, known to British intelligence for some considerable time. The couple were taken to an isolated bungalow in County Louth where Durrant was forced to instruct his captors in the finer points of terrorist bomb making. He had no choice but to obey.'

Marlowe moved across to the lower of the two bunk beds and sat down. Morgan stared directly at him, watching his owlish, intelligent eyes glittering behind the spectacles. Marlowe leaned forward as if taking Morgan into his special confidence.

'Last night Gordon Durrant and his wife escaped from the IRA using some ingenious method which we will no doubt hear more of in coming days. They turned up, according to our sources, at Dundalk's main police station in the early hours of the morning, dirty and shaken. They roused the local Gardai, who were so impressed that they have already mobilised a section of the Irish Army. The Durrants are now safe and are being held in an army camp in Dundalk. It would appear that they were very fortunate in that they made their escape while the IRA gang which held them was engaged in a murderous, drunken brawl during which some of them were shot dead, although at least one member of the gang is known to have escaped. Intelligence sources will probably conclude the drunken brawl was about money or control of material – these sort of things happen in terrorist organisations, and it appears that earlier that evening they assassinated a leading member of the IRA, P J O'Neill. He was a Maze prison escaper and a man thought to have enriched himself through his period in control of elements within the IRA. Something like that will no doubt emerge from reliable sources. Our intelligence certainly suggests pro- and anti-O'Neill factions fell out, either as a result of this matter of money, or possibly over what to do about the Durrants. One faction wanted to ransom them, the other to have them killed when they were no longer useful.'

Marlowe paused for a moment, then sat back in the chair, his eyes blinking in the harsh light. Morgan was quiet, listening to the civil servant structuring the botched up bits of reality into a coherent whole. He stared at him impassively, then made a sweep with his eyes round the room. It was a story as good as any other. It was not true, but something to believe which might be better than any truth. For the moment at least. When Morgan looked back, the civil servant was on his feet again.

'Well, that is almost all there is to tell. Except that one of the dead was a renegade British soldier, name of Barwood. Curiously he was a Protestant from Northern Ireland, a bit of a roughneck who had deserted his regiment a few years ago. Some thought he had gone off in search of adventure with the Foreign Legion, but it appears he ended up in the Provisional IRA and was unlucky enough to choose the wrong side in this little feud. That's the sad truth – except that we can go over the details with you again after you have had some sleep and before you fly back to London. I am told you start your new posting next week. I wish you well.'

'I must phone my wife,' Morgan interjected. 'We have things to discuss.'

'Tomorrow, of course.'

'As soon as possible.'

'Of course. Goodnight.'

Marlowe closed the door, leaving Morgan staring round the empty room. The light hurt his eyes, but he did not want to turn it off. The dark would be unbearable. He did not want to know any more about what had happened in Ireland. The country was nothing to him now, just a strip of ground too narrow for any real life, being fought over by packs of wild dogs. He would leave it and never return. All he wanted was to hear Emily's voice again, and those of David and Louise. He might have persuaded Emily that their marriage was worth saving and an abortion was stupid. A success. He would know within a few hours. A few long hours. Even if she had gone ahead, he could forgive Emily anything now. He just wanted to get back and live the life of a proper man.

He was too old for idealism. It had been gouged out of him, bit by bit, over the years. He was also too old for this crazy running around, trying to structure stories to fit the mass of incomprehensible details. He could not explain the world, or even little parts of it any more, not to himself and certainly not to an audience. That was now the job of the civil servant who had just left him. Or maybe it was the job of people like Crawshaw who made up lies to their own satisfaction. It was not truth any more, the scientific, forensic compilation of facts. It was more like religion. People would believe what they wanted and men such as the civil servant, Crawshaw, O'Neill and the others, would use every means possible to reinforce certain simple faiths. All the complications Morgan could see obstructed their religious experiences. He was too interested in the quality of doubt to be obsessed by their quality of faith.

What was left? To go to Rio and make his films on South America? The fact that he knew nothing about it and had never been there would be a great advantage, essential for what Capital Satellite Television expected of him. He could learn to be simple, unencumbered by any knowledge of the complexities. The peasants could be poor and honest; the landowners wicked and greedy; the governments corrupt. The aim was to reinforce stereotypes, not to overturn them. It was an escape. He thought he could handle it.

Morgan walked over to the mirror and looked at his face again. There was nothing remarkable about it – no fangs, no ugliness, just an ordinary man's face. He ran the palm of his hand down his chest until he could feel the regular beat of his heart. His breathing was in natural time, his stomach did not hurt. His mind did not ache. He closed his eyes and listened to the sounds of Landrovers starting up and steel gates opening and closing. There were boots on the concrete and men getting in and out of bullet-proof cars, army patrols coming and going on their nightly duties in aid of the civil power, unchanged over twenty years.

A hundred and fifty miles to the south and west near Castlebar in County Mayo, a thin-faced man picked up the telephone one more time. He had told Hughes. Now he must try to speak to Coffey. Larry Kennedy sat in the main room of a rough farmhouse. The farmer and his wife had opened the doors at his first knock. He had asked them for tea. They made it without questions, and had returned to bed. Kennedy took a gulp and began to dial a Dublin number. Outside, a pig grunted in the barn. Beside the barn walls, out of sight from the road, he had parked his car. It was still warm from the journey from the north. The rear window had been shattered and there were bullet holes in the boot. He would have to get rid of it.

To the east there was an edge of brightness to the night air. It would soon be dawn, and the day would be full of sunshine. The last of the rain clouds had passed. The Dublin number was ringing. A sleepy voice began to ask questions, and Kennedy responded in a kind of code. In the back of his car, coils of brown and white plastic sat curled in their bags.